# TRIPLE CROSS KILLER

## ROSEMARIE AQUILINA

FIERY SEAS
PUBLISHING

Visit our website at www.fieryseaspublishing.com
Triple Cross Killer
Copyright © 2017, Rosemarie Aquilina
Cover Art by Juan Padrón
Editing by Vicki McGough
Interior Design by MLGraphikDesigns (mlgraphikdesigns@gmail.com)
ISBN: 978-1-946143-38-9
Library of Congress Control Number: 2017951660
Printed in the United States of America
First Edition:
10 9 8 7 6 5 4 3 2 1

# Dedication

This book is dedicated to my brother and sister-in-law, Dr. and Mrs. Joseph W. and Susan Aquilina, for being positive role models, who inspire, care, and most importantly, are the best examples of parents that I know. You truly make a difference in the world.

# Acknowledgements

Linda Langton, President, Langtons International Agency, I couldn't ask for a better Agent. Linda, I appreciate your continued faith in me and my writing. You are an absolute joy to work with, and I treasure your staff as well. I thank you all.

Fiery Seas Publishing, and their remarkable staff, who made the publishing process simple so I could focus on what I like to do, writing. I couldn't ask for more. You are greatly appreciated.

Teresa Crumpton, Editor, Owner of Author Spark, Inc. and long-time friend. Teresa, your lovely laugh, writing lessons, constant editing, and patience with me have pushed my writing and my career to success.

Stuart Horwitz, Author of the Book Architecture series, and many other outstanding works, Editor, and amazing friend. Stuart, you taught me less is more, and that a "pantser" can have fun and succeed.

My immediate family: my parents, Dr. and Mrs. Joseph N. and Johanna E. Aquilina; my children: David, Jennifer, and son-in-law Aaron, and their children, Adalyn and Jack; Johanna, Marissa and Michael. My siblings, Joseph, his wife Susan; Thomas, his wife Carey; Helen, her husband Doug, and my ten nieces and nephews. Morgan Elizabeth Wilt Cole, my forever adopted daughter. Austin Cohen, my forever adopted son. A special thank you to everyone for your patience and support during my many hours of writing, rewriting, and tedious editing.

# TRIPLE CROSS KILLER

by ROSEMARIE AQUILINA

# Chapter One

CROUCHING AMONG LUSH RUSSIAN OLIVE trees behind a garage, several blocks from his Siesta Key condominium, Nick Mosiah Archer waited patiently. Ocean brine tanged the air, filling his lungs. He checked his watch. Any minute, mama would pull out of the driveway, with her daughter, Janie, riding shotgun. Stupid woman. Janie should still be in a car seat in the back. It was no wonder Janie's mother didn't know what was happening to her, what Janie had written to him, what Janie really needed. Why Janie needed *him*.

The garage door rose. Right on time.

Nick waited to make sure Janie and her mother drove far enough out of the neighborhood that they would not return for something forgotten as they had done on one other occasion when he'd performed his surveillance. He needed to verify the old man was alone. Nick had plenty of time. He decided to wait five minutes more for insurance—time enough to double check himself: khaki shorts, polo shirt, a day's growth of beard, and a clipboard cradled in his left arm.

Nick checked his watch. It was time. He crept around the picture-perfect Cape Cod, strode up the walk, climbed the steps, leaned on the doorbell, and whispered, "*Come on, rat bastard. I mean Rat Bastard, sir.*"

The bolt clicked free.

Nick pasted on his *your-new-best-friend* smile.

"Who's there?"

*Gruff old rat bastard.* "A petition to stop expansion along the public beaches, sir. Some of your Crest Drive neighbors have signed it."

The door creaked open, stretched the brass chain, and revealed the white hair and one wheel of the old man's chair.

Nick grinned at Janie's grandfather. He knew he was a good actor; good enough for Hollywood.

"There's no damned expansion planned around here, you idiot." The old man wheezed. He put an inhaler to his mouth and huffed a puff. He waved Nick away.

Unfazed, Nick slid his foot between the door and the jamb. "You can vote absentee ballot, sir." In his softest voice, Nick forced the old fart to strain to hear. "If you're registered."

"I was registered to vote before you were registered for kindergarten. Hand me that damn petition." The brass chain clattered free. The old man reached out his hand for the clipboard.

Nick pushed the door open wider with his left hand and with his right placed the clipboard into the welcoming withered hands. *Take it, you old pervert. It'll be the last thing you ever read.* He paused until the aged eyes appeared to focus on the petition and the old man became absorbed in reading the fine print.

With practiced poise, Nick stepped across the threshold and planted both feet firmly inside the foyer. He shoved the wheelchair forward and kicked the door shut behind him.

The scrawny man gazed up, startled, then threw the clipboard at Nick. "Get out of my house." He raised a gnarly fist, his head bobbling. The inhaler dropped and clattered along the tile floor.

Nick bent, his mouth close to the old man's ear. "Janie hates your guts. She detests everything about you. She's finished servicing you. She needs to forget you ever existed, you son of a bitch."

The old codger was little more than blotchy skin stretched taut over knobby bones. Nick grabbed his open collar. "I know you prefer hair grabbing, but you just don't have enough hair left."

"Unhand me." The old man's voice warbled.

"Now you know how Janie felt each time you touched her." Nick smashed the old man against the back of his wheelchair, wrapped strong fingers around his bony neck, and mumbled, "Just like an old turkey buzzard."

The old man struggled, but in less than a minute, he gurgled, his eyes bulged, and he went limp, hands falling to either side.

With one expert snap, a quick arranging of the body, and a double check of the premises, Nick finished. He picked up the clipboard and opened the door. Backing onto the stoop, sporting his Sunday-School smile, he said, "It was a pleasure meeting you, sir. Have a wonderful day."

# Chapter Two

SARASOTA DETECTIVE ABEL MENDOZA SPED toward the crime scene, weaving in and out of Sunday-afternoon traffic. What kind of pariah murders an old man confined to a wheelchair? Abel was going to find the creep and show him how it feels to be confined. He supposed he could have heard the emergency dispatch operator wrong but the odds of that were not high. He whipped his pristine blue 1965 Mustang into the driveway at 1816 Crest Drive, a middle-class Cape Cod, and climbed out. Emergency vehicles—some parked, some still arriving—inundated the cul-de-sac. With the exception of those responders, from the side-drive to the front door, he didn't see anything out of place. Uniformed officers hustled, and reporters skulked behind the yellow crime-scene tape. He stepped up onto the porch at the front entrance. Slightly overgrown shrubbery on each side held Christmas lights and ornaments. A few of the ornaments lay underneath the shrubbery. An officer with gloved hands opened the front door before he had the chance to knock.

"Break-in?" Abel asked.

"No sign of forced entry," the young officer said. "Victim is a foot inside the door. You're about to see him for yourself. He's about four feet over the threshold."

Abel stepped in and the officer stopped speaking while he watched him don latex gloves. The officer pointed behind Abel who carefully turned around, then edged himself near the victim in the wheelchair to brain-photograph the scene from every viewpoint. The old man's head was distinctly angled, his right arm hung, and his left hand was stuffed down the front of his unzipped pants. He reached inside his jacket for his notepad. He jotted notes, drew a diagram of the foyer, made a sketch the victim.

"Family?" Abel asked, without looking up at the officer.

"TV room. Down the hall, through the kitchen to the right. His daughter and granddaughter."

Abel headed down the hall as instructed, a large turn through the kitchen and he stood in an overcrowded family room. Abel introduced

9

himself, then perched half his butt cheek on the arm of a loveseat across from a woman he learned was Mrs. Savoy, daughter of the victim, on the matching sofa. He guessed she was in her mid-thirties. Her daughter, Janie, he guessed about six, lay with her head in her mother's lap. Abel conveyed his condolences. He learned she was divorced, her father was eighty-two, and she and Janie had returned home about three thirty after attending noon Mass and doing a week's grocery shopping. They'd returned late last night from a family holiday in Detroit and the shopping couldn't wait.

Janie squirmed and put her thumb in her mouth. She avoided his eyes.

"We'll need the Detroit address."

"Am I a suspect here? Really. You people—"

"No, ma'am," Abel said. "Procedure. To understand the puzzle and see the full picture we need to place all the pieces. That is really the simplest way to explain what we do. It is how we solve crimes."

She trembled. "I shouldn't have left my dad home alone. Not for almost four hours. I should've bought a damn house alarm."

Janie began to cry.

Abel touched her shoulder. "Ma'am, I'm very happy you and your daughter were not at home. You two are alive."

She mopped Janie's face with a tissue, then raised her chin toward Abel. "Call me Amy, please." She refocused on Janie, rubbing her shoulders, then her back. Then, she curled her body over her daughter, kissed her and smiled into her eyes. She lost that battle when tears fell from both pairs of eyes.

Janie wiped her own tears, then reached up to her mother's cheek.

"Momma, please don't cry." Janie's voice was strong.

Amy kissed Janie again, then stroked her hair and finally rested her cheek on the small girl's head.

"I killed grandpa; it was me." The tiny voice stretched into the silence.

"Hush child. Such a kind child, not wanting me to be upset." Mrs. Savoy pled her case to Abel. "She and I being gone—"

"No." Streams of tears fell from Janie's lashes. "I told Santa—"

"Santa? Janie?" Amy flipped her palms up in question. She stared at Janie.

Janie blinked and tilted her head at her mother's confused reaction at the mention of Santa.

"Detective, my child just lost her grandfather. Can we do this later?"

Abel eased back and crossed his legs. He studied them. *Was it so bad to let the little girl speak?* "Maybe your mother can answer questions first and when she rests, you can talk to me. Would that be okay?" Abel reached over and patted Janie's head, then raised his brow at her mother, knowing he'd pinned her in.

Her eyes narrowed at him. Her voice snapped. "That might work."

"Perfect." Maybe she knew if the old guy had pissed anyone off. He waited until they settled in.

"Have you found anything missing?"

Mrs. Savoy shook her head.

"Did you notice anything out of place when you arrived home?" He felt the deep sadness in her heavy eyelids as she considered his question.

"Dad's usually underfoot when I'm home, so I figured he'd fallen asleep. I asked Janie to tell him we were home."

"No sign of struggle." Abel swiveled his head. He could see the organized family room and into the clean kitchen. "Was anyone upset with him?"

"He hasn't always been easy to get along with, but he had no enemies that I know of."

"How did you find him?"

"I poked him and he didn't wake up," the little girl said without lifting her head.

Mrs. Savoy took in a long breath, squinted her eyes at Abel, ran her fingers through her daughter's ponytail, and then abruptly took her shoulders. "I can't hear this again. I'm going to make tea." She slid Janie off her lap, stood, and began to edge out of the room.

"Detective, I'll be in the kitchen if you need me." Five steps and she disappeared into the background.

Janie—deep brown eyes, barely blinking—stared at Abel.

"How old are you?" he asked. He used his gentle daddy voice.

"Six and a half." She twisted her ponytail around a finger.

"You are growing up. I have a daughter. She likes Lilo and Stitch."

Janie brightened. "I got both the DS and the Lilo and Stitch DVD for Christmas!"

"Well, my daughter Cassie looks just like Lilo."

Janie grinned. "Actually, you kinda look like Cobra. He really works for the CIA."

"I've heard that. But Cobra is smarter than me. I think he tells funny jokes. My wife, she's very pretty, like Nani." Janie was too small to have to go through all this.

Janie giggled.

"Do you think you could talk for a few minutes with a lowly Sarasota Detective?"

She raised her brows and squirmed upright on the couch, reached out and fingered his camel-skin jacket. She mouthed *soft*, without making any sound.

Abel smiled and waited until her fingers were satisfied.

"*Bueno*. Tell me about your grandfather." Abel picked up his notepad and pen again.

Wriggling deeper into the sofa, Janie exhaled, and her thumb started for her mouth, but she redirected it behind her back.

This was a child who was not fond of her grandfather.

She tilted her head and squinted at him. "Like what?"

"Like what happened when you went to look for him?" Abel asked gently.

Janie released a breath, fixed large eyes on Abel, and pressed several police badge stickers between her fingers. "After we got home, Momma called grandpa, and he didn't answer, so she told me to go get him. He wasn't where he usually watches television."

"Where—?"

"Bedroom." She paused and looked at his notepad until he wrote it down, and then she continued, "But he wasn't there, so I kept looking."

Long pause.

Abel waited, keeping his face relaxed and his mouth at a near smile.

Janie's voice dropped. "I found him in the foyer. Just sitting there. In his chair." She rubbed the tips of her fingers together in a circular motion and rested her eyes on their movement.

It was obvious Janie didn't like that chair. He guessed it might scare most children. "Did you touch anything in the foyer?"

Janie squinted and cocked her head.

She was in the habit of being honest.

"When grandpa wouldn't answer me, I touched his sleeve." Out came the thumb.

Wouldn't *not* couldn't, Abel wrote. "You did not want to touch him?"

She shook her head, stiffened her body, and retucked her thumb. "I thought he'd get mad. Mom told me to get him, and I figured if I poked him, he'd wake up, but he didn't, so I poked him again, harder. Then, I got really scared, and I screamed, and ran to the kitchen."

"What did your momma do?"

"I had to get the phone and bring it to her, and then she told me grandpa was dead."

"You are a very big girl to have helped your momma. What grade are you in, Janie?"

"First, and I'm the best speller."

"You look like a very smart girl. I'm very sorry about your grandpa. I'm sure he loved you very much."

Janie pushed her head into the soft back of the couch. Lifting her hands up over her head, she pulled her ponytail over her eyes, then lifted it high over her head.

"Is there something you want to tell me?" Abel sat back as if he had all the time in the world and patiently waited.

She peeked out, rubbed the palms of her hands into the cushions and scratched her nails into the fabric so hard Abel could see the pink of her nail beds flicker into white. Her tiny arms pulled the cushions forward as if they were sheets of paper that could rip off and wrap around her, but they firmly held on. A few anxious minutes later, she gave in. Petite fists tumbled to her lap with a stream of tears falling atop.

"I asked—well, I asked God to make grandpa go away, and I prayed to God every night. Now grandpa is gone forever." She pounded her fists onto her lap. "My fault."

"God is my favorite," Abel said softly. "Your favorite, too. I'm glad we share that. You ask God for help any time; he'll be there for you and your mom, too. I know."

Janie nodded, sucked her thumb, and rocked back and forth.

Abel patted her knee, but she flinched, so he stood, and stepped back. That would go into the notebook as soon as she calmed down. "You did great, Miss Janie." He pressed several more  stick-on police badges into her palm. "Wear these so you can be like Cobra."

"Cool." Janie's face brightened. "Can I see my mom now?"

"You watch the end of Sponge Bob." Abel twisted his head back toward the corner of the kitchen, and then back to Janie's questioning face. "I'll check on your mother and see if she is finished in the kitchen. If she is, I'll send her back here to you."

\* \* \* \*

Relieved Janie was in the arms of her mother, Abel returned to the foyer, where Dr. Milano, the Medical Examiner, leaned over the gurney. "Any preliminaries?"

Dr. Milano's sharp Italian jawline stiffened as his gloved hands unzipped the black body bag. "Strangulation, very little struggle. The old man didn't have much of a chance. Based on the body temperature only a few hours passed before he was found; there was no decomposition, no skin slippage; except for his neck, he is visually intact. Not much under the nails, but we scraped them before we bagged the hands. We'll do what we can to find DNA from his assailant."

"Anything you've seen before? I mean related to another case?"

"You know I stand mute." The doctor straightened and made a note. "Autopsy tells the story. You like conjecture."

"Even for a bottle of my family wine?"

"You drive a hard bargain, Mendoza. Argentinean wine is my favorite." Dr. Milano put demonstrative hands around his own neck. "Strangulation is a crime that takes strength and leverage—"

"Meaning—"

Dr. Milano interrupted Abel. "That crime in particular is quick, clean, and *very* personal."

Abel's partner, Rabbit, entered, tousled dark hair, wearing jeans and a stained, worn jersey, looking like he'd just been disturbed from a Sunday football game. "Victim was wearing a dark-brown, possibly handmade, rosary. A strong, silk-type cord around his neck is in an evidence bag. Thought you two would want to take a look at it once I've tested it."

"Was the cord used in the strangulation?" Rabbit flipped open his notepad.

"No ligature marks. Point is, daughter was surprised by the rosary and she didn't recognize it as one of hers from the house. She said her father wasn't a believer, that it was her mother who raised her in the church. Bagged and tagged it and watched her surprise while I did it." Dr. Milano sounded weary. "One more thing—ever heard of the Kissing Bug?"

"Yeah, deadly, bloodsuckers. AKA Assassin Bugs. My wife makes monthly donations to the Orkin man trying to rid us of them." Rabbit squinted. "Why?"

Dr. Milano eyed each of them. "Formal insect name is Conenose or Triatoma, currently found in only four states, including Florida. I found a few dead ones inside the old man's shirt. They are bagged."

Rabbit winced. "Gross."

"Told the family to get the house sprayed after you release it back to them. I can't tell if he's been bitten or not."

"Infestation?" Rabbit frowned, unsettled. He scribbled a note.

"No idea. Family was unaware." Dr. Milano cast his eyes around the room. "They show as the sun sets, attracted to the light in homes."

"Do these creatures have anything to do with the murder, maybe crime-scene dressing?" Abel scratched his head.

Dr. Milano arched a brow. "Your job."

"We'll stop in tomorrow to hear what other tidbits you find." Abel offered him his hand.

"And to deliver wine." Dr. Milano shook Abel's hand, then pointed a team toward the body bag. They began to wheel it out to the morgue van.

Abel patted Dr. Milano on the back. "Of course, my friend. I'd never stiff you. A strong lead will earn delivery of the premium label *and* the table wine. At capture, I'll deliver a case of each."

# Chapter Three

*Detroit*

IN JADE-GREEN TIGHTS AND MATCHING iridescent leotard, Rita Rose growled. After almost half a dozen years of yoga and extensive repetition of the twenty-six postures, her legs should be more limber, but stress had a way of tightening the most limber of parts—the brain was too complex to work free of lingering issues unlike a muscle that could be relieved of a knot.

Jaq kept staring at Rita and making intermittent funny faces at her.

"No giggling." Rita folded her arms, signaling she was now entering "calming mode."

The old downtown renovated warehouse where the two friends enjoyed yoga suited their needs for regular exercise, stress release, and girl talk whenever they could fit it into their chaotic work schedules—but it was not conducive to playground type behavior.

Jaq resorted to close-range googly eyes. "It's too cold and too early on Monday morning for you to wear that sour look on your perfectly made-up doll face."

Rita stretched out her current half-moon pose until she accidentally almost head-butted her best friend's forehead. "December first is supposed to be cold. There's nothing that will make me laugh. I need out of here."

"Forget Doctor Zeke Fazul, your badass, lying-ass, set-your-ass-up-to-take-a-fall-for-him-and-go-to-prison fiancé. That is a long-closed chapter. Get back in the lake with a new fish. You're twenty-eight; you're supposed to have fun." Jaq used her detective *just the facts ma'am* and *that's an order* voice.

"I don't acknowledge that name. You're no competition for Ann Landers. I'm done—outta here." Rita de-knotted herself, picked up her mat and tottered out of the room.

Jaq followed Rita into the hallway. "Hey, Thumbelina, couldn't you wait till the dead-body pose? I need to stay in shape for the mean streets I have to protect." She lowered her tone, kept it light with a note of seriousness. "No man is worth letting yourself go for."

Rita stopped, her infuriation drilling holes into Jaq.

Unfazed, Jaq dug through her bag for a comb. "My treat—Coffee and a sweet roll? Swear, I'll listen?"

"Maybe if you throw in Santa's whole bag of presents." Rita wriggled her arm into her furry coat. "I could use a few good surprises."

They stepped into the brisk December air and headed for the coffee shop with Jaq's arm around Rita.

* * * *

Inside the chic coffee shop, they sat at a round table in the rear. Cozy, conveniently downtown, and where the up-and-coming self-fortified before they headed off to corporate America. Jaq ran her forefinger along the edge of the fresh-cut flower vase and then patted the linen tablecloth. Rita looked as though she wanted to disappear.

Jaq waited.

They sipped coffee, nibbled on bagels and cream cheese, pecan rolls and mini-muffin tops. Rita's bites got smaller and slower. Convinced Rita was stalling, Jaq decided to press. "So, tell me before we eat enough carbs to put Yogi Raja into heart failure and us back into cleansing mode."

"Look, I'm angry. And, no, I'm not still mooning over Doctor Bad Medicine."

"Well, that *is* something new." Jaq thumped the table with two open hands. "But it's time you date a real man and drop your past."

Rita began talking with force, fiercely pointing her coffee spoon at Jaq. "When you found the evidence and got me cleared of all charges, I thought, 'Great! I can start over.'" She was trying not to cry. "I hoped people would forget. I knew it would take time."

"They will. Keep moving forward. Don't listen to hypocrites who believe that the rich, handsome Doctor Zeke Fazul would never set his fiancée up to save his own career."

"That's just it, I didn't commit vehicular homicide." She was getting louder. "Even those who know the truth—that he moved me into the driver's seat, and then walked home as if I was the driver—second-guess me."

"You will never satisfy those gossipy people. That's just life. As a detective, I see it all the time."

Rita pushed her plate away. "My career has tanked."

"I don't get it. You got your nursing license back. Your career's back on track."

With a vengeance, Rita snatched her plate back. "I live like a recluse. I haven't had a dram of alcohol since that damn holiday party twenty months ago."

"First, as to that fool Fazul, tell Santa you want a boyfriend for Christmas. Then, sign up for an online dating service and be happy. You deserve it."

Rita half smiled. "What's up with you and all the Santa comments this morning? Did you buy David a Santa Costume for Christmas?" Now, she mischievously grinned.

"Santa was just in to pick up letters to him and a load of toys from our Toys for Tots program. Sorry, holiday spirit, I guess."

Rita wrinkled her face at Jaq. "Online dating is an insane idea, especially coming from a law-and-order type like you: Miss Safety-first." Rita finally burst out loud in gales of laughter until she ran her hands over her face and stopped. Elbows planted on the edge of the table, she rested her head in her palms.

Jaq frowned. She suddenly understood Rita's earlier concern. "Is someone saying you're an alcoholic?"

"No." Rita covered her mouthful of cinnamon pecan cluster. "They aren't saying anything specific. When they assigned me as the charge nurse for the emergency room last night, the graveyard shift, mind you, I was thrilled, and so happy to return to work—"

"What's driven you to carb overload?" Jaq put a hand over Rita's and held firm till she stilled herself.

Rita cleared her throat. "Near shift change, this hulking, burly HR woman with chin hair, practically yanks me out of the ER in front of everyone."

Jaq gave a sympathetic grimace.

"Like I was some new-hire screw-up, she pushed her face into mine, and said, '*effective immediately you're assigned to Autopsy where you can't do any damage*.' In front of everybody."

"What is your take on why this happened—you returned to work without restriction, right?"

Rita nodded. "We'd just finished stitching, gluing and setting body parts from the four-car accident on the Lodge and chasing a misguided bird out the back door. The Chief ER Resident gave me an attaboy and a shoulder squeeze. Then, we took a break. Enough time for him to say hello to his wife, a nurse who works in hospital administration."

"And that gets you moved?" Jaq sat back in her chair and folded her arms.

"Her face couldn't hide the pleasure as she personally delivered the news to me. I think she doesn't want me near her husband."

"What'd you say?"

"Not a damn thing, I report this morning at nine sharp. I was so stunned. I wanted to deck her administrative ass. I immediately used my breathing exercises and my professional-self held back." Rita rested her head on her hands, elbows on the table.

"You could fight it," Jaq said. "I'll help you. So will my partner. You know David thinks the world of you."

"No fight left in me." Rita emptied her coffee cup. "I can't fight the hospital I work in."

"I understand." Jaq held Rita's gaze and surreptitiously slid the plate of pastries away from her. "Consider this reasoning: first, you are truly one of the most competent nurses I know."

Rita squinted. "Is this where you convince me a transfer isn't so bad?"

"Second," Jaq continued, "and most important, you'll be working with Dr. Towers, the Wayne County Medical Examiner. In our business, he's famous. Working a case with him is a rite of passage. No better ME in the state. Third, you'll see David and me all the time. Homicide detectives spend a lot of time in Autopsy."

"So I'm being traded, like some baseball player?"

"Working with Dr. Towers—" Jaq rubbed her temples. "Sorry. I need to take some Excedrin. Another damn headache." Jaq swallowed two pills she'd fished from her wallet. "Dr. Towers is an unrecognized superstar in Wayne County—maybe in this state. You should think of working with him as an honor, an achievement; like earning a high princess award."

"I'll take that under advisement. I think you've listened to one too many talk radio self-help shows on those stakeouts you and David are assigned to." Rita stood and scooted around the table behind Jaq. "Let me help relieve your headache—my hands are better than drugs."

"Just relax. Craniosacral therapy doesn't hurt." She laid her hands on either side of Jaq's face, fingertips gently resting on the temporal bone, right below her temples.

"Medical mumbo-jumbo," Jaq said. "If it hurts, I shoot."

Rita loved doing this. Not enough pressure to squish a bug, and patients were always so grateful. Rita held her position and waited until she felt the flow. Gently, gently she rocked Jaq's skull back and forth, back and forth, until it fell naturally into a healthy rhythm.

Jaq released a deep breath, and her shoulders relaxed. "Okay, oh wisest of redheaded women." The throb of her headache decreased.

Rita slid her fingers over Jaq's temporomandibular joint, applying gentle pressure until the angry fascia surrendered. "What, no bullets? No Thumbelina jokes?" she whispered.

"Haaah," Jaq said. "I think I'm in love, oh tiny friend of mine, tiny friend with mighty hands and magical fingers."

"You're welcome. You get to the station. I've got to get some sleep, but can't until after my plumber fixes the leak in my bedroom closet."

"Even your apartment is weird."

"Yeah. Some man designed the bathtub access door in my bedroom closet. No woman would have let moisture near her clothes. And Jaq, thanks. You helped me clear the clutter I couldn't see past." Rita released a deep sigh. "I have a new career. Autopsy. I tried planning. Didn't work out so well. Life, like cellulite is going to happen while I sit back and—"

Jaq waved her hand and interrupted. "Maybe it's time you give the 130 million males in America a break and go out on a date."

"Maybe." Rita stuffed a pinch of muffin top in her mouth. "If the plumber doesn't ruin all my clothes."

\* \* \* \*

Nick was glad to return home to his boyhood room. He lived, for the moment, in historic Indian Village, with his mother and twin brother. The neighborhood consisted of 352 stately households, four churches and two elementary schools that were still considered the showcase of Detroit, even since Detroit's well-publicized bankruptcy. He looked around his room and out the quaint leaded-glass bay window. He stretched the long Tuesday-morning flight out of his spine and positioned his uniform in the closet precisely in line with his others. Room to breathe between each. Orderly, sterile, safe, systematized—shirts perfectly folded, socks rolled, shoes shined and aligned. He kept his room like a showroom. Enveloped by its organization, comforted by its pristine state, he found solace in the smooth uncluttered lines of his belongings, each exactly as he'd left it. His sense of well-being, augmented by his mother and brother, helped keep him focused. He had important work to do.

As a matter of routine, he checked the markers he'd left to indicate if anything had been disturbed, and as always, he was pleased no one had violated his security. His mother and brother never invaded his space. The family had a pact, each respecting the other's privacy. Years ago, after their father had disappeared, at a family meeting they'd vowed to allow privacy and trust into their home, at least until he returned. There was no time spent looking for him, mourning his loss, or discussing his return; life returned to immediate normalcy—or almost—as if his father had never existed. His mother explained she married for life, she wouldn't remarry, they were a family, she was certain of his return, end of story.

Nick peered out the side window overlooking the backyard. Even the frozen, leaf-covered mounds of his mother's precious hibernating roses as they glistened in streams of sunlight, couldn't compete with the view of Sarasota waves cresting on white sandy beach.

His flight had gone well. The crew had complimented his landing, as always. Perfection. During his Sarasota layover, he'd had time to rest in the sun, swim in the Keys, catch up on his reading. He curled his lips. His ability to see into people gave his missions simplicity and allowed him to progress with ease. He returned to the flight bag he'd opened on his bed.

Carefully, unpacking the rest of his carry-on bag, he found the worn letter that had traveled with him for so long. *Too long.* He rested the sweetly written crayoned letter into the shoebox with the others.

"Hey, Nick." Chris pounded on the bedroom door. "You home?"

"Hey, Brother. Give me a few minutes to unpack." Nick hoped he'd remembered to lock the bedroom door.

"Mom wants to know if you're coming down to say 'hello' like a human being."

"In a few minutes. Promise." *Shoo.*

"Don't be too long."

Despite their mother's petite frame, neither son wanted to deal with her fierce temper or pouty mood, which had a habit of bursting when she didn't get her way or felt ignored.

"Tell her I'm cleaning up. It'll buy us some time. Now leave me alone so I really can make it down before she bugs you again."

"See you in a few." Chris sounded resigned.

Nick didn't want to open his door just yet, not even to his twin. Checking the door, he was relieved it was locked. He pulled the flight schedule from the hidden pocket inside his uniform jacket, reviewed his upcoming layovers and contemplated his days off. Would the next mission go as easily? Children trusted him to do what they couldn't; protect them because they couldn't; allow them to live a safe life which without him they couldn't. He slid the schedule back into the secret pocket, unlocked the door, and—with the early edition of the Sunday *Sarasota Times*—headed downstairs to his first cup of coffee. It was important to keep up with the local news in the cities he traveled to, and besides that, he needed some talking points this morning. Unaided, breakfast talk with his mother who expected details about everything in his life, could be a chore.

* * * *

He found his mother, as usual, in front of the stove using her chef talents.

"Good morning." Nick brushed a kiss on her cheek. "You're prettier than a rose in full bloom."

He accepted the platter of buttered toast and the jar of jam she handed him and delivered it to the center of the kitchen table.

"That flattery might work on your bevy of beautiful women." Evelyn closed the oven door and turned her head back toward him. "With me too, when you are gone so long."

"Four days, Mom. Not long, and I live here."

"At thirty-seven you still make me wonder what you're up to. You are so quiet about everything you do."

"Well, I'm *up to* six-foot-two, and as to flattery—no such thing. It's the plain truth. You look better than women half your age." Nick grinned at his mother.

"At eight you used a similar line on me just before I found the stray dog you'd tried to hide from me. It was still wearing the mud from burying his bone under my favorite rose bush."

Chris looked up for a tenth of a second.

"Age is a state of mind," Evelyn continued, "and you boys are closer to senior citizenry than I will ever be."

"The layover in Sarasota went well." Nick made his voice loud and upbeat. He could play any role required. He unfolded the *Sarasota Times*. "With my early flight time, I missed reading the morning paper."

"The kitchen table is for family time." Mother's voice got strident. "Not reading the paper, not computers." Then, her voice got whiny: "I miss real table talk."

Nick ignored his mother's comments, so frequently delivered they'd become part of breakfast like the butter on their toast. He observed Chris who was, as usual, buried behind his laptop. Their eyes met. Nick raised an acknowledging eyebrow.

"You've been off work all week?" Nick reached for the toast. "Vacation?"

"I have lots of time coming." Chris nodded. "I want to finish writing this game program. It might just be the one that sells. I can't get enough programming done on my regular days off."

"So, write full-time." Evelyn padded toward the center of the table where she carefully placed a breakfast soufflé. "Your father left us enough money—"

"Mom, stop," the boys said in unison. Another ritual speech ever since their father left. They were tired of those last two words—small, but powerful and held up too often.

"Don't disrespect me in my own home." She slammed a spoon next to the breakfast casserole.

"Our home." The twins continued in unison as if Evelyn had not interrupted.

"Damn lucky—flying three days and then having two or more off." Chris didn't look away from the laptop screen, and his fingers were flying.

"You're a freakin' computer guru." Nick filled his coffee mug and reached for the soufflé Evelyn set on the table next to the stack of toast. "Tell me again why you deliver mail."

"I get exercise and have plenty of time to think. I don't want to work on computers 24-7."

"You both work too hard," Evelyn interrupted. "I see more of your laundry than of you. There's enough money—"

"Okay, Mom," they said in unison.

"Once I sell a game, I'll get my own place. Then you'll miss my poor table manners." Chris slurped his coffee with a loud, wet, sucking sound and splattered a messy serving of soufflé over his toast.

"I'm not keeping either of you here by force. I'll be fine living alone in this big house. Then maybe when we're together, we'll have actual conversation—you know talk, exchange meaningful words back and forth, you'll both acknowledge I'm still breathing."

"Without us, who would eat this great food *and* protect you from all those men prowling around the prettiest mom in town?" Nick leaned close into her and kissed her cheek.

Evelyn blushed. "You don't talk about your dates, I don't talk about mine."

Nick grasped her hand in his and patted it. "When I settle into a more regular local flight schedule, I'm back into my own place, but, until then, I love the meals, conversation, and the laundry. Oh, and, you too, Mom."

"Wheelchair murder?" Evelyn gasped.

Nick's heart blipped. "What are you talking about?" That came out louder than he'd intended.

"The newspaper. Look at the headline."

Nick flipped the newspaper over. He skimmed the story before he read the headline out loud. "*Intruder Breaks Neck of Man in Wheelchair.*"

Evelyn nodded. "What exactly does it say?"

"Some old man in a wheelchair died."

"Someone broke his neck," she corrected. Evelyn crossed her hands over her heart, closed her eyes, and then slowly opened them.

Chris stared at his mother. "Mom, you really shouldn't read the news, or listen to it. You take it all too seriously."

"An elderly man who couldn't possibly hurt anyone. It's unthinkable." Evelyn's eyes began to well.

Nick looked between them. "Says here the guy was eighty-two." He fingered the gold cross hanging underneath his shirt, pressed it against his flesh with his thumb as hard as he could. It was there. It was all he had to remember.

Nick shook his head, met her eyes, and simply replied, "I remember some kind of argument when Dad—"

"You were very young." Evelyn sipped her coffee and avoided all eyes. "He was a good man, great father and provider."

Nick cracked his knuckles. "Dad disappeared when he was in his forties. Right?"

Making the sign of the cross, Evelyn nodded. "Heartburn?" Evelyn asked Nick.

Nick burned a stare at his mother without a response.

Evelyn pushed her plate away, placed her elbows on the table and began rubbing her temples. Her eyes stung with tiny drops of tears. She controlled them from spilling. "You know my emotions get the best of me when we speak of your father; let's not go there. And, let's not speak ill of your father or of the dead."

Nick returned to the newspaper article. "Killer probably did the old gent a favor. Says here he was sick, didn't get around much. He's probably thankful," Nick sneered. "Journalists report police delusions."

"They like catchy headlines, not facts," Chris put in.

"They never write headlines like: *Man Happily Meets Maker at Eighty-two.*" Nick disciplined his face not to give away his insider knowledge. Clearly, they wouldn't write: *Police Too Stupid to Figure Out Why Bastard Dead and Killer Is a Hero.* No one would understand, except the children who needed him. They understood, and that was all that really mattered, for now anyway.

Nick sneered behind the paper. *Merry Christmas, Janie.*

# Chapter Four

AFTER DINNER, NICK SAT ON Chris' bed next to a pile of colorful letters and two boxes. "So, still using letters to Santa to develop your game ideas?" Nick asked holding a handful of letters Chris had stolen from the dead letter bin at the post office.

"I've told you, I've shown you, I'll say it again: the letters children write to Santa Claus and the way their minds work is incredible, insightful, honest—better than any question, survey, or focus group. Trends—what children really want—change every year." Chris' shoulders melded into his overstuffed leather office chair.

Nick raised his hands, palms out. "Fine. Mom wanted me to check on you. Since I stayed a few days over in Sarasota, I thought we could go out, catch up with a beer, after you show me your game progress."

Moving forward in his chair, Chris grabbed the controls. "Watch and learn, watch and learn."

"Consider trying a new approach?" Nick reached into a box on the bed marked *save* and thumbed through a stack.

"Children have an innocent imagination."

"But, you've read hundreds of letters by now, haven't you?"

"Sure. Kids are intuitive, and I see it all, hear it all firsthand." Chris grinned and clasped his hands together. "Children are the world's best untapped resource, and they're all mine."

Nick stared at Chris, not knowing what to make of this side of him.

"What are you thinking?" Chris demanded. "It's *not* stealing—you can't steal designated garbage."

"You worry too much. I was just thinking that the possibilities of your brilliance are endless."

Chris cocked his head onto his shoulder. "Okay."

"You're right. But I'll shred them when you're finished just to make sure. Okay?" Nick stepped to the filing cabinet next to Chris' computer. "I can shred the ones in the box labeled *destroy* now. It'll save you time. My contribution."

"Only what is inside the destroy box." Chris half rose— "Do not touch any other letters, pictures, or my list of game ideas. Everything opened is organized and categorized, at least what I'm using."

"Okay. Letting me shred what you are not using is a good idea. Less clutter will make it easier to organize."

Chris rubbed his fingers over his eyebrows. "Whatever."

Nick slid off the bed and stood behind Chris. He leaned over Chris' shoulder. Together they stared at the computer screen. Nick settled his hands on the back of the chair. Chris' hands were working the computer's keyboard. "How'd you choose the name of the game?"

"*Hero of the Day*. First-person shooter game. The players have to think about how to get around evil forces with intelligent operations, not firepower. The more you kill, the more points you lose."

"No killing? Doesn't that defeat a game like this?" Nick leered into the screen.

"There are guns, other weapons, and muscular bodies everywhere. Skill matters," Chris said, and typed in a code.

"Firing weapons will heighten the fun." Nick pointed at the machinegun shooting on the screen as Chris worked the game.

"No way, Brother. The idea is that the players need to earn the highest level by finding the hidden door using tools and intelligence. There are messages. Riddles. Solve them—without killing—and earn mega points. If you choose to kill, you lose points. Eventually, the player earns each next level." Chris was matter-of-fact as he changed screens.

"Once through, why play it again?" Nick pushed.

"I'm perfecting endless possibilities of challenge."

"Elevate the stakes at each level and your dream will be realized." Nick was tired of giving his brother reality doses.

"I'm not into earning a high-warning label where no mother lets her child play it. That defeats my purpose." Chris saved the screen, closed that game envelope and opened another game.

"Maybe after you've finished it, and you're ready to teach me the game, I'll understand it better." Nick kept his voice steady. He tried to act interested. He needed continued access to Chris' room without causing a stir. "Meanwhile, let's go downtown for that beer. When we get home, I'll shred those unneeded letters."

"Not tonight. I'm going to work a few more hours. I've a few more screens to perfect." Chris didn't look up. "Uh—next weekend—if you're around. You want to shred, have at it."

"Tell Mom I'm out for the night." Nick grabbed the destroy box from the bed and quickly left the room. Midway down the hall he stopped and called back. "I'll shred in the morning."

Without waiting for a response, Nick tucked the box inside his bedroom closet, then sprinted down the stairs and into the night as swiftly as a ten-point buck in hunting season.

* * * *

Nick sat motionless behind the wheel of his Metallic Blue BMW. He wasn't sure where he wanted to go, just had to get out of the house. Away.

He plucked a red box of Marlboros from his jacket pocket. He needed to clear his mind of questions that had infiltrated without invitation. He hated smoking. He hated smokers. He hated their stained teeth and noxious odor. But he was not like them. He hated their lack of control. He had ordained control.

Once in a while he loved the taste, the smell, the thin smoke dissipating. He had the power. He dominated cigarettes, the direction of the smoke, the buttheads in this world. He sniggered and held the butt of the cigarette between his teeth letting it hang there as the smoke spread. He inhaled. Exhaled. And he was ready to see where the hum of the engine would take him and his control.

Nick slowly looked around the angular, custom-designed bar, décor: silver, pewter and black. He found exactly who he had been looking for and sat on the end stool near the drink garnishes, with easy access to the wait-staff. The auburn curls fell just right on her jade oriental-silk dress which didn't fit exactly right in the conservative room, but it did fit the petite redhead. He would dress her differently.

He wanted to reach out and grab her, sit her on his lap. Touch her in every way. Find places inside her and make sure she was for real. Her slender body reeled him in. She leaned over the polished black baby grand piano. His eyes followed the arch in her back to her buttocks, thighs, calves, ankles and heels. He would have her. Rule over all of her. She looked easy prey. As easy as the one-touch zipper that would release her body into his.

He paused, stared momentarily. Like the snake, he needed to move slowly, mesmerize her, and then capture her before she had time to rethink, time to think at all. Nick sat taller on the barstool, twisting the stool slowly, methodically from side to side. He'd known she came here. Fate intervened, just as it had once before. She was here, after all. His choice. His moment. His time. His control.

He concentrated, recaptured his plan, rethought his timing, replayed his script. He let his eyes catch hers. Nick grabbed his empty glass and raised his arm just high enough to attract the bartender's attention. In seconds, a full glass and a bowl of nuts were placed in front of him. He ordered a fresh drink for the exquisite naive redhead. No, not what she'd been drinking. He knew better: A green apple martini.

She appealed to him, and this moment was unique. Her look was unique. He liked unique. He loved different. Exotic enticed him.

Pulling his gaze from hers, he intentionally ignored her. He waited. It wouldn't be long.

Two sips and three minutes later, politely, she walked over. Vixen. Nick knew what she wanted. He liked to acquire his women of their own initiative. And here she was.

Nick raised an eyebrow at her as if surprised. A game he loved. A game he exploited. A game he mastered.

"I owe you a thank you." The exquisite woman tilted her head and offered the slightest of one-sided smiles.

"I apologize for taking you away from the piano," Nick said.

"No. You don't." She showed perfect teeth full-out.

Unusual. Direct. This is going to be fun. "Why do you say that?" Nick asked, as if genuinely surprised.

"If you wanted me to stay at the piano, you would've sent the drink over anonymously."

All that and intelligence, too. "What if I'd wanted to meet you?"

"You did want to meet me. You sent me the drink. You could have brought it over to the piano." Her voice was smooth as the marble bar top. "But you wanted me to do the work—thank you in person."

He'd toss her a biscuit. "Smart, analytical, and beautiful. I like it." Nick lifted the corners of his mouth just enough to keep hold of his serious tone. An opportunity to show off his expensive orthodontia.

Her ocean-green eyes stayed focused on his. She scooted up onto the stool next to him and wrapped her fingers around the drink.

He held himself steady, careful not to back away in the least.

She crossed her legs, close to his, very close to his, without touching, and the jade dress crawled up her black stockings, exposing sleek, toned legs.

29

He enjoyed controlling his inner emotion by not revealing recognition of her captivating erotic vision. She would have to try much harder. She was unaware he'd studied her and knew from hearing endless weary descriptions about her, she would.

Her ankles wrapped around each other above black stiletto heels perfectly poised above the bar of the stool.

On cue. It was time. He exaggerated the movement of his eyes from hers, down the length of her to the tips of her shoes, and slowly up again to her still-steady eyes. Then, he gave her half a grin. "Do you have a name?" She might as well have been an orchestra instrument.

"Rita." Her chin jutted out the tiniest bit.

Watch the master make her dance. "A last name?"

"Rose." Forming the R was like a kiss. Her delicate chin pointed at him further, and she drew out the O in rose.

She had watched one too many black-and-white movies. He'd watched them too, in the barracks. He could play, too. "Two first names." Pause. "I like it." Pause. "A lot." With two fingers, Nick smoothed a loose curl from around her face. "Cigarette?"

Nodding, Rita watched him take out a cigarette from inside his jacket. "You're naughty; those aren't allowed inside." Rita took it from his fingers. Keeping her eyes locked on his, she placed the unlit cigarette between her lips, leaving red lipstick print, then slowly removed it. "You have a name?"

"Nick."

"That's a nice name, Nick. Last name?"

A pusher. She likes to push. I'll fix that. "Just Nick." Nick Mosiah Archer, a name you'll not soon forget.

"Like Good Saint Nick?"

"Something like that," Nick said. Teeth clenched behind his smile. *Yes, I'm good, you wench. An expert on human behavior, seeker of redemption, protector of children, protector of souls. A saint? I like it.*

He needed to remain aloof, at least for now. He would know when the time was right to give her more, or take it all away. Rita Rose was not in a position to dictate anything to him, clearly not in any position to require him to divulge information. He'd give her what she needed. In time, she'd learn what she needed to learn. His eyes charmed her in. All in good time. She didn't really know what she wanted; no woman did. He sneered inwardly. I'll show her the way. Teach her what's really important.

"Dance?" Nick made his voice soft, put his lips so close to her face they brushed against wisps of hair.

"Sure. Can we wait until I've finished my martini?"

Ballsy bitch, harsher than he thought she was. I can't wait to tame her. "Anything you want." He lifted her martini and placed it in her hand. "Angel-teeny. Anything you want."

Nick raised his own glass in mocking toast. "To my beautiful, sweet, very tiny, luscious, new friend, Angel-teeny."

Rita's eyes were wide over the glass and she sipped her martini with her eyes held on his.

Nick chugged the Irish whiskey, slamming the glass down in exclamation. His fingers gently stroked the outline of her arm, elbow to fingers, and his eyes crinkled as he studied her.

Rita quickly finished her drink and set the cigarette down beside it. Nick favored her with a smile, stood and twisted a palm in her direction. She placed her hand in his palm and followed him onto the dance floor.

He wrapped his free arm around her tiny waist. Her curves melded nicely within his grasp. He leaned down, breathed in the scent of her hair. Roses and jasmine. Her flesh, young, pale and freckled, beckoned him.

He felt her breath on his neck. "Mmm, what's on your gold chain, just Nick?"

"No fair peeking inside my shirt," he said. A turn around the floor and he wanted more. "Want to get out of here?"

"What do you have in mind?" She had to tip her head back to meet his eyes.

"I'm a man of my word, like I promised, anything you want, Angel-teeny, you got it."

He gestured toward the street-side of the room. He had to raise his voice above the blues music; the five-piece band had begun another number and the couples on the dance floor had increased. Moveable space was quickly evaporating.

"Let's just enjoy the music. You're really a great dancer." Rita reached up and gently placed her hands on either side of his head and stroked gently.

Touch like a whisper. "Mmm, that's nice." He pulled her in closer, his hands still snuggly wrapped around her waist, a thumb stroking her lower back.

"I hate crowds." He leaned down again and whispered in her ear. "Tell Saint Nick what else you like to do with those magical fingers besides dance. Let me take you away from this. I want to make *all* your dreams come true."

"You're a funny guy, Nick." She cocked her head slightly and their eyes met in the dark.

She needs to learn her place. "It's a little warm in here, Rita Rose. How about a walk? Beautiful night." He grasped her beautiful hand and gave it a gentle squeeze. *For my beautiful plan.*

"Nick, there are things about me—" She paused and bit her lip. "I can't. I'm just not ready for more than a dance right now. We've had fun. Let's meet here, say next week. Drinks, dance, no strings?"

"Angel-teeny, you disappoint. You don't want to do that, do you?" He pulled away from her and stood at arm's length, pouted, refused to look away. He knew her resistance was melting.

She sighed and laughed. "So not fair. Okay. Let's stretch our legs outside. That's all I can promise for now. And about that name, Angel-teeny—"

"You're beautiful," Nick interrupted. He controlled all things, nicknames, where they went, what they did and how this date would end; if it ended at all.

She twisted away, slipping her elbow free of his grasp and clacked across the shiny terrazzo to the barstool where they'd begun their journey.

Nick followed behind her and watched other men notice her. She's mine, you Bozos. I've planned every detail, I've captured it, and I'm about to go in for the kill; stay away, there's a roomful of other daisies to pluck. He nodded and finger shooed away the two bartenders who approached them behind her back.

With conviction, she picked up the cigarette, as if a magical wand, then stroked it between her fingers. Her shoulder coiled into him. "You owe me a light."

He raised an eyebrow. The ladies loved that. "Sure, Angel-teeny. A cigarette and a walk in the night air might be just what we need."

# Chapter Five

THE STREET CROWD ON WEDNESDAY in downtown Detroit on Ladies' night, kept Greektown Casino busy. Regular gamblers, those out for a stroll, the homeless, addicts, prostitutes and various after-dark criminals were poised amidst the shadows. The brass strategically placed detective teams to hold down the body count. It wasn't a question of if they'd get called for a DOA, just how many and when. The high murder rate discouraged the influx of the casual user into Detroit for the illegal range of available street drugs like heroin, and crack-cocaine. Not that Detective Maxwell was cynical.

He read the text, thumb-keyed a few lines, clicked off, and pulled away from the curb. "We're off the Diego stakeout permanently."

"No way. After months of work and being here most of the night?" Jaq gulped the last swig of coffee, crumbled her cup, and tossed it on the floor of the truck. "Who's pulling us off?" She snapped on her seatbelt.

"The Chief. Crime scene at his sister and brother-in-law's house. His sister married a Rider, the last of the local hardware store owners—lives near Cadieux off Mack."

The Explorer lurched onto Gratiot.

Jaq recoiled. "Thought they lived in Grosse Pointe."

David rolled his window down, popped a red light on the roof, closed the window, and hit the siren. "Crime scene is the Detroit side of Mack—I'm guessing they're short teams who could timely respond on scene."

"Damn reality. Are we picking up our third partner—or should I say your dog partner?" Jaq pulled out her notepad and pen, made a note, slipped pen and pad back into her shirt pocket.

"You know it. We need Recon for those finely tuned scenting skills. If the perp has so much as sneezed, Recon will lead us to him."

\* \* \* \*

33

Fifteen minutes later they were on Bishop Street. The houses were spaced closely together, with each seeming more imposing than the last. Hundred-year-old trees signaled the stability of the place. Even in November the oaks and maples blended with massive pines to sing *this is a safe place*. A Neighborhood Watch sign stood on Bishop near Rosewood. Built in an era when care was taken in craftsmanship, the Hanusack-Rider two-story home with setback unattached garage, had been well cared for. Under the streetlamp, the driveway had obviously been recently repaired. Nothing looked out of place except for the crime-scene tape, half the police force, emergency crews, and the ever-hungry media. Uniformed officers were holding neighbors at bay; some of neighbors were crying, other neighbors were comforting each other. A few couldn't help but comply with willing camera crews for their proverbial fifteen minutes of fame.

David clasped Recon's harness, and Jaq followed. Stepping up to the front door, Jaq flashed her badge, and the uniformed officers nodded them in.

"Dixon, where's the Chief?" David habitually treated every officer with respect.

"Kitchen, with his sister; through the hall, make a right," the uniform said.

"Victim?" Jaq asked.

"Chief's brother-in-law. Same hallway, but make a left. Corner of the room."

In a corner of the long kitchen, with windows on two sides, Chief Hanusack sat at the polished oak table with his sister and her children. He slumped in the chair, his eyes distant, while he held a little girl about kindergarten age on his lap. She was upset and rested her head against his chest. He comforted her with news that he'd personally delivered her letter to Santa. She hinted at a tear-stained smile, then returned to sobbing.

His sister, Megan, sat across from him holding a slightly older boy who was mesmerized by the stained-glass lamp hanging over the center of the table. She rocked him swiftly and hummed a lullaby as if she and her child were the only two people in the room. The Chief stared at David and Jaq, but Megan didn't react, not even to Recon sniffing her feet.

"Chief?" David put a hand on the Chief's shoulder.

Jaq pulled out a small spiral notebook. "We'll get whoever did this."

"Whatever you need. Profilers, surveillance teams, canine unit assistance—I can try to locate Yucon, Recon's brother. Name it. We'll work out details later. Understand?"

"Yes, sir." David tried to meet his eyes, but the Chief kept his eyes on his sister. The burly man, always a tower of strength, seemed fragile as he stroked handfuls of his niece's long, silky-fine hair. He didn't seem to notice the hair tangle between his fingers as he tried his best to blink away the pain for everyone.

David cocked his head at Jaq and nodded her forward. Jaq whispered something to the officer watching the family, and then followed David into the family room. It was oblong, the focal point a brick fireplace, with book shelves on each side. Above the fireplace hung a canvas with a stormy sea and a ship caught in high winds. A large television in the corner, evidence of hours of viewing with the worn furniture and stacks of DVDs on the shelf nearest it.

David spotted Dr. Towers immediately. "Hey, Doc. What d'ya know?"

Dr. Towers' head of tightly clipped curls nodded. David handed Recon's leash to one of the uniforms, and he and Jaq stepped toward the victim.

Dr. Towers minimized his voice, slightly raising his eyes to David. "Chief's brother-in-law and best friend, Peter, was found by his sister about three this morning. No sign of forced entry or struggle."

"Were the wife and kids asleep?" David asked.

"Yes," Dr. Towers said.

"What brought him downstairs—I take it they all sleep upstairs?"

"Wednesday night bowling league. Wife says he usually arrives home around midnight," Dr. Towers said. "She woke up alone around three, figured he'd fallen asleep in front of the television and went downstairs to wake him up."

"Found him like this?" Jaq asked.

"Exactly," Doc said. "Seated in the corner overstuffed chair, slouched and surrounded with these books. She thought he was sleeping, felt how cold he was, and called 9-1-1."

"Time of death—" David was ready to note it.

"Best guess, between midnight and two." Dr. Towers always looked serious at a crime scene, but this one seemed to weigh him down. He and the Chief had served together in the Detroit riots at a time when they were neither liked nor respected. They'd seen each other as colleagues, not as

Caucasian and African American, living through very difficult times. That collegiality had never left them.

"Any chance death by natural causes?" Jaq obviously forced the words out because it had to be asked, but no way this bizarre setup was natural.

Dr. Towers pulled a pen from his pocket, bent forward, and with a gloved hand, pointed. "Blunt-force trauma to the neck. Bruising, swelling. You might be looking for a heavy metal object. Could be a pipe of some sort for leverage—not sure what was used—I will try to narrow it down at the lab."

"Broken neck?" Jaq released an exasperated sigh. She tapped her foot and her hand on her leg. Then, she ran her fingers through her hair.

"Strangulation—But the story lies in the tissue underneath. Broken neck, likely. Homicide."

"Weird setup." David stared at the victim and the scene clearly arranged to tell them something. But what? "Where'd all the books and clocks come from?"

"Wife said they are from all over the house. Perp spent some time pulling them together and placing them around him."

David craned his neck, taking in the whole room. "He wasn't worried about getting caught. Setting this scene was important to him."

David squatted, tilted each book with one gloved finger just enough to read the book titles. "Titles and authors are too diverse to have cohesion, obvious message tied to the book and clock theme, although it escapes me. After the photos, everything gets tagged into evidence."

"I'll let you do the reading." Jaq patted David's back. "I'll expect cliff notes."

"So, you're finally going to try to get by on good looks alone?"

Jaq peered closely at the victim's throat. "Did you find anything else on him?"

"He was holding his wristwatch between his thumb and forefinger." Doc demonstrated with his own right hand.

Jaq squinted at Dr. Towers as if she were trying to visualize it. "Any idea why?"

"None."

Careful not to touch anything, David squatted and inspected the carpet and under the edges of the furniture. "We'll need the profilers in on this one."

"What, no crystal ball?" Jaq jotted more notes.

"No short-cuts. You heard the Chief. Profilers at our disposal, without asking."

"Cleanest crime scene we've ever been to—that's for certain." Jaq spun in a circle, then edged very slowly around the family room.

"Got anything Recon can sniff and search, before I let him loose?" David asked.

Dr. Towers shook his head. "Check with your evidence teams. I am set to have him placed onto a gurney and into refrigeration if you can give me the green light. I'm not sure the CSI unit is willing to have Recon compromise the scene just yet."

David nodded.

"One other thing," Dr. Towers said. "I understand from the family Peter Rider was not a very religious man."

David didn't get the connection. "So?"

"He was wearing a silken rosary around his neck. One of the officers showed it to his wife before we bagged it. She was stunned."

# Chapter Six

RITA'S BEDSIDE ALARM CLOCK BLARED news of the murder of the brother-in-law of the Chief of Police. She stabbed the Off button. Peace.

She took a deep breath and opened one eye. Felt like there was gravel under the lid. She eyeballed the five on the clock and groaned. Welcome to Thursday in Detroit—Murder Capital of the USA, where no one was immune and dead bodies stacked up like layers of filo dough. Workday three, and she and Dr. Towers were already above ceiling-level in cadavers. She loved working with the living. How long until she stopped loathing the work with the dead?

She craned her neck, then rolled over and realized she was alone. Disappointed and relieved at the same time, she wondered when and where she lost Nick. How had he disappeared without her knowing it? Here it was: a neon reminder why she should never and had never, until last night, brought home a strange man. And, why she would never do it again.

She slid her leg into the empty portion of the sheets. Cold, really cold. He couldn't have stayed long after she'd fallen asleep. She hadn't felt him stir, not even to use the bathroom. She was very lucky she'd not brought home a problem.

Looking around the dimly lit room, nothing appeared to be missing. If he was gone, she deserved it. She should've stuck to: "No." She should've insisted on a hotel. She should've been the one to leave. Playing the role of a diva had been fun, but she doubted she could pull it off long-term. She didn't feel ready—yet. She should've taken better care of herself.

She was still strengthening, healing her wounds, and trying to turn into a better, stronger version of herself. Damn—it was hard work being a better you. It was too early to have sex with another man. She should've kept the blow-up hunk and battery pack from her bridal shower instead of asking Jaq to Taser him, then dumpster him in honor of the 'death' of her last relationship.

She pulled herself from the bed's warmth and steered herself directly to the kitchen, dragging the comforter. Consoled she hadn't revealed her past with its shortcomings, she was still distressed she didn't know Nick's last name, yet she'd let him enter her body. She bit her lip. "Ouch." She cried out. Damn it, another habit she needed to break.

Filling the coffee pot, Rita mused about women who have sex with a man who only gives his first name. She'd graduated to one of those desperate women she had no respect for. A good reason for him to have vanished and for her to strengthen her pledge.

The aroma of fresh coffee infusing her senses, Rita grabbed the newspaper from the front door. She returned to the kitchen, eyes on the newspaper, which she carefully unfolded. Once she was seated at the counter, her eyes focused on one perfect red rose and a rose-bordered Post-It note tacked on the headline.

Meet me for Sunday Brunch 2 p.m. Southfield Westin in the Town Center.

I'll make it up to you for leaving you without another round and breakfast.

~Nick.

Rita held the rose to her nose, then set it down. She studied the note, her relationship fears forgotten. He wants to get to know me. In deep-breathing pose, she inhaled and exhaled. Calmed, she poured coffee, almost overfilling her mug. "I'm letting work and all those piled-up cadavers get to me," she said out loud. "Well, no more. I'm going to focus on my new man." She gracefully twirled to the bathroom.

Stepping into the hot shower, her thoughts focused on the outfit she would wear to further entice Nick. It was Thursday; Sunday was three whole days away, plenty of time to plan. If Jaq were here, she would demand every last date detail, and then do a background check. But she wasn't, so Rita raised her arms, twirled, and performed a little happy dance. Time to date and venture independently.

# Chapter Seven

RITA WALKED AROUND THE COOL autopsy room and inspected the silver tray that held sterilized instruments wrapped in blue paper. She counted the slides and Petri dishes; everything was ready for autopsy. When she learned that Dr. Towers hadn't slept much since he'd spent time with detectives, then arrived early in the lab, she felt badly he hadn't called her in to assist him.

Dr. Towers had dedicated more than thirty-five years to the county. Had he ever tired of it? Cameras, slides, dictation equipment—it was all daunting to her because of its importance. She knew firsthand what it meant to be wrongly accused, to need the right evidence. Every move counted. This was a new application of the science she loved, a new facet of life saving.

Dr. Towers adjusted the headband over the blue mesh cap that held an immense magnifying lens. He peered through an acrylic face shield, leaned over the body, reverently pulling back the sheet. With a black marker, he drew on the body, dividing it into quadrants. He photographed, examined the head, external scalp, then made internal cuts and full examination. Together they analyzed, noted, swabbed, excised, pulled, labeled, and sealed, until she'd forgotten the cadaver was human. They worked for hours.

Rita followed Dr. Towers' orders, but his disciplined hands mesmerized her as he methodically administered the autopsy and dictated his findings for documentation. It was easy to assist with his direction. It was also easy to forget that this body had been among the living just yesterday.

Stepping back to take a break, Dr. Towers snapped off the overhead Dictaphone and looked at Rita. "Like winning the lottery to have you assigned to me."

She avoided his eyes. "I don't know what to say." It sounded like a compliment.

"In time, you could learn to like it here. And me, too."

She felt herself redden. "Oh, I didn't mean—"

He twisted his wrists, palms up. "You are fine."

"No, I'm embarrassed. My career is about all I have left. I'm sure you've heard hospital gossip—"

"I know you feel working here is a demotion. We do a lot of good here. In time, you will understand."

Rita's lip quivered, she bit it to make it stop. "I need to explain—"

"Maybe, sometime. What is important is the skill I see."

Rita raised her eyes to his and gave him a half-smile. "Thank you."

"I have performed, by now, likely thousands of autopsies. You are the first assistant to follow me flawlessly so early in our working relationship. I commend you." He gave her a very gracious head-bow.

Rita squinted up at him in disbelief. "It's you. You're easy to follow. I hardly believe what you're saying is exactly true, but it's appreciated. Thank you."

She exchanged the marked slides on the cold silver lab counter for a set of clean ones and checked the SD cards for memory on each camera. "Hard to believe we've used one full slide set already. I'm recharging the shaving set as well, just in case."

Dr. Towers scrunched his nose.

"Something wrong?" She couldn't imagine how he'd gone from giving her praise to nose-wrinkles in ten seconds.

Dr. Towers flipped on the Dictaphone equipment and aimed a scalpel toward the body. "I am verifying some curious markings through these magnifiers."

Rita stepped in. Dr. Towers pointed to some darkened areas.

"Clearly bruising patterns that resemble fingers from strangulation. But there is another shape." He pointed and made a rectangular outline. "A flat, heavy, oblong-shaped object was used to crush the larynx. But something was attached that left an imprint of very faint lines. I will call a few of them dots."

Rita strained to see. "The spots that look like the shape of a cross?"

"A cross?"

Rita looked up at him. "Okay, maybe an X."

"My first thought as well. See the high and low indentations—you can tell from the slight variations in color." He paused and continued to point with the small scalpel in his hand.

"I am guessing, just that, a cross, but particularly a crucifix. The difference is a crucifix has the body of Christ on it—it's not just flat."

Rita squinted and handed him a fresh set of slides. "And?"

"Explains the inconsistent markings and coloring. I will run a sample and do a comparison for the detectives. They are due here this afternoon."

"I don't see—I never would've guessed—"

"Stick with me and you will." He pointed and made a wide circle.

Dr. Towers flipped on the Dictation equipment, and they stepped back to the body. "I will need to incise them for demarcation, and then excise for microscopic examination."

Rita opened her eyes wide and listened to his medical description, and then bent as close as she dared. "I see discoloration. Almost looks like a birthmark."

"But it makes a pattern." Dr. Towers nodded. "We need to take special care photographing."

"This is very meticulous work." Rita blinked several times very quickly. "I see why we wear magnifiers."

He laughed. "Like small brush strokes on a canvas. Eventually, a picture comes together."

"How much time do we have to prepare the canvas?"

"Few hours, always too few. Detectives will be here just before we are ready to leave for dinner."

\* \* \* \*

"Thanks for staying late, Doc. We're counting on you, Doc, 'cause we got a boatload of nothin'."

David and Jaq sat at Dr. Towers' pristine desk across from Doc and Rita. Jaq and Rita exchange a whispered hello while David cracked his knuckles.

Doc tossed a glance out his window, then back at the detectives. "I plan on retiring with my wife in the sun."

David ignored Doc's hint of being tired. "Recon might as well have spent the morning chasing his tail. CSI photographed, sprayed luminal, and dusted for fingerprints—the usual protocol. Zilch."

"We interviewed a few neighbors," Jaq added. "No leads there. It's almost like he was murdered by a magician." She made an abracadabra gesture.

David nodded. "Very calculated."

"The silken-corded cross I removed from the victim might grow something that Recon could smell to identify your perpetrator if you leave it sealed in the bag to ripen long enough." Doc's brows furrowed together, and he squinted, as if he were looking into the sun. "That is what Recon does, right?"

David nodded. "It happens."

"Doc?" Jaq tucked her feet under her chair and leaned forward. "What's got you bugged?"

"The labs will not be ready for a few weeks. Nurse Rose will spend some time today cataloging film and slides to speed things up. I still have cross sections of organs to do, but there is no expectation to find anything in other extremities below the neck."

"But—" Jaq tried to interrupt.

"My guess is you two have a bigger problem than just this case."

David and Jaq tilted their heads at each other, then at Doc, who slid a few pictures toward them. He flipped through a stack and pulled out certain ones as he spoke.

"Not only did you see the staged crime scene, but the autopsy showed a crushed larynx, which takes some strength to do. The killer strangles the victim, and then—after he dies—makes sure his larynx is not broken or simply collapsed, but actually crushed."

"Crushes his windpipe after death." David rolled his head back and let it hang for a second. Without looking away from the doctor, Jaq fished a stick of gum out of her jeans pocket, unwrapped it, and popped it into her mouth.

"Exactly. Did you log into evidence any type of oblong device?"

They both shook their heads. Negative.

"The device he uses is for leverage. It may have a crucifix attached to it."

"How certain are you?" Jaq cracked her gum.

"Note the deeper markings, barely there, but visible." With the tip of his pen, Dr. Towers pointed to the photographs he'd strewn across his desk.

"Here are the exact markings on a test I ran with a crucifix." He pointed to a second set of pictures. "Compare the similarities. Not exact because I don't have the actual apparatus. A stretch, maybe, but you asked for early conclusions."

"What made you think of a crucifix, Doc?" David asked. "A bit curious, don't you think?"

"Not given the circumstance. The wife's reaction when she saw the rosary—it left a nagging impression. First thing I thought of when I saw the markings." His voice was deep and rich.

"Careful, Doc, you are showing your age by your wealth of experience," Jaq said.

"And the crow's feet and spirals of my white hair." He wagged a pen at them. "Age and wisdom or lack of it cannot be hidden, as my wife constantly reminds me on her way to dye her hair."

They laughed.

"Any ligature marks around the neck or indications he was bound and dragged?" David asked.

"None."

"You said bigger problem, Doc," Jaq said. "Have we missed something? Seems like Detroit just has another religious nut on the loose. Detroit has had its share."

"There is a message in this body. It has not spoken to me, yet. That is frustrating." Dr. Towers pounded a fist on his desk. "I am also keenly aware, however, that religious nuts have a tendency to deal in plagues."

Jaq thumbed through the pictures again. "You think there are others out there?"

David took the stack of photos from Jaq and set them back on the desk. "You praying for more business, Jaq?"

She shook her head at him as if he belonged in the time-out chair. "Bad pun."

David examined his palms. "Serial killer?"

Dr. Towers' face was solemn. "This office can't keep up with autopsy demand, so selfishly I hope not, but in my experience when the message is in a body, the sequels reveal the who and why."

# Chapter Eight

Sarasota

THURSDAY'S PERFECT FLIGHT LEFT FRIDAY for a play day in the sun—cloudless skies, mid-80s on land. It had been relaxing, but now it was time. Almost midnight, the clock would soon strike Saturday when he would return to Detroit—but not until he took care of business in Sarasota.

He tapped each pocket to ensure he had everything. Then he slipped out the condominium door and down six flights of stairs. Hearing the frog under the bottom stair, he bent, scooped him up, slid him in his pocket, and zipped him in. Under the watchful eyes of the stars Nick escaped through the parking lot without as much as a squeak. Great night for a jog along the water. It usually was.

He meticulously counted the light posts while he jogged on the path he'd planned on Thursday night's jog-and-scout. Up the winding street, around the steep block, then down a long overflowing pink hibiscus curb. Waters' Edge.

Surveillance. Corner house. Quiet. Destiny. Lights off inside the house. All tucked in their little beds. Lights on in the back of the house. Jog in place, turn thirty degrees, and peer through the heavily flowered Spirea bushes. She was swimming her nightly laps. On time.

He slipped into gloves from his back pocket, then hopped over the low wooden fence. Neatly tucked into a shadow, he paused against the brick patio wall. She finished, pushed herself up on the ledge and flipped off the swimmer's cap protecting her bleached hair, then stood and retrieved her towel.

From behind, he grabbed her wet body. Firm, nicely toned, too bad. Any other day a spin on the sheets might be desirable. Today, oh wet one, you don't deserve my gentle touch.

"What?" She squealed like a stepped-on rat.

He blasted his forearm against her throat and hugged her to his chest. He knocked the breath out of her. Nick clenched his teeth. His voice was low and strained. "A lesson for you, little lady. Your little girls don't like it when you beat them with the handball paddles—meant for the game, not their behinds."

She tensed, tried to fight—hard to do without oxygen. Her neck jammed forcefully in the crook of his arm, the compression caused her head to bob up, then over. He crushed the life out of her, and she went limp.

The weight of her lifeless body dragged on him. He placed her in a lounge chair, then positioned her. Not satiated until he felt bones cracking under the force of his fingers, he swiftly lifted the crucifix that dangled near his heart. He kissed the three cross points, rubbed his fingers over it, then dropped it beneath his t-shirt. He retrieved the oblong marker from his inner jacket lining and positioned it on her neck. His fingers smoothed over it until he was satisfied the markings were level and indented sufficiently. Lifting her head, he dangled a rosary from her neck, arranging it between her breasts. The frog's neck, easily snapped, was placed over her mouth. He headed to the corner shed.

The shed was exactly as it had been described in the letter: organized pool and game equipment. He grabbed two handball paddles and ambled back toward his prey. He tied the paddles to her wrists with a large safety rope. He gazed upon her. Satisfied. Mission complete.

His jaw set, his voice low, he spoke into the warm night air. "Good night, Lesley. Your husband and little girls will have a happy life without you." He turned the pool light off and hopped back over the fence. He had a jog to finish and a restful night of sleep before his return flight to Detroit.

# Chapter Nine

Detroit

NICK SHIFTED HIS WEIGHT, UNFOLDED and refolded his handkerchief as he waited for his reservation to be called. He checked his watch, paced, and hawkeyed the hostess and the door. He hoped to be seated when she arrived. If she came. Maybe he should've called her. He checked his watch again. She saw the invite, held the rose. She will be here.

"Hello—Just Nick." Rita's voice was as soft and sensuous as he remembered. "Your invitation was the nicest surprise I've had in a long time." She reached up and kissed him lightly and placed her hand on his head as she'd done the evening they met. She worked her hand slowly down to the small of his back, then let her hand rest for a few seconds before returning it to the top of her purse.

"There's more where that came from, if you're this easy to please."

Rita laughed. "A wonderful way to make Sunday special."

He sensed she felt awkward. Nick's hand caught hers. He planted his arm around her waist and guided her behind the beckoning hostess. "Timing is everything. Yours is perfect, just like you, Angelteeny." He held her chair for her, and she sat. He bent and kissed her neck.

He rounded the table and sat across from her.

"What? If I were late, you'd have left?" Rita cleared her throat and gave a little laugh, as if he'd made a joke.

"It's very important for my women to be on time."

"Your women." Rita leaned forward. "Excuse me?"

"When people make plans together and one is late, that person devalues the other and the relationship."

"Relationship?" Her curiosity was piqued, or maybe her anger. "You've decided we're in a relationship?"

47

"Of course that, my dear, depends on you." Nick gently pulled her hand into his; the waiter poured ice water into their glasses. "You look beautiful, by the way."

"Thank you."

Her blush made her radiant.

"You said 'my women'. Does that depend on me, how I behave, as well?"

Nick squeezed her hand. "Now you are getting the idea. Smart and beautiful."

"Just how many women do you have? I won't be part of a crowd."

"A crowd of one, unless you decide to become the quiz-master. You'll find, I quiz. I don't answer."

A burly mustached waiter offered each of them a menu and began to explain the specials. Annoyed with the interruption, Nick promptly returned the menus to him.

"We'll have the buffet. I'll have coffee and a diet cola with a slice of lime. Both drinks served during my meal, and, I only drink fresh cups of coffee, so I'd like a fresh cup, no coffee added into the old cup as each is emptied or gets cold."

"Yes, sir." The waiter stood statuesque. "What would the lady like to drink?"

"I—"

"She'll have the same." Nick dismissed the waiter with a hand and arched back with an instant change of focus to Rita.

"How did you know what I wanted to eat and drink?" Rita held him with her eyes.

"I'm sorry, did you want something else, something different? I can snap back the waiter for you." She was snippier than he'd remembered.

"Not really—" Rita's voice trailed.

It was clear she wasn't sure what to do. He'd help her feel more secure. "I just hate wasting time."

Rita raised her brows and curved her lips. "That was clear Wednesday night."

"Like the buffet, I'm a man who has everything you need, or want." Nick paused, curved his lips and reached across the table and squeezed her hand. "Promise."

"I may need to try everything on the buffet, and then move right on through the menu." Rita paused, then burst into laughter.

He shook his head at her and flashed perfect teeth. He paused his every movement until he saw her pupils enlarge. She blinked and smiled at him. *They can't resist me.*

"So, tell me something, Nick. How is it we've spent the night together, now we're sharing a meal, but I still don't know your last name?"

"What's in a name anyway?"

"Everything." She pushed her chair away from the table, stood, and headed for the buffet without looking back.

Nick cocked his head and waited. She still didn't look back. He tossed his napkin on the table, stood, and followed her. He'd found himself a challenger. He was up for it.

"I like a girl with a healthy appetite." Nick fell in line behind her and began filling his plate.

"I'll work it off." Rita tossed her head back and met his gaze. She popped a strawberry into her mouth.

Nick flashed her the same 'thank you for flying the friendly skies' smile he'd flashed to thousands of travelers as they either boarded or deplaned. Patiently, he waited for her to fill in the silence. Experience taught him that women like Rita who made it their mission to learn more about him didn't let many moments pass with tranquility.

Rita leaned into Nick and whispered, "Look, I don't usually sleep with men I've just met. And, I never bring them home with me. I just don't. I'm not like that. For whatever reason, with you, I did, literally on blind faith. You could be married for all I know." She plated a final roll and headed toward their table, her tone serious, a gasp released with her final word.

Nick chuckled and followed her. "You, young lady, should trust me. Trust yourself. That simple." They arrived at the table. He arranged his plates in front of him, then sat.

Rita sat poised as a mannequin.

"I just want to get to know you. I'm not married. I find you enchanting. Going home with a woman—sex on a first encounter, is rare for me, too. Promise."

"Really?"

"Actually, I've never done it—promise. Scout's honor—cross my heart."

"A Boy Scout, too?"

"Eagle." Nick grinned.

Rita laughed.

"If you feel upset, I'm sorry. But I want to maintain the magic before we get entangled in the humdrum daily boredom. Especially since we got intimate right away."

Rita nodded. Her cheeks pinked and a half-smile emerged. "Okay. I think I understand."

"After Wednesday night, when I saw you, I felt as if I'd been looking for you all of my life. Cliché, yes, but sometimes it is what it is."

Rita nodded.

He reached over the table and gently stroked her hand. "When you came over and spoke to me, I knew I had to have you. Not just for a night. I'm hoping, yes, a relationship."

"Wasn't difficult—remember you sent me a drink. Saying thank you was the least I could do."

"Now who's playing games?" Nick wanted to catch her off guard. "You don't thank everyone who sends you a drink. And, I'm not the first guy to send you a drink."

"No—"

"Or, am I the only one feeling this way?" He frowned and his eyes focused on his plate.

Rita's eyes focused unblinkingly on his and she waited until he looked up at her to speak.

"I'm just not accustomed to all of this attention." The waiter replacing the coffee cups didn't break the gaze between them.

"Come on, Angel-teeny, that ain't true. No games. Just truth." Nick held his eyes on hers.

"About that name—please look for a different one?"

"My, you are a demanding one." Nick ignored her request; he was in the controller seat, not her.

"Look, it's been a long time since I've been in a solid relationship. I've been hurt—I can't just jump in because it looks good or feels nice."

"We've all been hurt. You have to trust someone, somewhere, sometime. That is here, now, and it's me, Angel-teeny." Nick tracked her focus. "I'm the one you're looking for."

"I need to know someone, his family, and friends before all of this. This is fast—for me." Rita bit her lip, and then softly added, "It doesn't feel like me."

Nick watched, amused by Rita's sudden loss of words. "Relax. Just know, I'm your new world. Learn to believe it." He winked. "I keep my promises." Nick slid next to her and kissed her neck.

"Promises and trust. Two big things to keep on a first-name basis," Rita said.

Nick squinched the corners of his eyes in slight amusement. "Archer. Nick Archer." He kissed her neck and earlobe. "Proof of my good will and your good fortune."

"Nick Archer." Rita repeated his name with a smile. "Our good fortune."

"Ready for the dessert part of the buffet? It's only the beginning of getting everything you want, answers included. Promise." Nick gave Rita's hand a friendly squeeze before they headed back toward the buffet, hand-in-hand this time.

Rita patted Nick's arm after she sat her desserts down before sitting in her chair. "Mmm, from those fingers you can't keep off me, I'm thinking you mean an exercise dessert before a fattening dessert?"

Rita laughed. "I was just thinking I can't afford either one."

"You need to give in to your inner pleasure center and enjoy. Think back to the other night. You still feel the chills I gave you, don't you? There are so many, many more you need to enjoy." He set his pointer finger on her wrist, moving its nail edge against her flesh, slightly twisting it until it reached her armpit.

She jumped, then flushed.

"I won't disappoint, ever." He made his voice an octave lower than it had been. "Promise."

"Just Nick, you might be too naughty for me." Rita stood, tossed the napkin from her lap onto the table, and returned to the dessert buffet.

\* \* \* \*

Relieved to be alone in the comfort of her bedroom, Rita was pleased she'd held her ground. She shed her clothes, donned her oldest cotton jersey, flopped on her bed, and grabbed the television remote. She clicked on the TV and flipped through channels. Her mind kept pace. Internal alarms wrapped her in paralyzing conflict.

She shuddered. Hell, two hours after their brunch date he'd called, and she'd agreed to another date, despite every instinct to duck and cover. She hid her face with her hands. What a day. She wanted answers to questions.

She wouldn't be controlled like some life-size remote-control Barbie—not ever again. She had almost been sent to prison for trusting the wrong man.

Nick had resuscitated vanquished feelings, causing simple desire to override intellect. She huffed at herself. What was she doing with a gorgeous specimen with offensive

mind games?

His caring nature cured the rough spots. Nick wasn't a cheater—he took her out in public places. If he knew about her past, he didn't mention it. She gazed up at the ceiling and at last resolved: there was no harm in a "relationship" with Nick, especially with safety nets in place, and she had plenty. She held out her hand and ticked them off one by one on her fingers: a best friend in Jaq, an important job, a boss who was a strong father-like figure and mentor, the telephone number of a good therapist—no one knew she hadn't called yet—her secret. Four fingers up. Withhold sex until she had answers. Her thumb up—she formed a fist. Good plan.

She yawned, stretched her body taut across the bed, and wrapped her arms above her head, then around a pillow. Content for the moment, Rita fell asleep adrift with possibilities.

# Chapter Ten

Detroit

ELBOWS ON HIS DECAYED DEPARTMENT desk, Detective David Maxwell took in a deep breath, exhaled, and shook his head. An array of files and a collage of photographs strewn across his desk dared him to make sense of the senseless murder of Chief Hanusack's brother-in-law. For hours, he struggled to find a solid lead before Dr. Towers' prediction of another victim. This time only netted him frustration and a stiff neck, not the simplest connection, or bit of inspiration.

It was near midnight. Sunday was like a silencer for crime in the city, a detective breather. He planned to meet Jaq early, but the murder of a cop's family member was always unsettling. "What was the message in that bizarre scene?" he said out loud in sleep-deprived hope he'd hear a mystical answer.

David rubbed his face hard—a rush of fresh blood to flush his lethargy away. He collected the hodgepodge of information and shoved it into his desk drawer. "Engaging for fresh eyes—exasperation for fatigued eyes," he muttered as he locked the drawer.

He stood, stretched, and grabbed his worn black leather jacket, headed toward the door and called out to the Desk Sergeant in the adjacent room. "Check me out, Sally, and have a good night—what's left of it, anyway."

Before he reached the door, his desk phone rang, and he motioned to Sally to cancel the audacious thought of going home. "Homicide—Detective Maxwell." He glanced at his Timex, immediately sorry he'd picked up the phone.

"You still giving those faded blue jeans a workout in the hard office chairs when you could be giving me a back rub?"

He cocked his head, hearing his favorite female voice. "You know damn good and well why I'm here, Detective."

Jaq laughed. "Superheroes don't take breaks."

53

"There's something obvious we missed." David yawned. "Didn't find it."

"We made a deal," Jaq said. "You're no good to me burned-out. You taught me fresh is best."

"Is this a grief call or a booty call? I'm too tired to figure it out. Leave the light on. I've got one foot out the door to sleep."

"Too late. I wish I could give you my choice." Jaq sighed. "Lieutenant called. Homicide. Meet me corner of Mack and Harvard. You'll see the black-and-whites."

"Is it—?"

"I need your assessment after you do your keen-observation thing to see if we are on the same page. Don't make me wait. I need a David fix and a caffeine fix."

Promptly re-energized on the brink of new intel, David darted past the Sergeant on call. "I'm out, Sal."

Pulling keys from his pocket, he raced to his vehicle and popped on the siren. A murder in Detroit is hardly rare. What were the odds this murder would resolve the Chief's brother-in-law's? What made Jaq so animated over this particular crime?

David smacked his lips.

\* \* \* \*

Lieutenant Winston swaggered toward David. "About time, Maxwell."

"Can't you guys keep things under control? I need some sleep." David matched the Lieutenant's gait toward the house.

"Your partner's anxious to see you. At first, I wondered if she was going to call you."

"No doubt. Women in and out of uniform get pissed off so easily." David kept in step.

"We're all going to be working overtime till the Chief is satisfied. You two need to stay on top of the case, not each other."

"Eat soap and go see your mother." They pumped up the front steps of the house. "About the case, what'd Jaq say?"

"When she arrived, she mumbled something about this being another drugged-out killer. Then suddenly, she started bellowing orders and grabbed her cell. Threw out an obscenity with each number she pressed. Figured it related to tracking you."

"Hey, Jaq, what's up?" David entered the foyer and hastened past the uniforms.

"Welcome to our Sunday night thriller." In jeans, sweatshirt, and ball cap, she looked delicious and impressively in control.

"Shall I pop corn and wait for intermission?" David followed Jaq's motioning finger and eyed the area as they progressed through the house into the square living room.

"You tell me." Jaq's voice had some verve. She was geeked. "Let's see if we reach the same conclusion. If you do, I'll buy the coffee. If you don't, you buy breakfast."

"A bit unfair, don't you think, Detective?"

Jaq raised an eyebrow. "Nope."

David understood: there was more here, but she didn't want to discuss the case until later. Their eyes locked, and her intensity closed the gap between them. She strode away, and, with a wiggle of four fingers, prompted him to investigate. He took a deep breath. He loved competence and she wore it beautifully. Her tall, lean body and tight ass didn't make her hard to look at either. His eyes followed the curves of her backside until she disappeared. He released a sigh.

He pressed forward. With each step into the bowels of the house, he tucked away his feelings for Jaq, for later. The house was small. David guessed about twelve hundred square feet. Two bedrooms down and one long room upstairs. The outside had seemed undisturbed, and the inside was clean, unlike most murder or crime scenes they investigated. Unusually clean. No disturbances. Each room, tidy. No telltale signs of a quick cleanup, even for fingerprints.

"So, surprise me. Where's the body?" David stepped toward Jaq. "Or, did you let the forensic guys take the stiff without me?"

"I wanted you to observe the premises before you viewed the victim." Jaq's eyes and head-nod pointed him toward the hallway closet. She handed him a pair of gloves.

With a gloved hand, Jaq released the closet door like a cat presenting a treasured mouse.

David stared at the body hanging in the closet as he heard Jaq's voice. "Saved the best for last."

He stepped back for the picturesque full view of the hanging, then inched forward, squatted, and squinted, to absorb every detail. He pulled out his notebook and pen and jotted: Death by hanging. Middle-aged

W/F. Plain. Brown, thick coarse hair, cropped shoulder length. Blunt cut, recently colored—no visible grey. Pudgy body, with heavy bone structure, but not really overweight. Clean, blue sweat suit, worn, no label. Her only jewelry—a wedding band: thin-plain gold. He stopped scribbling, shifted his weight, then faced Jaq.

"The hand is quicker than the eye. Is that it? 'Cause this ain't no magic show, nor is it a suicide. She's wearing a handmade rosary, clearly our killer, now serial—like Doc predicted."

"Exactly. We're still waiting for Dr. Towers and the rest of the forensic guys."

"You could've at least taken the body down. She's not going anywhere. Did CSI get photos?"

"Done. All photos, fibers, and scrapings are complete. I wanted you to see this. As is. Not just from pictures."

"I get it." David fixated on the victim and wanted to scream. Damn bastard, not again. Not on my watch. "She's hanging by a black leather belt. Looks worn, but the leather and the big buckle are strong enough to hold her up."

"Keep going," Jaq nodded.

"I'm assuming it's as much what I don't see as what I see." David took a quick look inside the shirt of the victim. "Am I right?"

"On target, as always," Jaq responded, then peeked out the window. "Medical Examiner just pulled up. Let's hear what Doc Towers has to say and leave together."

\* \* \* \*

Dr. Towers leaned forward and twisted to see more of the unfortunate woman's body. "Didn't want to take her down?"

"Jaq likes Halloween." David leaned in just above Dr. Towers' perfectly sheared Afro.

The encroachment of his personal space caused Dr. Towers to immediately turn back and peer over the top of his bifocals at David. "It does not look like there was a struggle, nor did she die by hanging from that belt. If the cause of death were by hanging, whether murder or suicide, the face would be blue." Dr. Towers turned back to look at David. "How is that for Halloween?"

"Blue?" Jaq interrupted.

"With a quick hanging, the face would not turn dark. Most are slow," the doctor said. "Death results in eventual strangulation, causing swelling. The face turns dark blue or black. Very painful way to die."

David gave Doc space to work and scanned the room. "Any idea where she was before the closet?"

"Likely the body was moved. We will run fiber and tissue samples. Bruising marks make me suspect she was strangled from behind." Dr. Towers made a clenching finger motion. "Surprised, then, for whatever reason, hung by the sick bastard who did this for display."

"A message." Jaq squatted and examined the woman's feet.

"That's really your area," Dr. Towers said. "I will get a better look once they place her onto the gurney."

"Message, like the Chief's brother-in-law." David looked from Jaq to Dr. Towers.

David pressed on. "Strangled. Larynx crushed, and hung by the throat. More straightforward. Something like: Don't speak. Because of the crushed larynx. Or, maybe it's two messages: don't speak, don't hit. Because there's also a belt. She pissed someone off, they retaliated."

"Not bad. But, how does all that relate to the Chief's brother-in-law and all those books?" Jaq's smile bordered on a smirk. "Maybe you should put in for Motives Specialist."

Dr. Towers sidled in past the assistants to take a closer look at the victim, now encased in a black body bag atop the gurney. "The dead do talk, and this one has lice." Dr. Towers held up a finger toward his assistants, stopping them from zipping up the bag. They stepped back, making room for him. "David, your guess is interesting. I will let you know if the evidence concurs. For now, come in closer to our victim for just a minute."

David and Jaq stepped in and stood shoulder-to-shoulder with Dr. Towers. They leaned in and he pulled out a magnifying glass and a silver pen, which he used to point to the part in her hair. Signs of lice, eggs. He combed his forefinger through areas of her scalp. "I don't see it throughout her scalp, which is unusual."

Jaq and David looked at each other, and then at Doc, who now kept his forefinger raised and pointed the pen with his middle finger and thumb toward the victim's neck. "Look at the tiny cuts and slight redness."

"Okay, Doc, what are we seeing?" David asked. They all peered through the large magnifying glass.

"Actually, the markings are slightly more pronounced than on the last victim—I did not see those till autopsy. The magnifier makes these quite apparent—same crucifix."

"How sure are you?" Jaq interrupted.

"Never certain till lab confirmation." Dr. Towers outlined the markings. He stepped back, tossed the gloves into a nearby trashcan, and returned the magnifying glass and pen to his pockets before motioning his assistants to finish with the body bag. Doc and the detectives stepped aside as the assistants zipped, tagged, and wheeled the black bag out.

Dr. Towers edged in toward Jaq and David. "You two want a preliminary verbal? My only comment is—you have the same perp."

"Any possibility you'd priority this case, please?" David crossed his fingers and held them in front of Doc. "We can't afford to be in the county backlog."

David felt the anger of an adrenaline rush. When he spoke, a note of urgency laced his hushed tone. "Damn perp's speaking in evil forked tongues. Silken rosary around the neck. Same?"

They'd solved countless murders with Dr. Towers and David knew his serious tone would clue the doctor in.

"It will find its way into an evidence bag. Let me swab it at the lab," Dr. Towers said. "It will keep in the Ziploc—Recon protocol. Eventually, you should find something that builds enough scent. See you after autopsy—yes, prioritized."

David and Jaq made their last round for proof, paying special attention to spots where trace evidence should have been collected. They ensured the crime-scene team sprayed for blood, brushed for fingerprints, took pictures, and combed for trace evidence from specific areas. They instructed CSI to leave a cast of all footprints with the Footprint Analysts.

Jaq and David paused to review the evidence bags marked for the lab. Twenty minutes later, they said goodbye to the teams and paced the perimeter of the house in the frigid night air, separated into their own vehicles, and headed for warmth and rivers of fresh, hot coffee.

# Chapter Eleven

WHEN DAVID AND JAQ DRAGGED themselves through the door from the parking lot, the Breakfast Bar Restaurant was nearly empty. David was relieved the weekend crowd was tucked away, preparing for a new week. He never understood why the place stayed open all night, even on holidays. Except for the cops and the after-bar crowd, there wasn't much business in the wee hours of the morning, for which he was grateful.

David tried to read Jaq's face. "So, what's your big yank with what's now our serial killer?"

Jaq tilted her head toward him. "A very methodic serial killer—"

"Hence the name serial killer—"

"This one has vivid religiously bent messages and—well. Is recreating an actual plague." Jaq released a sigh as if she were relieved to have said it out loud.

David rubbed his chin and laughed. "The power of suggestion? You're taking Doc's off-the-cuff comment about a plague of bodies to have a larger meaning because of this murder?"

"Look, Vanna White's not asking for a letter so we can solve the puzzle. Logic, common sense and Doc's comment locked in the idea."

"Building a cohesive message, a logical connection between these victims is fuzzy at best, and you want to add sheer sarcasm into the mix? You can't be serious." David pushed his shoulders into his seat and scowled. "It's been a really long day, and we're into another day. Give me facts."

Jaq put both palms flat on the table and leaned toward David. "This second one clued me in."

"Clue me." David cleared his throat, filled each of their mugs with coffee, then folded his hands.

"The ten plagues of Egypt." Jaq lowered her tone to a whisper. "This victim had lice. I asked the Chief and discovered his brother-in-law was firstborn. Both murders were committed under cover of darkness."

"I missed the bible on your nightstand. Been staying up with the big book after I fall asleep?"

She slightly raised her voice. "I've read the bible, been known to pray. And when any murderer leaves rosary calling cards, the bible's where I go calling." She dropped her mug with a thud. "This perp is haunting my darkness, keeping me awake, while you rest peacefully."

David arched a brow at her. "Me thinks we should go recreate some of those delightful squeals you make in the dark." He paused and smacked his lips as if tasting the last bite of sweet chocolate. He didn't wait for her response. "Most murders occur at night. Lots of people have lice. And being firstborn, well, that's just an accident of birth."

Jaq shook her head. "If you want to hear any squeal other than me stepping on your feet, I wouldn't brush the plague idea off. Chief Hanusack's important to both of us." She pressed the end of her spoon handle causing it to flip. She seemed pleased that it clambered loudly onto the floor.

David laughed. "Okay, if you're right, biblically, the message is for some wrongdoing. Right?"

Jaq nodded and clapped her hands, then folded them. "Expect ten victims without any history connecting them, except, of course, for their broken necks, a handmade rosary, weird positioning, and a tie to the Plagues of Egypt." She paused. "We need to figure out what the victims were doing wrong."

"What the perp *perceived* each victim did wrong, you mean."

Jaq nodded. "Revenge is a good motive."

"So?"

"Two crosses. Get it? Double cross. The cross he indents and the cross on the rosary. The message could be that the victims somehow double-crossed the perp. A connection, maybe a lead."

"We need to prove the victims knew the assailant. Could be there was some kind of business dealing that went bad or he—"

"Or she," Jaq added resolutely. She rapidly batted black web-like lashes at him. It both distracted and annoyed him. He emptied his mug in gulps, then refilled both mugs.

"Fine. He or she gained each victim's confidence, so much that they allowed him or her entry into their homes. Maybe a salesman, public official—police, fire, mail carrier."

David paused, squinted squarely at Jaq. "Love the double-cross idea, and the profilers will, too. But, you are wrong about the she."

"And, you are an ass."

"A woman acting alone couldn't string up anyone the size of our latest victim."

"You're too quick to rule people out; women can be as strong as men—even stronger."

David chuckled. "I wish we could rule someone in." Raising the emptied coffeepot, he flagged the waitress. "It's exhausted."

Jaq shook her head. "The issue or the coffee pot?"

"Don't ask questions if you don't want to hear answers."

Jaq folded her arms in front of her on the tabletop and leaned in. "I know you, Maxwell. What's the plan?"

"Doc gave me a few medical search terms. I used those with a few of my own, like: strangulation, crushed larynx, cross, clean crime scene. I sent the computer searching statewide, then nationwide for murders fitting our facts."

"So, the night wasn't wasted." Jaq paused while the waitress put fresh cups and a pot of coffee on the table.

"Worked with our profiler." David sighed. "I could do that work all day."

"Too speculative for me. What'd you take a stab at?"

"Goes something like this. Serial killer makes victims' deaths appear random, but they're not—each victim lives with or has a relationship with a child. Our perp lives or works in close proximity to the Detroit, Wayne County area. Had a troubled childhood. Leaves each crime scene sterile, like his feelings—he has none because he had to shield them from what he endured in his childhood," David said. "It's not much, but it's more than we had."

Jaq shrugged. "Pretty basic. Anything else?"

"Yeah. He thinks the Crusher, as he calls this serial killer, crushes voice boxes because somewhere in his own life he lost his own voice—couldn't speak up—was a victim himself until he got out of whatever situation he was in."

"Makes sense." Jaq webbed her hands out and stretched her fingers, then locked them together in a ball in front of her.

"Family discord, violence—"

"Yeah. If this gets worse, I'm sleeping with the lights on."

"I'm your light." David reached out, gave her hand a gentle squeeze, then gently tapped his fingers on the rim of his coffee cup.

"Did you and the profiler interpret the strangulation without any relationships among the killer and victim, or are you now saying the Double

Cross Killer—our name for this serial killer, is related to his victim, now victims?" Jaq fished through the pink packets looking for real sugar.

"Serial killers don't kill randomly, and they don't kill relatives or people they know." David shook his head at her. "Why are you always contrary?"

"Lots of people live with their families and have relatives visit. It's not unusual. Criminals clean the crime scene before fleeing, and some serial killers get off by setting the scene." Jaq raised her brows at him and nodded. "I enjoy being contrary."

David tapped his forefinger on the table. "We'll need to check it off the list. I doubt there's any blood relation or any other between the victims, even remotely. Likely, they crossed his path."

"Unlocking that connection is going to be tough." Jaq nodded.

David agreed. "Need to hear more profiling about the perp taking continued chances by setting the scene, getting kicks by doing the deed knowing he could be caught."

"And the kids aren't harmed or snatched." Jaq squinted as if trying to see through him. "We need to determine if the children of the victims knew each other."

"I love the way your dimples come out when you frown as you work things out."

Jaq pressed right through the emerging blush. "And check if any of the relatives lived in any of the other victims' homes at any time."

"You get the prize for most obvious questions." David made fish lips at her, and then reverse puckered them into a half smile. "Process of elimination."

"Obvious, I know. But teasing you gives me pleasure, especially when you owe me breakfast." Jaq stuck out her tongue and snatched the bill. "Admittedly, though, the child aspect adds a new dimension."

David grabbed the end of the bill. "Hey, not so fast. This wasn't breakfast, just coffee— my treat. A really nice breakfast my treat, your call. Now, let's get some sleep."

"I intend to keep you up just a bit longer," Jaq taunted with fond sarcasm and released the bill when he grabbed it.

David met her eyes across the table, swigged the last of his coffee, and cocked his head and the mug at her. "Honey, you have the ammunition to do just that." He slid out from the booth and strolled toward the register.

# Chapter Twelve

Detroit

UNDER THE BRIGHT LIGHT ABOVE the Medical Examiner's autopsy table, fascination laced through the gore factor. The victim, now evidence, the human factor secondary, yet treated with great respect, pulled medicine and law together. The cold, sterile room had just enough maneuverability for everyone to have the proper vantage point and work space.

"Like my dry cleaning—Sunday night murder, autopsy Tuesday afternoon," David said. "Thanks for taking this matter so quickly."

"Kindly, do not spread the word." Dr. Towers raked a stern eye over the top of his glasses at David.

"I don't know how you do this, Doc." Jaq shivered. A blue mask covered most of Jaq's face. "I can't dispel the vision of the victim's body looking more animal than human sprawled out in this dissection position."

"A carcass carrier of messages, crudely put." Dr. Towers' focus didn't waver, he remained bent over the body. He wore magnifying glasses. "I have heard it all—I am a means to an end, a puzzle solver, the key to riddles—shall I keep going?"

"Doc, we mean no insult. Just need answers." David needed the chatter to avoid thinking about his swirling stomach. He wondered what made Jaq so strong. Dr. Towers held her close attention as he pulled and pointed at bruises, organs, bones, burns, and cuts.

"I have always said, I am the true ventriloquist of the dead—a simple conveyer of their stories."

David grinned. "How do you reconcile the fact that your lips always move?"

"As predicted. Cause of death: Homicide. Body moved after the murder," Doc said. "Both bruising and the concentration of blood indicate she was kneeling when she actually died. She was then laid down; an oblong apparatus with a crucifix was pressed into her throat. Then, she was dragged until she was finally hung in the closet."

"Court-certain about the crucifix?"

"Yes. I'll testify. These wounds are slightly deeper. Each victim has the same markings, but these are clearer."

"On purpose?" Jaq asked.

"Likely. Takes control and calculation, practice and planning." Dr. Towers stopped and stared at them.

Jaq took a deep breath and slowly exhaled. David could see her mind churning. He scratched down some notes with his gloved hands.

With deliberate respect for the deceased, Dr. Towers folded back the white sheet, fully exposing bare legs, thighs, and hips. "Her heels. Ankles. The lower portion of the right leg. You can clearly see surface scratches." He paused and pointed. "And, where the color is more intense on the right side of her leg and arm, that is rug burn. Fresh marks. Given her weight, one hundred eighty pounds, skin injury was inevitable."

Jaq nodded. "She was dragged."

"Right. I found fibers inside the burn areas consistent with the carpet in the home."

David forgot his queasiness. "How far was she dragged?"

"Estimate, five feet. Any farther and we would see deeper, more intense rug burn."

David scribbled in his notepad as fast as he could, and shuffled uncomfortably in the blue sterile garb. "Can you guess the height of the perp?"

"At least six feet."

"Man or woman? I think we should be open to either." Jaq folded her arms, hugging herself. She looked cold.

"You tell me," the doctor said. "Scratches on the victim, likely caused from changing position. Perp simply needs upper and lower body strength to drag, lift, and hang her."

Jaq shivered. "Did the dearly departed tell you why she was on her knees?"

"See the bruising on each shoulder?" Dr. Towers stepped forward and pointed to the shoulders.

"Fingerprints?" Jaq followed David from the end of the metal table to the head of it.

"Pushed against her will to her knees by pressing her shoulders down with such force these bruises resulted." Dr. Towers stopped and pointed. "Quite painful."

"Knocking the wind out of her, the bastard then reaches across her and breaks her windpipe? Double whammy," David said.

"Not before strangling the poor woman." Dr. Towers entwined his fingers to demonstrate the strangulation. "Tiny broken blood vessels in her eyes confirm strangulation."

"Bare hands, damn bastard," David said.

"Killer is a thrill-seeker," Dr. Towers said. "He uses his hands instead of a weapon because he gets a thrill from actually touching his victims as he literally squeezes the life out of them. From the way he hung this victim, my guess is he sees himself as Godlike—all powerful."

"Up close and personal fits the Double Cross Killer." David leaned in to see the prints with Jaq.

"The victims were off guard and out of shape." Dr. Towers pointed to the length of the body. "No tricks—sheer logic, plain science. By the way, Double Cross Killer is an apt name for your perpetrator."

"Jaq gets the credit for that," David said. "How did he break her windpipe?"

"Punched it in until he felt it crackle. A few seconds of intense suffering, then no more pain, ever."

"Doc, what do you make of the lice you found at the scene?" Jaq asked.

"Interesting issue," Doc said. "Rita and I took additional pictures of the scalp. I scraped the lice and spent some time before you arrived this afternoon under the microscope looking at the slides we made."

"Was she infested?" Jaq asked with a frown.

"Not at all. My hunch is the lice was simply scraped up and planted at the hairline. No active infestation." Doc's brows furrowed. "The scalp and hair follicles are very clean."

David interrupted. "My guess is our Double Cross Killer will escalate, begin to kill more frequently."

Dr. Towers finished David's thought. "He seems to have a meticulously detailed plan." He pulled the white sheet over the body. The trio walked out of the examination room, into the outer lab and work area, with a quick removal of gloves, masks, and blue paper garb before final trash bin disposal.

"The shoe size fits your height theory. But we have partial prints that indicate a wider width, size-thirteen shoe," David said.

"Actually, we now have two different shoe sizes, eleven and thirteen," Jaq said. "Each crime scene had a different size print."

"We're building a fairly specific Double Cross Killer profile. He gets a sick thrill out of making the victims so comfortable, there's no struggle when he kills them." David stepped over to the lab counter and scanned the sample slides Doc had labeled. "Could be a plant—shoe sizes are so easily changed."

"True, smart monster. Undoubtedly knows any struggle means trace evidence and a loss of control, so he has to get trust and within striking distance," Jaq said. "He's got a mix of high IQ and a very low valuation of the world around him—walking nitroglycerine."

Dr. Towers sighed. "What do you know about this victim's personal life?"

"Single working mother." David reached in his jacket pocket, grabbed his notepad, and flipped back several pages. "Lower middle-income. Daughter in the second grade. Ex rarely around. Had lots of boyfriends—strong possibility she was supplementing her income with the oldest profession in the world. Victim's mother is in Florida. She's been called and will take the child back with her after the funeral, child seems great with that."

Dr. Towers frowned and nodded.

Jaq interjected. "Child seems more excited to live with her grandmother than distraught about her mother's death—but at that age most kids don't understand death."

"Mom have any criminal history?"

"Several calls to the home—domestic. No arrests. Not one officer filed an official report. No particulars."

"I have not mentioned it recently, but as a bit of a closet profiler, this case has come to intrigue me." Dr. Towers snapped up his bifocals and rested them on his forehead. "Like hanging by belt. A belt can be used to whip someone into shape. Could be a double meaning."

"She got hit by someone she hit?" Jaq said.

"Exactly," Dr. Towers said. "Just a thought."

"We had that same idea. He has the need to silence his victims, the throat, voice box—crushing it speaks deliberately to us." David cut his eyes from Doc to Jaq.

"He could want to stop them from talking to the wrong people. But the nonsensical things, like the lice—" Jaq paused, turned toward David, then focused her attention on Doc. "You inadvertently sent me into an interesting direction when you used the term 'plague.'"

"Excuse me?" Doc scratched the back of his neck.

"I'm researching the religious angle. He's causing a plague of death and using the Plagues of Egypt to send a message," Jaq said. "David thinks I'm way out in left field."

Doc raised a brow and his face seemed to brighten. "Interesting concept, although I did not mean anything by my comment."

David surprised, studied Dr. Towers. "What I said—"

Jaq tapped her temple and interrupted David. "We operate on proof, we're finding evidence. For me, the lice, advances my plague theory. Wait and see."

Doc shrugged. "To expedite, my nurse assistant, Rita Rose, is personally following up with toxicology."

Jaq tiled her head. "How's she working out?"

"She is a gem. In fact, I had a call from the Mayor. He suggested these Double Cross Killer cases become a priority of this office, and to ensure limited staff involvement I assigned Rita to be my only assistant on these cases, assuming there are going to be a number of them."

Doc continued. "Someday give me the female perspective on how all the beautiful women end up with all the jerks."

"She told you—" Jaq began.

Doc interrupted. "About her former fiancé, who left the scene of an accident and left her to take the fall for driving under the influence causing death." Dr. Towers straightened up and stretched. "She was honest with me and I read the papers. It was highly publicized and gossiped about in the hospital."

Jaq bit the corner of her lip. "She couldn't talk about it for a long time, still can't."

Dr. Towers nodded. "Sad. Better human than most. Shattered her confidence."

"Tough case to figure out. I almost didn't believe her." Jaq's gaze fell to her feet. "She still has nightmares about her incarceration and the jogger's death."

"You might recall, I performed the jogger autopsy," Dr. Towers said. "At night, wearing dark clothes, joggers, even at age nineteen should know better. Dr. Fazul was too drunk to have the reflexes to drive a straight line or to stop. As a passenger, there was nothing she could do. She was too intoxicated to intervene."

"Sheer loyalty and instinct helped you solve it. It was a miracle you figured out it was Dr. Fazul in the driver's seat." David stepped toward the outer office.

"It was my magic decoder ring. I still feel guilty it took me so long."

"The facts simply were not on her side." Dr. Towers' voice was protective. "You stuck in there till you got it right. All that counts. Rita knows."

"We need to head out." David pointed a thumb out.

"I will review the tissue samples of both victims. Final written results to you ASAP." Dr. Towers shook Jaq's hand, then David's. "Keep me updated on any new evidence."

"Thanks, Doc." Jaq leaned against the heavy glass office door.

"I asked Rita to compile a computer search and pull the charts of all deceased with broken necks that have come through this hospital, regardless of cause or year of death."

"Great minds think alike." David grinned. "I ordered that through our computers."

David pulled open the weighty door and followed Jaq into the hallway. The dimmer light of the wide corridor made the oversized baroque-framed antique art seem haunting and Dickensian. A few minutes later, the hallway emptied them into Jaq's special-edition Jeep. David grabbed her keys.

"We have our working theory." Jaq ignored him and kept talking while she slid into the passenger seat and clipped in the belt.

"What theory?"

"Children living with the victims."

"Or visiting. This victim had her child, a parade of boyfriends, and an ex lurking somewhere," David said.

"Something Doc and you said about the belt made me think," Jaq began. "About kids?"

David pulled the jeep over and parked it. In the darkness under the street lamps, Jaq explained. "Lots of people hit kids with belts or threaten to. Belts and kids, make sense—that's how I grew up."

"Begs the obvious question." David scanned her. "How does he know them?"

"My sister runs her life by her kids' schedules," Jaq said. "You could run an army just by watching her garage door."

"So, the perp watches the house a few times—"

"Exactly—school, daycare, family shopping outings with mom or dad," Jaq said. "I always know when it's okay to stop over for a hot meal or to do laundry."

"And the perp can easily stake out the place, get in and out virtually unseen amidst family chaos. That's also how he knows there's enough time to arrange the victims' bodies," David said. "You got all that from a belt?" He felt her excitement.

"And my magic decoder ring."

He saw her shoulders relax into case confidence. He revved up the engine and pulled out into traffic. "We've got a lot of work to do."

Jaq grabbed onto her seat. "Hey, slow down there, hotshot."

Several minutes later, David wheeled the Jeep sharply into Jaq's designated parking spot at Central PD and cut his eyes to her as he pulled the keys from the ignition. "I'm thinking it's time to order anything that can be delivered—your choice. Put dinner out of the office on my future tab."

Jaq nodded and grabbed her keys from him. "Daycares, churches, Child Protective Services reports, schools, sports, YMCA camps—that's a lot of ground to cover looking for common activity. Double Cross Killer's targeted area is in there. I can feel it."

David punched in the elevator code. "Then let's crush him."

# Chapter Thirteen

Sarasota

DETECTIVE RONALD RANDALL WASN'T A large man, and he was okay with that. His ability to hide in a crowd, create his own burrow, and investigate unnoticed, allowed him to work unhindered, causing his colleagues at the Sarasota Police Department to nickname him Rabbit. They celebrated his ability to solve multiple cases at the same time; despite the Department's efforts to limit him to one key criminal case at a time, he habitually resolved matters not assigned as well as his own caseload, to the dismay of some and the amazement of others. Rabbit and Abel Mendoza, his partner, worked in sync. Others tried to keep up with them, but failed.

Scratching generous waves of salt and pepper hair atop a high forehead with one hand, while flicking cigar ash into an overfilled ashtray with the other, Rabbit stepped away from the kitchen table to take full view of the notes he'd made on the opposite wall.

"Not again, Ronnie," his wife Tammy said. "Every time there's a conundrum, I get a kitchen full of notes, ashes and cigar butts."

Rabbit grinned at his wife of five years. Frustrated yes, but she wasn't mad, despite her tone. "Yeah, but you know I am good to finish the remodel after I solve this case." Rabbit grabbed her petite waist and twirled her toward him. Softly kissing her, he lost his fingers in her long blonde curls.

"My poor kitchen was supposed to be ready for Thanksgiving, and it's two weeks to Christmas Eve."

"Look, Goldie, I have a bad feeling about the cases we've been assigned."

"Serial killer for sure?"

"No one's safe until this perp is found. That includes you, relatives, and friends. Two families have been torn apart. There'll be others. A phantom killer who leaves a message, then disappears."

Nodding, Tammy massaged her husband's shoulders. "You'll find what you're looking for. You always do. Just do one thing, for me?"

70

"What's that, Goldie?" Rabbit chuckled.

"Well, first of all—just because that nickname worked when we were in college, don't think I'm not wise to your plan to soften me up."

Rabbit fondly remembered the day he'd given his wife that moniker. He reached an arm around his chair, scooped her forward and pulled her onto to his lap. Tammy seated across his legs, locked eyes with him. He looked squarely into the large hazel eyes he'd loved for what seemed his whole life. He swore they shone more brightly than the finest cut diamond. "Now, what were you saying?"

"For me, I'm going to love this bigger kitchen. But next, we need to add a study, with a bar area so you can hibernate, make coffee, grab a beer, whatever you do when you go into crime-solving mode. We either need to add another room or—"

Rabbit frowned. "Or, what? This sounds like something between serious and ominous. Should I grab the hard liquor before you go on?"

Tammy remained sitting on Rabbit's lap and pressed her chest into his. She wrapped her arms around his neck and hugged him tightly, then whispered in his ear, "Look, honey, I love watching you stress and work around the clock. I love how your mind works at solving things. But, here's the thing; I just don't want the baby to stress out or smell cigar smoke. They say—"

"What did you say?" Rabbit asked. Feeling a warm tear fall against his chest, he pulled her away from him enough to place them eye-to-eye. They'd tried for so long he'd given up, taken it for granted it would just be the two of them. "Are you sure?"

Unblinking, Tammy nodded.

"If it's a girl, we'll name it after her beautiful mother, Goldie." Rabbit pulled Tammy to her feet and twirled her with him around the kitchen until they were laughing and weeping.

\* \* \* \*

Rabbit watched as his wife lay in his arms sleeping. Although it was the middle of the night and his body was spent, he couldn't sleep. His mind flicked back and forth between the two victims. An old man in a wheelchair and a woman in a pool. There was no commonality except the signature containing the message—a signature they couldn't read. Where would he strike next? There had to be a way to get ahead and stop him.

Rabbit gently rolled his wife onto her side of the mattress and slipped his arm out from under her. He threw back his side of the covers, stood, and ran his hands through his hair, scratching his scalp as if to massage the brewing questions into answers or push them into oblivion. He had to move forward despite the early hour and the still-sleeping sun. Tammy was breathing the regular deep inhalations of someone fast asleep; Rabbit grabbed his robe and pajama pants from the foot of the bed and headed for the kitchen.

Clicking on the kitchen light, he immediately focused on the notes he'd made on each victim. His ritual was to tape case notes to the refrigerator door, review, and modify. He scanned the door, opened it, and retrieved the orange juice.

Jonathan Willow, 82, Crest Drive, Grandfather. Murdered in Wheelchair. No sign of struggle. Hand in pants. Lived with daughter, son-in-law, granddaughter. Broken neck, strangled, crushed windpipe, bruising in the shape of a cross on neck, silk macramé rosary.

Lesley Vincent, 33, Water's Edge, Mother. Murdered Poolside. No sign of struggle. Handball Paddles tied to wrists. Lived with her husband, their two children. Broken neck, strangled, crushed windpipe, bruising in the shape of a cross on neck, silk macramé rosary. Frog, broken neck placed over victim's mouth.

Gulping orange juice from the carton, Rabbit walked from the refrigerator to the cabinet where he'd affixed a map. He scrutinized his notes and the family interviews. The victims lived within a five-mile radius of each other. Each victim lived with children, who were not at home at the time of the crime. There were no witnesses. Like a shadow creeping in and out, unnoticed, the perpetrator took lives, left a bizarre encrypted message, then vanished.

Rabbit tipped the orange juice carton for its final drippings, crushed the carton in frustration, released a belch, and planted himself at the kitchen table.

Glaring at the dates, he pulled the crime scene photographs from the files and lined them up across the table. Why hadn't he flagged it before? He grabbed a calendar and verified: weekends. Both murders. The first, Sunday; the second, Friday. Killer with a weekend schedule. A commuter, transient worker, long-haul truck driver, weekend worker, vacationer. Someone who doesn't leave their home until the weekend—travels or works on specific weekends. Military—he'd previously thought of that—too easy, and easy was not usually the answer. Pondering the macramé rosaries—a religious nut. Again, too easy. He pounded the table. He spied his cigars, but vowed to give them up with the gift of the baby. Damn.

National Guard—weekend warriors. A trained soldier could creep in and out unnoticed, had enough discipline to do a tidy job, and likely had intelligence training.

Rabbit popped open his computer and pressed the On button. The Google search for military units in and around Sarasota, Florida didn't take long. He hit one link after another. As the computer crunched its data, he reached for his cell and dialed Bennie Wayland, the Special Agent assigned to assist him.

"Hello?" a raspy voice whispered at the other end.

"Bennie, you awake?"

"Rabbit, again? What the hell are you doing now? It's four a.m. This had better be good."

"No time to explain. I need you to get to your desk, pull up all murders with neck injury that have occurred on a weekend—Friday, Saturday, Sunday. Look for any similarities to our serial killer."

Bennie yawned. "Did you figure out what he is communicating?"

"Bennie, listen. When he communicates something other than murder, I'll let you know. Got it?"

"Yes, boss."

Rabbit blew his frustration into the receiver. "Print up all military bases, units, training centers, whatever Florida has around the Sarasota area. Get the logs, photos and films from all weigh stations and tollbooths within one hundred miles of Sarasota. I want travel logs for any truck that's been through the Sarasota area on the weekends of each murder, and the film from every tollbooth on those weekends."

"This couldn't have waited?"

"No, it's Tuesday. We can expect another dead message as early as Friday."

He heard a pause, and then Bennie exhaled. "Okay, I'm leaving already. What branch? Army, Navy, Air, Coast Guard?"

"All of them. But focus on the National Guard, doing their weekend thing, and full-timers who regularly travel."

"Their weekend duty," Bennie interrupted.

"Whatever you want to call it. Just do it. Then, any remaining military. Next, tollbooth film. Finally, truck drivers and weigh stations."

"You think there is a military connection? Terrorism? Maybe he's communicating a sadistic message?" Bennie paused. "Dots don't connect. Truck driver makes more sense."

"Bennie." Rabbit clenched his teeth. He was trying to be patient, but the thought of another lost life on his shoulders was a heavy weight. "On task. We can talk later?"

"I just get excited when you do your thing—"

"I'll keep you posted—but right now we have to stop a delivery."

"I need a few days."

"Twenty-four hours. Get it, all of it, enlist help if you need to— without explanation—in the order I've outlined. Be there in a few hours." Rabbit clicked off, tossed the cell aside and pushed his chair from the table. He yawned and faced the refrigerator door, then glared at each victim list.

He clamped his eyes.

An image of the frog jumped out at him with the Assassin Bugs.

His eyes popped open. He scribbled Assassin Bugs at the end of the first victim's list. He rubbed his temple—overtired and overthinking—?

Assassin Bugs and a frog, a bad fairy tale—more like a Grim Reaper calling card. He touched his toes, then stretched up. Another yawn. Time to return to bed and his wife.

\* \* \* \*

At the station shortly after eight, a seemingly bottomless Mountain Dew in front of him, Rabbit sat behind his oversized worn-oak desk, polishing off his second raisin bagel stuffed with butter and cream cheese, scrutinizing data. He wiped a butter stain off his jeans and tossed a pile of crumpled napkins in the trash bin beside him.

Bennie piled a second stack of computer data on the corner of his desk. Rabbit angled up. "You did good." Rabbit wanted to show his appreciation, but he didn't have much time. His eyes were already focused on the neatly labeled files and bulky printouts. With a thumbs-up to Bennie, he began to attack the files.

"Military information is complete. Eh—" Bennie hesitated, his uniform as neatly pressed as his voice. "I'm waiting on logs, photos, and films from the active weigh stations and tollbooths, not easily accessible. I assured them we would keep it quiet, if they would."

"I don't cut deals or promises." Rabbit paused, file in hand. "Especially if circumstances don't allow me to keep them."

"Don't think like that." Bennie always skewed reality to avoid issues. "A little insurance to get info without drawing media attention. Otherwise, you wouldn't have any info, and nothing expedited without court orders and subpoenas. Followed your orders."

Rabbit nodded, without looking up. "Just can't be boxed in. When will you have the rest? The first victim made everything past-due."

Benny's thumbs were looped in his back pockets. He shrugged. "Being delivered. I had guaranteed all information would be signed for by one of the three of us, with proof of identification or it was a no-go."

"They watch too many detective shows. Think we solve crimes by hanging around waiting for information that magically appears. What if we're not available?"

Bennie muttered. "I will be. I assured them."

Rabbit growled. "Hope you've got your sleeping bag and toothbrush."

Bennie sighed. "The hell of it is, the military's making me come in. They want my fingerprints, my official ID, driver's license, and a certified-as-true copy of your ID and an order-to-work on the files before they'll release anything. Seems since my inquiry, there've been some discussions with the two-star general, who finally gave approval—his way or no way. Surprisingly, the military offered help."

"At this rate, we might need a battalion or two."

"General said it would be good training for their profiler. Wonders if this is tied to any national security issues and would be happy to circumvent the CIA, if they're involved. Interesting group, the military. More closed-mouthed and controlling than the feds."

Rabbit winced. "Maybe we should make some tea-sipping time with the two-star to enlist their help." Rabbit held a curled pinkie finger up. "If I really get stumped."

Bennie took a step toward Rabbit. "I'll be damned. You're onto something. I can see it in your face. Gonna share any time soon?"

"When I know, you'll know. I'm mulling over a few things. I've got pieces; I'm missing fittings for them. Where's Abel this morning?"

"It's seven thirty. He's not obsessive-compulsive."

"When you see Abel, tell him I said to save the siestas for Argentina. Don't you have some place to be?" Rabbit's eyes were back in the files.

"I'm already gone." Bennie jammed his notepad into his back pocket and charged toward the door.

\* \* \* \*

Shortly after nine thirty, Abel clomped in and called out to Rabbit as he approached. "I've got the ticket. Si. But it's on a really long reel." He set an A&W bag on the corner stack of papers on Rabbit's desk.

"Spending time at the American movies again?" Rabbit stuck a straw in the soda lid. "Explains your bearing gifts of soda and chili dogs this early. Americans prefer donuts, bagels, and eggs for breakfast."

"Si. I'm not married to two women for a reason. You're beginning to sound like my other wife. I'll wait till we go to counseling to answer?" Abel's face contorted like it did when he'd emptied the dog bag. He pushed the bag at Rabbit to take the first helping.

Rabbit reached into the A&W bag. "You're forgiven, my stomach thinks it's lunchtime. Try thinking about the phrase: you are what you eat." He took a long drink. "This additional Mountain Dew will replace my lost hours of sleep."

Abel lowered his voice. "My wife put me on a diet. She makes green food. This is my only real food." He reached into the duffle bag slung over his shoulder, grabbed a stack of logs in a rainbow of colors, and sat across from Rabbit.

Rabbit grinned at the sight of the paper in front of Abel. "Guessing, truck logs?"

"No. But your idea of National Guard, trucks and travelling spun the notion—" Abel was cut off.

"How—" Rabbit began, but Abel interrupted his interruption.

"Bennie sent me a text to calm you down. It woke me. After I called and he filled me in, I spent the rest of my night going to various cab stations." Abel reached a handful over to Rabbit. "I spoke with many dispatchers and cabbies—some we know, many new. These logs are from twenty-four hours before and after each murder. Your visitor theory may be right. A visitor needs transportation. Cabs."

"Cabs?" Rabbit squinted down at the papers in his hand. "Cabs. Great idea."

"Si. I think—what would I do? Taxi cab, unless perp has his own or rents. If we find nothing, perp might be a local."

Rabbit nodded. "Good call. Perp could call cabs to avoid tollbooth cameras on his license plate, trace evidence left in his vehicle, or to claim he and his vehicle were home."

"Smart. Calculates everything. Premeditation, no heat-of-passion crap. Plans every detail, or he would've made some mistake, left a fiber or a print."

"Cabbies also fit the profile for a traveler in and out of the area."

"Si." Abel stuffed the last bit of mustard dog into his mouth and lifted his brows.

"Cabbies don't ask for names or ID. And invisible people pay with cash. Cabbies tend to travel the same destinations, like the airport run."

Abel let out a sigh and rolled his dark eyes. "Just a start to help you pull another rabbit out of the hat."

"Wish we had months, weeks, not hours."

"I'm just in it for the accolades and the hot dogs."

Rabbit crumbled the empty bag, tossed it in the trash bin next to his desk and watched it land. He raised his eyes to Abel. "I'll pull a team to look for patterns in the cabbie logs. You get the rest of them, then pull a profiler for the information we have."

"Two teams? One team?"

"Two. But, find everyone you can to help. Weekend is close. Different perspectives may help find something we haven't been able to."

"Good idea." Abel grabbed his soda, shoved the final dog into his mouth. "I'm out," he said with a stuffed mouth.

# Chapter Fourteen

Detroit

RITA AND JAQ CRUNCHED DOWN the snowy sidewalk in the crisp December air about an hour before sunrise Thursday morning. Worn brick building fronts held shopper phantoms, engaged now with white-collar businesses, varied eateries, and for lease signs. Snow and ice build-up left only a thin sidewalk path where the little salt that had been spread worked some magic and cleared a cement river for them to walk along. Rita could see her breath and was thankful she'd worn thermal long underwear. Jaq's ponytail bobbed along, but Rita wondered whether Jaq could hear with the thick black wool band over earmuffs doing double duty. "I had to keep him to myself for a while before I told anyone, even you," Rita shouted.

Jaq nodded slowly. She pushed her lips in and out a few times before she spoke. "Sounds like you really like Nick, but I think you kept him to yourself because you have serious doubts." She placed her hand on Rita's arm. "I can't blame you."

"Don't make me sorry I confided in you. I really like this guy."

"Good income, handsome package, and enough of a smooth talker to immediately bed you."

"Jaq, you make me sound awful."

"Don't unravel—no judgment, just observation and concern. If you don't want the truth, don't ask me questions." Jaq stepped up the pace and the passion in her voice. "He lives with his mother, but claims to be worldly. Something's not right."

"You've been a detective too darn long. Not everyone's a criminal."

"No one's perfect—"

"Nick—I've seen it, tested it, and will testify." Rita giggled. She had to lighten the mood.

"You slut." Jaq trotted a circle around Rita.

"In my defense, I'm not sleeping with him again—till I know more."

"Too late. You already gave away the milk."

"Okay, Grandma. I'm not using sex to get him to marry me. I want to really know him, not just have great sex with him."

"Now we're talking. The sex is fabulous? What else?" Jaq faced Rita, batted her lashes quickly, and grinned.

Rita stopped and swiveled in front of Jaq almost knocking into her. "Enough. Exactly why I didn't tell you. I want to make sure this relationship is the real thing before the world finds out about it. When no one knows, there's nothing to explain. Not like last time."

"Look, I couldn't be happier for you, as long as you keep your antennae up. It's about time you dated. Once you date one, other men will want to date you. Circulation, it's a good thing."

Rita reached into the snow bank next to her, grabbed a handful of clean snow and flung it onto Jaq.

"Hey, not fair, you're the one who needs cooling off, not me." Jaq brushed the snow off her hair and shoulders.

"Keep up the interrogation and there's more where that came from. Remember, I'm much closer to the ground than you." Rita ran a circle around Jaq, dodging her attempts to return the snow shower. Quickly, they fell back into step, walking.

"So, when can I meet him?" Jaq leaned her face into Rita's.

Rita squinted at her. "You have selective hearing, you know that? Not just yet. I mean it, Jaq. All mine right now. We've hardly dated. Can you and David even publicly double date?"

"You know department rules—"

"Are meant to be broken—what they don't know can't hurt." Rita stepped up the pace this time as they rounded the corner. "Just being near the two of you is like being too close to a bonfire. It's a question of time before the wood at the top bursts into flame in front of the whole department."

"Okay, Freckles," Jaq said. Jaq stopped, pulled off her insulated gloves, reached into her pocket for a tissue, and blew her nose.

"You and Dr. Towers getting along?" Seriousness returned to Jaq's voice.

"You must've said a lot of nice things about me. He's been great. Said the hospital was full of it. Wants me to work with him permanently."

"And you?"

"I prefer the living, but I'm intrigued by the dead. He makes it fun, if you can call what we do fun." Rita followed Jaq and began stretching. "I'm researching criminal pathology."

Jaq nodded and motioned Rita to return to walking.

"How's therapy?" Jaq raised her forehead.

"Wind's changing." Rita's voice had a definite edge. "Let's head back to my apartment."

They reversed and headed back mid-block.

"Too perfect?" Rita asked. "Is that what you're thinking?"

"I don't pre-judge." Jaq followed Rita into the warmth of her apartment. The spacious foyer served as the gateway to a massive living room, and a welcoming dining room and kitchen entrance were also visible. A hallway with a guest bath leading to the master bedroom easily configured into the overall design. "You deserve to be happy—you need to realize it."

Rita wriggled out of her winter layers. "I'm beginning to roast."

"Me, too." Jaq laughed. "Rita—it's a new relationship, you're still running on IRA: idyllic romantic adrenaline. Trust your INP: inner nagging parent—if something doesn't feel right, it's not."

"Okay, *ONF*: old nagging friend." Rita flung her jacket at Jaq.

The phone rang in the kitchen, and both women's attention converged on it.

"Who calls you at six thirty in the morning?" Jaq laughing, slipped off her own jacket, grabbed Rita's from the floor and tossed them both on the coat rack to the side of the door.

Rita pointed at the phone. "Could be for you." She didn't dare suggest Jaq pick it up—she wasn't ready for Nick and Jaq to meet, even over the telephone. She put the receiver to her ear.

"Hey, Angel-teeny."

"Hey you." Rita bit the corner of her lip and focused on a corner of the ceiling.

"Ready for an early morning rise with me before work? A little erotica over the phone is just what my morning called for."

Rita turned and bulged her eyes to plead with Jaq, who obviously understood. "I'll make coffee," she whispered, and tiptoed into the kitchen.

Rita breezed back to the front door, kicked off her running shoes, then scampered into the living room and curled up on the sofa. "Actually, I'm up, getting in my exercise." She pulled off her socks and tossed her grandmother's displayed crocheted afghan from the back of the couch onto her feet.

"Good girl. Who's there with you?"

"Just Jaq—Jacqueline," Rita said. "My best friend for years—we met at yoga. We're on a pretty strict exercise routine." Impatiently, she tapped her fingers on the arm of the couch.

"You ought to jog with me. Walking and yoga aren't real exercise."

Rita paused before she answered, wondering if he was joking. "When Jaq's tied up—Yoga's a tough workout."

He laughed. "You wouldn't be cheating on me, would you, Angel-teeny?"

*I'll cheat, with yoga, yes. I bet I can out-jog you.* She tapped her fingers faster. Was Jaq right? Had she acquired another fruitcake? A little chill prickled her spine; she clutched the afghan and spread it over her. "I'll let you know when Jacqueline becomes Jack." She tried to laugh, but it fell short of normal.

"You and I aren't the cheating kind." Nick's voice was almost a whisper.

Saliva was collecting in her mouth, she swallowed hard. She was glad he wasn't there or she might impulsively spit in his face; instead she cornered him. "Are we talking exclusive?"

"I'm not a player. I thought you understood that. I didn't think you were either." He paused. "I know our first date—" His voice was slower and deeper still.

Rita interrupted. "When we met, we were both playing roles. They were fun, but we were not ourselves." She paused. "I like exclusive."

Rita felt more creeping chills, she pulled the afghan closer.

"You know I trust you, don't you?" he asked.

*Then where are you going with all this?* "Yes."

"Then you trust me and us. Right?" Nick's voice was deep.

"Yes." Rita focused on the ceiling and wondered which of them was more insecure.

"Thank you." Nick said it like a command for more.

Rita decided she wasn't going to say anything else. She craned her neck around the room to ensure she was still alone. She bit the inside of her lip.

"Be sure to tell Jaq you have my permission to spend the early hours of the morning with her when we're not in bed together, which will be soon. Right?" Nick's voice commanded.

*That's right, I'll ask an Officer of the law for your permission.* "There's always hope." Rita laughed.

"No fair teasing. Make sure to remind Jacqueline I could join you at any time, so behave." Nick smacked a kiss into the phone.

Rita opened her mouth, but before she could say goodbye, she heard a click.

Jaq entered with two mugs of coffee, one of which she offered to Rita.

"So, did Nick have his mommy's permission to call?" Jaq took a long sip and peered over the mug as she sat at the opposite end of the couch.

Rita accepted the mug, but barely registered Jaq's presence. Should she end it now? The chills became nausea. Was this her usual pattern with men or was this caution, creep at large? She managed a smile.

"He hasn't answered any of those all-important questions yet, has he?" Jaq pressed. "You're letting him get away with it because he's that good in bed. I'm right, aren't I?"

Rita put the coffee mug to her lips and gulped. She didn't care that it was a bit too warm. It was worth a bit of a burn.

Jaq smacked her lips. "When I meet Nick's mother, I'll hand her a list of what Rita wants to know."

\* \* \* \*

Evening darkness was the perfect time for a gentle reminder, after their morning conversation, that he would always be watching—Rita had nowhere to hide. Nick stood firm and tall in the mirror, he saluted, then paused in reflection as he thought of her and his plans. He checked his watch and moved forward.

Nick smoothed his lightly gel-glazed hair, letting just a wisp of a curl fall onto his brow. He liked the fallen curl—he craved watching his plan come to fruition as his prey smoothed the trained curl back. Rita's touch was unique. He wanted more.

He maneuvered his vehicle to her apartment and parked with precision. He followed a hurried woman into Rita's complex and counted four steps up a landing, and then through a revolving door. He climbed to her floor and walked down the long hallway. He pushed the buzzer, sounding a chime until he was certain he heard movement inside. Then, he tapped on the door with the knuckle of his forefinger and grinned into the peephole to allow her full view of him.

Door opened, on cue. Innocent eyes, gorgeous face, even when I catch her with curls piled on her head and a makeup free face. He held her eyes allowing her to speak first.

"What're you doing here?" Rita clutched her robe, peered at Nick, then into the hallway.

"Missed ya, Angel-teeny. Any Jacks around?" He didn't wait for an answer. He stepped in, flashed a grin, closed the door, then leaned in for a kiss. "You're all warm and pink—I caught you in bed."

"What are you up to? I need sleep."

Her voice was timid. He liked it.

"I worked a twelve-hour shift. Let's play tomorrow." Rita yawned. She stepped back, headed to her couch and sat.

Nick parked himself next to her. He pulled her onto his lap as if she were a small child who'd just climbed out of bed. He kissed the top of her head. "I know you worked out early, then worked all day, but with me, I figured you'd be up for a late-night stroll. I have pent-up energy after landing my eight o'clock flight early. I wanted to share it with you. The fresh air will wake you up. It'll be fun."

Rita tipped her head back so she could see his eyes. "Go for a jog and let me sleep. I'm working in the morning." Her eyes squinted, but her lips half curved to a smile. "Come back for breakfast or meet me for lunch." Her voice was firm, bordering on crabby, her body language contradictory with robe hung open and hands nestled on his chest.

He was wearing her down. Her heart-shaped face glowed in the ambient apartment lighting. Rita had a cool, yet innocent air about her. She inspired him, felt like home. He was her soul protector. He'd been enticed when he'd heard about her, and his idea clinched when he saw her. "Not without you, Angel-teeny. After the walk, we can have breakfast, dessert if you prefer."

Rita laughed. He yanked her hair tie out and curls fell all around her. She cooed as he combed his fingers through the curls and her lashes fluttered. "You make this hard."

Her resolve was melting. "Move a little lower, hard is the point." His turn to laugh.

She placed her hand under his and nestled her head against his shoulder. "Not fair."

Filled with her evocative scent of lavender and baby powder, with his free hand Nick reached down into the bag he had carefully set at his feet and pulled out a box wrapped in paper reminiscent of Monet's watercolors. He lifted it onto Rita's lap.

She sat upright, then clapped. "What's this?"

"Reminded me of you." Nick watched her fondle the fuchsia ribbon. He worked to hide the smirk of accomplishment: All women liked gifts, especially unexpected ones.

Rita raised her head and kissed him. "How thoughtful." Her voice softened to a musical purr. She pulled the ribbon apart and released a beautifully scented fuchsia candle rimmed with delicately painted roses. She pulled out a white porcelain base with matching rose images, held the set in her hands, and gazed at it. "Thank you. Roses are my favorite."

"Something to light your way." Nick met her smile. "Especially when you're in bed without me."

Rita blushed. He loved making her blush.

"Small symbol that you're important to me. Know I'm always thinking about you. We are not a one-night stand. We are providence—meant to have found each other."

"I love the sentiment and the candle." Rita's voice was soft, her eyes downcast on the box.

Nick scrutinized her, satisfied he'd made a lasting impression. "Go back to bed. I'm assuming I'm still kicked out." He held his eyes on hers and didn't move them until she blinked and looked away. Nick slid her off his lap, like a fragile ornament, and stood.

Rita sat the box on the coffee table, retied her robe and followed him to the door. "I love the gift."

"What's not to love? Sleep well." Nick bent, kissed her on the cheek, and closed the door. *Worked better than sex,* he smirked.

# Chapter Fifteen

BACK TO THE PRECINCT FROM the frigid night air, David plopped a stack of paper and a large White Castle bag onto Jaq's desk. The thud rippled through her body. "Gee thanks. Any harder and the bomb squad would be arriving." Jaq reached into the bag for burgers. "What's got you so explosive?"

David grabbed one of the burgers from her. "Printouts from every state for the past twelve months—every homicide victim with a broken neck." He sat a tall coffee in front of her and placed his own on his desk. His black leather biker jacket was water-beaded and still speckled with freshly fallen snow.

Jaq closed her eyes for just a second to enjoy the burger and jumped as she felt his icy-cold hands on her warm face. "Not here," she hoarsely whispered under her breath.

"Cold outside." David laughed, bit his burger, grabbed fries and sat. "You're such a hard ass—learn to break a rule."

Jaq evaded his eyes and ignored him. She took a long warm drink of coffee. "Your balancing skills are outstanding enough for the circus. Your caffeine timing impeccable. Eighty-eight strangulation victims?" Jaq couldn't help but feel incredulous. "Is that how you got the Chief to give us the meeting room all to ourselves?"

"Now, what are you talking about?" David stared.

"When you dropped me off, this note was posted on my computer announcing the meeting room was ours until further notice." She handed him a yellow note. "Chief must be feeling pressured, because that's what I'm feeling."

"Yeah, that's how you look. He wants his sister's husband's killer on a platter with a side of airtight case."

"No forgetting that." Jaq didn't want to be disrespectful, but damn it was the least he could do.

"The list isn't bad, really. Fascinating that of all the ways to die, strangulation is third in the Top Ten Ways to Die list." David flung his jacket on the back of his chair, grabbed his coffee, then walked behind Jaq as she read.

"I asked for enough data to rule out cases. Unrelated crime victims should scream at us. Let's organize everything, then begin fresh in the morning."

Jaq cracked her gum and nodded. *Read your own stack, I can't concentrate; your cologne is interfering with my space.* "When are you updating the profiler?"

David scrunched his face, shrugged, and sat at his desk.

"I'm wondering if the religious theme can help predict the Double Cross Killer's next victim. I want to address the cross issue, since there are two of them," Jaq said.

"Silk rosary and the neck-cross findings." David lifted a report and waved it at her. "Adding the seven deadly sins and the Ten Commandments complicates everything."

"Hey, ten plagues—get it right and lose the dismissive tone." Jaq grabbed the report she just closed and flung it at him.

Jaq wrung her hands together, then ran them through her hair. She opened and closed desk drawers as if she were looking for something, a frustration-letting ritual she'd picked up as a uniformed officer on desk duty. When she'd slammed enough, her fingers grabbed the top half of the sheets from the pile and slid the rest onto David's desk. "Divide and conquer."

David stood, snatched the stack and a few miscellaneous items from his desk. "Bring your things. We're headed to the meeting room—spacious, quiet, and private."

"Another order? We're partners. Remember?"

Once in the room David latched the door, dropped his things on the long conference table, and then set a white board up. "If it's a clean crime scene, tack it on the board. If it's not, toss it into this box." He folded a page into a plane and watched it land in the box.

"Ego-maniac," Jaq muttered. She sat, placed a hand on each side of her face mimicking blinders, then bent over her stack and began.

\* \* \* \*

An hour later, Jaq eyed David from behind the clutter of notes, pins, papers, and files, and threw a handful of papers across the room. "I'm blind, I've blown a bulb." She rubbed her eyes, rolled her chair away from the conference table and stood.

David stretched. "Who knew there were so many strangulation cases?"

"Mild ones by comparison."

"What kind of maniac crushes windpipes, not just strangles them, but takes the time to crush their windpipes and imprint a cross, then set a scene?"

Jaq glossed her lips with a stick from her pocket. "Does it to the victim dead or alive."

"Being ordered to concentrate solely on the Double Cross Killer cases is a bonus." David stood up, walked to Jaq and held her close to him.

Jaq wrapped her arms around David's waist and locked her hands together. She leaned her neck back and her eyes travelled up. "Scuttlebutt is we're scorpions. No one wants to touch us and fall prey to—"

"Bad-duty syndrome, like high school-locker searches? Their loss." David laughed. "I love privacy with you, but hate working under threat."

"Lately when I walk into the locker room, everything stops. Literally. People turn and exit. Whole department's feeling the same pressure—hearing ultimatums since Hanusack's brother-in-law fell prey," Jaq said.

"Men's locker room, it's the silent treatment." David kissed the top of her head and the day's stress between them fell away.

Jaq shot David a half grin. Their eyes met briefly, then wandered toward the day's paper mess.

"We'll succeed. We always do." A spirited kiss left her wanting more but she withheld and clomped to the wall map with giant steps to refocus.

"Our signature crime breakdown and tact needs transformation." David followed her to the United States map he'd tacked up next to the Wayne County map.

"Suggesting?"

"Stick a pin in the map representing each file, regardless of any relation to the Double Cross Killer. Later, we eliminate any pin that doesn't fit."

"Tedious—"

"If we've removed a pin that fits the design—the line by the pin's hole—will tell us to take a closer look at that specific file—clear picture."

Jaq visualized it. "Maxwell, you must've liked your art teacher. Good point. I'm counting on phenomenal after-hours artwork." Electricity merged with heat and surged through her. "I'm exhausted."

"It's almost midnight—" They both stiffened hearing the telephone ring. David grabbed his cell from his back pocket, clicked and answered it.

Eyes on Jaq, he clicked off. "Chief's ordered us to meet Winston—Bedford Street, end close to Mack Avenue. We need to run by my place, pick up Recon and get there ASAP."

# Chapter Sixteen

Detroit

DAVID COUNTED THE SONGS JAQ interrupted, not one ended before she clicked to another radio station. He was more disappointed their night together was interrupted. He patted her hand, and then slammed the door behind him to retrieve Recon.

"Did you take a few winks up there with Recon?" Jaq asked when he returned with the dog.

"Any winks I'd have taken would've been with you." David stroked Jaq's hand.

"I wasn't promised winks." Jaq's lips curled.

"Killer's escalating." David turned right onto Hemingway, then tossed Jaq the note where he'd scribbled the address.

"This address is three blocks from the hanging vic and near the Chief's sister's house."

Within minutes, David plunged onto the crime scene, parked, and ordered Recon out beside him. Jaq buttoned her jacket and climbed out the passenger side.

They ran toward the house with David holding Recon's harness in one hand, stopping only to flash badges to the knot of officers standing outside the two-story brick colonial. David envisioned the wall map they'd just updated and noted this location didn't change the trajectory. It confirmed the perp was local.

They stomped snow off heavy boots before entering the house. Instantly, David met Lieutenant Winston's scrutinizing eyes.

"Welcome," Lieutenant Winston held out his hand. "Chief wanted me to see how you two and Recon are getting along and bring him a personal report. He and the Mayor have an early breakfast to plan a press conference."

"You look more mortified than our last corpse." David ignored the rest of the team. Recon sat at attention awaiting orders. Jaq disregarded them and poked ahead, notepad in hand.

Lieutenant Winston folded his arms over his chest. "Recon for McSween—good trade. Less arguing."

"I heard that," Jaq called back.

"Ouch. Two bitches to argue with." Lieutenant Winston shook his head at David.

"Both are trained to bite." David edged his shoulder within an inch of Winston's.

Winston tipped his head. "You three are freaks. Can't solve a little serial-killer case. Double Cross Killer: three corpses. Your team: zero leads, zero arrests. All talk, only fumbles."

"Before NBC scoops you up as their new sportscaster, Man with the Stats, lead me to the new corpse." Jaq having disappeared, David and Recon followed Winston through the foyer to the staircase.

The Lieutenant lumbered up the stairway that bisected the house. The bathroom. He paused outside the closed door. "That mutt better not contaminate the scene."

David and Recon were two steps behind. "Get off it, Winston. You know she won't pulse a muscle without my signal."

Winston scowled.

David signaled Recon. She sat at attention and waited patiently outside the bathroom door. David kept his tenor monotone. "What do we have? Or should I ask one of these rookie cops?"

Winston twisted the knob and pushed. The door swept into a long, narrow room ablaze with a trio of makeup lights inset in a mirror-covered wall. It smelled of warm strawberries and rubbing alcohol.

Winston scrutinized from the hallway. David solemnly stepped into the luxurious bathroom and found himself returning the vacant stare of a large, dark, brown-eyed woman semi-submerged in a white, claw-foot tubful of blood, electrical cords of all sizes hovering like sinister snakes. Her wrists were slashed. "A staged underwater goddess of serpents." Alfred Hitchcock sprang to mind.

David squinted to focus. He took in a deep breath and tried to remain calm despite rising enragement. This was not bloodless like previous scenes.

Winston snapped his fingers. "Impressions?"

David wished he had a muzzle for Winston and a magnifier for the corpse. He wanted to punch the wall and take Winston out with it. Trading the softness of Jaq and a few hours of sleep next to her for having to tolerate Winston's dislike for them to look at this serial creep's handiwork was infuriating.

Amidst the cords floated a silken, handmade rosary. David scanned the bathroom, then squatted and bent in toward the woman's neck. Visually bruised, broken; clearly marked. David needed Dr. Towers. His stomach churned. Bodies, blood, death—repugnant part of a job he loved.

Lieutenant Winston called in again, blandly. "Followed protocol and the Chief's orders. Left it as discovered for you and your… canines." He was sarcastic and thin-lipped. Recon might just have an accident at this rate. One small bite out of that pest, one giant laugh and lowering of blood pressure—hell of a medical cure, and cheap too—but it wasn't worth the write-up, or the extra training time for Recon.

"Finger marks on her neck—bruises caused by the Double Cross Killer. The electrical cords—another weird message. Slashed wrists, part of the message—or meant to throw us off. Cause of death, we need Doc."

"Hey, Recon." Jaq's voice was gentle, she scratched behind her ears. She peeked into the bathroom. Jaq's wavy hair now loosely knotted atop her head, a few fallen curls framed her face—on most women a mess, but on Jaq, rugged and natural.

"What's up, Jaq?" David watched Jaq stroke Recon's neck. The dog stayed at attention.

"The kitchen, and most of the other rooms in the lower part of the house have been dusted for fingerprints, photographed, and searched for trace evidence—"

Winston interrupted and stuck his sneer-puckered round face inside the bathroom. "I expect a full update. I'm going to locate the ME." He arrogantly twirled an index finger at the officers standing guard like wallpaper a few feet away on the other side of the hallway outside the bathroom, and then stuck his head back in. "Wrap up ASAP." He disappeared and clomped down the stairs.

Jaq joined David next to the tub. "It's a bring-your-own-cord party."

"Bloody mess." David was weary.

"I'm gonna clock Winston." Jaq's eyes scanned the bathtub, then the room.

"Inferiority complex; missed out on being breast-fed. Can't handle pressure."

Jaq laughed. "I'll bring him a bottle of milk next time."

91

"First vic with significant intrusive injury—no one had as much as a scratch, nothing close to slashed wrists." David stood, flipped open the medicine cabinet and began pulling out prescription medications. "Perp's not a drug user. Several barely used scrips in here with some serious street value."

"Scene's definitely weird enough for our Double Cross Killer." Jaq pounded out of the room leaving her clearly annunciated words behind. "Fits with my plague theory. Likely Doc'll confirm."

David followed her. "Plague—and, message?"

"Plague: water to blood. Remember, take thy rod and stretch out thine hand upon the waters that they become blood—uh, that's the very short version. Anyway, pools of water became blood in vessels of wood and in vessels of stone." Jaq's eyes widened. "A fit."

David motioned the officers to close the bathroom door and stand in front of it.

Jaq curved back at David. "Let CSI do their thing. Let's go to the kitchen and figure out where the cords came from—which household appliances— or if the Double Cross Killer brought his own. And let Recon find a scent— or did you already do that?"

"Waiting for you." David grinned, then he and Recon proceeded behind her down the hallway.

"Who else lives here?" As Jaq noted the family pictures on the walls, they paused, slowly venturing further down the hallway.

"Four bedrooms." David pushed a door ajar with one still-gloved hand. "This looks like an all-purpose room. The other three inhabited. No one home at the time of the murder."

"Children?" Jaq squinted into a collage of photographs.

David peeked into the rooms. "Two rooms look like they belong to children—stuffed animals and a boatload of toys, DS games. Third, the vic's room."

"Nine-year-old boy, a four-year-old girl." Jaq sauntered into the victim's bedroom and began opening drawers, flipping through hangers, boxes, and books. "Uniforms are questioning neighbors."

David stepped into the room. "My God, you're a mess-maker. Looking for evidence or shopping?"

Jaq stuck her tongue out at him, then continued searching. "We need to talk to the neighbors ourselves?"

"You get a name?"

"After enough taunting, Winston will get it to us," Jaq said. "The officer in charge told me the next-door neighbor's not sure where the kids are. Says they haven't been around for a couple of months. Father never married the victim, but frequently comes and goes, along with many other males. She peeks through the curtains a lot I gathered."

David nodded. "Helpful citizen and good neighbor."

Jaq reached into the nightstand drawer and sealed an address book and cell phone into evidence bags. "Gotta love curious neighbors living vicariously through others' tawdry lives. CPS and a LEIN check. If there's a criminal history of solicitation, likely CPS has been called in and it's been placed on the network by state police." Jaq held up the evidence bag. "We need to find the children, father and victim's relatives. These will help."

"I'll go into the boy's room, you into the girl's room." David slipped out.

"Okay," Jaq called after him. She finished, then strolled on to the girl's room.

"CSI gave the 'all clear' in the bathroom. Recon can do her thing," David called out. He walked out of the boy's room into the girl's room, where he found Jaq digging through a toy chest. "Headed there—Did you hear me?"

"Don't need my permission. I just got caught up reading a few letters to Santa the little girl started. Wanted to get it just right, kept starting over. I just kept thinking, now all she's getting is a deceased mother and how sad is that at Christmas."

"Jaq, you're exhausted."

"Recon, get'em." She patted Recon's head before David and Recon exited and headed toward the bathroom. She returned the letters to the toy chest and continued sifting through it.

"Stand back," David called out. The officers cleared the area. "Recon, search." Recon, freed of the harness, inched and sniffed.

Recon catalogued, promptly dismissed each upstairs room, then anxiously headed toward the stairs, then the bathroom. She barked urgency, her snout pointed to the bathroom rug. Jaq fell in behind her.

"Okay boys, mark it, and then seal it in the extra-large Ziploc." David pointed. "Let's see what organisms grow. Good dog." He scratched under her neck and handed her a treat from his jacket pocket.

David, Jaq, and Recon descended the stairs and plodded toward the kitchen. They checked cupboards, drawers, and small appliances for cords. Where they were detachable, cords were missing.

With a gloved hand, Jaq opened a long, narrow broom closet. She pointed at two utility hooks. "Appliance cords could've hung there."

"Looks like hooks were added when needed so it's possible, unless they were stored with the appliances themselves. Either way makes organizational and logical sense." David shifted his attention between the cupboard and Recon, who was methodically sniffing the kitchen.

"Many appliances store better without cords. How could the Double Cross Killer know the victim does that?" Jaq tracked Recon.

"Bastard knows his victims more than casually." Following Jaq's stare, David stepped toward Recon.

"Or, like Recon, takes his homework seriously." Jaq rubbed the back of her neck.

"Let's hope the team fingerprinted the inside of this cupboard and these appliances. Recon's bothered by this area." David stroked Recon. "I'll Ziploc the dish towel hanging on the broom-closet knob. I'm betting Recon's telling us the Double Cross Killer touched it when he opened it and grabbed the cords."

"First thing we do back at Precinct is review each position vics were found in with each object. Line them up, look for something we've missed." David frowned and stared at Jaq.

She focused on Recon. "The plague indicator is what I'm considering. He's playing with us."

"We need to look for the tiniest intersection with the children—eating at the same ice-cream parlor, shopping at the same mall? Small, bizarre—I think we're missing it." David clasped his hands together and cracked his knuckles.

"Quit it, Maxwell. Awful sound—gave me chills." She shot him a sour face. "Winston cracked his knuckles; you shouldn't do anything he does."

David laughed. "He's only man enough to crack his thumb—might as well suck it and go home to mommy with his need for milk."

Jaq half smiled. "We'll add a corresponding list of child activity info on our wall map and include CPS, and daycare centers, look for mutual kid places—like where they gather for swimming lessons, dance and sports activities, summer camps and birthday parties."

"Get real, Jaq. A profile of the perp, yes. If you're even remotely thinking profilers can identify a probable next victim who we can find, write that request at the top of your Santa wish list because that is impossible," David snickered. "I need to talk to Doc. I hear his voice coming from the stairwell."

They dodged through the kitchen to the front door, handing over the evidence bags and leaving directions with crime scene technicians.

Jaq yanked David's sleeve. "Maxwell, I understand talking with Doc, but he'll know more after autopsy. Winston's hovering and I'm done playing for today."

David laughed and fondly squeezed her elbow.

Jaq staved off a yawn. "We'll absorb more in the morning."

"Fine, only because I don't have the energy to carry you to bed over my shoulders again." He shouldered toward the front door and opened it, hearing Jaq follow behind him.

"The bed warms up really quickly when I wear flannel pj's." Jaq pursed her lips at him. "Our lives are about to go from crazy to insane."

"Flannel's not in any man's vocab unless he's wearing it and hunting." David stepped into her. "It's after four. Let's escape now, bribe Doc with a lunch break."

Jaq squinted. "Deal. I need sugar." She closed the door behind her, followed him to the truck and climbed in while Recon settled in in the back. As she crooked her neck and shoulder to buckle in the seat belt, David pressed his hands up her neck, and then worked them down, sliding his fingers below the collarbone. He maneuvered her jacket just slightly off her shoulders. "Sugar delivered soon." She was hungry, but too tired to protest, his hands were soothing.

"Ease out of that work adrenalin of yours." David massaged her shoulders, letting his thumb imprint his sensuality deep into the muscles, just enough to make her body crave relaxation and release stress. Just as her eyes fluttered, he stopped and realigned her jacket onto her shoulders, fit his jeans squarely into his seat and pressed the pedal toward home. He didn't need the heat from the engine to warm him; he could feel it emanate from Jaq despite the separateness of their seats. He was confident the bed would immediately heat and Recon would enjoy nuzzling with the flannel.

# Chapter Seventeen

Detroit

RITA STUDIED DR. TOWERS' FACE as she spoke. "Double Cross Killer cases fascinate me." She paused, leaning so far forward their blue masks almost touched. "Even under those goggles I can see you've got bags under your eyes from being up all Thursday night with police, then coming in here to perform the autopsy."

"Detectives—priority case—may appear any time. I am expediting to help avoid public panic. Follow me out of this chiller." Dr. Towers' shoes clacked out of the autopsy room with Rita close behind. Protective garb peeled off, he tossed it in the bins. "Thank you for assisting me in the dark hours on a Friday morning."

Rita nodded and removed her mask. "We'll be ready for the Detectives."

"Exactly why you are assigned to these." Dr. Towers pointed to the slides and files. "You comprehend there is no choice but to remain focused. Old-school mind in such a young body."

After two more hours peering into microscopes, moving slides and making notes, Dr. Towers scribbled the autopsy identification number, then read it out loud and handed it to Rita. "Final notation. Verification: cause of death, homicide—strangulation. Crushed windpipe and slashed wrists post mortem. Where are the previously identified Double Cross Killer files?"

"On your desk." Rita collected the notes, dissections, and slides, tidied the room, and then retreated behind Dr. Towers.

"I could not have finished these preliminaries without you."

"Make the body talk, just like you say." Rita bit her half-smile.

"Follow the crosses, last to first victim." Rita grinned.

Dr. Towers swiveled his head toward her. "I never argue with a beautiful woman, even if she is young enough to be my daughter."

* * * *

96

"I woke up with clarity: answer lies with children." Jaq unsnapped her seatbelt.

David pulled into the authorized personnel parking spot at the Wayne County Medical Examiner's Office. "Need evidence." David pulled the keys from the ignition and grabbed his coffee.

Jaq's brown eyes glistened into hazel, then gold; David had to look away or become hypnotized. "I knew hot Krispy Kremes would entice you out of bed."

Jaq's lips glistened with glaze. "Be nice and I'll share."

David leaned in and kissed her, then grabbed a donut from the open box on Jaq's lap. "We're either going in or making out in the parking lot."

Jaq batted her lashes, giggled and blushed as she jumped out of the Explorer with the boxes.

"Perp's ability to get in and out makes me think military or police training. Special Forces. Kills me to think he could be one of our own."

They crossed the parking garage, treaded through the entrance and down a long hallway with multi-colored arrows at every intersection to the elevator.

Jaq frowned. "Double Cross Killer's a thrill-seeker—greater danger, higher delight."

"Vics aren't killed at work, in a parking lot, or while jogging, where they're easy targets. It's at home, where their family lives." David pushed the elevator Down button. It opened almost immediately, and they stepped in.

"Victim's habits, friends, business associates—everything has to be checked. I've asked the Chief to assign additional officers to help with the interviews," Jaq said.

Jaq stared at David as the elevator hummed. David was mindlessly banging the already-lit Garden-level button. The elevator bell rang. Jaq turned toward the door. "We know there's some part of serial killers that kill because they want to get caught. Double Cross Killer might have a buried conscience emerging, longing to be stopped."

The door opened, they stepped out and headed down another long corridor.

"Assuming he poses each victim to send us a message." When they reached Dr. Towers' suite of offices, David edged in front of Jaq and forced her to face him.

Jaq hesitated. "You okay, Big Fella?"

David continued. "At this point we haven't stopped him and now the Double Cross Killer is daring us. He kills, arranges, cleans, and leaves without worry."

Jaq's Red-Alert stance softened as she nodded. "We're on the trail of a black cat in a fur factory."

"Maybe Doc has our feline." David pushed the heavy door open.

They approached Dr. Towers' office through rows of sterile chrome counters. David called out, seeing him sitting behind a desk of organized chaos with layers of vials, slides, and books. "Hey, Doc, you feeling all right? You're definitely a pale African today."

"Concern noted." Dr. Towers didn't look up. "Rita and I have been here since the wee hours of the morning. Finished the primary autopsy on your latest. Awaiting labs. She assisted working the cross aspect backward to include the priors."

"You're worse than us." Jaq shook her head. "No break since we left you."

Interrupting what David thought might be the beginning of an interrogation of Dr. Towers, David ignored Jaq. "Trade your findings—" he intentionally elevated his voice, "for warm Krispy Kremes and fresh hot coffee?"

"Earned at least that." Dr. Towers stood up behind his desk. "Go to the conference room."

Rita fell in behind them and put a hand delightedly to her neck at the sight of the donuts. She laughed. "Double yoga workout this week, Jaq?"

Dr. Towers followed the line into the conference room. He tossed a stack of plates and napkins into the center next to the open donut box and coffee cups, then sat at the head of the table and began. "No unusual or unmatched fibers. Double Cross Killer made sure his victim was dead, he crushed the windpipe, slashed the wrists, tossed in the cords, and cleaned the scene, but there is more to the story."

Jaq jumped in. "Like turning water to blood?"

"Ah, your Plague theory." Doc motioned to Rita, who stepped in behind him. "Certainly fits."

Jaq raised her brows to David.

He returned a nod.

"Victim files, by date." Rita organized them in front of Dr. Towers, grabbed coffee and a donut and sat next to Jaq.

"We took special precaution to organize these photos so you can follow the theory. Pay meticulous attention to the close-ups of the neck." Dr. Towers lined up each photograph, like a zoom lens: from full frontal, to tight head, to neck, to close-up, so each pore was clear. "Advance through each victim carefully."

David and Jaq craned and scanned.

"Look close." Doc asked. "Begin with last night's victim."

David fingered the photos. "Bruising."

Jaq nodded.

"Go further. What shape?"

David and Jaq looked at the photographs, at each other, at Doc, and then back to the photographs before David answered, "Cross."

"Yes," Doc said. "Definite. Not an X, a crucifix. Same one. Markings comparable with each victim. Working backward, confirms it. Magnified each neck. Same artwork. Photographs are like developing negatives: with each corpse, they become one level clearer."

David squinted and looked through again. "On purpose?"

Dr. Towers nodded. "Very calculated. Difficult to accomplish. Never have come across this. Computer techies are trying to work the images into a negative of sorts to see if there is something special about the crucifix your perp is using."

Jaq turned to Rita, then Dr. Towers. "Impressive." Jaq scanned each set of victim photos as David finished with them.

"Perp has the hands of a surgeon, knows the body. The wrist cuts are also clean, not jagged. If they had to be stitched and heal, they would leave a clean scar."

"Medical training?" Jaq asked.

"Likely." Dr. Towers shook his head. "He knew where the veins release the most blood. Quick and clean."

David sighed. "What else?"

Dr. Towers lifted a page in his report and read down the list. "She ate fast food—hamburger, fries. No alcohol, no drugs, prescription or otherwise. No defensive marks. Aside from the neck region, no unusual bruising; rug burns from being dragged after death to the tub. Fibers match the home."

David huffed. "Rug burn—common theme."

"Right. Slight as well. Dragging to position. Dead weight—excuse the pun—is absolute weight, difficult, not impossible, to relocate without an accomplice. Double Cross Killer is able, and if working alone must be extremely physically fit."

Jaq grinned. "Do you think he's acting alone?"

"Likely. Fits the serial-killer profile. Loner. Likes control. Working alone gives him absolute control." Doc's tone was matter-of-fact. "Exactly like the control he shows in leaving the marks on the body."

David nodded. "He gets high on taking risks, but hides inside the victims' houses because of a weird aloofness."

Rita shuddered. "So, you're waiting for him to kill in the open?"

"For the subtle to become the obvious?" Dr. Towers clasped his hands and leaned in. "Excellent question."

"It could escalate that way if we don't solve this quick enough." David sighed.

"Serial killers remain an overall scientific fascination because they are exotic, rare, and deadly." Dr. Towers paused and rubbed his hands over his face. "A drastic observable change like that would be unlikely."

"The Double Cross Killer plans out every operation like a battlefield mission or a surgical operation. He has an initial plan of attack with a backup plan in the event of failure with the ability to maneuver without detection." David stopped talking, folded his hands and considered the concern in the room.

Jaq wagged her leg. "Victims are not random."

Rita sat back in her chair and rested her head in her hand. "Can you stop him?"

Jaq turned her chair toward Rita. "He's getting anxious—continuing to kill."

David nodded. "The murders are deliberate, connected messages that likely will be sent closer together until we find the answer to whatever riddle he's queued up."

Jaq leaned her head back into the chair. "Agreed. The ante is up."

"Double Cross Killer's responding to something specific about each victim that triggers a deadly rage in him and voila—murder with a message."

"Maybe a riddle." Jaq shot a sideways glance at Rita, they exchanged smirks.

"Either way, he is the director," Doc said. "Discern the connection between message and murder. If you do not, David's increased body-count theory is our reality—"

"That's unsettling." David gulped the last of his coffee, crushed the empty cup and tossed it into the metal bin behind him.

Rita set down her half-eaten donut on the plate in front of her and wiped her mouth with a napkin. "This may be procedure to the three of you, but I'm in the business—at least I used to be—of saving lives. I can't casually integrate into my brain the idea of waiting for bodies to emerge so we can solve a puzzle, like it's some kind of game."

Jaq wheeled her conference chair closer to Rita. She leaned toward her. "As a nurse, you heal by making the sick physically feel better. We work it from the other side. We bring closure. It has a real place in the emotional healing process."

"It's one of those things that make sense in a textbook. I comprehend it. I just can't fathom waiting for homicide." Rita wrapped her arms around her chest.

"It is never easy, Rita. Remember, doctors take oaths to do no harm." Dr. Towers kept his voice soft. He clasped his hands in front of him. "Assisting the dead to have the last word is immensely gratifying."

# Chapter Eighteen

Detroit

RITA'S FLUSHED FACE EXPOSED HER anxiety about Nick's arrival. She streamed away from the full-length mirror, but snapped back with a wrinkled nose and pouty lips. Black fitted dress, lacy nylons, stilted pumps, what's not to love about this outfit? Plumped, red lips; high-gloss red Ruby Slippers nail polish, even Dorothy's shoes should be jealous. Rita giggled and graded herself an 'A+'. She shook her hands. She hated the schoolgirl jitters and her inability to hide her emotions. She hated how hard she had to work to appear confident. The bottom line—she was falling hard for Nick.

Hearing the phone, she was happy to hear her friend. "Hey, Jaq."

"Get stood up?"

"He calls to check on me more than my mother. Picking me up after his flight."

"I'd squash any man who did that. It doesn't bother you?"

"Funny thing, I'm kind of into it." She held back that his deep voice added to the growing sexual tension from the erotic intimation. Fun, playful, and something to look forward to. She'd give the calls up if she got bored and she could always ignore the ringing—or call it quits—? She had plenty of time to make up her mind—didn't she?

"Must be getting serious for you to date someone who keeps closer tabs on you than a parole officer. So, what else is up?"

"I can't get the latest victim out of my head."

"Gruesome," Jaq said. "Tell Doc if you need a break. You're new to corruption and corpses."

"I'm intrigued. It's helping me refocus. Makes me feel I've been selfish and single-minded."

Jaq laughed. "You'll be trouncing criminals with stiletto heels and a scalpel soon enough."

Anticipation of Nick and what she would actually report to Jaq fluttered through her. "Anyway, you're a good friend. Report at six for Monday-morning yoga." Maybe then she would have the courage to ask Jaq for that background check. Rita bit the inside of her cheek.

\* \* \* \*

With a calming deep breath, Rita double-checked her makeup and hair, straightened her nylons and stepped into her polished black pumps. Contented, she smoothed the short black dress, pleased it wasn't too short. Unconsciously, she ironed the silk with her hands, slowly down her petite frame. She checked herself again in the full-length mirror adjacent to the door, puckered her lips, and raised her chin at an angle to verify her chic French twist. Back and forth across the foyer floor, she paced.

Where was he? He hated lateness. She'd never been stood-up by any man. It wasn't happening now. She strolled into the living room, kicked off her pumps, and curled her feet into the couch.

What she would say to Nick when he finally appeared? Rita's first instinct was to not answer the door and tell him later, if and when he called, that she thought their date was for tomorrow, and she'd fallen asleep. He believed tardiness devalued the relationship, so truth was she wasn't valuable. That left one question: was she willing to end the relationship?

A firm knock on the door. Her answer: "no." She stood, slipped into her pumps, and strode toward the door. *Breathe,* she cautioned herself. *Breathe. Hold ground.*

A second pop landed on the door. She unlocked it and whipped it open. Before she formed words, the largest bouquet of flowers she'd ever seen swooped toward her. She stepped back.

"I'm truly sorry for being late." Nick bowed his head, hat-in-hand, literally. "Nothing I could do about it." Nick stepped inside without invitation. Half his face grinned. "It was after all, your fault."

"Usually is." She knew how to make her voice sultry.

"I passed by these beautiful flowers and had to have every one, for the prettiest woman I know." He handed her a bouquet made up of five smaller ones. "Am I forgiven?"

"Twice forgiven." She collected the flowers, then smelled them.

"Twice?"

"Once for being late, once for not calling. Calling is a sign of valuing a relationship." He followed her into the living room; she set the flowers on a side table.

"That's another thing I like about you." Nick looped his arms around her and kissed her.

"We're keeping a list?"

"A long one. Easy to please."

"I'll have to rethink that."

"We both know I'm easy to forgive."

She released herself from his grasp and picked up the flowers. "Clearly easy for you to buy forgiveness." She sank her face into the flowers and drew in their perfume. She hoped he not only heard her but listened. She crossed the room, to the kitchen, selected a vase and arranged them. The beauty and bounty of them softened her. By the time she returned, Rita had to stop herself from leading him to the bedroom. She desperately wanted to feel his flesh against hers, but she was still in cleansing mode. Her guilt from that first night still pestered her. Her grandmother's voice echoed: proper ladies don't do those things, and her mother's voice crept in adding: especially if they want to marry well. She hated those inner voices, but they kept her levelheaded—most of the time.

Returning, vase in hand, she set it down on the coffee table in front of the couch. "Feed me?" Rita gently began to massage Nick's shoulders and back.

He pulled her around to face him. "Whatever you want, Angel-teeny. I'd rather have you for dinner." His large hands slowly crept up and down her back and weakened her with each pressing inch they covered.

"Mmm, I'd love that, but there'll be nothing left of me. I worked all day and haven't eaten since breakfast. I'll be more fun if you fuel me." She had to get them out of the apartment, or her resolve would dissolve.

"We're out." Nick grabbed her elbow, and Rita flung her tiny black bag over her shoulder.

"I've always wondered what the Grosse Pointe Hunt Club was like." Rita admired the crystal wall lighting and multiple ceiling chandeliers against antique wood and classic paper and paint. It gave a regal, elegant atmosphere that made her feel like she was in Great Britain.

They were seated in front of a roaring fireplace. Did Nick need this kind of attention?

"Get used to it. We deserve the best. Old money and history in here." Nick grinned, showing perfect white teeth. "I'm a regular. We're seated at the best table in the room."

"Great view, yet fairly private." She turned her head. "I feel a bit on display."

"Exactly." He motioned the waiter over. "When you have the best, show it."

The waiter barely had time to settle at the table before Nick ordered. "Wild Mushroom Quesadilla, two French Onion soups, and two of the Barn Sirloins. No alcohol tonight. Two diets with lime. We'll be ordering dessert and coffee."

The waiter eyed Rita, then Nick. "Thank you, sir, madam." He retrieved the menus. With a flick of his fingers, Nick dismissed him.

Warmth rose from Rita's throat into her face, and Nick drew in closer. She hated eating the food he ordered without asking her. She tried to accept it, but realized it wasn't just about the food. There were so many commands. The clean scent of his cologne melded with the sizzling aroma from the portrait-perfect New York strip steak being delivered to the next table. She pushed down her anger with the thought that it was what she would likely order anyway.

His polished grooming, handsome features, and constant evasiveness fit the profile of a secret agent. Rita tittered at the picture she'd created.

"What are you giggling about?" Nick asked. "Did I miss something?"

Rita needed a few seconds to recover from her thoughts and to change the subject. "I was just thinking about the funny shapes the crystals make on the walls above the glow of the fireplace. It's like dancing warriors—an around-the-room pow-wow."

Nick did a 360. "I've never noticed." He sounded pleased she liked the room. He placed his hand over hers, and then worked his fingers together around her wrist. "Here's something else to sparkle around the room."

Nick slid a glittering bracelet on her wrist.

Rita gasped. "It's extraordinary. All the Christmas colors."

"Specially made for you. Diamonds, like your soul, pure and peaceful. Rubies like your hair and spirit, red and fiery. Emeralds, like your eyes, green, brilliant, mesmerizing. Sapphires like the Virgin Mary, blue, calming, accepting of all good." He rotated the bracelet around her wrist and stroked her hand. "Three of each stone, like the Wise Men, but you're the star I'm following."

"Nick, this is the most thoughtful gift I've ever received." Rita ran her fingers over the stones. "I love the sentiment." Their eyes held. She released a slow, deliberate smile. She was genuinely touched.

"You've grown to mean everything to me." He squeezed her hand.

"You're important to me, also." Rita placed her other hand over Nick's.

"Together we feel like family. Family's everything." Nick's voice was very deep.

"I know you're close to your mother and brother," Rita said. "What about your father?"

"He left when we were quite young. Never said goodbye."

"And, growing up without a father?"

"Painful. Don't misunderstand. My mother was great. Still is. As strong as she is, she's not my father."

"Hence your reason for living with your mother?" Relief, a great reason. Hooray for sex and sleeping with both eyes closed.

"In part." Nick sipped his drink and replaced the glass—calculated by his plate—precisely at two-o'clock. "I like my Sarasota condo. That's enough to take care of along with the family home. For now."

"Your brother helps?"

"Great guy, my best friend, but he's never taken on much responsibility. He writes computer programs and is kind of a loner. He relates better to books and equations than to people. Always has."

Rita was surprised Nick had offered this much personal information without protest. "He must be very smart."

"If he didn't work at the post office, he might never leave his room. A little, but his heart's in the right place. You'll like him."

Rita nodded. "I'm certain of it." She wouldn't dare to ask about meeting his family.

"Any siblings?" Nick sat back as the waiter placed their appetizers toward the center of the table and soup in front of them along with fresh drinks. Nick waived him away without a word of thanks.

"Four, three in Colorado."

"You're the oldest."

Rita watched the waiter disappear behind what she guessed were kitchen doors, then returned her attention to Nick. "Good guess."

"Understand—I don't guess. I'm right about everything. Like you and me."

Rita felt her cheeks pink, her glance fell to the center candlelight. "I have a brother and two sisters—close in age. The two youngest are still in college, taking the long way through. I earned my Masters in Nursing and Administration with my Nursing degree—special program."

"Makes sense." He nodded and placed a quesadilla triangle on his appetizer plate.

"Really." Rita deliberately forced her eyes to de-squint. She wouldn't let him read her emotions. "Why?"

"Because I was right. You're an independent over-achiever."

"You've figured out the obvious." She laughed. "I've spent my whole life being accused of being too independent for my own good and striving to reach goals to prove I've made it."

"Independence is a remarkable attribute."

"For women, it's not often seen that way. Nursing, arguably depends on doctor's orders and patient's needs."

"You're skilled and confident. Doctors and patients trust. You've built a life—That's independence." He raised his arms in a *voila* gesture.

"Maybe," Rita said slowly. "I've never thought about what I do that way. I've thought about attending medical school."

"Then go."

"I want a family. Children. Doctors are rarely home. Nurses can work three or four days a week, have a good income, and raise a family. No absent mother or wife." Abruptly, Rita stopped speaking. She'd broken another personal rule—never be first to talk marriage or children. What was she doing?

"Don't stop. I like listening." He leaned in closely.

"I don't like listening to me." Rita's eyes locked on his. Her forefinger rubbed the rim of the appetizer plate. She steered the conversation in another direction. "I'd rather learn more about you. I need to know more."

"That's a good sign."

"A sign? Of what?" Rita bit her lip nervously. Had she offended him?

"You care, that this is a lasting relationship. You really are different from the women I meet who want only what I can provide. Men are not very different from women when it comes to relationships and needs. I want someone who wants me for me—good and bad."

"Of course." Rita stirred her soup and spooned up another bite.

"Someone who isn't easily impressed and ready to toss me aside for the next guy who has a nicer car, more money, or a more impressive title. Those are only things. They don't last."

But it seems you need me to prove it to you. "I agree." Rita curved a half lip up.

"You do, exactly why this relationship will work with us."

Rita nodded but didn't wait for Nick to speak. She surprised herself and pressed on. "I know so little about you."

"You know I'm a Captain with Delta Airlines. I joined the military, ROTC, when I was seventeen and eventually went into an Army Aviation Special Forces unit because of the training and the flying hours I could log. I love the freedom of the skies. Military, civilian—I don't care how I fly."

"Isn't the saying, 'fly the friendly skies'?"

"For United Airlines, not Delta, but the idea is right. There's nothing like the open sky in any weather, on any day of any year, for any reason."

"I've thought about that. Flying and the military tell me you like your freedom and structure at the same time. Does that clash at times?"

"Not really. In each you have to be organized and think ahead. Both agree with my sense of adventure. With Delta, my schedule changes every month, depending on what I bid, but that's okay. I hate anything that becomes too routine and predictable." Nick paused. The waiter retrieved their appetizer plates and replaced them with the entrées. "My work, although predictable, is very flexible. Fits my sense of the world."

"Doesn't your flight schedule keep your life in a sort of holding pattern?"

Nick scrunched up his face in fake disgust. "That's puny!"

She laughed.

He rubbed the back of her hand with one finger. "Seriously, flying gives me more freedom than any job I can think of."

"I'm happy for you." Rita tasted her entrée. "What a wonderful choice. Everything's cooked perfectly."

"I'll send a message to the Chef. I like a woman who says what she means."

Nick took Rita's hand and pulled her closer to him across the table. "How about dessert?"

*I'm in too good a mood to have you order me something.* "I couldn't. Maybe later."

"Your place?" Nick kissed her hand, then motioned the waiter for the bill.

Rita nodded. She understood it was an order, not a question—like ordering her food. He liked to take charge, so unlike Fazul who had actually mandated her independence. She didn't mind Nick taking control. Not totally. She was progressively more drawn and excited by him. He was the one.

Still holding Nick's hand, she rose from the table and gave him a squeeze. Finally, fate stepped in and granted her wish for a good man to build a life with. She would make it work.

Walking arm-in-arm to his car, she rubbed her bracelet, and then snuggled close to Nick.

"I enjoyed our time together. I know you're feeling the same," Nick said.

She wished he'd let her hold up her side of the conversation. She slipped into the seat. He stared at her, patted her neatly folded hands on her lap, then slammed the door. He jogged around the car and slid into the driver's seat.

"Me too." Rita kept her eyes downcast on her lap. Nick's eyes penetrated and unnerved her. Her fingers began to fidget with each other.

"I know we got off to a rather quick and uncertain start. But, in part, that intrigues me." Nick maneuvered through icy roads toward her apartment.

"We did jump in, but you, this relationship, is different. Our chemistry—"

Nick interrupted Rita, he pulled into a parking space near her apartment door and clicked off the ignition. "Our chemistry is immeasurable." Nick stroked her cheek gently with his thumb.

Rita unclicked the seatbelt, grabbed her purse and the door handle. "Thank you for the lovely gift and a memorable evening."

"You forgot the dessert you promised."

Rita paused, tilted her head, and breathed in a steadying breath. She'd expected this difficult moment. She conceded she wouldn't resist his touch. "Oh, dinner was so lovely, I forgot about dessert."

"The kind of dessert I want was not on the menu. Surely, you won't deny me. Only you can satiate my appetite." Nick tenderly gripped Rita's arm but it stopped her from exiting the vehicle. "Besides, I was hoping we could compare work schedules. You need to join me on my next Sarasota flight. I'll extend a few days. You'll be my guest—won't cost you anything."

Rita tilted her head. "I can afford my own trip. I support me."

"My treat. I want to share Sarasota and my Siesta Key condo with you. You'll love the beach. Trust me, there's nothing better than pressing your toes into flour-soft, white Sarasota sand. Number one beach in America."

Rita wanted to enjoy their limited time together, especially if he was about to invite her on a trip. She softened. "I'll check for something sweet while you compare schedules. You might have to settle for ice cream."

"You're sweet enough." Nick laughed. "Ice cream will make me so cold you'll have to warm me up." They exited the car and walked toward the apartment building arm-in-arm.

Rita laughed, fit her key into the lock, and cranked it.

Before they stepped into the apartment, Nick grabbed her, kissing her full-mouthed. Nothing she'd been through, imagined, or anticipated prepared her for his intensity, strength and persistence. Even more than their initial night together, Nick's force was overwhelming. Her common-sense and cautious nature were no match for his absolute charm, tenderness, fortitude, and logic.

"You, enchanting woman, need to deliver your indelible magic." Nick's breath steamed through her. His soft lips brushed her ear as he whispered.

He picked her up and headed for the bedroom. Rita wanted to object· but what was the harm? No time to reason it out as his shirt fell to the floor and his hands massaged their way up her legs. Logic abandoned in the act of sex, she grabbed his belt buckle and tugged it apart.

They were good together. She needed him, and he wanted her. That's really all she needed to know. She groaned and her breathing quickened with his. Their mouths joined in. They kicked the covers back. Relaxed, Rita laid back, her body beginning to arch in pleasure. Nick's hot breath bit her neck, and his urgent voice whispered, "Come on, Angel-teeny, talk dirty to me."

Rita felt her pleasure sensors beginning to convulse but to her confused surprise, hot tears fell from the corners of her eyes.

# Chapter Nineteen

Detroit

WEDNESDAY MORNING RITA AWOKE TO an empty bed and the smell of coffee. In the four days since their dinner at the Hunt Club, Nick had become a fixture in her apartment. They set a comfortable routine. Nick spent every night in her bed. When he was flying, he was late, and she enjoyed that time to herself. She was clear, they had a relationship. She quickly learned he was a creature of habit and of ritual. An early riser, late jogger with an emerging jogging pattern. Although she had not yet perfectly tracked it, she would.

Stretching under the sheets in the darkness, she craved a hot shower and a drowning in her first mug of caffeine. She froze, surprised when the radio blared the weather report: thunder and hail that resulted in downed wires, an impending ice and snowstorm, closed schools, treacherous driving. Sleep had cocooned her. She hadn't been remotely aware of the harshness the night tendered to the new day.

She flipped back the sheets and faced the clock. Six—ninety minutes before she had to leave for work. She'd better leave early.

Nick timed everything perfectly so they could share the first meal of their workday. She wondered if he'd accounted for the storm. She grabbed her robe, stepped into her slippers, made the bed, and lifted the curtains. Even in the darkness, the glistening view was breathtaking. Like a snow globe, she wanted to flip it and watch snow fall onto the peaceful iced-over scene. She turned toward the shower and thoughts of Nick.

Being with Nick was a remarkable contrast to the relationship she'd had with her medical resident fiancé, which she still thought of as the Fazul Fiasco. He was always working, barely had time for her, and repeatedly reminded her of his investment in their future. Until she almost deposited her life in prison for his mistake. Nick made her feel whole. He didn't notice the missing pieces inside of her. If she had her way, he never would.

111

Rita immersed herself under the pulsating shower water. She closed her eyes and found herself humming while she massaged her scalp under a growing mound of bubbles.

"Talking to yourself?" Nick stepped into the shower, put his hands on her hips, and scooted her so he could share the spray.

Sheepishly, Rita grinned. "I admit it. I talk to myself, occasionally answer myself. Does it bother you?"

"Not if it doesn't bother you. What was the topic?"

Her chin was tucked; she rolled her eyes up at him. "Don't laugh. Okay?"

He Eagle Scout saluted her. "Promise." He suds-upped his palms and explored her body.

She wasn't about to admit anything about False-tongued-Fazul. "Do I snore? I mean, I'm worried." She paused to put cream rinse on her hair. "I sleep so great with you. I can't believe I missed last night's storm."

"I'm better than warm milk and dull TV. You're supposed to sleep deep and sweet."

"So are you, but you don't." Rita rinsed her hair and soaped his back.

He faced her, pressed his body against hers, and kissed her neck. "What are you talking about?"

"You leave my bed—"

"Oh, I get it." He removed his hands from her, lunged forward and briskly washed his body at such an angle she couldn't wash his back. "No other man has left your bed. Just me. You like control that way."

"What?" Rita was perplexed. She rinsed herself, stepped away from the water, reached a hand out of the shower and grabbed her robe. "Not even close. I just miss you in bed. I sleep so well, and you sleep so poorly, you leave early."

Nick spun and faced her. "When you talk about something, you really should know what you're talking about, and then be clear." His tone was didactic, like an angry father instructing a disappointing son. A twelve-year-old son.

"I thought I was." Her confident voice had abandoned her, left her with a vapor voice that couldn't stand up for anyone.

"The truth—if you're interested in truth—is that I sleep so well with you I have the energy to get up, jog, read the paper, and brew coffee. Does that sound like a man who didn't get a good night's sleep?"

Rita stared into the steamed mirror and towel-dried her hair. "No," she called out over the still-roaring shower. In the mirror, the foggy reflection of Nick's head sticking out of the shower stared.

"Exactly." Nick just stood there, his face pointed toward her, but vacant, as if he'd been disgusted, but the feeling was so profound he had to abandon it. All that was left was a face, totally blank.

Rita looked down at the belt of her robe and retied the knot. *Why are you such an ass-hole to me?* Slowly, as if stunned, she bent forward and turned the blow dryer to her hair.

"One of the stewardesses brought me a special blend of coffee. Jamaican Me Crazy. Obviously, appropriate this morning." Even loud, his voice was suddenly tender again. "I'll be out in a minute to try it with you." He pulled his head back into the shower.

A few seconds later, the water turned off, Nick reached out for a towel.

*Will the real Nick step forward? I like this sweet Nick, stay this way— please? Dumping your ass would be painful.* "Should I be jealous?" Rita yelled over the noise of the blow dryer.

"Her name's Julia. Her boyfriend spent some time with me in the cockpit. She rewarded me with coffee beans." Nick stepped out with a towel wrapped around his waist. "Glad to hear you'd be jealous."

Rita widened her eyes at him, felt the confident Rita coming back. "Me? Not a bone in my spectacular, made for you, body."

Nick sidled up to her. "Set that blow dryer down. You need a reminder of just how good we fit together."

Rita turned off the hair dryer, yanked at the sash of her robe and let it fall open to ensure an eyeful. Then, she pressed herself against him, tipped her head back to capture his gaze as she ripped away his towel and pressed hard against him. "With the proper leverage, I could jump you right now. I want to straddle you, twist my ankles behind you, feel your hands on my buttocks." Then, she dropped to a sultry whisper. "But I'm putting in extra hours this week so we can leave early for our weekend in Sarasota." Rita pulled back and knotted her robe and turned out of the bathroom.

"Oh, no, you don't." Nick was loud and his grasp on her shoulders was strong. He pulled her back by her curls.

She refused to wince. She pointedly looked down at his middle. "He isn't up for a workout and I can't be late." She made her face reveal deep sadness in a pout. Then, she edged back, grabbed a makeup brush, and put her face close to the mirror. "Hospital's counting on me."

From the ceramic floor, Nick snatched up the towel and left the bathroom.

Rita dropped the brush and supported herself, both palms flat on the counter to stop trembling. Breathe deep. She looked into the mirror, but shifted her eyes down. She didn't like to lie, but she liked to fight even less, and her gut warned her a fight was brewing. At least she'd drawn her weapon first. A few minutes later, she thought she could keep her voice steady, she called out to him, "I've got just enough time for breakfast with you. Remember, I mentioned the shift trading so I could take the time off?"

"You'll make it up to me tonight."

He's just stomping around. *How the hell does he change like that?* She ran fingers through her damp hair and arranged it.

"Actually, your timing's good. I'll surprise my mother with a mid-week brunch. She's been feeling ignored."

*Well, I can play nice as well as you can. And I need to know more about your family.* "Let's have your family over for dinner some night." She crossed into the bedroom to get dressed.

"In time. Right now, you're mine. If it makes you feel better, they've been asking about you, too."

Feel better than what? Arrogant sob. But I want marriage—a family—the mother-in-law to complain about. The weird reclusive brother-in-law, Uncle Chris, who our kids will whisper about. Now dressed in hospital scrubs, she returned to the bathroom. Nick was shaving. "You actually told them about me?"

"You're kidding, right?" Nick gave her his I'm-so-damned-tolerant smile. "Again, use the brain inside that beautiful head of yours. Utter intelligible words. Think, Angel-teeny. How could I explain my sudden long absences from my mother's home? Never been much of a liar."

"Happy to hear that." Rita reached next to the sink, grabbed his dirty clothes from the countertop, then turned to leave the bathroom. "Please work on a new nickname. I'd hate to explain how you came up with that one." *Besides it's icky.*

Nick laughed. "Then earn a different one."

"I'm inventing a better explanation—"

"What the hell are you doing with my clothes?" Nick barked. His right hook punctuated the gruff undertones from his voice.

Pain jabbed the left side of her chest and ricocheted into her jaw. She braced herself against the doorjamb as his hands fell from her stiff body. "Throwing them into the washing machine." Her face drained, and she'd have to work hard to retain any dignity in her voice. "That's what I do with dirty clothes. The clean ones go in the fridge." With a dull thud, she returned his dirty, yet-folded clothes to the bathroom countertop. Fearful that tears would spill, she avoided eye contact. The growing ache in her throat caused her to hastily exit into the bedroom.

"I'm capable of washing my clothing." He stood in the hallway scolding her backside. "Remember that and we'll get along. Forget it, even once, we're finished."

She didn't turn to face him. "Share a mug of coffee before I leave? I'll be in the kitchen." She wondered if she'd bruise and how she'd explain it.

"Look." Nick caught up to her, put a hand on her shoulder. He didn't turn her, instead edged in front of her. He bent ensuring they were eye-to-eye. "You know I'm particular about my clothing. Living between your apartment, my mother's house, and my Sarasota condo, it's difficult to keep track of my things." He nodded his head at her. "I love that you want to take care of me. I need a little space for some quirks of my own. Okay?"

Rita looked up at him and gave him a non-committal smile. *If you were a girl, I'd pull your hair out.*

"I really am sorry. Everything's great. Promise."

Interesting that he's dubbed himself dictator of my home, my space. He's a nut. But almost everything I've wanted. Better than growing old and feeding the squirrels. She took a deep breath and looked up at his uneasy face. Smiling larger, compliantly, she nodded, then patted the hand he'd placed on her shoulder. "I'll bring your coffee to drink while you finish shaving. I'm sorry, too."

"Forget it. Let's make the most of our time before you leave."

Rita nodded, then fled to the kitchen. She heard the echo of Nick's words: He didn't like to lie. She wouldn't intentionally lie either, not on important things. Who judged what was important?

For what felt like several long moments, Rita sat still at the breakfast bar, evaluating what she'd dubbed the bathroom incident. Wasn't laundry, laundry? Had she been crowding Nick? Was this a reaction to something else she'd done… or hadn't done?

"Coffee smells great." Nick, clad in designer jeans, black turtleneck and leather vest bounded into the kitchen and planted a kiss at the nape of her neck. "You need a refill. I'll toss the bagels in the toaster and grab the cream cheese. Butter and jam, too."

Rita stared in awe of Nick's instant ability to forgive and forget. She didn't want to ruffle any more feathers. "There's freshly washed berries draining in the sink. I'll grab them."

Nick pressed the toaster button. "Perfect."

The strength in his square jawline accentuated by his boyish grin, tanned skin, and perfectly white teeth, was hard for Rita to resist, especially when it came in jeans and leather. His deep-blue eyes—sending the I'll-love-you-forever message—an entire package that made her want to crawl back under the sheets with him and hibernate. She already forgave the bizarre bathroom scenario, because everyone had oddities. So, she wouldn't touch his clothes. Not if she became a washing-machine neurotic and he begged her to do it. She clutched her mug and clenched her teeth, sending an idyllic smile back at him. An honest man, almost normal, a home, and children—she wanted that—this would work.

Playfully, Nick grabbed Rita's hand and kissed it with a loud sucking sound. "Forget the sugar. You're sweet enough. Sit close to me with the goods."

"Cute." Rita batted her lashes at him and kept her voice light. She was getting good at portraying a strong persona, regardless of her inner turmoil. "Keep that nibbling up, and you'll need to go on a diet."

"Hey, about that laundry thing." Nick's voice wavered as if he were trying to sound casual, but wasn't succeeding.

"Forgotten." Rita sipped coffee to hide residual emotion. "Really, it won't happen again." Rita stood to put her emptied dishes in the dishwasher.

"Yes, forgiven, but I have an idea."

"Okay." Rita, dishes in hand, turned back. *I guess it's not over till it's over, and he has the last word—message received.*

"I'll buy two hampers. One you can wash, and one you don't touch. I mean really don't touch—you don't open it, bag it, clean it, whatever. I handle whatever's in there. Avoids problems and cuts your work. Win-win."

Nick ran his forefinger lightly from her forehead down to her cheek, landing just under her chin, teasing it just a bit. With that finger, he guided her chin up to his face and kissed her. "Deal?"

She nodded. Too damn hard to stay mad. *I must be out of my mind.*

"There's that beautiful smile that completes my morning." Nick pulled Rita onto his lap. She teetered the dishes. Noticeably pleased, he embraced her forcefully. "My pretty Angel-teeny."

The hug continued. Worried he was going to break her and the dishes, she tugged back, he clasped her closer to him. Just as she contemplated her skin might be on the verge of blue, he freed her.

"Happy?" His brilliant, toothy smile took up half his face.

Likely her vivid imagination, but the subliminal smile messaged: See, I could crush you if I wanted. Woozy, she bobbed, smiled—worked hard to make it a warm, accepting smile—two shades shy of worship. "Can't be late to work. You disapprove of tardiness, so does the hospital."

\* \* \* \*

David unzipped his worn padded biker jacket, but didn't take it off. He and Jaq, already sans coat, entered Dr. Towers' office and seated themselves across from his desk.

Dr. Towers peered above his bifocals at them. "Five o'clock on the dot. You two are weekly fixtures in those chairs." Dr. Towers met David's eyes, then Jaq's. "As I said last night at the crime scene: I'll meet you anytime, but dinnertime Wednesday. Surprise steak night at my house. Wife expects me six thirty sharp. It has been a date with her for thirty-five years, and I will not break it."

David did his one-eyed squint. "How's it a surprise if you know you're eating steak?"

"We could not always afford steak. Dating or married, Wednesday was the one day each week we enjoyed a protein meal. We named it Surprise Steak Day."

Jaq chuckled. "Cute. With what you do, I'm surprised you aren't a vegetarian."

Dr. Towers spied his wristwatch. "Travel time cuts our time. Here are the preliminaries. Rita is pulling the labs together that have to be sent. We will prepare the final reports including the comparables with the other victims, but there are some areas of interest for you."

David nodded. "That's all we asked for."

"Clearly matches your serial killer, crushed larynx and so on, slightly more pronounced marks of a crucifix, as expected." He handed David the photographs.

David shivered and passed them to Jaq. He hated even touching the photos.

"I'll get to the differences in a minute. Time of death, between eight and eleven, Tuesday evening—"

Jaq stood and paced. "You know what this means—last night's storm. The perfect killing night for the Double Cross Killer. Thunder and hail. Planned perfectly." She sat and folded her arms.

"I bow to your woman's intuition and bible reading. Good thing we're a team, cuz that never would have occurred to me." David swiveled toward the doctor. "What else, Doc?"

Jaq interrupted. "We can expect ten bodies total for each of the plagues, and we'll have our message."

Dr. Towers resumed his explanation. "No signs of struggle from the handcuffs found on the victim's hands and feet. Likely placed on him after death. His back, however, revealed whippings, again, after death. The balance, much the same as the other victims. Despite being six-feet tall, no rug burn. He was wearing heavy denim jeans, which could account for that."

"Toy handcuffs." Jaq sat and flipped out her notepad. "Victim has two children, boy and a girl, likely theirs."

Dr. Towers' voice was soft. "Where was the family?"

"Holiday season. Kids had their all-school Christmas Choir." Jaq swung her right hand up and down as if it were wearing those handcuffs. "They had to be at school at six. Bad weather didn't start till seven. Dad had to work and didn't join mom and the kids at the school."

Dr. Towers tapped his fingers on his watch and pushed his chair away from the desk. "My bride awaits." He stood, stepped out from behind his desk, removed his lab coat, and placed it in on the hanger behind his office door. He grabbed his heavy coat and walked out the office door. "Shut the door when you leave, please. It will lock."

Dr. Towers stuck his head back into his office. "Just a thought, if the Double Cross Killer is leaving you some sort of religious message, and these bodies are leading up to one big Christmas present, Christmas Eve is a special Wednesday. I am unavailable all day." Dr. Towers waved. "The dead are as respectful and patient with me, as I am with them."

David called after him, "We're hoping for a no-show on the holiday cadaver delivery."

# Chapter Twenty

Detroit

F RIDAY MORNING RITA WOKE EARLY in anxious anticipation of spending a long weekend in Florida with Nick. In the kitchen darkness, listening to the gurgling of the brewing coffee, she ticked through her mental to-do checklist as the first strip of yellow sunlight slipped through the windowpane. Her vow to Nick to travel light, a purse and small carry-on, nagged at her. She needed to hold her ground and trusted it would occur naturally through the course of their relationship.

She poured herself a large mug of coffee. Although she thought of herself as a person with abundant common sense, Nick seemed to make better sense. She admired his ability to rationally organize the world.

She bit her lip. Was that true? One fear among many in her struggle to move forward and learn from the past.

Rita grabbed the bottle of Excedrin for Migraine she'd slipped into her bathrobe and tossed two into her mouth. All this self-talk was giving her a headache. She closed her eyes, centered herself on having a good time, deep breath in—then out. Simply being with Nick. An honest, intelligent, principled guy was a relaxation focal point. Ready for happiness with a right to be scared. It would be the first time they traveled out of town together and—releasing another deep breath—she would meet people he worked with. What if they didn't get along? What if his colleagues didn't like her? She didn't have a backup plan—she inhaled and held a long breath. What could she say to fit in, make Nick proud? What to do—deep breath out?

Fourth ring, Rita grabbed the phone and clicked in. "Hello."

"Hey, big day, did I wake you?" Nick was so cheerful she immediately felt guilty.

She put a hand over her heart and felt it flutter. "Packed and on my second cup of coffee. How are you?"

"Counting the hours till I see you. I'll pick you up at nine sharp. Flight leaves at 12:40. Gives us plenty of time. We're checking space available first-class."

Rita set the phone down. They were really going. Nick's sexy voice comforted her. She wondered if he'd guessed she was unsettled. Hearing his voice gave her goose bumps—the good kind.

\* \* \* \*

In unison, the copilots shut down the controls. Nick nodded at the other pilot. "Another perfect Sarasota landing. See you in a few days."

His copilot asked about Nick's long weekend. Nick ignored him. He unlatched the door, grabbed his flight bag and stepped away. Elated to find Rita still latched in her seat, as directed. He leaned in and kissed her. He appreciated a woman who understood command. Her brows were taut and her body tense until she returned his kiss. Their eyes met, her whole person blossomed and her face radiated delight.

"First-class treatment for my first-class girl." One hand on the overhead storage bin, the other unlatched her belt. "Enjoy it?"

"Perfect flight and service." Rita laughed as she stood.

"Think I'd forgotten you? Shutdown and security procedures take a while. Pilots wait till the passengers are off, before we leave the cockpit. Takes longer since 9/11."

"I wondered about that." Rita reached in her purse and grabbed a tube of lipstick.

Nick frowned and tapped on her wrist. "What's that?"

"Freshening my lipstick—"

"You have God-given berry lips. Why cover them? I detest kissing lipstick. I need the real thing. Mind?"

Rita giggled. "Berry? The name of my new color. No problem." She raised a brow. "Chapstick okay?"

"Perfect." He grabbed her hand, kissed it, ran his fingers down her back, and then pinched her buttock. He put his lips to her ear. "Chapstick, we can both wear." He lightly bit her earlobe, burst into laughter, and led her off the plane with a jolt of her hand.

\* \* \* \*

During his army years, Nick had listened intently. It led him to mark and perform as planned. Rita had exceeded expectations; in fact, the stories he'd heard during his military service years hadn't done her justice. His desire to fulfill his destiny with her by his side to cause the demise of the one that cast him aside, exalted him.

"I'm thrilled to be away from grey Michigan. This heat makes me want to chuck my clothes and run into a wave." Rita walked beside Nick through the double airport exit doors onto an extensive sidewalk.

"I like that idea, seeing you run naked into the water. I'll be the envy of Sarasota." Nick laughed and grabbed her tightly around her waist.

"Hardly." Rita laughed.

"You're blushing? You have a model's body," Nick whispered, his warm breath tingled in her ear. He blew cold air down her neck and back, then brushed a kiss on her cheek and squeezed her right buttock.

"Honestly," Rita whispered, "the way you look at me, I'm publicly naked." She gripped his hand, guided it up to her waist, and held it there.

"Nothing wrong with that either." Nick pinched her waist.

Across the street waited a rented Ferrari convertible. In the evening light, it shone like cerulean silk. Top down, they zipped over to Glen's Market and picked up milk, eggs, Coke, bottled water, Special K, shelled pistachios, and strawberries.

He bounced through the tour of his luxury condo across from the public beach on Siesta Key. She *oohed*, *aahed*, giggled and clapped at all the impressive places he zipped by. They did some bouncing in the bedroom, took a short nap, showered, and hopped back into the Ferrari for a Persian dinner at Star's Terrace on Siesta Key.

Nick wordlessly observed Rita dipping pita into hummus. He propped his chin in a fist and enjoyed that, like a young child, she so obviously enjoyed every bite. She was so alive, open to the world, open to him.

"Why are you staring at me?"

"I don't mean to make you self-conscious. Women often pick at their food. You eat and enjoy it. I envy how full of life you are." He needed her to feel his yearning to be with her.

Shades of pink bloomed on her cheeks. "You make me feel like food is dripping down my face."

"Only charming freckles." He blipped the tip of her nose. "We should get back and exercise this meal off—" he paused. "First, let's take turns in the restroom before the bill arrives."

"Good idea." Rita pushed her chair away and spun toward the ladies' room.

Nick snapped up the waiter and ordered two White Russians festively decorated. They arrived just before Rita with whipped cream, sprinkles, shavings of chocolate and twin cherries hanging over the side. Nick sprinkled his own special mixture into Rita's, perfectly masking it.

"How beautiful." Rita bent toward the drinks; she grabbed the back of her chair and moved it closer to Nick, then sat. "We're staying?"

Nick playfully fingered Rita's long, wavy hair. He tucked a few wisps behind her ear. "Quick after-dinner drink."

"Too pretty to drink." Rita dangled the cherries between her teeth and Nick eased in toward her and took the second one.

Laughing, they each ate their cherry. Rita set the stem on the saucer. "There'll be plenty of time for that, I promise." Rita held up two crossed fingers. "Geez, now you've got me making promises."

The pair laughed again, the waiter cleared their table and laid the bill next to Nick. Slipping a crisp hundred-dollar bill into the leather holder, the pair finished their drinks. Nick grabbed Rita's hand and she rose from her chair.

"You should let me pay once in a while, Nick." Her eyes were full of appreciation.

She was always so generous and appreciative. "My father left us a lot of insurance money. It's been invested well. Money's nothing for you to worry about."

Rita nuzzled his bicep. "Thank you."

Nick thought he should be doing the thanking. Already she felt safe being affectionate in public with him. "Ready for a slow walk back by way of the beach?"

"Absolutely." Rita suddenly grabbed the back of her chair with one hand and Nick with her other hand. "Guess I had more alcohol than I thought. That last drink dissolved my legs."

Nick squeezed her hand tightly. "You're just tired." He wrapped a steadying arm around Rita and studied her. "I don't think you can walk back."

"I'm queasy. Can we return to the condo?" Rita asked. "Sorry to spoil your night."

They exited the restaurant toward the Ferrari, Nick's arm firmly around her waist. "No problem."

"Thank you." Rita rested her head against him and they walked in silence.

"Your carriage awaits, m' lady." He opened the Ferrari's passenger-side door and steered her in. He jogged around the front of the car and jumped in.

He put his hand across her forehead. "You look pale. I've got a little something to help you feel better and get a good night's sleep. You'll be good as new in the morning."

\* \* \* \*

Just after two in the morning in the masculine master bedroom, Nick pulled his arm out from under Rita in the massive super-king-sized sleigh bed and carefully centered her head onto her pillow. Almost instantly she rolled over as if they'd never been joined. Tenderly, he placed a chain around her neck, letting the attached gold locket dangle just above her breasts. He brushed her hair back from her face and stroked her cheek. Her skin was soft, delicate, milky white, except for the subtle sprinkling of freckles. He loved touching her face. He loved touching her hair. He loved touching her all over. Mostly, he loved her reactions to his touch.

Certain he wouldn't be missed, he rolled out of bed, tucked his pillow next to her, and clicked the timer on his watch. Easily, he slipped into his dark jogging suit. He double checked his provisions and tied on oversized running shoes. He grabbed the perfectly folded address and map from the bottom of his shaving kit, then slipped outside.

His mission area wasn't far, a nice little jog around Siesta Key. Roads were clear, beach waters, calm; deep breath in. He'd timed it, scouted it, mapped and catalogued it twice. No guessing, mission first. Children depended on him. He'd never let them down. His breathing, stride, and eye movement in sync, he neared his destination. Rita invaded his thoughts just for a second, she loved children, too.

Another block. He rounded the corner, slowed his pace, and reached into his pocket for the letter. He rubbed it to intensify the potency of his power, reciting the words scrawled in heavy pencil: "Daddy hits me and Mommy. He makes purple bruises on us. Santa, please bring him nice pills to make him stop."

The house on Shadow Lawn Drive was well lit. Running in place emulating taking a break or waiting to cross the street, he studied the house. No signs of guests or a party inside. Too few cars parked on the street and none parked in the driveway. Nick evaluated the rest of the property, lighting, neighbors—everything that might cause interference. He stopped running in place, checked off mission points, then completed a few stretching exercises as if to alleviate a sudden charley-horse. All this to entertain any alert nosy neighbor.

Christmas lights, a street lamp, and the stars to guide him.

He slipped into the shadows and found the hidden key just where mom left it the last time he scouted around. His intelligence training had never failed him.

\* \* \* \*

Saturday morning Rita was still cradled in the crook of Nick's left arm. The alarm clock was blinking. "Good morning, sleepyhead."

"We forgot to set the clock." Rita sat up. "What time is it?"

Nick checked his watch. "Almost eight. Feeling better?"

"Wandering between groggy and hung-over." She pressed manicured fingertips against her temples. "Much better than last night."

Nick ran his hands through her wild hair and kissed her neck. "You didn't move all night. I was thanking God I know CPR."

"I sleep so soundly with you. Your famous coffee, please."

"Coffee it is." Nick slid out of bed into a robe and headed to a very modern open granite and steel kitchen.

Once out of her sight, he shoulder-danced and snapped his fingers— both hands. The last piece of the plan had fallen right into place: Rita was unaware of his absence. "Bagel's toasting," he called out. "The bread will help settle your stomach."

"Thanks. I'll shower and meet you in the kitchen."

He'd have to reinforce he was the boss. Nick prepared a breakfast tray. Waiting for the bagel to toast, he expertly plated the tray for their relaxing breakfast on the lanai. Wanting flowers for the tray center, he remembered the bushes around the building plush with bright orange and red flowers. He unlocked the door, scampered down six flights, reached around the corner of the bottom stair, plucked a handful of Hibiscus, and returned whistling, climbing two stairs at a time. Again inside, the water still running, Rita was humming. He tried to figure out the tune, but couldn't match it. He grinned, completed the tray with the flowers, then dropped the tray off on the lanai table before heading into the master bath with a mug of coffee. The rich aroma infused the steamy air.

Sliding the mirrored shower door open, Rita beamed. "Now that's what I call service." Rita accepted the mug, shifting to avoid shower water spilling into it. "Nick, I adore the gold locket."

"I was afraid you didn't find it."

"I really was out of it—didn't feel you put it on me. I'm sorry."

"I look forward to seeing you wear it." Nick reached in to retrieve the mug. He slid the shower door closed.

"Your coffee worked magic." She sounded excited. "I'll be right out."

"Breakfast is served, madam." Nick kept his voice low and deep. "Meet me on the lanai."

Rita emerged click-clacking in low summer sandals wearing a black bikini with blood red trim and a sheer beach cover-up that doubled as a summer dress. She slipped through the open sliding-glass door to the lanai and draped her arms around Nick, kissing the back of his neck, working her way to his cheek, and finally his lips. "This is perfect, thank you. You even found flowers."

"So, what's your heart's desire after the beach?" He gazed steadily into her pupils, drinking her in, owning her.

"You choose, as long as we're together."

*Of course it is my choice.* "Dinner and a movie?" He cocked his head, trying to look boyish.

"Great. You can jog before we go to the beach."

Nick glowered at Rita. "Why would you think that?" His voice was hard and demanding. He didn't care that her eyes immediately cast down and her demeanor darkened. He needed to send a message, he was in control, and it would stay that way. Early lessons were the best ones—if she could just remember her place.

Rita raised her lids and their eyes clashed. "Your routine at home: a jog, then breakfast. I've never seen you eat before you jog. It's not healthy."

Acquiescence, he'd hoped, but he heard a hint of brashness. Wasn't time to end the relationship. Nick stared, expressionless. "I'm not in Michigan, I'm in Florida. Different state, different routine." *Understand now or there's no relationship, no Rita.*

Her face lost its animation. "Okay. I didn't know. It didn't occur to me."

"So now you do, and now it will." No change in tone at all.

"Won't happen again." Rita picked at her bagel. She finished eating it in silence.

After a few minutes, Nick cut through the awkwardness between them. "Coffee?"

She didn't answer.

He didn't tolerate stubbornness or pouting. He held up the carafe as if he were going to pour it on her lap.

She snapped a hand up like a traffic cop. "I'm fine."

"You're cold." He gave her no time to respond. "You're shaking and pulling at that dress too tightly to warm you. Let's go inside."

"One more cup, then the beach?" It was her pretending-not-to-be-scared voice.

He knew she'd give in. "After you show me how much you appreciate the locket."

"I hate to dampen your weekend, Nick, but I still feel nauseous, and my head hurts. I need a little time, and the ocean is so—"

Nick wrapped his hand around her tiny wrist and twisted ever so slightly.

"Nick—"

He yanked her out of the chair, spun her so her back pressed against his front. He sent his fingers from the crest of her lips slowly down her neck, and then under her suit, finding the tip of her nipple.

"Please—" Her voice was quiet, but urgent.

"I deserve inspiration," he whispered. "Here we are in this beautiful, secluded area, far from home. You wouldn't want to disappoint me again, would you?"

She gazed at her feet.

He loosened the grip on her wrist and led her to the bedroom.

\* \* \* \*

Saturday morning, Rabbit and Abel sped down Midnight Pass Road, then curved from Northview onto Shadow Lawn Drive, parked next to the CID van and jumped out. The home looked undisturbed except for the response teams. Flashing their badges, they cruised past the uniform at the front door and were ushered by another uniform into the bedroom. The Sarasota Criminal Investigation Division Team members were busy documenting while the coroner's people awaited instructions outside the bedroom door. On the high-speed ride to the scene, they'd done everything short of cutting a blood covenant—this time there'd be a clue. They weren't leaving the scene without a clue. A meaningful lead to the arrogant, insane murdering bastard.

Dr. Milano shook his head at the detectives. The creases under his bloodshot eyes underscored sleepless nights, his down-turned lips begged answers.

Rabbit returned his look. "It's barely eight; you're already chewing sour balls."

"It's your serial killer—strangulation. Same rosary." Dr. Milano's voice was a notch above despondent.

Rabbit, in a commanding voice excused everyone from the room. When the bedroom was emptied, he addressed Dr. Milano. "Tell us what else you've got."

Dr. Milano waved in Rabbit and Abel to stand next to him and the victim, who lay in his bed. "The basics—my written report will be in your hands in a few days."

Abel leaned over the victim. "Perfecto."

Dr. Milano nodded. "Caucasian, male, age thirty-seven. Home alone, family at a holiday event in Tampa. He had to work. Wife called him around five this morning, when he failed to answer she woke a neighbor, with a key. Neighbor dialed 9-1-1."

"You came in special for this?" Abel raised his eyebrows.

"Officer noticed neck bruising and I got called, same as you two." Dr. Milano pointed to the victim's throat. "Strangulation. Very little struggle."

Rabbit's eyes burned. "Sleeping when he was attacked?"

"Time of death estimated between ten and midnight." Dr. Milano lifted the sheets and the victim's t-shirt. "Take a look."

Abel squinted. "Cigarette burns—"

Dr. Milano interrupted. "Chest, stomach, legs, arms. At autopsy, we'll count and list them." He pointed to multiple marks and areas. "Also strewn all over him—ashes."

"Meaningful." Rabbit kicked the dresser. "In some world where killers run amok." He walked around the bed. He scanned the floor, the sheets, the bed, and the body. "Any cigarettes to go with those burns?"

"Not my area." Dr. Milano sounded as if he could use a regimen of Prozac.

"Butts might have DNA." Abel huffed frustration. "Any cigar-size burns?"

"Consistent." Doc shook his head. "Cigarette, maybe small cigar."

"Doc, what about these?" Rabbit bent over the body. "They look like hand prints?"

Dr. Milano nodded. "Several. Crime-scene scrapings and photographs already taken. More at autopsy. Reminds me of a child's handprint—the kind where a teacher paints the hand, and the child places it on paper to make the print."

Abel stooped and got his nose close to the body art. "These hand prints are made in lipstick."

Dr. Milano bent, magnifier in his eye. "Likely wore gloves over his hand, careful to avoid leaving a print or DNA. I'm not hopeful. Every hand print is smeared to his design."

"He was after a specific age hand size?" Rabbit squinched his eyes closely measuring the prints. "Guessing age five, maybe six?"

"Possibly." Dr. Milano flipped through his notes. "I will measure each."

Rabbit clenched his fists. "Damn it. I predicted he'd strike on a weekend. This is his Friday Night Special."

Abel crossed the room to the bedroom window. "We're about seven blocks from the poolside victim."

"What's your perp trying to communicate?" Dr. Milano always tipped his head sideways when he asked a question.

Abel caught Rabbit's eye. "Not a clue—but that's a great name for this one. The Communicator."

Rabbit forced air out through his nose. "Or non-Communicator the way we're receiving his messages. We'll pick up the autopsy report quicker than your printer spits it out." The detectives left Dr. Milano to prepare the body for transport.

"Rabbit, it's not like you to sound discouraged this early in a case." Abel stepped in front of Rabbit to stop him from walking outside the home.

"Hey." Rabbit almost stepped on Abel's shoe. He placed a hand on his shoulder. "Child's handprint. The Communicator just told us, this killing spree is about children." Rabbit released a sigh. "And he has us in the palm of his hands." If Rabbit was right, he didn't like the message—or the fallout they were about to receive if he didn't decipher this further.

# Chapter Twenty-one

Detroit

RITA REACHED OVER AND HANDED Jaq a t-shirt. "Got us matching ones this weekend in Sarasota. Great yoga cover-ups."

Elbow planted on the hospital cafeteria table, Jaq snatched the offering with one hand and popped up an index finger with the other. "First—on Friday—I get a text from you from the Sarasota airport."

Rita turned both palms up. "I missed you."

A second finger wagged in Rita's face. "Then you show up with this for Monday-morning yoga and can't stay after for coffee and details."

"You can't always stay for coffee and details." Rita tried to mount a defense without laughing.

Jaq waggled three fingers, and twisted her mouth to keep from laughing. "You put me off till lunch so we can chat between cadavers, and then you show up in your building cafeteria late, late, late."

"Sorry. Working your Double Cross Killer cases is overload." Rita gasped, then swiveled to ensure no one heard her.

"Chief keeps harping he wants a GPS tether on David and me. I'll get one for you. Then I'll know exactly where you are."

Rita leaned her head and shoulders forward and crinkled her forehead up. "You've forgotten what it's like to be in a new relationship."

"No, I—"

"He's a really good guy. We had a blast. No worries, really."

"Just a few days ago, you said you were taking things slow. Next thing I know you two are traveling across the country." Jaq squinted at Rita.

Rita unloaded her cola, sandwich, and salad and removed her empty tray to the nearest table.

"Here's an idea." Jaq bit the corner off her egg-salad sandwich and waited for Rita to pop a forkful of salad in her mouth. "Remember the first time we had coffee after yoga, when we first met? We told each other about our best and worst date ever?"

Rita swallowed hard, took a drink, and wiped her mouth. "Oh my God. I'd forgotten about that." She laughed. "Your point here?"

"Tell me the high-point and the low-point of your trip." Jaq reached across the table and tugged on the edge of Rita's sleeve. "Girlfriend, it's only fair."

Rita pointed at Jaq. "You're a bona fide pain."

"With a gun."

"Fine. High-point…" Rita reached just into the neckline of her scrubs and lifted the gold heart-shaped locket. "Saturday morning—woke up with this locket, then a wonderful breakfast with fresh flowers. Question is: which one of dozens of pictures on the white-sand beach will land inside the locket."

"Sounds romantic." Jaq had both elbows on the table, her chin in her hands. "Low-point?"

"He's very religious."

Jaq jerked upright and said too loudly, "You go to church—the problem?"

"I believe in God, but I don't spread the word or memorize the bible or quote scripture. Nick recites scripture at the strangest times—It grinds at me. Just when I think I should step back, he does something so kind I think: better a God believer than an atheist, I guess."

\* \* \* \*

It was almost midnight. The tip of his nose felt frozen as David stood at Jaq's front door loaded with bribery. His thoughts about Jaq and the six years they'd dated and been partners warmed him. He balanced coffee cups and rang the buzzer, no free hand to fish for his key. Never show up late without coffee: the first of the "rules about Jaq." It helped that Jaq lived on Detroit's eastside, close to a 24-7 Dunkin Donuts.

"Timing's everything," David called out, and the door creaked open. "Recon and I bet you fell back asleep."

"Sleep. That's why I forged ahead, alone—you were supposed to join me inside, not take me outside." Jaq stepped out, slammed, then locked her door, and grabbed a steaming cup. "Early wake-up is not on our agenda." She followed him to the parking lot.

David laughed. "I've guaranteed you'll enter my truck." He opened her door and waved it open and closed, open and closed.

Doors slammed, Jaq checked their safety gear, and David revved the engine.

Jaq sipped her coffee and got comfortable. "You didn't say much on the phone. So the Double Cross Killer crucified another vic?" She found her way into the donut box and lifted one into the air. "Recon wanna Fetch?"

"Hey, you know the rules: no donuts to Recon." David swerved the truck and pulled over.

Jaq laughed, took a giant bite of a frosted donut, then gulped her coffee. "Fall for it every time, Maxwell—Have I ever shared a donut with Recon?"

"Hell, you hardly share one with me. You can trail behind her after she eats donuts—it's like giving an old man beans."

"Take a breath and brief me. If there's a stiff, a few more minutes won't make any difference."

"Message I got was the uniforms on scene couldn't decipher if it was just another domestic squabble or our perp."

"You didn't ask for details?"

"Would you ask the Chief for details?" David did the one-eyebrow lift. "I did a lot of yes sir, no sirs, before the big click."

"That's not good." Jaq dabbed away raspberry jelly with the back of her wrist.

"Streets are empty. Hang on to your..." he banged on the accelerator, "...coffee."

Jaq held her cup in front of her. "I take it the call didn't include leads?"

"Chief got a couple of calls he's not happy about." David accelerated.

Jaq slammed back in her seat. "Like?" Back to serious, sarcastic, and sexy.

"The usual suspects."

"Okay, Bogey. Let me take a stab at it: Detroit News, Associated Press, Mayor, FBI—shared unhappiness, and we're getting an earful."

David nodded. "At the scene."

Jaq banged her head against the headrest. "I need a vacation."

"If we don't solve this soon, that won't be a problem—we'll earn ourselves a permanent one."

Jaq chuckled and licked custard off her fingers. "Looks like we're on our way to Denby." David agreed and pulled onto Kelly Road.

"Practically in the high school's backyard. Seymour Avenue, just ahead." David swerved the truck and cut the lights.

Reporters, crime-scene units, and curious neighbors crammed the constricted space in front of the dilapidated two-story brick colonial. David edged into a neighboring space between emergency vehicles stretched diagonally over pavement, curb, and lawn.

David, Recon, and Jaq quickly exited the Explorer and ducked behind the yellow crime-scene tape. In tandem, they shielded their faces. Reporters snapped pictures of them progressing toward the house.

"Don't let that mutt compromise the crime scene," Chief Hanusack bellowed. "Make sure you feed and walk her before you release her."

"Seriously Chief, you know how we operate—" David met the Chief's stare, but held his tongue with Recon's leash.

"You'll understand once you're in there."

"Double Cross Killer?" David pulled his notebook and pen from his back pocket.

Hanusack scowled and began walking. "Intriguing work of art. Kitchen."

With a firm hold of Recon's harness, the team followed him through the center corridor to the kitchen in the rear of the house. Crime-scene photographers, technicians, and Dr. Towers repositioned themselves to allow full access.

David handed Recon off to an officer, then ambled behind Jaq. Together they circled the victim, careful not to disturb anything. David wanted to tell Jaq he'd investigate elsewhere. She understood his revulsion with corpses, but he couldn't until the Chief left.

The pungent odor of stale beer overwhelmed the crowded space. Cracked eggs, shredded cheese, beans, lettuce leaves, and miscellaneous leftovers acted as window dressing, some stuffed inside the victim's mouth, where a fork and knife were planted like victory flags on a battlefield. Mounds of a dirty white crystal-like substance were strewn over everything.

"Picturesque—" Jaq turned slowly. "In a demonic-frenzied sort of picture."

"Obvious message," David said. "Hungry, couldn't decide on the menu. Ordered everything."

Jaq leaned in for a closer view.

"What's all over the top of the food—street salt?" David frowned.

Jaq grabbed a few pieces in her hand. "Exactly. Let's find the container it arrived in."

"Find the cause of this meal-deal or your next assignment may be short-order cook." Chief Hanusack pressed in his ear-bud. "Criminal Investigations wants in."

"You assigned us—exclusive." David worked to keep defensiveness out of his voice.

"You've got my support—tonight." The Chief stared. "Don't make the Department look like we're idiots. FBI wants in as well. We need to at least show 'em the crimes are limited to the Great Lakes State, that there's no big drug or gang cartel, so I can keep 'em backed off." Chief Hanusack gritted his teeth. "So far there's an impressive lack of evidence so they're speculating big."

The Chief jabbed toward them with the business end of his unlit cigar. "Get a handle on this perp. Now."

"Yes, sir." David tried not to sound belligerent. "A psychological profiler's decoding the perp's picture-messages. We're unraveling him."

Hanusack sounded dispirited. "There's panic out there, real panic. I can feel the fear in the city. Detroit can't handle another hit like this. Legislators at all levels are calling." He paused and assessed the room. The support teams understood the silent hint and exited the kitchen. "Media's demanding a press conference, details, an official statement—"

Jaq turned and locked eyes with the Chief. "They can't force you to speak, Chief—"

David attempted to be the poster-boy for old-fashioned, dependable detective work. "Any premature announcement will put us months behind, draw out the nut jobs, copycats, create more fear and corpses."

"In fairness to the public, the Mayor and I will cautiously meet the press. We want to limit panic, put out safety reminders, maybe produce a lead."

"We are getting closer." David kept his voice level with firm conviction. "I can feel it."

"I've assigned additional officers and overtime. I want real proof of just how close you are." The Chief studied the floor, then shot razor eyes up. "Realistically, should we just turn it over?"

"You can't be serious?" Jaq's voice was sharp. She then pursed her lips. "Two weeks."

"David?" The Chief's eyes darkened, his brows furrowed, his stare held David's. "Thirty days." David's voice was level but firm.

Chief Hanusack blinked at David, then Jaq. "Two weeks. Thirty days if I receive a solid lead in two weeks."

David and Jaq agreed in unison, each holding out a hand for a firm shake with the Chief. No further debate was necessary.

"Understand if this case isn't locked down by Valentine's Day, you two'll have a sweetheart of a vacation." The Chief dropped his still-wrapped cigar inside his jacket pocket and smacked his hands together. "I'll make a brief statement about how we're closing in. Ask for patience."

"Thank you, sir," David said.

"You two work around the clock. If you're not on the streets, you're locked in that damn conference room. Don't care if you, eat, sleep, bathe, or call your mothers. I want regular reports even if Recon delivers them in a mini-keg strapped to her collar."

David cracked his knuckles. "Yes, sir, if you're not available, carpenter bees will drill the updates into your office."

Chief Hanusack pointed a finger at Jaq, then David. "Don't disappoint my sister or her family. Or me." Their eyes fell to the ground like disobedient children. He stomped out of the kitchen, the reverberation of his heavy gait echoing.

Dr. Towers treaded toward them and bent over the corpse.

Jaq crooked her head at the ME. "Double Cross Killer?"

"Likely." Dr. Towers snapped on latex gloves.

"Anything new?" David's voice was flat; he was ready to move on.

Dr. Towers arched his head and pointed to the neck markings. "Same dark bruising. Same knotted cross."

"More visible," Jaq said. "Plague, too."

"I don't recall food fight or salt being one of the ten plagues," David said.

"Think photograph. The way I see it, in pictures, the salt will look like mounds of hail. Hail was one of the ten plagues."

David sighed. "Duly noted."

"Still not a believer?"

David swiveled his head. "Your plague theory still has to translate. Besides, hail was part of our last vic."

"Biblically speaking it was a tremendous hail, so no one knows how long it lasted."

"Double Cross Killer is telling a story." Dr. Towers' voice was rushed. "Food distribution plays a role. Going to the morgue to await transport."

"Everything is photographed, combed, dusted, and bagged." David swung his arm backward. "Recon's ready when everyone clears."

Dr. Towers nodded. "I'll release the body once they bag the hands. Did you learn anything from the family?"

Jaq squinted. "I didn't see any civilian types."

Dr. Towers pointed a finger up. "Family's upstairs. The little girl found the body—her father. Grandmother and mother called 9-1-1."

"I'm on it. See you." Jaq leapt through the kitchen door, muttering thanks.

"I will call after autopsy. You call if Recon finds anything." Dr. Towers pulled off the rubber gloves.

"Will do." David nodded and retrieved Recon.

\* \* \* \*

Bounding up the stairs, Jaq stood at the top; she heard noise. Sobbing emanated through the hallway. She gave a one-knuckle knock, then pushed open the bedroom door. A young girl was being rocked in her mother's arms. Her grandmother stroked her hair with the hum of a soft lullaby. With the nod of grandmother's head, Jaq stepped inside the long bedroom. The mother and little girl seemed unaware of her presence.

"Very sorry to interrupt you at this difficult time. I've a few questions. Would you mind?" Jaq, about to repeat the question, followed the grandmother who slipped off the bed and motioned her to a sitting room across the hall.

"What is it? My babies be in no shape to answer anything now." Grandmother's finger was in front of her mouth and her voice was a barely audible whisper.

"Yes, ma'am," Jaq began. "Just have a few questions so we don't waste investigative time. We want to find who did this. Will you help?"

"Later be best. We need some time."

"Ma'am, I understand. Statements can be taken at the station after you have all had time to get over the initial shock. I'm very sorry for your loss." Jaq spoke in a soft voice, slowly, as if they had all the time in the world.

"Child, I'm not sorry." The old woman's mouth was wrinkled and her warm eyes seemed to stare right through Jaq.

She could see the old woman had a piece to say. "Ma'am?"

"A very bad man died. Always cattin' around, drinkin'. Never kind to that sweet grandchild of mine, unless he ordered her to grab him a beer."

135

"I understand there was a history of domestic violence." Jaq pulled out the LEIN sheet from her back pocket, unfolding and skimming it. "Your son-in-law had a history of getting charged, but all charges got dismissed."

"Ever' time he hit her, he made her feel like she done him wrong. I raised Claire to be strong. He beat her weak." A tear rolled down the dark cheek. "I taught my sweet Annette to trust in God, and me, 'cause that's all she got to hang onto."

"Annette is your granddaughter?" Jaq instinctively reached for her notepad, but changed her mind.

"Yes, ma'am." Annette's Grandma reached into her robe and handed Jaq an unsealed envelope. "Annette writes regular to God and Santa Claus, askin' for help. Makes me pledge to mail the letters. I ain't never broke a vow I made to that child. This is one that I ain't yet mailed, but it's jus' like the others. I reads 'em all. Don't tell her I ain't sent it yet."

Jaq nodded, opened the letter and began to read.

Dear God:

My grandma told me that you are everywhere and I can ask you for help. I asked Santa for help too. I don't want any toys. I want my daddy to stop hitting me and my mommy and my grandma. He makes me eat off the floor when I spill. I try hard not to spill things. Can you make my daddy nice? I love you.

Annette Price

"I told that child God would answer her prayers. And so He did." She paused, resting the back of her palm on her forehead. She closed her eyes briefly, and then spoke. "Thank you, Jesus." She raised her arms up high, and then lowered them. "We be going up to the Grosse Pointe Baptist Church to make our offerings—you know the one? They be good people up there."

Jaq bobbed her head slowly. "Nice church. Good people and support system for your family." She held up the letter. "Mind if I hang on to this?"

Her hands on her lap, prayer-position, voice, barely audible. "She won't be needin' to write another."

"May I call the minister for you?" Jaq gentled her voice.

"Oh no." She shook her head in broad sweeps; sat back quickly, put her hands up to her hair, then down her chest. "We all needs to clean up. Can't be seen a mess at God's house, especially when He done us such a favor."

"About that favor—" Jaq began.

Annette's Grandma cut in. "I never did know what my daughter saw in him. He was like a skunk—had the markings of evil in him, he did. My daughter had her education, a good job. Claire was going places. People recognized her. He knuckled in all her dreams, all those possibilities every time, too many times. I prayed an' prayed for him to disappear right into her bruises. God answers prayers."

"God took daddy away," the little girl whispered from the doorway.

"Come here child, sit on granny's lap."

Wide-eyed, arms up in the air, the tiny frame tottered to the comfort of her grandmother's lap. When Annette finally attached her ear to the comfort of her grandmother's beating heart, she closed her eyes, and the old woman began to rock and talk. "As I was sayin', you police people don't need to look for no killer. God made that mean man, an' He took him away." She hummed. "Plain and simple. Praise the Lord Jesus. Halleluiah." The white-haired woman shouted, raised one arm, and jolted her face up. Her granddaughter looked at her, and then the ceiling with a smile.

Jaq stared at the smiling duo and squatted to meet the old eyes. "I'm sorry, ma'am, I have to ask you this question. Did you have anything to do with the death of your son-in-law?" Her voice slow, soft, filled with compassion. "Before you answer, you may want to call an attorney."

The expression on the old woman began to morph.

Confused, Jaq continued. "You aren't a suspect at this point, ma'am, but you do have the right to talk to an attorney if you want one. If you can't afford one, the court can appoint one for you. Any statement that you say or write could be used against you in a court of law."

"Am I under arrest?" She began with a chuckle, and it grew, then blossomed into a laugh. "You don't get to be my age without an understanding of the world. I watched my share of television when that monster of a man wasn't home putting the fear of the devil into everyone. And I'm not senile. I know what I am sayin', ma'am. He was a very bad man, but I didn't bring any harm to him. I let God do His work. I did mine. I prayed until I couldn't pray no more. That's all I'm guilty of. That man's with the devil now. It's a certainty."

"Did anything unusual happen last night?" Jaq was still hunkered next to the chair.

Annette looked up. "I was bad."

"Hush child. You was perfect as always. You are only six and such a smart child, doing well at school. Perfect marks." Grandma addressed Jaq. "Her mother and I are proud. Proud like the parents of the Olympics winners."

"Why do you say you were bad?" Jaq asked the little girl.

"Mommy made pork chops for dinner, and I wanted to cut my own meat. I tried really hard." Annette paused. "But I couldn't, and it fell on the floor."

"That devil of a man screamed at his daughter, banging and throwing silverware and food, swearing and stirring up more evil than the under lords."

"Did anyone get hurt?" Jaq scribbled notes.

"Made this innocent child finish her dinner right there where the pork chop fell, right there on the floor."

"Where was her mother?"

"My Claire just brung him another beer. Ain't nothin' else to be done. I brought Annette upstairs and got her a decent dinner when I could."

"Did things like that happen frequently?"

She nodded. "Roger had a short temper. Everything set that man off, 'specially at dinnertime. Hardly had a quiet meal."

"Momma."

Claire entered the room timidly. "Hush now. We can't be speaking ill of the dead, or we ain't no better than the evil that got him to his early grave."

"We're finished for now." Jaq stood. "Can we take you somewhere? We can wait until you pack what you need for a few days."

"We got nowhere to go," Annette's grandmother said. "He didn't let anyone make friends. I'm lucky I could go to church and the senior center while he was at work. I hid my bingo money to buy what little we needed. My Claire and me can't afford to take Annette and go nowhere. We be fine, now that he's gone."

Jaq explained that the house was a crime scene, and police would set the family up at the Sheraton until CSI was completed. An officer would be posted outside their house. Jaq told Annette's grandmother and mother about the mess the team would make and that home insurance would pay for cleanup. She asked both women not to give any information to anyone else. The women agreed. Jaq turned back. "An Officer will provide you with forms to apply for financial assistance through the Crime Victim's Compensation Fund."

Grandma's worn face showed relief. "We'll be needin' some help."

Jaq couldn't find her voice. And she'd thought her co-workers were brave.

\* \* \* \*

"Astonishing." David positioned the key in the ignition and revved the engine.

"For a murder scene?" Jaq clicked her seat belt and flipped through her notes, fake reading. She was noticeably upset.

"Not only are we right about the kid angle, but the Double Cross Killer's a freaking Robin Hood on steroids." David screeched the tires with newfound exhilaration. "And, Recon was damn beautiful."

"Sorry I missed it."

"The rosary this vic was wearing has the Double Cross Killer's scent. When she sniffed it, Recon went wild."

Jaq snapped her fingers. "Killer's over-confidence is making him sloppy."

"There's violence here, against the wife and child."

Jaq nodded. "Things go very wrong in the family. According to Grandma, the child writes multiple letters asking for help from God and Santa. Grandma prays every minute she can."

"We end up with dead dad—request granted." David pumped his fist in the air, as if he were sounding the horn on his Big Rig.

"Grandma mails all the letters. Keeps praying."

"Are you sure she didn't give the letters to someone, not the postmaster?" David swiveled his head to Jaq, then back on the road.

"Positive."

"Suspects: the Postman, Grandma, God and Santa." David's raised brows deeply creased his forehead.

Jaq looked at her watch and harshly tapped her pointer finger on its face. "It's almost three. We're sleep-deprived and missing the killer's connection to Santa and God."

He waved his hands above the steering wheel, then plopped them back on. "Not aware of any post office or church break-ins or for that matter, stolen Santa suits or impostor Santas."

"Postal employee." Jaq pulled her notepad and wrote as she spoke. "Access to mailboxes and schedules of residents. New angle."

David was barely listening. He blurted the image he envisioned. "Regardless, he kills for what he believes is the right reason—becomes judge, jury, executioner, taking the law in his own hands—like Robin Hood."

"No wonder we can't find him. He's without his merry men," Jaq grumbled. "Maybe we should interview God and Santa Claus. After all, they seem to be intercepting all the mail."

# Chapter Twenty-two

AFTER A FEW HOURS OF unsettled sleep, Jaq left the warmth of her bed, preferring to cocoon herself at headquarters with the autopsy notes and CSI evidence. Her hunched shoulders ached; she straightened them long enough to slam a stack of faxes at David as soon as he entered the conference room. She pointed a long-handled contraption at him. The two thirty reading on her watch caused her to shriek. "Only two days before Christmas. I'm exhausted, famished and we're no further."

"Ho, ho, ho." David set a box in front of Jaq and removed the oversized protractor from her hand. "Your favorite Greektown salad and lemon soup."

Jaq seized the meal. "Jingle bells. Several states released case information in the Weird-and-Unsolved-Crimes category with varied broken bones in the victim's upper torso. I didn't request anything more specific because of copycat crimes and its ugly cousin: Confusion."

David shifted his jaw and flipped through a stack.

"I sent a uniform to the courthouse." Jaq handed him a document. "Signed subpoena ordering the Wayne County Post Office to deliver reports of lost or stolen mail, employees who failed to return for work on the dates of the murders and those on leave."

"Nice."

"The first five states have no Double Cross Killer features." Jaq pushed those stacks of paper aside.

David smirked.

Jaq huffed. "Hey, at least I'm trying." She picked up the protractor.

"New weapon?" David studied it. "I'll don my Kevlar vest."

Jaq headed to the pinned area on the wall map. "Last night's victim," she said, her pointer finger resting on the new pin. "Perp's living in close vicinity to the pins."

"Quandary's figuring distance."

"Goal-oriented serial killers stay close to home, employment, and their handiwork. Aim that contraption at the map. Try two miles around each pin."

Glad he's not suffering from self-doubt. "That radius could bleed together hundreds of houses."

"Hundreds is better odds than eight hundred thousand Wayne County residents." David gulped his last swig of coffee as if it were a shot of bourbon. He crumbled and tossed the cup, thudding it in the trashcan at the other end of the map.

"Why two miles?" Jaq adjusted the protractor with the map coordinates and measurements listed alongside.

"Profilers say we're not looking for an obvious oddball. Likely an upstanding, highly intelligent, over-achieving control freak. Military training or Police Academy training. Throw in Ivy League, charity organizing, churchgoer."

Jaq washed her hands over her face. "Okay, does that widen our net or send us in circles?"

"Immediate areas around each victim's home." David waited until Jaq faced him. "From Jack the Ripper on down—they live near their victims. He is here among us."

David tapped his fingers on the wall, mimicking seconds on a ticking clock. "Point and draw already."

Jaq placed the protractor tip in a pinhole and drew a circle. "Any area that overlaps multiple times dictates our beginning location."

David studied Jaq as she drew.

"Let's find the common denominator and become the eleventh plague—his nightmare.

Maybe then you'll believe in the plagues." Jaq removed another pin and drew another circle.

"Honey, I didn't say I don't believe in plagues; I want a message that leads me to capture."

"Put on a cape and ponder one yourself, Batman. I put out a theory, you made fun of it, don't act like you suddenly approve."

David leaned against the wall, folded his arms and his eyes edged along her frame until their eyes met.

His eye-crawling quickened her breathing.

"Should've brought your silken pj's. It's going to be another long evening."

"Get out of my drawers." Jaq threw a handful of pins at him and watched him duck. Thankful for the lack of mistletoe, she tucked her hormones and returned to work.

* * * *

It seemed to Jaq to be on cue as the call rang in at nine thirty, interrupting their work. Jaq stiffened as she listened to David's end of the conversation. David tapped his phone off, tucked away a few photos, snapped files closed and grabbed his jacket.

Jaq almost pirouetted out of the conference room beside him. "Christmas is about twenty-eight hours away. Killer's escalating on cue."

"He sensed we've been cooped up in that damned room all day and didn't want us going stir crazy." David pushed the Down elevator button. "Hero that he sees himself."

Jaq stepped behind him into the elevator. "A gruesome reason to liberate us from our hideaway."

They sauntered side by side toward David's Explorer.

"Recon first, then the site." David zipped up the underground parking and around the corner toward his apartment. "I should have brought her to work with us. Thought she needed some solid sleep."

"I could've used some. These crazy hours are interfering with my astuteness." Jaq yawned and shouldered into the passenger seat with closed eyes.

Within a few minutes David pulled over, parked, and retrieved Recon. David directed her to the back and clicked himself in.

"Recon's wide awake, looking as anxious as we feel," David said. "I love how she gets excited each time, like it's the first time."

"I can't survive on dog naps." Jaq yawned again.

"Your adrenaline will be running higher than Recon's by the next block. I have it on good authority the Double Cross Killer changed tactics."

Jaq peered over and sat taller. "Do tell."

"Scoop is there's a new twist we have to see to believe." David slowed, cut the lights and rolled down the window. "Hey, Doc, we're right behind you."

Dr. Towers cut in front of a parked Detroit police vehicle and made an about face toward David's voice. "My wife's ready to find the Double Cross Killer and crush his windpipe."

David parked at the edge of the driveway. "Are we going steady yet?"

"Let's hope we don't make it to the engagement stage."

"Too cold, move inside." Jaq slammed the vehicle door. "Doc, I don't see the CSI Van or your LX. Did you need a ride back?"

"Van will arrive soon. New car. Combination Christmas and early birthday present from my wife. I will not insult you by informing Detroit's prize detectives which vehicle. I will let you two sleuths figure it out—no calling in for help."

"Geez', can't a girl be curious without being challenged to a duel?" Jaq laughed. "Game on."

The trio walked toward the house, followed in harness by Recon. They stopped in front of the open garage.

Dr. Towers handed David his medical bag. "Make yourself useful while I walk in and take a few pictures. You two and Recon follow behind and do your thing."

"The garage?" Jaq didn't believe it at first.

David gestured toward the garage. "The change I mentioned."

They drifted toward the Animal Control truck that had just pulled into the driveway behind the Explorer. Two men jumped out, donned protective clothing including gloves and masks as they made contact.

David waved to avoid contaminating their fresh gloves and made introductions. "Were you called?"

The blond, older man pushed up a cheek with the corner of his mouth clearly spewing "Duh!" without actually saying it. "Report of vermin removal at a crime scene."

"Diseased livestock." Jaq's gaze pounced from David to Dr. Towers, then back at David. "Plague. Plain and simple."

After they produced their ID to David, he checked it. "Vermin? Defined as bugs, livestock, what?"

"We'll know soon." The blond handed masks to David, Jaq and Doc. "We've extra boots and gear as well. Dog needs to stand clear."

David stood between the Animal Control Team and the garage. He began engaging the blond. "We appreciate your work. This crime scene can't be compromised. Nothing can be removed, even a carcass, until evidence is documented and collected."

The blond man stopped and spoke very slowly like he was instructing a new cadet. "And we appreciate your work. We will let you investigate, but this could be a contamination site. Health regulations and protocol must be followed. You fall in behind us, after we give you the all clear."

Dr. Towers nodded at David and Jaq.

"Just great." David's belligerent tone exposed his protocol disapproval.

"Damn, I'm ready to rock now." Jaq felt certain this unique scene would reveal valuable intel. She pulled out a notepad, leaned against a wall, and used her jottings to keep her annoyance at bay. It'd be frowned upon if she were to kick some Animal Control Team butt. Not getting the first full view of your victim was like not seeing your newborn—or so she'd heard.

David handed the uniform at the door Recon's leash and leered over Jaq's shoulder.

David sighed. "Garage could be a copycat."

Jaq kept her eyes focused on her note-taking, which at this point was more of a series of questions and doodles.

"What's going on in the never-ending conga-line of questions in your brain?" David whispered.

"Murder in the garage, in a van—close to the house, but, outside of the actual house. Sloppiness, maybe? Break in the plan? Did someone come home and spoil his plan."

"Won't know till we get in, but I don't buy that—he's too calculated." David got loud. "Doc's waving us in."

They stepped up to the door and placed the masks over their faces, and entered the garage. Despite the winter cold, the stench burned their eyes and noses. David gagged.

Dr. Towers pronounced the official situation. "Carcasses of a collection of road kill at varied stages of decomp—everywhere. Take a quick look because Animal Control is anxious to remove them."

"Not exactly livestock." David winked at Jaq.

Jaq searched the garage. "Maybe you should learn to salsa dance so you can move more quickly out of the range of the camera lens." Jaq more easily juggled viewing the body and staying out of the photographs than David as Dr. Towers rhythmically snapped photographs of all angles.

"Perp crushed the windpipe, transferred the victim, then set the scene. Handcuffed the arm of the victim to the steering wheel." Dr. Towers sounded disappointed, like maybe this time they'd find the victim in time to save him. "Very methodical. Exactly like the others, including the silk rosary." He grabbed his medical bag from David. "Thirty-two-year-old Caucasian male, worked at a local bar—night shift. Got out early. Wife found him around nine when she was checking the locks and getting ready for bed."

"Family?" David asked.

"Kids are with grandparents. Mom was finishing Christmas shopping," Dr. Towers said. "She was planning on an early rise, cooking all day. They celebrate Christmas Eve."

"No signs of a struggle." Jaq craned her neck and twisted it around the garage. "Maybe the Double Cross Killer is on a killing spree of his friends."

"Against profile." David's voice was gruff, as if he were taking the kill personally.

Dr. Towers' voice was bland and precise, like his movements. "You are not getting the message. He kills. Sends another message."

Jaq used the toe of her boot to lift the edge of some wet paper on the floor. "What are we supposed to do?" She looked up at her team. "Send a reply body?"

"Did you find a common victim link?" Dr. Towers didn't sound hopeful; more like he had already decided there would be no definitive answers this night.

"Lack of grief by the close family, about the deceased—in fact they are relieved—that is a common link." David turned back toward the garage door entrance where he'd deposited Recon. "Fact is, Recon isn't disturbed by any relatives' scent, and there's no evidence pointing to any relative so that's not our direction at this time."

"We think we're looking for someone who's protecting children from violence because of an emerging domestic assault history of a few victims— reported—unreported—it's there," Jaq said. "Also exploring a CPS angle— reporter, investigator—not sure."

"Mmm. Have you considered a forensic interviewer of any child?" Dr. Towers asked.

"Good thought." Jaq pulled out her notepad and made a note. She wasn't going to let one thread of this horror slip.

"Still doesn't explain how anyone would know all the children and what's going on inside the home," David said.

"Same social worker, CASA worker—Court Appointed Special Advocate?" Dr. Towers offered.

David nodded. "Checking."

*God and Santa Claus have eyes everywhere.* Jaq thought back to little Myra's letter.

Dr. Towers raised his brows. "Let me know the results of the interviews."

"I'll check with CSI on evidence collection." David was eager to get Recon in the garage.

"Compromised crime scene—" Dr. Towers began.

David held up his hand, palm-side up. "Don't say it, Doc."

"The animals here may set Recon off despite her training." Dr. Towers clapped his palms against his pant legs. "I have placed these cases ahead of all others. Rita is working overtime on Christmas Eve. She is off Christmas Day and weekend."

David half-mooned a smirk on his face, then smacked his lips. "Sorry, Doc. When I can sleep, I dream in cartoons that mock this investigation. Makes me irritated and impatient."

"I feel the same pressure you two have. But, from work and home. I owe my wife a very long, very expensive vacation. If you two stop the chitchat, you can do your job and we will both finish before the media mob frenzy descends."

\* \* \* \*

Carcasses removed and evidence gathered, Dr. Towers shook the hands of the Animal Control workers and gave directions to remove the gurney. "Recon might want to warm up in the garage and do her thing," Dr. Towers said. "I'm headed home and will call you in when I have a preliminary report."

Jaq patted Dr. Towers' shoulder. "Thanks, Doc."

David walked around the garage, then, after clearance, retrieved Recon.

Recon sniffed the air and entered with her head held high. She was on alert. David released the harness, and everyone stood back and observed her work.

"Bag it." David pointed. He momentarily stuck his head in the eggplant-colored van. Upon exit, he spewed orders. "Just pull out the whole ashtray and bag it. Recon's extremely interested in the contents. An assortment of coins, but my girl-pal is never wrong."

"Hopefully, the Double Cross Killer touched it?" Jaq edged in to take a closer look.

A gloved CSI officer cut between them to follow orders.

David didn't answer, his eyes focused on Recon. When Recon seemed disinterested, David re-harnessed her, praised her, gave her a treat, and refocused on Jaq.

"Anything from interviewing the vic's wife?" David pulled away from the van and Jaq followed him. They stepped outside the crime scene in the opposite direction from the CBS News truck and headed for the Explorer.

Jaq filled him in. "Victim is second husband and stepdad to her two daughters—ages seven and eight. Only dad they remember. Claims no domestic violence."

"Where were the girls? I didn't see any kids in the house?" David asked.

"Vic drove them up north to their grandparents' house Saturday morning, returned that evening. Girls spend a few days with grandparents, and then mom and stepdad arrive before everyone is awake Christmas morning. Girls have done that the past five years since their dad died." Jaq flipped through her notes.

"We need to interview those girls." David clicked the doors open. Recon jumped into the back before they climbed in.

Jaq snapped her seatbelt and set her cell phone in the cup holder. "Agreed. Forensic interviewers—Doc made a good point. If there's evidence of an abusive situation, let the experts handle it. We'll get permission to tape the session."

"And any CASA volunteer who may have been assigned to work with a family and report back to the court. That would be in court files, easy enough to access." David revved the engine. "Did you figure out Doc's birthday vehicle? You put our reputation on the line."

Jaq laughed. "While you were going gaga over Recon, I found it."

"Dead giveaway." Jaq shook her head. "Doc's wife hasn't lost her sense of humor. Black Hummer, license plate 1032 ME."

"So?"

"1032 is code for 'Homicide'. ME, well, even you can figure out that's 'Medical Examiner.'"

David grinned.

"Let's get an early start in the morning since it's Christmas Eve. Interview any neighbors the uniforms come up with." Jaq snuggled in the seat and closed her eyes.

"Do you ever stop thinking about work?" David made a sharp turn and parked in her lot. He whistled for Recon and they all climbed out. David clicked the alarm on the truck. With a quick pace, they headed toward the building.

"I'm going to dream of cranberries and candy canes." Jaq yawned.

"Only if they're mine." David wrapped his arm around Jaq's waist.

"Jingle bells." Jaq giggled in the darkness.

# Chapter Twenty-three

RITA PLACED HER LUNCH TRAY on the table, then stretched and slid into the booth across from Dr. Towers.

"It is not easy waking up to these long morning autopsy sessions." Dr. Towers smiled warmly at Rita. "Thank you for coming in early once again, especially on Christmas Eve."

From the pocket in her green scrubs, Rita whipped out her pager and flashed it at him. "I understand the urgency, but I may lose a terrific boyfriend over it. He doesn't understand early-morning hospital calls and pages."

"You will be home in time for dinner and midnight mass." He hesitated. "Have you told him what you really do?"

Rita shook her head, held her bent thumb knuckle between her teeth, then released it. "I just can't seem to tell the truth about this career shift. Maybe after this wave of murders, so it doesn't seem so—"

"Dangerous?"

"Creepy. Sorry." The thought of Nick reminded her she'd brought a Sarasota Sun Times article for Dr. Towers. She pulled it out of her oversized shoulder bag and reached it across the table. "I almost forgot."

Dr. Towers grabbed the paper and immediately unfolded it.

"I traveled with Nick to his Florida condo. I grabbed this newspaper at the airport. I read my novel instead. When I finally did read it, I thought you should read the headline." Rita tapped on the paper.

Dr. Towers pulled his reading glasses from his pocket. He read the headline out loud: *Serial Killer Strangles Third.*

Rita watched his expression change.

With an unexpected rage, he articulated the last word of the headline. He read to the bottom of the page.

Rita sat stiffly, hands folded in her lap. "I'm sorry I didn't read it sooner." She bit her lip and kept her eyes on him. "I think there's a correlation, but I don't know how—coincidence, copycat, the same murderer?" She stirred

148

her soup and squeezed lemon into her water. "Maybe I am just out of my element."

"Good instinct is what you have." He refolded the paper, set it on his lap, then looked over the top of his reading glasses. "May I keep the paper?"

"Sure."

"As with the Double Cross Killer murders, keep this confidential— don't discuss the Sarasota similarities with anyone, including your boyfriend."

Rita nodded. "Of course."

"Or have you already talked to him?"

"Nick? No, we don't talk about things like murder. He's very OCD—a bit of a neat freak. Totally into religion. My interest in murder, a sin and a messy part of other people's lives, could lead to specific questions about where I work now. I haven't found the nerve."

Dr. Towers sipped his tea, gently set down the cup, and slowly curved up his lips. "Do not find it right now."

"No chance." Rita forked up a bite of her chicken salad, then stared at Doc. He was reading the article again.

"Jaq and David will be very interested in this." Dr. Towers thumped the paper.

Rita wasn't sure she saw fear, but she certainly heard concern and urgency. What was really going on? Had she actually found a link? "Don't worry. I'll not mention it to anyone. In fact, I'll forget about it until you make me remember." Imagining her mind like a computer, Rita dragged the knowledge into her brain trash folder… but didn't empty it.

Dr. Towers swallowed the last sandwich corner, wiped his mouth with a napkin, folded it, tossed it on the plate, and pushed it to the end of the table. "Rita, let me know of any other articles you come across. Be aware of your surroundings. Understood?"

"We're on the last flight tonight for the long Christmas weekend." A flutter started in the center of her chest and streamed to her arms and throat. "I'll stay alert."

"Good." Dr. Towers stood and picked up his tray. "Now, if you are finished, we need to get back. Our detectives are expecting my call to come in this afternoon."

* * * *

Wednesday crawled. Jaq waited for Dr. Towers' telephone call, and David did his I-should-be-hibernating grumpy-bear act. Anticipating the Double Cross Killer's next attack wasn't easy, nor was being cooped up with ill-fitting evidence in a conference room that felt more like an isolation cell. Desperate for an interruption, Jaq phoned Sally Walters, whose husband was killed while she and her children were at a Christmas school function he couldn't attend because he had to work late. Sally was available. Yes! Jaq poked the grizzly with a verbal stick, and both detectives dashed for the door and escaped onto Woodward Avenue.

When Sally Walters opened the door to her Grosse Pointe Woods home, she was a portrait of composure. David and Jaq followed Sally to a kitchen brightly painted with sunflowers, and an oak table and six chairs in a window-wrapped nook. Jaq paused for a moment to take in the décor. David scooted past her and took a seat with his back to the windows.

Sally gestured toward the kitchen like Vanna White showing off a prize. "I'm an artist at heart, and I like things bright."

"Sunflowers are friendly." Jaq made her voice warm and enthusiastic, ran her fingers lightly over the sunflowers, and sat facing the windows. She wanted Sally at ease.

"The children have gone through a—something big." Sally sat across from David, Jaq on her left. "The home needs to be cheerful for the children."

"You have a great eye. The flowers look so real, and the accents are splendid." Jaq placed her hand over one of Sally's.

"I got lucky. Seems sunflowers are suddenly fashionable. Found everything to match." Sally paused and visibly craned her neck around the kitchen, her voice was timid. "Maybe I overdid it—too matchy-matchy? My husband wasn't fond of flowers."

"Not at all. It gives me a very warm feeling. I bet the family spends a lot of time in here. I know I would."

Sally's face brightened and she stood and hurried to the kitchen counter. "Let me get you something to drink."

"It's not necessary." But Jaq quickly realized Sally needed to keep her hands busy. "Can I help?"

"No, I'll just be a moment."

In seconds, Sally placed a platter of sliced cranberry-nut bread and festively iced cutout cookies on the table, then teacups, silverware, and linen sunflower napkins in front of each of them. Finally, she brought a china teapot with freshly brewed hot tea. "When you called, you said you had questions about my husband's murder." She kept her eyes on the teapot and sat.

"We've been gathering information and—"

Sally interrupted, talking fast. "Have you found the murderer? I haven't read anything about it in the paper. Just the new murder."

"Actually, no." Jaq detested having to tell this poor woman they hadn't caught the man who'd blasted the family boat onto the rocks. "We're reviewing all of the cases and victims. We're hopeful."

"What we need is to ask you some follow-up questions from the other night." David got right to the point. "We're mostly interested in talking with the children of each victim, including yours."

"Excuse me? 'Cuz that's not happening." Her voice got high-pitched and she flagged her hand, upending it into a stop sign. "My children have been through enough. We need time." A tremble ran through her, she shook out and refolded her napkin.

"Maybe we could explain, before you make up your mind." Jaq placed a cookie on her plate and poured a cup of tea. She wanted Sally to know they weren't leaving anytime soon. Jaq would eat the whole platter and bake more if she had to.

"Haven't you asked enough questions?" Resentment tinged Sally's voice. "My children are too young. They've nothing to add."

"We wouldn't ask, if we didn't need you. We're getting closer." Jaq stopped and waited until Sally met her pupil to pupil. "The killer has killed again. We need to stop him. Your children might know some tiny thing that could really help us out." Jaq sipped her tea, and locked eyes with Sally over the rim of the teacup.

They waited.

Sally released a gurgly cry from her throat but her voice was surprisingly firm when it emerged. "Fine. *But,* I pre-approve *everything* you ask my children *if* I decide to let them talk to you."

"Verifying the ages of your children—?" Jaq looked up from her open notepad.

"Seth—seven. Suzanne just turned nine."

"How are they doing?" David's voice was quiet, slow, and gentle. It sounded as if he had all the time in the world and his world revolved around her children's welfare.

For a second Sally's face softened. Then, obviously thinking, she stared at the duo. Her body stiffened and her grey eyes roamed back and forth between them. "Are my children in danger?"

"Really, you can relax." David was nodding so slightly it was almost imperceptible.

He was so hot when he showed his caring side… Jaq mentally slapped herself and focused. "Neither you nor your children are in danger, Sally."

"We're profiling the perpetrator. For the best picture, we need very specific information about each victim and their families." David made the word "families" sound sacred.

"I'm confused." Sally twisted the napkin.

"Truthfully—" Jaq bit into another cookie and spoke with her mouth full. After all, what says *just plain folks* better than talking with your mouth full? She had to keep Sally engaged. "We're confused, too. But your help will make our theories get us closer."

Sally tossed the napkin onto the table. "So, you don't believe the murders are random, do you?" She bit her lip and rested her hands on the rim of her teacup. "Oh my God." Her hands trembled. "He always said he'd get me from the grave."

Jaq reached over and gently touched her arm with an index finger. "Who'll get you?"

"Look, I don't speak ill of the dead. But my husband was very controlling. It was because he loved us so much. He had a temper. He always said I should pray he'd die first." She paused. "And then he did."

"What did that mean to you, 'to pray he'd die first'?" Jaq kept her voice non-threatening.

"Because I—we—the children and I, were his property, and if we didn't do what he said, do exactly what he wanted, well, there were consequences."

"Consequences." Jaq set her cookie down. "Did he harm you?"

"He didn't mean to. It was mostly my fault."

"I didn't find filed reports of domestic violence calls to the house or any history of violence, only 9-1-1 calls reported as mistakes." Jaq talked just like they were discussing sunflower curtains. "Many cases go unreported. Is that what happened here?"

Sally suddenly needed a tissue. She slid her chair from the table, stood, and turned her back to them.

"Sally." David's voice was warm.

She lifted her blouse revealing the long, thick welts crisscrossing her bare back.

Jaq swallowed hard, but kept her composure. Her cheeks stung with instant heat. "I'm so very sorry. How long did you endure the lashings?"

"Just the past few years. He was a great man until he lost his job. Then I couldn't do anything right. I didn't even know how to leave." Sally paused. She dug a tissue from her jeans pocket and cleaned up her face. In a much stronger voice she continued, turned around and returned to her seat. "I'd have left and reported him if I'd thought the kids were in danger. He never touched them."

"Did anyone ever hear him threaten you or hit you?" Jaq asked.

She shook her head *no*.

"What about the kids? They are like little gremlins—they see and hear things. Adults think they are invisible, but they aren't."

"No, but as he became angrier and more withdrawn, he had less to do with them. I was happy about that. So, no. They would've told me." Sally looked from Jaq to David. "I'm sure."

Jaq nodded. "Your children attend University Liggett School?"

"They're happy there. I'm involved in the school. It's exclusive, breeds a lot of Harvard graduates."

"What about extracurricular activities?" Jaq felt a deep frustration rise. *Where's the connection—give it to me, damn it—I can feel it, you have it right here.* She looked around the kitchen to avoid leaping out of her chair, then placed her hands under her buttocks. Sitting on her hands made her feel less likely to lunge at Sally and shake the information she wanted out of her.

"My kids are into all sorts of things, and the school brings in a lot of events for the children."

Ever-patient, David moved forward. "Like what?"

"Programs that benefit the community. Like Meals-on-Wheels. Or the delivery of a message, a poem, or a story to seniors and other shut-ins."

"That's so nice!" Jaq meant it, but she also needed to press for more details. "How lovely to receive something from a child."

Sally continued proudly, "The local community groups gather the artwork from University Liggett School and other Grosse Pointe schools the last Friday of each month, or the Friday before a holiday, and deliver it to the Program Director. As I understand it, the Children's Home of Detroit and the Grosse Pointe University Women continue this in June, July, and August."

"Is this program unique to the Pointes?" Jaq feared her fingers on her right hand had numbed so she pulled them out from under her and reached for cranberry-nut bread.

Sally made a mouth shrug. "I don't know. One of the younger teachers, who did her student teaching in California, brought the model to the school, and they sent home a flier with an informational packet. They asked for volunteers and permission to give away our children's artwork and writings. I'm sure Principal Severs will give you a copy of the program if it's important. He might know about the other school districts, if that's what you're asking."

Jaq wrinkled her eyebrows together for just a second. She had no time to apply anti-wrinkle cream day and night. "I wonder why we haven't heard anything about it before now."

"Seniors and shut-ins aren't exactly the top of the news, are they?" Sally let a lame smile escape. "That's why it's such a good program. The children only receive the reward of giving, not receiving, except for a thank-you letter. And a visit from Santa, who thanks them for their good works."

"Really?" Jaq sounded as if she'd just heard some extra juice gossip. Things were coming together. At last. She pulled up her left hand, took the final bite of cranberry-nut bread, then jotted down a few notes.

"They had a party just before the Thanksgiving break." Sally was back in mom-mode now and spoke easily. "Each child sat on his lap. They brought in a photographer, and the children gave him their letters along with their wish lists. Saved us all the dreaded Christmas mall visit and the mile-long lines."

"Do you have the pictures?" Jaq asked lightly, as if it were of no consequence whatever. Woohoo! She was having trouble keeping her seat, but she schooled her face.

David flicked her a glance. She refused to look at him. Not yet.

"Sure. All the parents got pictures." Sally swirled something in the bottom of her teacup. She seemed to be drifting. "We all ordered packages. It was a school fundraiser. Made a lot of money."

"Would you mind if we get a picture of each child with Santa?" David finished another cookie.

"Sure. I have extras. Just give me a minute." Sally stood woodenly and left the room.

Within a minute she returned and handed Jaq two five-by-seven pictures.

"Thank you." Jaq took the photos and held them with respect. She smiled kindly at Sally. "We'll get them back to you when we can. You've been a big help."

The front door opened.

Sally looked at the detectives wide-eyed, alarmed. "My children. We're out of time. We have a lot to do to get ready for Christmas tomorrow."

"Hey, Mom," the children called out in unison. "Did you see our snowman?"

"In the kitchen," Sally called back. "I'll look outside in a minute."

Bounding in, they plopped off their chunky, snow-filled coats and spilled their boots onto the floor. It took them two whole seconds to notice the plate of baked goods. Only then did they realize there were strangers present. Jaq had forgotten how in-their-own-world kids could be. It was fun.

Sally placed an arm around the shoulders of each of her children. "These are the detectives who are trying to figure out who took your daddy away from us. They stopped by to see how we're doing. Say *hello,* and then go wash your hands while I get plates and hot cocoa to go with these cookies." Sally smiled. "Deal?"

"Okay, Mom," Suzanne said, turning toward the bathroom with Seth following closely behind.

"Please," she whispered. "I don't want my children upset. I, we, really don't have anything else to tell you. They don't know anything."

"We understand." Jaq edged a half smile up at David. They uniformly sat back to make it clear they were not ready to leave. "I just have a few questions about Santa Claus. Then, we'll leave," Jaq said.

"And I have one more question." David glared at Jaq, and then turned his sweet attention to Sally. "The handcuffs that were around your husband's hands and feet. You said they were the ones your children played with—that they were from their toy box. Do you recall when the children got those handcuffs?"

Sally's visible discomfort shifted Jaq's attention away from her irritation with David.

"No idea. They like to play cops and robbers, like most kids, I guess."

"How do you suppose the killer knew where they were?" Jaq asked.

Hearing the children, Sally shook her head. "No clue. The children are always leaving their toys around. Andy always hated that. Could've been in the toy box or on the floor."

"Did your husband ever use handcuffs on you?" Jaq asked gently.

"Uhm, yes, he—" Her voice trailed off. The children bounded in and headed straight for the cookies.

Jaq watched each child grab a cookie. When they headed for the table, she began. "Guys, your mother showed us pictures of you with Santa."

Both children set their eyes on her and waited.

"I was wondering if you could tell me anything about Santa," Jaq said.

"Like what?" Suzanne's nose crinkled. "He was nice. Some kids said he wasn't the real Santa, but was his helper. I didn't care."

Seth shrugged one shoulder. "Yeah, Santa was nice, I guess."

Jaq didn't press Seth, but wondered what his hesitation was. "Did you each write him a letter to take with him to the North Pole?"

Both children nodded. "Yeah. Part of our assignment in English. Teachers said they weren't going to read them, but we had to write them," Seth explained. "The whole school had the same assignment. Kinda dumb as homework."

"Can you tell me what you asked Santa for?" Jaq asked.

"I don't like to write much, so mine was pretty short. Computer games and a new bike. Pretty much what I ask for every year." Seth grabbed another cookie. "Can I go now? My shows are on."

Sally nodded. "One show, then help set the table for dinner."

Jaq sat across from Suzanne. "Do you remember what you asked for?"

She looked from Jaq to the cookies to her mom and back to the cookies. She squeezed her hands together. "I don't think I'm supposed to tell."

"It's okay, honey. Christmas is tomorrow. I'm sure Santa has already packed the sleigh. Your gifts are safe inside. It's okay to tell." Sally wrapped an arm around her daughter's shoulder. "Whatever you asked for is fine. Whatever you want to say is fine. Santa will be okay with it, and so will I."

"Okay." Suzanne paused, looked up wide-eyed at her mother and ignored Jaq and David. "I asked Santa to give daddy nice pills so he wouldn't hurt you anymore. That's all I asked for."

A hundred tiny mice ran up Jaq's spine.

* * * *

David and Jaq remained silent until they were clear out of the neighborhood. David was the first to break the silence. He accelerated onto I-96. "We've got him."

"I know, but tell me how, exactly." Jaq tried not to get her hopes up. Hell, this was the first real hope they'd had on this case; she'd forgotten what hope felt like. "It's not as simple—"

"Santa is the Double Cross Killer."

"Okay, Sherlock. So, we go to Liggett, and we figure out which Santa suit they hired. I doubt he gave them the right name or that they can ID him. Likely, they never saw Santa out of his suit."

"Santa had to get a paycheck," David sang in a girlie tune.

"In a real name to a real address. Hot damn—it's a start—big if—if he asked for pay—" Jaq froze at that thought.

David made a formal proclamation. "It's the American way. A solid lead. Not the first time we heard about Santa letters, either."

"Santa letters lead the Double Cross Killer to the kids." Jaq pounded her feet on the truck floor. Her whole face brightened. "He's a wacked-out Robin Hood with a red hat and white beard."

"Instead of green tights. Good move for Santa." David laughed out loud. Jaq wasn't quite ready to join him.

Realizing this perhaps, David's attitude sobered. "Motive?"

"Save the kids. A kid like Suzanne asks Santa for help, not toys, books, or clothes. Gives Santa details—enough to know why help is needed and how to find them. Double Cross Killer finds them, scopes them out, and kills whomever the kid claims causes the harm."

Jaq was practically bouncing in her seat. "And the bastard leaves a calling card. A reverse message to the victim's victim."

"Like whipping this victim's back and cuffing his hands," David said. "Those children knew exactly what daddy was doing to momma."

"Exactly. The kids might've understood the message all along. They must've been terrified. Double Cross Killer announced he's stopped the abuse."

"Explains the lack of grief we've witnessed," David said.

Jaq rubbed her hands together. "How does someone hire a Santa?"

"Employment wanted lists and checks it twice," David said. "Let's go see Doc. We've finally got something to say."

* * * *

Within the hour Jaq and David sat across the conference room table from Dr. Towers and explained what they'd deduced.

"Remarkable." Dr. Towers straightened. "Fascinating." He leaned forward. "What can I do to help?"

"We need to keep this very quiet, limited access. You, maybe Rita. Even then, we're keeping a few details under wraps." David gestured as if he were pushing down air.

Doc nodded. "Certainly."

"Is it possible for you to go through the evidence and look for any type of leaf or soil sample, anything we may have overlooked that might help us zero in on one of these areas?" Jaq pulled out a sheet of paper, unfolded it, and placed it in front of the doctor.

Doc reached for his bifocals, then focused on the picture.

"This is a picture of the map we made with the murder indicators and the circles. You can see where they intersect. Those are the areas we're concentrating on." Jaq felt proud of the whole map idea and told herself—rightly so.

"Nothing wrong with that concept." Dr. Towers nodded and traced a few intersections with his fingers. "Solid plan. At this point, I'll search high and low, think upside down, stand on my head with my clothes on inside out, if it helps."

"You always leave us with such great visuals. Ever consider creative film director?" David thumped the table.

"By the way, fabulous birthday present, the Hummer. License plate's a dead giveaway, don't you think?" Jaq winked at Doc.

"I will tell my wife you think she has good taste in presents and husbands."

Jaq slid to the edge of her seat toward Doc's desk. "We hate to pressure you, but the preliminaries on our latest?"

Dr. Towers laughed. "Well, actually, I have a theory that will astound you."

"Astound?" Jaq's chills were revisiting. This was good. Very, very good.

Dr. Towers opened his desk drawer and withdrew a newspaper.

"I called Nurse Rose in early to assist me and we had lunch together." Dr. Towers paused and met Jaq's gaze. "Have you met her new boyfriend?"

Jaq and David looked at each other and nodded. "Nick Archer? No, but she talks about him plenty. I've threatened to do a background check on him if I don't meet him soon." Jaq wondered where this was coming from. "Why? Have you met him?"

"I don't know much about him." Dr. Towers shook his head. "What I do know is this: he is a pilot for Delta, and Rita recently travelled with him to Sarasota, Florida—"

Jaq interrupted. "If she's not doing her work, I can talk to her—Double Cross Killer cases have to come first."

"No problem there," Dr. Towers said. "Let me get to the point. At lunch, she pulled out the Sarasota Sun Times she'd brought back with her. She asked me to read an article about three recent murders in Siesta Key."

"We don't have any jurisdiction there," David said. "And—"

"David." Jaq watched Dr. Towers slide the paper toward them. "Read the headline." Jaq leaned into David, so they both could read.

Dr. Towers shook his head again. "I think you will find there is a relationship between our Wayne County murders and the Sarasota murders. I asked Rita not to speak to anyone about her theory."

"Her theory?" Jaq remembered Rita mentioning the trip, but no mention of murders or newspaper articles.

"Well, she asked me if there could be any relationship between the Siesta Key murders and the Wayne County Double Cross Killer murders."

"Excuse me?" Jaq felt dumped. She was the best friend. Rita should have been talking to her.

"She has good instinct. Honestly, I think she may have stumbled upon a connection we were not able to find."

Jaq and David looked at each other, then Dr. Towers, then back at the newspaper. Neither spoke. They absorbed his words and read.

"It is either a copycat, or the Double Cross Killer is a traveling man," Dr. Towers said.

They finished reading and lay the paper on the table.

"Copycat is always a possibility and will waste a lot of time, if that's what it is. But, traveling fits our theory." David pointed down the columns and skimmed the article.

"After I released Nurse Rose for the day, I searched the Internet and made a few calls to Sarasota and waited for you to arrive."

"And?" Jaq nibbled on a fingernail. Her mind was racing, and her stomach gurgled. Was this real?

"I spoke with the Sarasota ME, who forwarded me his preliminary findings from the autopsies of the victims in the articles—confidentially, of course. I made a list of every similarity I found, and I sent our findings to him as well."

"Can we see the notes?" David asked.

Dr. Towers handed David a file. "Dr. Milano is the Chief Medical Examiner. I was intrigued hearing his tone, but after reading the autopsies, they might as well have been prepared by my own hands." Dr. Towers turned to Jaq. "Including your plague theory."

"No way." Jaq threw her hands in the air. "Did anyone use the term 'plague'?"

"No. But the autopsy notes and preliminary report make notations of findings without conclusion." Dr. Towers paused and looked at David, then Jaq. "An argument can be made that fits into your plague theory. Victim one, assassin bugs. Victim two, a frog. Victim three, cigarette burns and ashes—"

"That's a stretch." David interrupted.

Jaq huffed. "Not really. Technically, it dealt with boils but begins with handfuls of ashes from the furnace that were to be sprinkled toward the heavens—"

"Did you tell this Dr. Milano about the plague theory?" David asked.

Dr. Towers shook his head. "Not my theory to tell, nor my line of work. Kept it medical."

David sighed. "Yeah well, if all of that is true, then I'm guessing this so-called plague is the Double Cross Killer's subtle message to tell everyone to change their ways—wasn't that the biblical theme, too?"

Jaq tilted her head. "It was more of a let-my-people-go thing, but it's a teeniest bit possible that somebody who crushes windpipes and stages freak shows where innocent children can find them just may not really know his bible all that well." She shrugged.

Suddenly, she felt her excitement swirl right down the flusher. "Just because it finally makes sense, it still doesn't bring us closer to him."

Dr. Towers lifted the article and handed it to David. "Take the newspaper. It belongs to your investigation. Sarasota investigators are as baffled, actually more baffled than you about these crimes. If you don't call them, they will call you."

Jaq scanned her watch, then looked back and forth at the men. Instinct tugged at friendship and yanked at her to rush outside and call Rita before dealing with the Sarasota Detectives. She wanted to hibernate in the War Room, all evidence in hand. Mostly, she wished this wasn't the day before Christmas. The world—with the exception of the killer—was about to literally pause for twenty-four hours.

"What's got your tongue tied and your face red?" David stared at her as he sat on the corner of Dr. Towers' desk.

Dr. Towers tilted his head in echoed question.

"Christmas Eve is upon us, literally hours away, Christmas Day the world stops—and this is dropped on us. We have no idea how long it'll take us to reach anyone you spoke with, Doc. Most workforces have a skeleton crew from now till January."

Dr. Towers knitted his brows. "True. I have overworked Nurse Rose so we are not behind. Today I released her until Monday."

"Many county employees take advantage of the long weekend," David said.

"Exactly." Jaq lifted her chin. "Here and in Sarasota. Double Cross Killer knows it, too."

* * * *

Rita, exhausted from the long workday, napped and was reenergized. When Nick hadn't arrived by six o'clock, she worried, since he assured her six would be perfect. She'd packed and was ready for the late-night flight. She'd prepared a light preflight dinner. His elevated mood reminded her of his tenor when they were in Florida overlooking the beach from the lanai or after sex. The appetizer dinner would show him he was appreciated.

Since Fazul, she hadn't spent a happy holiday season. Finally, it seemed that would change and yet now she sat paralyzed on her living room couch, staring at her cell phone, hoping a ventriloquist's voice would emerge to answer her worry.

She checked her prized grandfather clock, stood, and rechecked dinner, glad it would hold. A few minutes later, she sat at the counter with her cell phone in one hand, hot tea in the other. She closed her eyes and to calm herself she savored the thrill, the sheer adrenaline rush she had felt when they first met. She still felt it when he was near and hoped it would never dissipate. Realistically, she knew it would, but for now she intended to remain immersed in good feelings.

As time went by, the whirlpool of questions swirling inside her rushed more strongly. Looking objectively at her new beginnings with Nick, she was having difficulty sleeping. She slept great with him, but her dreams lived somewhere between enchanted and cursed. Deep in contemplation, she was startled by heavy footsteps. The unlocked door flew open. Nick bounded in. He brushed snowflakes off his charcoal grey wool overcoat, then peeled off his black leather gloves, shoving them into a pocket and setting down his flight bag. Before Rita could say 'hello,' Nick picked her up and twirled her around the foyer.

Relief—he was OK—and joy—he was happy—tumbled around in the surprise and the swirl. "What has gotten into you?"

"You have." He held her face in his big hands and tilted it up so she could look into his eyes.

"Really, Nick, what is going on? You're almost giddy." She laughed. "Did you win the lottery or something?"

"Or something." He reached into his black leather flight satchel and pulled out a small black velvet pouch. "I can't get you out of my mind. With my eighteen-hour layover last week, I did a little shopping."

Rita gasped, then reached toward Nick's extended hand. Nervous fingers untied the bow made of satiny gold twisted rope. A small leather box with smooth rounded corners peeked out. Looking from the box to Nick and back to the box again, she tingled like a freshly shaken bottle of soda. She wasn't sure her reaction was appropriate for the amount of time they'd been together. But she was excited and the joyful flutters felt right. She concentrated on the gift.

"What did you do? May I open it now?"

"Of course, silly girl." He looked entirely pleased with himself. "Merry-early-Christmas. It's to open, not to be stared at."

"I know, but it's not Christmas, I can wait a few hours—"

"Christmas is every day, if I want it to be. Open it." Even under his heavy coat, she could tell he was puffing his chest out. She loved that he loved fun.

"Not before I kiss you." She stood on her toes. "Whatever it is, I already love it."

"You'd better." He wrapped his arms around her.

Rita pressed herself against him, could feel the heat of his flesh, the pounding of his heart, his yearning lips against her own. He picked her up and carried her from the kitchen to the living room and gently set her on the couch. He sat next to her, then pointed toward the box.

Their eyes met. Something deep inside her thumped. Rita dropped her eyes, refocusing them on the box. Her fingers, usually graceful, felt clumsy under Nick's watchful eyes. She couldn't help shaking. The leather box felt soft. When she released the silken cord, the open box unleashed a row of glittering reflections. She gasped. With abandon, real joy, she flipped around, flung her arms around his neck and planted a firm kiss on his lips. She giggled.

Laughing with her, he stroked her hair, gently prying her off him. "Try it on."

Rita studied the brilliant marquis-cut diamond ring surrounded with two bands of equally brilliant, but smaller, alternating square and round-cut diamonds.

"I've never seen anything like it." Rita pulled it from the box and matched the eye of the diamond with her own and handed it to Nick.

"You don't like it?"

"I love it. It's exquisite." Those emotions that had been swirling before, collided. Her inside-self waved a big red warning flag, but her outside-self was too in love to take heed. "We have so much to learn about each other."

"Your answer is no?"

Round innocent eyes stared. "Is there a question?"

"Marry me. We're made for each other." Nick looked noble, commanding, and certain. "No question. The ring's almost as beautiful as you. And one of a kind, like you—specially designed. Just as you were designed by God for me." He looked grateful.

"Yes." Rita held her eyes on his and nodded. "Please put the ring on me." She held her left hand out.

His broad mouth grinned. Gently taking Rita's hand, he placed it over his heart. Then, as if her fingers were thin pieces of exquisite china, he positioned the ring. Pulling her hand to his mouth, he kissed the ring.

With both hands, he pulled her forward. Her body fit neatly into his, she could feel his heart pounding. With strong arms, he enveloped her, then whispered, "He who finds a wife finds a treasure and receives favor from the Lord. Proverbs 18:22. It's important you understand."

Rita tipped her head back and kissed him long and hard and more deeply than ever before. He lifted her into his arms. She was certain this was the taste and feel of home.

Across the room, down the hall and into the master bedroom, he carried her.

Now on their bed, he removed her clothes, almost tearing them, as her body surged with chills and her mind raced. His thumbs teased her nipples before sensually moving on to explore the rest of her.

Rita's eyes rolled back. All of her questions dissipated. Instinctively, she arched her back. Flesh met flesh. She needed him inside her. Drawing him in harder, tighter, farther, she began to quake. He sank so deeply inside that she almost lost consciousness. With each sensual touch, fear was lost and doubt dispersed. Finally, the volcanic eruption melded them into one, and she felt herself emotionally join with him. Hearing their hearts pounding in tandem, Rita wasn't sure where her flesh began and ended, until he kissed her lightly on the head and pulled free of her. Wet warmth spilled to the outside with him, while Rita slowly inhaled, exhaled, confident their souls had touched.

Minutes passed. She traveled back across some kind of mind-tundra. Finally, the brain numbness evaporated. "Dinner—I made a surprise dinner. And our flight?" she whispered.

Nick still lay on her. "Mmm. I just had dinner."

"Really, they're light appetizers."

"Very thoughtful." He played with her hair. "You know that, Rita. You're so thoughtful. Wrap it up."

"Anything you say, big guy."

Nick smoothed his nail over the length of her, then drew her in close and tugged at a handful of hair at the nape of her neck. "Get dressed quickly. We've a flight."

\* \* \* \*

Rita settled in the cabin of the airplane. She waved her engagement ring into a crack of light from the overhead, enamored with its sparkle and his exquisite taste. An extravagance she'd never imagined. Marriage was about the man, not the ring—a lesson easily learned from the failed marriages of her friends and family members, and her own failed relationships. A simple gold band would've satisfied her. Likely, couldn't wear any ring to work. Nick, likely wouldn't hear of her not wearing a ring at work. She'd deal with that later—triple layers of gloves?

Rita beamed every time she saw that sparkle which shone like a star, even in the dark. A glint of the love he felt for her. His words. They'd become heavily entangled in each other's emotions since they'd flirted their way into bed too soon. She slid the ring on her finger back and forth, back and forth...

Rita twirled the ring around her finger. Her inner-self and her never-ending doubts; a ring, band or rock, should not have such power. But it did have power, and with each sparkle she garnered more confidence in Nick and discarded her doubt. She was too excited to sleep. Time to plan which skimpy item, of the many lacy treats she'd packed, she would wear when they woke up together in Sarasota on their first of many Christmas mornings.

# Chapter Twenty-four

AFTER THEY LANDED, NICK AND Rita laughed arm-in-arm in the cool but star-filled Sarasota Christmas Eve night.

Nick tossed their luggage into a Jeep he'd rented, and Rita climbed in. "I'm exhausted, but thrilled to be away from Michigan blizzards." She ran a quick brush through her locks and secured them with a shell clip.

"Lucky, we weren't grounded." Nick slammed the rear door and jumped into the driver seat. "These few days will be great. And, back in time to spend the New Year with our families."

Rita yawned.

"A celebratory drink?" Nick asked. He revved the engine and backed out of the space. "Or, are you too tired?"

"Excited and tired." She placed a hand over his, then angled her head toward him. "A toast sounds lovely."

"French Champagne coming up. Condo's well stocked. I'll set up while you freshen up 'cause I expect a reward for that smooth flight."

Rita tousled his hair, worked her hand to his groin, then her fingers outlined the stitching of his zipper. "You got it."

Nick removed her hand. "No fair. If I get arrested for swerving, I can't get my reward."

Rita yawned. "If you stop for food, please pick up a newspaper. Let's see what's playing at the theatre."

"Sure, but I'm not thinking there'll be time for movies, unless they're X-rated."

* * * *

The calm sensual night developed into one of distorted dreams, slinking shadows, and threatening weather. It lasted a long, long time.

But Rita awoke to a sense of serenity and the aroma of brewing coffee. The night's storm was replaced by sunshine and the sound of gulls feasting on treasures brought up by the storm-lashed waters. A perfect Christmas morning.

Rita reached to the foot of the bed and grabbed the red silken teddy and thong she'd so fervently tossed many dark hours ago. She was a kitten about to purr. She stretched, basking in the remembered warmth of Nick's touch against her flesh. Running her hands through her hair, she thought about the night. She slept especially well with Nick. No tossing. No turning. No staring at the ceiling for hours at a time—it was like a wonderful coma. Maybe that's what being happy does. No more long nights alone, no being fearful; no wistful dreaming, she'd had hers.

She eased into the bathroom. She didn't sleep well when she was alone in Detroit. Lately, the Double Cross Killer invaded her sleep, her thoughts— but not when she was with Nick, and she was not about to break her happy spell. It had been a long time. Taking a final gaze at her peaceful face in the bathroom mirror, she emerged from her private thoughts and plunged into Nick's world.

"Merry Christmas, sleepyhead," he called out from the lanai. "I need you to place your star on my tree."

"Didn't you get enough last night? Why didn't you wake me? I seem to have slept in rather late, especially for a Christmas morning." Rita stuck her head out of the bedroom.

"You needed sleep after our late flight. Besides, I love to watch you sleep." Nick sent a kiss through the air. "I'll never have enough of your perfect body."

"You like to embarrass me." Rita ensured her voice was cheery. She wanted to maintain his good mood. She hastened into the lanai, pushed her chair next to his, kissed him, and then sat.

"You were like an all-night tidal wave. I did try to wake you up. You mumbled and rolled over."

"Really? I know I slept deep—I feel wonderful. The storm helped lull me to sleep. My sleep here with you is very different than in Detroit." Rita lifted the small glass of orange juice and gulped it down.

Nick laughed. "You're just begging for more trips." He ran his fingers through her hair, repositioning the long tresses over just far enough to plant kisses on the nape of her neck.

Rita wrapped her hands around his neck and her fingers playfully tangled in his gold neck chain.

"Hey..." Nick's right shoulder rose. "Don't break my chain. I've told you before it's old and fragile."

Rita released the chain, removed her hands from him and changed the subject. "My throat's really parched. Maybe I'm getting sick—or maybe it's just really dry here?" She refilled her orange juice glass.

"Just the flight and the change in climate. I can explain the science of it to you."

"I'll travel with you more often, if you promise not to explain it." Rita's voice was slow and rhythmic, a smile painted on her face.

"You're beautiful in the morning." Nick planted his face right in hers.

"Okay, what exactly do you want?" Rita leaned into him. She grinned.

"Firm wedding date." He kissed her.

The thought of a wedding woke notions of white roses and sunshine. "Nothing fancy. Agreed?"

"Promise."

"I'll work on it." She reached for a piece of toast and pulled her head back. She bit in. Swallowing hurt her throat.

"My mother, after you meet her, will help plan the wedding—take over if you prefer. Let's get our families together, make the announcement. We can give them assignments. We'll make everyone happy and save us lots of time."

"Okay, now I know you're kidding." She dropped her napkin and talked with her hands. "I want a small, personal wedding—but not one that's thrown together." Rita had waited a long time for a wedding.

"The important part is the marriage." Nick set his mug down and folded his hands on his lap and stared at her. "What we both want."

"I want it—no, I need it, to be special from beginning to end, not just something we had to do to get our lives in ord—"

Nick's cold stare blew in like a cold front. Rita stopped talking.

When Nick finally did speak, his voice was pedantic. "A wife of noble character is her husband's crown, but a disgraceful wife is like decay in his bones." He paused. "If you're not sure, let's hit the Delete button right now."

Rita felt belittled. Was he out of his mind?

His eyes burned through her.

"Nick, I'm definite about our marriage. I'm also firm the wedding must be special."

"I'll get my flight schedule. Find a date. We'll plan an announcement party."

Although seated, she felt as if standing on a fault-line— "So much to think about, so little time."

"I have faith in you. I'll help." He kissed her, pulled her to her feet, and twirled her around. "Promise."

Rita nodded, but her cheery mood evaporated into a headache and gastrointestinal bubbles. There was no hiding from her internal volcano. She rubbed her temples, then pressed fingers against the nerves in the back of her neck to short-circuit at least one end just as Nick's arms enveloped her from behind.

"Tomorrow the shops reopen. I'll buy you a late lunch and a couple of dresses from the boutiques. You'll need new things for engagement parties, dinners—mostly for me. I love to dress you in things I buy for you. Almost as much as I love to undress you."

Rita leaned toward him and returned a kiss. More stomach gurgles. "You're amazing. You always know the right things to say."

"This is only the beginning." He grabbed her hand. They stood, and she followed him into the bedroom. "Time for Christmas appetizers before we venture."

Once inside, Rita grabbed at his robe. "I think the tree needs unwrapping."

\* \* \* \*

Nick stood over Rita in the darkness. She was peaceful as the clock struck midnight. Her chest rose and dropped in rhythmic cadence. He lifted her arm, felt her pulse, and let it flop onto the bed by her side. A typhoon couldn't wake her. Good to go. He zipped the new jogging suit, grabbed the extra suit, checked his equipment, and sprinted.

In seconds, he was free of the condo, taking the stairs into the starry night. He jogged through the parking lot and into the pool area until he reached the exercise room and punched in the owner's code. Leaving the lights off, he clicked on a pocket light and focused on an empty bottom corner locker. He placed the extra suit inside, closed the locker with the tiniest of squeaks, then exited into the evening air that filled his nostrils with the scent of forsaken fish.

His mission called. His maneuvers had prepared him. It was time to take flight, protect the night's children. He placed his hand over his heart and felt the folded letter in his breast pocket, then slid his hand over and pushed the cross into his chest. "Never again." He began the long jog ahead.

\* \* \* \*

The three-bedroom ranch was easier to find every time he scouted it. Well lit, floodlights accentuated peach-painted stucco and walls of climbing roses. Lower windows were closed, but many upper windows remained open. Inside, there was only darkness with the exception of one small light. Her bedroom. There it was. Target.

Moving between the shadows, Nick snapped on leather driving gloves. Gripping the decorative rocks beneath the windows, he rearranged them slightly and lifted the stone bench. Decorative once, now functional. He maneuvered like a trained acrobat, lifting himself undetected onto the roof, then through the open window into the home.

Slinking against the barely shadowed walls, Nick found his way to her—Katherine Quinn, grandmother, caretaker of her grandchildren while their mother worked. Stupid woman—leaving her windows open. An even more stupid woman—hitting defenseless children with her cane. He'd teach the old bat a lesson.

He peered in through the slit of the partially opened bedroom door until his eyes focused. His sleeping prey in full view, relaxed, he pushed the door just wide enough to creep in sideways. The door creaked.

Damn it. Creaks were as bad as alarms. He hoped the old bat was deaf. He stood, he listened. He timed himself, waiting until the house stilled itself. He knew creaks were not to be trusted. He paced each act, then neared her bed.

Katherine jumped. Her wide eyes made her whole face a mass of craggy wrinkles.

He lunged toward her, his hands reaching for her neck while his body plowed on top of hers.

A board swooped at him, connected, and ripped flesh.

"Eeoow. Shit."

She whacked the board at him again, but he blocked it.

The board clambered to the floor. Shit. More noise. Stupid old bat.

He braced one arm across her and pummeled her face with his fist. Damn radar-hearing Bitch. His jaws ached. Damn Bitch. Damn creaking. He didn't know where he was injured or what exactly she'd struck him with. He had to act fast. She wouldn't foil his mission. The old woman's gruff voice tried to scream, but the sound was dry, the attempt feeble. The raspy crackle was hardly audible.

Time congealed, mesmerized and sealed the whirlwind of space they shared.

And in those next few seconds she was stilled. The air filled with the final release of her lungs and the dull thud of what he'd deduced was the dropping of the nail-spiked board she used to strike him. He kicked it across the room, out of reach. Mission rules: take nothing for granted. Take no prisoners; leave no trace. Back-up plan, now in place.

"Striking out is what you do best, isn't it, Grandma Quinn?" He laughed, but it came out distorted. He hated her for that, too. He reached for the cross that dangled from his neck and rubbed it until he felt the pulse-pressure of his own thumb ache, then he grabbed its replica, again seized hold of her neck and branded her. "You've whacked your last victim, you old bag. I decree you'll not touch another child with your cane, nor any human with your rage."

Looking at the stilled figure in the rumpled bed, he carefully anchored the cane over her neck, firmly locking her into position. In the darkness, he couldn't decipher if his driving gloves were torn or how badly he was cut or bruised. He had to make an immediate assessment. Aware he needed time to wipe over everything and check his body, he yanked off the jogging jacket and shirt and scanned for cuts near the searing pain that stung every movement.

"Damnation." He stared at the holes in his arm and the streams of blood. Tearing the shirt with his teeth he bound his forearm, stopped the bleeding and zipped his jacket over it. Reaching for the penlight in his pocket, he surveyed the room and grabbed a blouse from the rocking chair near the bed and a bottle of rubbing alcohol from the medicine tray on the nightstand. He wiped over everything he'd come in contact with until he was satisfied. With his foot, he felt the tossed board. Cautiously he grabbed it, married it with the items he had to dispose of and gave the room a final inspection with his penlight.

He prepared the body, triple-checked his work, then whispered to her. "You're one badass old lady. Would've made a fine foot soldier." One final look, and satisfied he was detection-free, he disappeared, evidence in hand.

\* \* \* \*

After a quick shower, bandaging, and changing into the fresh jogging suit he'd hidden in the exercise room, Nick felt powerful as the adrenaline surged through him. Combing his fingers through still-damp hair, his wicked grin leered back at him in the mirror.

He checked himself over. The gouges were mostly superficial and would heal. The already thickened blood on the opened flesh didn't look any worse than the rose-bush cuts and holes he'd sustained when he'd landscaped and properly established his mother's rose garden. In that very soil lay the gold crucifix, waiting for him on the old man's decayed chest. He deserved to rot under the roots of his mother's prized roses. His evil growing into thorns, the love his mother had for him blossoming into roses. He'd yanked the golden treasure and slipped it over his own crown; it was in this instant his path was clearly ordained. Nick lifted that unearthed cross from his own neck now, brought it to his lips, pressed it in until it cut against his teeth and he tasted blood. Then, he kissed and released it. Sucking in a deep breath before leaving the room, Nick eased the door into its frame, ensuring silence.

Nick scurried into the darkness across the courtyard to the adjacent condominium units, and slid into the foul-smelling room that contained the fly-feasting dumpsters. He disposed of the blood-covered evidence. Early Monday morning it would be landfill. Until then, thirty-three units would spill garbage onto it, and lots of paper, boxes and leftovers, what with all that Christmas joy and giving.

Returning to the lighted sidewalks of the condominium complex as if finishing his systematic jog, he headed to his building and climbed the condominium stairs two at a time. When he reached his unit, he pushed open the door he'd left slightly ajar. Quietly, he tossed aside his clothing and slid into unrumpled sheets, gazing upon Rita's pale flesh in the moonlit room. She hadn't stirred. He lay an ear to her chest to check her breathing. Then tried to arouse her, making groggy, muffled murmurings like he'd just awakened from a deep sleep. No response.

It was time for his reward; he needed to release the adrenaline he'd earned or he'd never sleep. He crept his hands slowly to exposed supple pink breasts and began massaging the petal-soft flesh.

Rita stirred slightly. Nick repositioned her body closer to him. She was too lethargic to make any overt movements. That was okay. He didn't need her to assist him in his pleasure. He didn't care if she remembered; he didn't want her to—she wouldn't with the heavy dose of forget-I'm-not-with-you pills he'd given her. He laughed out loud. A truly great night. He thrust himself onto her to ensure no space between them and inhaled her scents. He massaged her skin and quickly became aroused, rolled her limp body onto her back, removed lacy panties, raised her knees, and spread her legs.

Every nerve ending fully aroused, Nick moistened his fingers, placing them first inside Rita. Feeling himself grow, he rubbed himself harder, faster. He moistened his flesh, then hers and filled her wholly, taking everything he needed, his heart pounding, breath quickening. He plunged in, pulled out, and chanted rhythmically: "He who loves his wife loves himself… a woman must be silent… He who loves his wife loves himself… a woman must be silent…"

\* \* \* \*

Peaceful skies showered streams of sunlight over everything Nick could see. The gentle waves lapped upon the white sandy beach. Such beauty gave Nick a sense of affirmation of his course. Soon, his journey would include an obedient wife. Kissing Rita, he wrapped one arm around her, weaving their fingers together with his other hand.

"Wake up, sleepyhead. I can't wait to spend every minute with you— wakie, wakie," he whispered in her ear, kissing it. He shook their interwoven fingers together back and forth.

Rita wriggled around under the covers. Her eyes fluttered, she yawned, and finally opened her eyes. "Mmm. Morning already? I slept so deeply I don't remember sleeping. I had weird dreams. But I still feel tired, like I didn't sleep at all."

"I promise you, you slept."

Rita reached up and kissed Nick. "Can we just lay together for a few minutes?"

"Sure. But first, I'll start the coffee. When you smell it, you'll wake up." He kissed the top of Rita's head and kicked back the sheets.

"I'm not sure I can get out of bed." Rita's voice was weak. "I'm parched— like I haven't had anything to drink for days."

"Well, then we'll have coffee in bed. Juice too, for that thirsty throat of yours." Nick tapped his forefinger against her throat, drew a line down to her breasts, then drew his hand back. "If you're not better, I'll stay in bed with you. We'll make a day of it. Promise."

Rita laid her head on the pillow and closed her eyes.

\* \* \* \*

A few hours later, Nick sat a clanking tray on the empty bed space next to Rita, and she opened one eye. "Mmm. Sounds like unsteady dishes, smells like coffee, looks like my very favorite delivery man."

"You ain't seen nothin' yet."

"Oh yeah? Show me." She used both hands to scoot to a sitting position. She reached toward him, one hand curled around his neck, the other snaking upward underneath his t-shirt.

"We've a dilemma, my dear." He laughed. "At least let me move the tray to safety so my hard work doesn't go to waste."

She giggled. "Okay, I do need that juice you promised before we do anything." She removed her hands from him. "I see you've been a busy boy, picking flowers from the garden again. They're beautiful. I didn't hear you leave."

"I came in to tell you I was going downstairs to get the paper. You were sound asleep. I took my time and didn't bother you. I figured you wouldn't miss me. The flowers called your name. They'll never be missed."

"They're beautiful. I'm glad to know that you, who I doubt has ever had a parking ticket, can pick someone else's flowers." She gulped the whole glass of juice without taking a breath. "I like that about you."

"That's a curious comment." He squinted as if he could see right through her.

Rita shivered. "It's a good thing. I always feel so imperfect around you. It's nice to know that you—" Rita stopped.

"What? That I can cross the line?"

"Yeah." Rita tilted her head, and tried for a come-hither look. "Something like that."

His eyes fixed on her.

She felt exposed, and not in a sensual way. More like being naked on the gallows. *How does this keep happening?* "What?"

Nick raised his eyebrows.

Dammit, she wasn't going to live her life afraid to speak. "What?"

"Nothing. I like that you think of me like that. You know, pure, good. Always doing the right thing."

"Mmm." Rita nodded. She focused on his face for a sign of secret buttons that she somehow kept inadvertently pushing.

"Finish your coffee. You need to be really awake. We have plans."

Rita put her finger to his lips and Nick crawled under the covers next to her. She ran her fingers through his hair, gently massaging his scalp. Gently kissing his cheek, she breathed him in, letting her eyes close and then open. His scent streamed through her. "You are such a wonderful man. No man has ever cared enough to really take care of me."

"Trust me. You deserve all good things. I plan on taking care of you for a very long time. Promise. Get out of that gown. Time to show me just how much you appreciate me."

Rita giggled. He pulled off her flimsy gown with one hand. She grabbed his shirt and began lifting it. Moving his flesh to hers, Rita felt the bandages on his chest. "What's this?"

"Nothing for you to worry about. Tripped this morning when I was out for my jog."

"Fell? What happened? Why didn't you say anything? Can I look at it?"

"Unleashed dog chased me while I was jogging. I couldn't shake him. Tripped on the pavement into a large rose bush. Pavement and thorns won the battle."

"Let me have a look. I'd hate to see you get an infection because it wasn't cleaned out properly."

"You worry too much, Nurse Rita. I showered, cleaned the scrapes. Used antibiotic cream under the bandages. Pilot and veteran, remember? First-aid training."

"When was your last tetanus?"

"I said pavement and rose bushes, not metal." His voice now had an edge.

She knew she was close to one of those miserable buttons. She needed to know she could bring her medical knowledge into the relationship— "I know. Bacteria can get into the bloodstream. Lots of bacteria on pavement and in dirt. Medical protocol is to make sure there's a current tetanus shot and an antibiotic is ordered for about ten days—sometimes a painful shot of Rocephin, then ten days of antibiotics."

"Slight overreaction?" He was trying to sound seductive.

But it was just a mask over—something. She could tell that much. "I don't want anything to happen to you." She made her voice gentle, but it came out almost childlike. Not what she'd intended.

"I appreciate that more than you know." Nick stroked her hair. "But, Nurse Rita, you haven't completed your examination of me. Aren't you first supposed to deal with the most critical aspect of a victim? It appears I have at least one protruding part that needs instant care and attention."

"I know just what the doctor will order for that."

# Chapter Twenty-five

"**F**OUR DAYS SINCE HANDPRINT IN lipstick strangulation. Weekend's almost here." Rabbit paced, his head shooting from ceiling to floor with stress-vibrato. "Bennie's compilation of weekend travelers should be completed."

"No reason to be mad at Bennie," Abel said. "He's provided as much information as fast as any human could, same as us."

Bennie nodded. "I'll dig into license plates, video footage, travel logs, tickets issued—whatever I can find, as long as he's out there, if it's the last thing I ever do for you and the Department."

Rabbit pressed his forefingers firmly into the back of his neck. Abel's gaze shifted between Rabbit, Bennie and the stiff old woman in her bed, a cane across her bruised, bloodied face and broken neck. "Mad? No time to be mad. We're witnessing our madman's handiwork. It sickens me that I've predicted weekend deaths and can't stop them."

"This murder's not exactly the weekend, it's Thursday—" Abel interrupted Rabbit.

"Christmas night." Rabbit shook his head and rubbed his temples. "So damned predictable. We predicted the Communicator would murder Friday—the beginning of the weekend. Here we stand staring at his handiwork and it's Thursday." Rabbit blinked, disbelieving it even as he repeated it. "I should have factored in Christmas, not just the weekend."

Bennie looked at Abel, then back at Rabbit. "You're the best mind reader we've got—you'll solve it."

"I feel as guilty as I'm sure he's gleeful at remaining leaps ahead of us." Rabbit couldn't contain his emotions. "Notice this victim was wrapped up in sheets secured by square knots?"

"Military angle?" Bennie bent down and peeked under the bed.

Rabbit clasped his hands in a tight ball and squeezed so hard his knuckles turned white.

"Hell man, it ain't your fault. Never is. None of us can afford to get emotionally involved." Abel's cheeks pinked. "Maybe you need a day away from the mayhem?"

Rabbit gave Abel an exaggerated scowl, but remained silent. He knew the more Abel's English became broken or he interjected Spanish, the more his Argentinian partner was upset by his frustration. Rabbit tried to calm himself, if only for his partner's sake.

Abel shuffled his feet. "Man, you okay? You've solved cases more complicated than this. But never guilted yourself—anything I should know? You ain't lookin' so good."

Rabbit did his best work under pressure, but this time things were different. Abel truly partnered with him, followed leads, added to his theories, and spun his own viable theories. Rabbit rubbed his hands, twisted around the room surveying the investigative team still brushing for fingerprints, taking photographs, and spraying luminal. This feeble woman couldn't have possibly done anything to deserve being cocooned in her own bed after being punched and strangled, while her grandchildren were sleeping in the next room. What message was the Communicator displaying? Most important, what the hell had he missed? Serial killers don't leave a clean trail every time, nor did they change message. Rabbit's mind plowed through the facts: this time children were present—sleeping, present at the scene. Not his usual mode of operation. Mistake or purposeful—no way to distinguish. Never before had he struck when anyone else was home. Rabbit couldn't focus. Questions kept zooming in. They needed a break.

"When perps get careless, they become bolder." Abel seemed to answer Rabbit's contemplation.

"If only we could force a mistake," Rabbit said. "Communicator's headed in that direction."

Abel nodded. "Si." He streamed toward the Medical Examiner. "Anythin' interesting?"

"Defensive bruising marks on her arms. She tried to fight back. He punched her. The basic steps appear to be the same as the others. Crushed larynx. The rest is for show," Dr. Milano said in his thick Italian accent. "I get autopsy results to you, same as the others, priority one."

Crime-scene technicians continued to snap photographs and dust for fingerprints. Rabbit directed matter-of-factly. "I don't care how many pictures you take, I want every millimeter at every possible range and angle. Develop duplicates, every size you can—in print, on slides, and CD." He turned to José and pointed. "Please immediately deliver a set of everything to me. I don't care what time it is. Understood?" José nodded in clear response. Rabbit shook his hand. They'd been through this before, and Rabbit trusted him.

Rabbit turned toward Bennie, who was now preoccupied and artfully moving around the room like a Native American scout. Intrigued, Rabbit watched Bennie position and reposition the forensic lamp containing ultra-violet, visible, and infrared components of light.

Finally, Bennie uttered a deep throaty, "Gotcha."

Rabbit immediately strode behind him. Abel, José, and a few of the uniformed officers, fell in step with him to see the glow under the light source.

"Blood. The old woman hit him, injured him with something." Rabbit's excitement underscored his words. "Double—no triple-check—under her nails. I want blood samples from everyone in the house. I want to know what she did to cause him to bleed."

"She's an old woman. Could be blood from her, from some other time," Abel said.

Rabbit shook his head. "Don't think so. Lucky-charm-luminal works every time. Bring the daughter in here—let's chat. Then, she needs to do an inventory. I want to know what's missing, if anything's been left behind." He made a camera lens by combining his thumbs and forefingers and looked through the crime scene piecemeal.

One of the officers scrawled a few notes. "I'm on it." He headed out the door.

Bennie silently walked around the glowing bodily fluids and darkened spots around the victim's bed. Photographers began clicking.

Abel ordered two uniforms near him. "Look for somethin' he used to wipe down the area: towels, cloth, paper, anythin'—could be discarded somewhere close by. Doesn't jus' disappear." He sighed. "DNA, our silent defender against crime."

"Let's see how far he blundered." Rabbit was geeked now. "Secure the crime scene after the collections are sent to the lab. Detail every available uniform to check garbage cans, alleyways, dumpsters, with a florescent light. Search every crevice the Communicator could've discarded his cleaning paraphernalia."

Rabbit shuffled his feet and stopped when he was inches from Abel and Bennie. "Get all this wrapped up and back to us, pronto. Abel and I are going to cut through the media and head back to the station. The victim's daughter, Veronica Quinn Riley, is meeting us to make a statement after she settles her children at the neighbor's. She's beyond shook. I've asked one of the black-and-whites to stick around and drive her in."

\* \* \* \*

The Sarasota homicide detectives sat across from each other in a conference room at Adams Lane Police Department Headquarters, scribbling in notepads and sifting through reams of paperwork. "Bennie really came through. Now we need to fit it all together." Rabbit stared at the mass of information.

Rabbit clamped his eyes closed. "I feel it. I just can't see it, can't pull it together."

"Rabbit, man, no one does it like you. You the man. You always figure it out. You have a gift. You're just bent that way. Ain't never seen nothin' like you."

"Quit saying that, you know we're partners—in this together." Rabbit's voice always had a bit of a bark. He hated to lose victims to criminals.

"Si. We're gonna solve it, together, like always."

Rabbit lowered his head between his hands. "Not in time to save this last victim, maybe not his next one. He's escalating. The answer is simple and I don't see it."

Abel jingled change in his pockets.

Rabbit opened his eyes and lifted his head with a sour face and cracked his knuckles. He waited to speak until the jingling stopped. "This many people murdered, one on Christmas—when Sarasota's spilling with tourists and activities. I've been missing something critical."

"We've looked at it too long. We need a break. Good night of sleep. New morning perspective. Si?"

Rabbit rubbed his temples. "No messages on the answering machine, no calls made to or from the house phone for at least three hours before she was murdered. Nothing distinguishing about any telephone call, except for one short call from one of those over-the-counter cell phones. Exactly, like the others, but with a different area code and cell number. Could virtually be anyone."

"We'll ask her daughter to verify, maybe she overhead that call before she left for work, or maybe the kids heard something." Abel jotted a note in his pad. "Bennie's checking for cell matches with the other victims."

Rabbit squinted. "Everything else in the home is routine."

"Predictable, giving the Communicator his pick of opportunities." Abel shoved the notepad inside his shirt pocket.

Somebody knocked.

The glass-paneled door opened.

The daughter of the victim walked into the room directed by a young uniformed officer. Her bleached-blonde shoulder-length hair swung jauntily along with her tall lanky body but her facial expression looked more like one entering a confessional.

"Thanks, we'll take it from here." Rabbit did his best to smile at the young officer.

Abel began. "Ma'am—"

"Veronica."

"Veronica, we're very appreciative you are here—" Abel pointed to a chair at the end of the conference room table. "Please sit."

Veronica grabbed a package of tissue from her purse. "I want—need— to help. I can't go home, not right away. My children are so—" She paused, visibly upset, trying to find the right words.

"Understood." Rabbit sat opposite her. "We know talking's difficult right now, but every minute we lose investigating, we can't prevent this from happening again."

"Again?" Veronica's eyes opened wide. "There are others?"

"Possibly." Rabbit put his large hand near hers, without touching her. "We need more information about your mother. Her recent activities, phone calls, friends, clubs she belonged to."

"Not much to tell. She couldn't go far. Her mind was sharp, but her body declined these past few years. She did what she could to help raise my children since my husband left. She opened her home to us. Except for working nights, an occasional date, or necessary shopping, I never left her alone with the children."

"Any unsettling messages or phone calls?"

"I hate to be bothered at home. My mother loved to know what's going on. So, she usually answered the phone. She left me detailed messages on my cell. I don't recall anything about strange calls."

Rabbit flipped through his notepad. "Do your children ever answer the phone?"

"Rarely, we discourage it. They usually hang up before they give us the phone. We're working on that."

Abel brought over a pitcher of water and a glassful for Veronica. He handed the glass to Rabbit.

"Was there any mention of a cell-phone call that was garbled—hard to understand or a 'dropped in the middle' call?" Rabbit handed her the glass of water.

"No. An occasional hang up, like everyone. We don't have Caller ID. Sometimes we press star sixty-nine, and other times we don't. We hang up on our share of solicitors, but, again, nothing unusual." Her face looked strained.

Abel sat at the side of the table. "Anyone you make angry by being too tied to your mother?"

Veronica paused, as if she hadn't heard the question. "No."

"Anyone your mother may have angered?" Rabbit made his voice gentle now.

"No. We haven't even been here the past few weeks. My children had early holiday visitation with their father. We arrived back in Siesta Key on Christmas Eve. It was horrid weather in Michigan. The flight almost didn't take off."

"All four of you?" Rabbit was careful to keep excitement out of his voice. He calculated its importance.

"Yes. While they were with their father, my mother and I spent time with relatives and friends and shopped. Nothing we haven't done dozens of times before."

"Michigan?" Abel asked. "Where in Michigan?"

"Detroit. Direct flight between Detroit and Sarasota. Very easy to travel with children—and my mother, she tires—uh, tired easily."

Abel scribbled notes. "What were your travel dates?"

Abel and Rabbit nodded at each other, then at Veronica, who remained silent except for the slant of her head and her hand dropped into her purse to retrieve an airline envelope.

"I haven't fully unpacked. Here's the Delta envelope with itinerary and ticket stubs." She pushed across the white-and-blue envelope complete with stapled baggage claim tickets.

Abel grabbed the crumpled envelope. "Bueno. May we keep these?"

"Sure. I don't need them. The flights were great. Delta Captain entertained my kids in the cockpit and let them sit in the copilot seat. They were so happy; they're still talking about it. At least our relatives got to see Mom before she—" Veronica's voice trailed. She blinked blankly at the floor and tears began to spill.

Rabbit grabbed a handful of tissues and gently placed them inside her right palm. Abel refilled her water. They remained silent while she composed herself, busy reviewing the travel information.

"One more thing?" Rabbit leaned in. He folded his hands and placed them on the table.

She nodded.

"Did your mother have any weapons—you know, for protection?"

"Like a gun?"

"That—or anything else? She struggled, may have injured her attacker. We aren't clear how."

Veronica frowned, studied the floor, then her lap. After a few minutes, she looked at Rabbit. "She kept an old board under her bed. It had these grotesque rusty nails protruding outward. I thought she got rid of it because I nagged at her. I was fearful the kids would find it and get hurt." She closed her eyes, tears falling again freely. She struggled to speak, "I'm sorry."

Rabbit studied the grieving woman. "Spend time with your children. When you're ready, in a couple of days, we'll continue this."

\* \* \* \*

Flipping through the stacks of papers piled high atop his desk, Rabbit realized Bennie acquired everything he'd requested, except similar murders in other states. Veronica and her mother's Michigan itinerary was a key he needed to turn. If the Communicator was not a Floridian, but rather a traveler in and out of the state, Michigan was a logical focal point.

Rabbit felt Abel's distraction etching into his concentration. "If you're trying to send me straight into the forensic center, you're doing a great job. Quit staring at me."

"You know it's like the thing you're supposed to ignore becomes the thing that's most conspicuous. I try, but I have to wonder what you're thinkin', man, and then I stare. You know, like I try to read your mind and there it is—it looks like starin', but it's really thinkin' about what you're thinkin'."

"Huh? Been eating funny tacos? Here, focus on these." Rabbit handed Abel the statewide printouts. "Find anything that says Michigan."

Abel reached, grabbed the stack of papers, and fanned through them before mounding them on his already loaded desk. "Bennie said he could get any specific file we need within twenty-four hours. Fill me in?"

"A hunch. We need to go outside of Sarasota—"

"The victims all are within a four-mile radius of Sarasota, with Siesta Key Beach being one of the boundaries, man."

"Not outside of Siesta Key, we've done that. I mean outside of Florida. Look at other states. Beginning with Michigan. Last victim's daughter says they were just in Michigan. We had another victim, Jonathan Walters, the old man in the wheelchair, found by his granddaughter after they arrived home, who was also from Michigan. We need to double-check each victim and look for a Michigan connection, specifically Detroit. Look for any activity, recent vacations, trips of any kind, phone calls, even relatives." Rabbit was feeling solution energy. This was the right direction.

Abel shook his head. "I have no notes mentioning a trip. I don't recall seeing luggage."

"It was the reason Walters was at home alone." Every time he recalled the conversation, he felt his hunch solidify and his ear tips sear red as if electric current singed through him.

"Okay, I didn't give that much thought at the time."

"Maybe a coincidence—but—doubtful. His family was in Michigan."

"Bueno. I knew you'd find an angle."

"It's the shot we got—"

"The break you use—Rabbit out of a hat." Abel nearly gleefully interrupted. "A late Christmas present, but a good one."

"Don't get too excited until we unravel the traveling habits and locations of all the victims." But Rabbit continued to feel the surge as well.

# Chapter Twenty-six

RITA OPENED HER MOUTH TO speak, and then closed it. Monday again. She wasn't ready to be back to grey Michigan skies and work. Florida sunshine-filled days and star-filled, sleep-fast nights were simple.

"What's made you so quiet?" Nick grabbed Rita's waist from behind and planted enticing kisses from the nape of her neck down to her shoulders.

She stepped away from the stove, spun toward him on tiptoes, placed her lips on his, and smooched. "Good morning, sleepyhead. I wanted to make you a nice breakfast and thank you for the wonderful Sarasota Christmas. Wish we were still there."

"We'll be back soon." Nick filled his mug and carried a plate of toast, bacon, and eggs to the table. "Ask for time off. New Year's and another long weekend's only days away. I get my bid days this week. We can schedule all the time you want in Sarasota. If I don't get what I asked for, I'll trade. You'll make it worth my effort."

"I'm glad you think so." She set her mug in front of her plate, then angled toward him and unbuttoned the top button of his uniform shirt. "Would you like a sample, Captain, sir?"

He laughed, pulled her to his lap by the small curls at the nape of her neck and kissed her hard. "Save it. I've got an early airport meeting, and we're all on call in the event of illness and delays. Quirky time of year in our industry. We count flight hours very carefully. Keep your cell on you. I'll check in."

Rita took the chair next to his. "This is nice." She sipped her coffee and juice, but set her fork back on her plate without lifting any food.

"You're not eating?"

"I'll eat. I'm queasy. Change of temperature, I think."

"You look a bit pale. Eat. Can't have you ill. I need you rested for my evening treat, remember?"

"Yoga will return me to working order."

\* \* \* \*

Rita locked the door behind Nick, then turned toward her bedroom to grab her purse and check her makeup so she too could leave for work. She spotted Nick's garment bag flung over the back of the living room couch, his flight bag on the floor next to it. She studied the bags. Nick hated it when she touched any of his things without specific permission. He hadn't given that permission. His exact words were: "off limits, forbidden." Like his laundry, she'd promised not to touch anything of his—they were simple requests. He was meticulous about his things.

But that promise was made before they were engaged. An engaged, about-to-be married, couple had no secrets. Besides, Nick hated disorder more than anything. He would've put the garment bag away, at least hung it up, but they'd been exhausted from traveling. Hanging up the bag wouldn't hurt anything, she reasoned. Reaching for the hanger, her booted toes hit the edge of the flight bag. She cast her eyes down and they caught a folded newspaper sticking out of the flight-bag pocket. She grabbed it. Sunday's headline. Sarasota Sun Times: 'Strangled Christmas Woman Makes Four.'

Frozen, she read the article. Rita's heart pounded heavily and her breathing thickened. She tried to remain calm by sitting still on the couch, but hyperventilation began. She needed a small bag over her mouth, but her knees were weak and locked. She needed to update Dr. Towers.

Having her head between her knees for a few minutes slowed her breathing. This was important; she needed to function. And she was getting stronger—inside and outside—every day; leaving the past behind. She could handle this.

She picked up the newspaper and skimmed through it, staring at it with an uneasiness that crept into her like a glass shard. Rita knew there was no way to rationalize her discomfort. She followed her intuition, kept her promise, and neither hung up the garment bag nor touched the flight bag again. Nothing good could come of it, she said out loud. She stood. Her mind was racing in so many directions. Time and distance would bring clarity, but she lacked patience. Her wristwatch screamed tardy. This craziness had to be set aside or she'd be late for Jaq, yoga, and work.

\* \* \* \*

"Yo, Rita." Jaq's hair was bunched in a scrunchee near the top of her head, like a lop-sided pom-pom. "Over here."

Rita's observed the makeshift warehouse before echoing acknowledgement. "Hey, Jaq. Surprised to see you so bright-eyed and bushy-tailed early on a Monday. You're usually dragging with some excuse of a late Sunday night call."

"Something about a text that read: at the airport, we'll celebrate when I get back. Merry Christmas. Monday-yoga." Jaq cracked her gum. "You didn't return my texts, emails or phone calls, and I don't have jurisdiction outside Michigan. I wanted to be here to make sure you weren't kidnapped or something."

Rita unrolled her mat. "Be happy for me."

"I'd like to meet this man who is edging me out." Jaq was already stretching.

Rita laughed. "There's room for both of you." She paused and watched Jaq stretch. "It's inexplicable. You look awesome."

"Maybe I'm finally growing accustomed to adrenaline rush and sleep deprivation." Jaq frowned. "You, on the other hand, well, your excessive lifestyle and all those cadavers are wearing off on you—you look like somebody's mummy."

"Ha-Ha." Rita shook her head. "Jaq, you can do better than that."

"I'm serious. Are you sick or something? I haven't seen bags like those under your eyes since—" She paused. "Well, never."

"Okay, yes. I'm creeped out. I don't sleep well with your serial killer on the loose." Rita watched the class slowly fill. "You're all better people than me. I happily assist Doc. I like the idea of solving a puzzle, like he says, but I prefer the living. Less Halloweenish."

Jaq lowered her voice. "I understand you—"

"Doc told you about the article?" Rita began to roll up her mat. "Skip today—talk at coffee?"

"Thought you needed the workout?"

"Need to chat more." Rita's voice was somber and almost childlike. It was the place she only went with Nick and she surprised herself hearing it spill to Jaq that way.

Jaq reached up and patted Rita's arm. "I should've guessed since you've been playing statue while I've been a stretching fool. Sure. And, yes, Doc gave us the article with your idea."

Rita nodded. "I'm expected at work, so we can't be too long. Can't be late. Doc's counting on me. So are you in a weird sort of way."

"Gotcha. Plenty of time." Jaq rolled off her mat and picked it up. "If we run late, I'll call Doc. He'll be fine. If he's not, I'll send David over with a peace offering."

\* \* \* \*

Jaq pushed open the heavy Starbucks door.

"Okay, first things first." Jaq stepped through the open door and walked with Rita to the coffee line. "Enough small talk, I'm about to charge you with blinding-by-diamonds if you don't start talking."

Rita clenched her left hand, and then opened it. "Oh my gosh, Jaq, I'm sorry. I should have shown you right away. Everything happened so fast. Just before we left for Florida, Nick surprised me. He couldn't even wait till Christmas to exchange gifts."

"It's been what—how many weeks—" Jaq held Rita's left hand and scrutinized the ring.

"Doesn't take long to know when it is right."

"Are you happy?" Jaq squeezed her hand and met Rita's stare. The women didn't blink, twitch, or glance at the coffee board until Rita answered.

"Yes." Rita took her left hand back. She turned toward the coffee board and ordered without waiting for Jaq to respond, then dropped a twenty with the instruction it was for both orders. Rita walked to the end of the counter and waited. A minute later, Jaq padded in behind her.

Jaq began speaking to Rita's back knowing she would turn. "Let me sum it up like this: You and I, brought together by yoga and running, kept our quirky friendship out of the mainstream. Been like sisters since we met. Now you get a rock, the size of those bewitching-green eyes of yours with extras to spare, and you don't share—except, I might add, for a rather benign text."

Rita turned and faced Jaq. "I know. I'm sorry."

"Sorry's for mothers, I deserve answers. Start talking."

The barista slid Rita's coffee toward her. She grabbed it and laughed.

Jaq received her coffee. "And—" Jaq inspected the coffee she was handed, relidded it, and shouldered Rita toward a table.

Rita looked up at Jaq. "And what? I'm more than happy to divulge details." They sat at a corner table.

"Again, for a blushing bride-to-be, I've never seen you looking this pale and worn. Should you go to a doctor or something? I can drive you, flashers and all."

"Nothing sleep won't take care of. Nick and I just vacationed for four days. We packed too much in. And, I slept like the dead. I'm a nurse. Don't you think I'd know if I were ill?"

Jaq cracked her gum again knowing it irritated Rita. "Aren't doctors and nurses supposed to be the worst patients? Maybe Doc can check you out."

"I'm not dead yet." Rita squinted. "Jaq, there's something—I mean before we talk about Nick, the wedding—"

"Okay."

Rita shifted her position and drew in a breath. "What Dr. Towers told you about my—"

"Your theory, the Double Cross Killer travelling between Sarasota and Detroit."

Rita looked uncertain. "Am I right?"

"It fits what we've been thinking, the direction we were taking. Thanks to you, we're starting in Sarasota. We have a call in to detectives there. And I have a few questions for you."

"From Sarasota, I only know what I read in the papers—except for this morning."

Jaq folded her hands and waited.

"This morning as I was about to leave, I noticed Nick brought the Sunday paper—well Section A anyway. I pulled it out and the headline was about a fourth murder Christmas night in Sarasota. Sounded like another Double Cross Killer murder."

"Do you have the paper?"

Rita pulled back in her chair and stiffened. "Oh no. I can't ask for it or let Nick know I read it."

"Why in the hell not?" Jaq was way over the loud limit for the crowded shop.

Heads turned.

"We have a pact not to go through each other's things."

"But you did."

Rita's eyes were wide. "But he'll never know." She bit her lip.

Jaq didn't press the issue. "I'll Google it. How many cases do you think you've read about that sound like the Double Cross Killer cases?"

"Just the ones I've told Dr. Towers and now you about."

Jaq nodded.

★ ★ ★ ★

Abel flipped through the messages twice, pulling three from Detroit, Michigan to compare them, all from the 3-1-3 area code, two from law enforcement, and one from the Medical Examiner. "Hey, Rabbit, did you see these messages?"

Rabbit didn't look up. He sat preoccupied, scrawling notes behind piles of documents Bennie had dropped off earlier. "Anything interesting?"

"Remember that Delta flight?"

"The one Veronica mentioned?"

"Detroit-Sarasota. We've got three messages from, guess where—Detroit."

Rabbit, tossed his pen across the notepad. "Dial already."

"At least I check the messages." Abel's large fingers punched in the numbers. "Loco en la cabeza."

After leaving messages for both Jaq and David, Abel dialed the final number. "Must be they don't work between Christmas and New Year's in Detroit. Neither detective is at the station, no answer on their radio or cell phones, which I was assured are with them at all times… Wait, I'm being patched through to the ME. I hate elevator music."

Abel didn't hide his agitation. He occupied his free hand by scribbling phone numbers into his notepad before wadding the separate messages into a ball and tossing them into the overfilled waste can.

"Pathology, Nurse Rose speaking. May I help you?"

"This is—Si—can I speak to the pathologist in charge?"

"Dr. Towers speaking. Who is calling?" Dr. Towers demanded without waiting to hear the voice.

"It's about time we reached someone in charge. Anyone working in Detroit?"

"Is this some kind of crank call? I am the Chief Pathologist, Wayne County Medical Examiner, and I am too busy for this. State your business or I am hanging up. You have ten seconds."

Dr. Towers hit the speaker button. All eyes—his, Jaq's, David's and Rita's—focused on the phone.

"Detective Abel Mendoza, from Sarasota Detective Bureau. My partner, Detective Randall and I received a message from some Detroit detectives. Maybe you know them?"

Dr. Towers eyed the curious trio as he answered. "Detectives Maxwell and McSween?"

"Yes."

"I am working with them. I spoke with Dr. Milano, the Medical Examiner I understand you work with."

"What do you have?"

"Serial killer. Thought you could help."

"We're interested."

"We read a few articles in the Sarasota Sun Times about murders by strangulation. Detectives think your perp has the same MO in the Detroit area. They are looking for a date with your team." Dr. Towers' eyes circled the pupils fixed upon him, not hearing anything at the other end of the phone. "Hello? Are you still there?"

Abel cleared his voice into the phone before responding. "We just began to consider Michigan. We have two victims linked to Detroit."

"Traveling?" Dr. Towers' eyes widened. They all leaned in, closer to the speaker.

"Yes."

"Dr. Milano and I exchanged and compared autopsies. We concur same perp." Dr. Towers closed his eyes and pursed his lips for just a moment. He grabbed a notepad.

"Detective Maxwell here," David chimed in.

"And McSween," Jaq added.

David continued. "We've joined in on speaker phone. We appreciate your help. Check your e-mail. We will forward what we can. Then get on the Internet. Google the Detroit News and Free Press. Several articles will appear."

Jaq held up a hand with parted lips to David. "They'll sound similar to what's been going on in your neck of the woods—sorry for the pun." Jaq paused. "The newspapers will give you a quick, although dull, overview. We'll fill in the rest when we meet."

"Feds want involvement. They've been sniffing around. If there's any reason for them to intervene, all hell will break loose." Abel's voice was pained. A few seconds of silent understanding passed between the detectives.

"We feel your pain." David bent toward the phone to be heard. "Mayor and the Governor, too. We talk on a need-to-know basis."

"We don't want to look foolish or scare a wide net." It was the Hispanic partner. "My partner and I will take a trip there, if not you come here. Let's see who gets clearance first. Although the weather is nicer down here this time of year."

"Agreed," David said. "Our Chief's brother-in-law was one of the victims. A priority case—he may not approve our leaving because that death was in this jurisdiction."

Jaq interjected. "We trust you'll keep your pathologist involved and they can continue to share information. We'll exchange any remaining data and evidence when we meet."

Punching the telephone Off button, Dr. Towers scratched his beard thoughtfully. "Sounds like Rita's hypothesis may have cracked both cases."

"I only read a few news articles." Rita put her hands in her pockets.

"Rita, never doubt your ability to make good sense out of nonsense," Dr. Towers said.

Jaq put a hand on Rita's shoulder. "You have common sense, an intuitive kind of smart. It's a rare thing."

"That is why we get along so well," Dr. Towers said.

"Meanwhile, I have more lessons to learn from speaking cadavers." Rita walked across the room and pulled out a drawer of slides.

"From the sound of the call, things may be sticky, but not stuck," Jaq said.

"A race to the next victim? Our state or theirs?" David frowned. "Not easy to catch an invisible killer with wings."

"Just capture before the trail leads to more bodies in either state—or he moves to a third one." Dr. Towers leaned back in his chair and swiveled his head between them.

"Could already be multiple trails," Jaq said. "Feds may need an invite, for that reason alone."

That announcement clearly irritated David. "Not today." He stood and stomped toward the door.

"By the way, they are threatening to send bodies to the University of Michigan." Dr. Towers rubbed his hands together, then clenched his fists and set them on the table.

"Meaning what?" David stepped back.

"Meaning the Wayne County Medical Examiner's Office is not keeping up with the overwhelming body count from the regular crime roll call, and then there is the hospital work. So there will be a farming out of bodies for autopsy."

"But you'll keep the Double Cross Killer cases, right?" Jaq asked.

Dr. Towers reddened under his dark skin. "I will keep them my priority as long as I can."

"Mayor says—" David began.

"One thing today, different thing tomorrow. Doesn't matter which mayor or where he comes from. Double talk." Dr. Towers frowned. "I am truly sorry."

"Back to work we go." David reached out a hand to Doc and the men shook hands. "We got you covered." He gave Jaq the leave nod.

"We'll send a flare when northern detectives meet southern detectives." Jaq stepped behind David, waved to Rita and closed the door.

\* \* \* \*

Abel handed the stack of news articles to Rabbit. "Tie's there. I matched the dates of Detroit and Sarasota murders."

Rabbit scanned the articles. "Both ME autopsy reports are critical."

Abel's voice was excited. "Compared murder dates, they never overlap. Time for travel, murder and return flight."

Rabbit smacked the desktop. "Another day's work." Abel placed the grid of dates he'd made on top of the articles Rabbit had. "So—last murder in Florida we go to Michigan, the opposite state, his next target."

Abel nodded. "Agreed."

Rabbit stood. "Unless the uniforms find an immediate body."

"Let's be ahead of him." Abel could hardly contain his excitement.

Rabbit tossed the articles and grid in a file. "I'll book the trip. You get permission. If anyone gives you the run around, speak Spanish really fast like you don't understand—you know the drill—then thank them profusely."

Abel laughed. "I feel used. Bueno. Estar todo en la mente. On it. While I get permission for our Detroit honeymoon, you advise them to expect us. Tell them to send a limo and book a room near their station. It's the least they can do for a fifty degree drop in temperature." Abel sprang from his chair and escaped through the door with a renewed gait his clunky body had lacked for weeks.

\* \* \* \*

Rabbit lifted the receiver and dialed the number for Veronica Riley. "We were wondering if you'd be willing to answer a few more questions? Short notice, but we may have a lead."

She exhaled reluctance into the phone but agreed.

Detectives were distracted when Veronica Riley arrived earlier than expected. She was calm and well groomed. They were already seated at opposite sides of the conference table organizing their files, ensuring the tape recorder was in working order, and there were enough pens, notepads, and water bottles. Bennie sat to the left of Veronica who he'd directed to sit at the head of the conference room table. Now seated, her composure was that of a mouse about to be pounced upon by three shrewd felines. He reached across, placed a comforting brotherly hand on Veronica's forearm. "Veronica Riley?"

"Yes?" Her forehead creased.

"I'm Special Agent Bennie Wayland. My pleasure to meet you. I do research for the detectives so they can focus on their cases and follow leads quickly. I'm what you might call a police step-and-fetch-it." He grinned at her. "They treat me very well."

She nodded. "I see."

"When they told me about you, I thought, well, maybe I could help." Bennie patted her arm.

"Thank you. Nice to meet you." Veronica held out a well-manicured, freckled hand and he shook it. "I just don't know how I can help." She reached into her purse, pulled out a tissue, then folded it neatly into her palm and clenched her fingers around it.

Abel, seeing a downward forefinger stroke sign from Rabbit, pushed the Record button. Abel made no excuses and plunged into the heart of the matter.

"Ms. Riley, may we record you like the other night?" Abel sat across from her.

Eyes on the machine, she nodded. "Yes."

Rabbit sat on the other side of her. "We've confirmed the perpetrator travels with consistency between Detroit and Sarasota."

Veronica's head cocked slightly to one side, and she brought her left arm up, resting her head in her hand. "Are you implying we—I know the killer, maybe the killer was—is stalking us? Do I need to move—hide—till you capture him?"

"No." Rabbit bounced one hand lightly up and down on the tabletop. "We're implying there are similarities between murders in Detroit and Sarasota. We're leaving for Detroit in a few hours."

"There are murders in two states?" She eyed Bennie.

Abel jutted his chin up to Bennie. Bennie leaned into Veronica. "Yes. Please, do not say anything to anyone."

Abel folded his hands together in front of him. "All information—including our discussion, must be completely confidential."

Veronica looked scared. "I understand."

"Your mother's the last known Sarasota victim. Your family flew the same round-trip Sarasota to Detroit route as one other family," Rabbit added.

Veronica paled. "Am I—are we—suspects?"

Bennie replaced his hand on Veronica's forearm. She left it there.

"No. We, the whole investigative team, are double checking everything to verify we didn't overlook anything." Rabbit folded his hands in front of him and smiled.

"The more we learn, even trivial matters, the more we question." Abel paused, then leaned toward Veronica. "We've gathered a lot of evidence. We continue to rework it with criminal profilers. Background checks on everyone remotely involved."

"Sometimes we can overlook something because we know too much. Does that make sense?" Rabbit met her eyes and held a thin smile; he kept his voice slow and steady.

"Can't see what's right in front of you. It happens even to me."

Rabbit raised his eyebrows. "We reconsider, revise everything until we get it right."

Abel reached into a stack of paper and retrieved the blue-and-white envelope containing the itinerary and plane tickets she had given them. "We used the flight information you gave us to subpoena a passenger list each way. Since each is a direct flight, there are two lists. Every passenger, flight attendant, and pilot is listed. Do you recognize anyone? Take your time."

With a shaky hand, Veronica grabbed the paperwork. She fingered it, then settled in and read every line.

The room was silent, all eyes upon her. She focused on the lists, one at a time, methodically reviewing each name. She pursed her lips. After several long minutes, frustrated sighs and nods, Veronica handed each list to Bennie. "Nothing. Not one name is familiar, even remotely. I tried to think back. I don't recall my mother mentioning or even writing down any of these names."

"Thank you for trying," Abel said. "If you recall anything or when you feel up to it and you go through her things—paperwork, old letters—please call."

"I'm not sure—" Veronica bit her lip. She extended her arm to Rabbit. "I found these Delta tickets from the last year I traveled with mom—once a month."

"You saved them?" Rabbit was full of surprise and elation. He accepted them.

"Custody battles. If you ever go through one, you'll know. I save all documentation related to my children. I'll need them back."

"Of course," Rabbit said. He could barely remove his stare from the envelopes in his hand.

"Was she involved in any neighborhood dispute? Anyone disgruntled?" Abel asked.

Veronica drew in a breath, releasing in thought. She closed her eyes and clenched her hands in a ball. Momentarily, Veronica slipped into her own world.

The room viewed her in silence. Another deep breath and her eyes fluttered open. "Nope. My mother was an old woman in pain. Her body was failing her, but her mind was clear as rain. She wasn't always pleasant. She often complained, but there were days she was resigned to the pain. She had a walker, canes and lots of pain medications."

"She cared for your children. She interacted with other parents and neighbors. No disputes with them?" Rabbit spoke quietly.

Veronica rubbed her hands together. "I work. I didn't see and hear everything. My mother took good care of my children, despite everything. It's not like she was changing diapers and lifting them all day. I couldn't afford regular childcare. If you don't believe she was competent to care for my children, call DHS and get the reports, their investigation."

Bennie's forehead wrinkled. "The Department of Human Services was involved with your family?"

"I think one of the neighbors called, or maybe the school. I'm not sure. They don't tell you that sort of thing. They said reports are confidential, yet they have a license to cause chaos in your life, investigating fabrications." She pointed a finger. "You're guilty till you prove yourself innocent."

"Were your children removed from you?" Bennie asked.

"No, but we took drug tests, proved my mother took her meds as prescribed, and that they were in child-proof bottles. They opened my refrigerator, checked for healthy food in the cupboards."

Abel wrote notes. "Everything was in order?"

"Yes, we passed. My children were questioned. Their closets, bedding and beds were checked. Their clothing and toys were checked. Social workers scrutinized sleeping arrangements. Even my garbage was checked. They contacted doctors, hospitals, schools, and talked with neighbors. You name it: we had to prove it and disclose it."

"Did they check out your mother—I mean is it possible there was a serious problem between your children and your mother?" Rabbit asked.

Her eyes narrowed. "No." She remained frozen for a few seconds, then added. "They disappeared almost as quickly as they appeared."

"Were you aware of the allegations?" Rabbit asked.

"Yes. Said my mother let the children run wild in the house while she was drugged up. Accused her of beating the children with her cane."

"Find bruises? Broken bones? Malnutrition? Any medical documentation?" Rabbit folded his hands.

"None, never." Veronica's fist pounded the table. "I'm a good mother. My mother loved her grandchildren. My children were the reason my mother was hanging on to her painful life."

"That must've been a difficult time," Abel said. "Process is imperfect. You did the right thing, cooperating with them. Sometimes people report to be vindictive. Maybe that happened here?"

She shrugged. "Anything's possible." Veronica fisted her tissue; there was a deep catch in her throat.

"This conversation stays confidential for all of our sakes?" Rabbit paused and watched Veronica nod. "Leaks could seriously hurt our investigation."

Veronica swallowed hard. "Of course. If I think of anyone, anything, I'll call." Her voice was barely audible, hidden tears begged their exit.

Rabbit's forehead creased again. "Do you know anyone with the last name Walters?"

Veronica arched her brows at Bennie. "Other than Barbara Walters from television? No." She slowly shook her head. "Another victim?"

Bennie nodded. "Jonathon Walters. His daughter and granddaughter found him after they arrived home from a trip. Detroit-Sarasota—several similarities to your mother's murder."

"Except, your mother had time to fight back. Mr. Walters didn't," Rabbit added.

"Same Delta flight—like I gave you?" Veronica's voice was low, shaky, her cheeks pink, and tears began to well.

Rabbit pressed a thumb on the tickets she'd brought. "We'll know soon."

# Chapter Twenty-seven

TUESDAY AFTERNOON AND DETROIT METRO Airport was overrun with upcoming New Year's passengers preparing for Wednesday night. Rabbit spotted their luggage in bin three through the baggage frenzy and pointed in that direction. After plucking their bags, Rabbit and Abel landed next to the street doors. Detroiters wearing black worn leather fit the description of hundreds in the room so the Sarasota pair stayed put, feeling they were more likely to be found by the Detroit detectives than vice versa.

The crowd was thinning. Rabbit stepped toward a pair heading toward them, the woman extending her hand out as she approached. "Detective Jacqueline McSween. Call me Jaq. How was your flight?"

"Perfect." Rabbit shook her hand, grinned and struck a chin-up to Abel. "Hey Abel, I must've done something wrong to have to work with your mug. I'm Ronald Randall. You can call me Ron or, as I'm fondly called at our station, Rabbit. My partner, Abelardo Mendoza, our local Argentinean, we call Abel."

"Hey, man, thanks for the beloved intro." Abel grinned.

Jaq introduced David. "Detective Maxwell, my partner." They shook hands.

"Call me David. Appreciate you arriving so quickly. Toss your bags in the trunk." He pressed a button and the truck back popped up. "We'll catch up on the way to your hotel suite."

They climbed in. David navigated his way out of the airport and onto I-94.

Abel leaned forward from the back seat. "How far to the station?"

David expertly wove the vehicle in and out of traffic. "Half hour. We thought we'd give you some time to check in, unpack, and rest. Then, we'll pick you up and over dinner compare what we've got—"

Jaq interrupted David. "Unless you want to meet for breakfast and begin right now?"

Abel raised a brow at Rabbit. Rabbit shook his head. "Si. Let's call and verify our hotel reservation or maybe you can send an officer over to check us in with our bags. We're anxious to see what you've got."

"That's easily done." David opened the window, attached the lights to the roof. "Hang on." He hit the gas, clicked the blinker into the downtown exit lane. "Precinct coming up."

Rabbit continued in a louder voice. "We've a working theory. If it holds true, it isolates occupation, home base and next hit, which is why we're here and you're not in Sarasota."

"I thought it was because you wanted to experience the Michigan winter," David said, careening around curves with a practiced hand.

Jaq eyed David, then positioned her back between the seat and the door to better observe their Sarasota hopefuls. "We are anxious for you to see our war room. Exactly what makes you positive he strikes here next?"

Abel pointed to Rabbit as he spoke. "Dates, frequency, Rabbit's travel theory. We booked the same direct flight we think the killer takes."

"Direct Sarasota-Detroit?" Jaq asked.

Abel nodded. "Si. Delta runs direct flights high season—November through April for the snowbirds."

David squinted. "Snowbirds?"

"People who winter in Florida, return home to summer in Michigan," Rabbit said. "You're obviously not one of them."

"So?" Jaq asked.

"That's the brilliance of it. Rabbit just starts flirting with the ladies—"

"Abel." Rabbit interrupted. "Your point?"

Abel grinned. He didn't care much about formalities, and sometimes he mumbled on. "Okay. Rabbit, from this sort of bantering with this beautiful stewardess, well, he figures out the perp is a pilot."

"A pilot?" David asked, and then repeated, "A pilot, perfect sense."

Jaq repeated under her breath. "A pilot." She rubbed her temples. Fear climbed into her heart and triple-paced her adrenaline. She craved caffeine, a heavily frosted cookie, and a tranquilizing gun for her best friend.

With the conference room door shut, the detectives formed a line in front of the up-to-date mapping and evidence boards. Rabbit reorganized and aligned the Detroit and Sarasota maps and evidence boards. Every few minutes his hands formed the telescope lens and Rabbit stepped back, then forward peering through it.

"Our maps and timelines are like two matching halves." Rabbit pointed. "Look at the dates—they fill in gap times perfectly."

"Rabbit, your theory is—" Jaq ogled the two timelines tacked together. "Perfection."

"Snowbird theory wins." Abel grinned. "No surprise."

"Also, two or maybe three fields of training." Rabbit held up three fingers. "Pilot with medical and military training."

"More, maybe religious?" Jaq folded her arms. "Maybe just well-read?"

Abel turned to Rabbit. "I bring the file. You tell it."

Rabbit raised his shoulders and put his palms up. "You found rosaries, same as we did on each victim?"

"We did, but haven't tracked them." David planted his right buttock on the edge of the conference table and folded his arms.

"Military," Rabbit said. "Designed, created, handmade by family support groups. Identical one on each victim. After we spoke, I had a hunch. I found the original group in Michigan, a US Army National Guard Family Support Unit. It spread like wildfire across the country."

Abel handed David a file. "Another Michigan-Florida connection."

"Perp's a highly trained soldier or former soldier," Rabbit explained. "Fits profile and resolves both surveillance and leaving without detection abilities."

Abel nodded. "Active military could fly in and out with layovers. He locates the target, formulates plan and easily executes under our radar."

"How far back do the rosaries go?" Jaq asked.

Rabbit pulled out a chair and sat. "Began in Desert Storm Army National Guard. Thousands of soldiers have them—now all branches."

Silence fell, shoulders drooped. Eyes connected. "How about a bite before we take you to your suite?" Jaq asked. "You can't experience Detroit without eating a Coney Dog."

Rabbit rubbed his hands together. "She's a mind reader."

"I never turn down a dog." Abel beamed.

Jaq angled her head toward the Sarasota list of victims and read the notations. "Plague. Your list fits into ours."

Rabbit returned his hands to lens position. "What?" The room stopped.

Jaq began. "Assassin bugs, frog, ashes, the last victim tied into her sheets. It all fits. We've similar evidence that doesn't fit the usual crime scene."

"I looked at the military angle on the sheets—perfectly tied knots— almost too perfect." Rabbit held up his lens and looked through it. "Your theory intrigues me."

Jaq grinned and bowed. "Thank you."

David grabbed his keys. "This must wait till dogs are down. Gets complicated and a little gross before we eat. Jaq's theory is the Double Cross Killer, as she's aptly named him—"

Jaq interrupted. "He's a religious nut on a mission to save children—maybe send a message—as God did, biblically speaking—for people to do better—treat children or the family better—so he leaves a plague notation, so to speak."

"We found a domestic violence thread and a complete lack of sorrow over the loss of the loved ones," David added. He moseyed toward the door, entered the hallway and began jingling the keys.

"Not as pronounced in our cases." Rabbit could barely take his eyes off the plague lists. "Grief seemed real—" He paused, then looked up toward the three ahead of him. "In most cases."

David stepped up his pace down the hallway. "Getting back to pilots and flights, pilots have control, although somewhat limited, over their schedules. There's a bidding process. We need to subpoena Delta Detroit and Sarasota pilot schedules and bids for the past two months."

"Good thought," Rabbit said. He pushed Down on the elevators, heading to the underground parking garage.

"Politicians are expediting everything. These murders have all but squashed Detroit tourism. Casino traffic is frozen and downtown development is at a standstill. Detroit can't afford any more financial hits," David said. "Mayor authorized unlimited man-hours with unanimous support of the county commissioners."

"Greektown and Indians are kicking in from their gaming and other profits. There's talk of offering a significant reward," Jaq added. The bell rang and they entered the elevator.

"Better not." Abel scratched his head. "Rewards cause quacks an' false leads."

"We need to push him out. His murdering frenzy's escalating," David said.

Rabbit nodded. "Think grounding. Pilots can't fly every day. They're restricted. Every move we make needs to count." They stepped out of the elevator and followed David in line to his truck.

Jaq called out. "Yeah, media's trailing right behind. You'd think we were Brad and Angie—"

David cracked his knuckles. "You wish."

Abel raised a brow at Rabbit. They ignored the idle chatter. That was what was great about having a male partner. No hormones, no complications. "I checked with the Walters family. They confirmed same Sarasota-Detroit route. Travel itinerary's on its way."

Jaq stopped and faced Abel, who turned to Rabbit. "There's another victim with the same travel pattern?"

They stopped and Rabbit explained. "Victim was an old man, wheelchair-bound. It occurred to me days later that restocking the kitchen and the large grocery shopping was the result of a vacation." He paused. "Found with assassin bugs inside his shirt."

David clicked open his vehicle. Satisfied, Jaq shook her head and within a few paces they joined David. "I understand earning the nickname Rabbit—deducing that from an obscure comment—even remembering it with everything going on—really is pulling a rabbit out of a hat." Jaq laughed. "My apologies for you working without food—Coney dogs are my treat."

David clicked the locks, fastened his belt, and turned the engine key. He pinched Jaq's waist and met her eyes. "You'll soon learn, my partner always apologizes in food. Keeps me on the treadmill."

# Chapter Twenty-eight

I T WAS A TYPICAL EARLY Wednesday for Rita and Dr. Towers, except that it was New Year's Eve, and except the fact that Rita sat with Dr. Towers at the Central District precinct amidst graphs and charts in a conference room with four detectives. To Rita, the intimidation factor was daunting. After an hour of listening to evidence, ideas, and 'where we go from here', Rita decided to unequivocally offer Nick's assistance, despite knowing she'd likely have to coax him. "My fiancé, Nick Archer, is a Delta pilot. I'm sure if I ask him, he'd meet with you, give you the inside scoop, answer questions about process, schedules, where everyone stays—"

Rabbit raised a stop-signed right hand. "Your fiancé's a Delta pilot?"

"Yes—several years—Northwest, now Delta. He can help. Although—" Rita bit her bottom lip. "I seriously doubt any of the pilots could commit these murders. I've met a few of them and some of the regular stewards and stewardesses. They're wonderful."

Rabbit, with wrinkled forehead and half-grin, nodded. "At this time in the investigation we can't risk any unknowing tip-off by anyone. We don't know who—what exactly we're dealing with. This information and conversation's highly confidential, same as your work with Dr. Towers."

Rita nodded and kept her focus on Rabbit. She entwined her fingers and began circling her engagement ring around her finger. Nick. A pilot. Delta. Military training. Sarasota and Detroit. He fit the profile. She flattened her hands on the table to still them. Many fit the profile. She was firm, like her flattened fingers.

Dr. Towers folded his hands in front of him. "I trust Rita implicitly. She understands confidentiality."

"I'll have no discussions with my fiancé or anyone else. I'm new at detective work, but not the medical field." Rita's mind raced and her heart fluttered.

Rabbit's lips rose in a half moon. "Thank you."

Rita avoided Jaq's eyes and spun toward Dr. Towers. "I'm meeting Nick, my fiancé, for an early lunch. Do you mind?" She feared being late, but dreaded the consequence of Nick discovering she wasn't a floor nurse, rarely worked in the hospital, and, she spent the morning at the First Precinct.

"Enjoy. I will catch you up after lunch—at our offices."

\* \* \* \*

Thankful she was allowed to leave work early, Rita immediately hailed a taxi and flawlessly maneuvered her way to Henry Ford Hospital with enough time to warm up from the cold. Rita steadied her trembling hands and quickly grabbed a lipstick from the pocket of her scrubs. Once satisfied her makeup was freshened, she ran her fingers through her hair, swapped ID tags, and straightened the shoulder strap on her bag. Stepping out of the elevator, she saw the familiar gait a few steps ahead of her.

"Nick."

She caught up to him and he wrapped an inviting arm around her and met her kiss.

"Hey sexy," she whispered. "Thanks for meeting me for lunch. I grabbed my jacket if you want to run out—I have some extra time."

"My pleasure seeing you in the middle of the day." Nick grinned. "Cafeteria's fine. I hoped to catch you on the floor, see you in action."

Her mind raced. "I'm floating. Likely, you'd have ended up on the wrong floor. As usual, your timing is impeccable."

Nick stared at Rita while the elevator carried them down to the cafeteria level. "Anything you need to tell me? Did you get fired from your floor or something?"

"Or something." She stepped back from him. "Nursing shortage causes floating."

"Makes sense. Maybe flexibility too? We can travel more often." He ran the back side of his hand, softly, slowly, down her cheek.

Rita smiled. "It's too new to know schedule-wise, but I will check it out." Avoidance was the best policy. Harmony and lots of time was what she needed.

"How can I reach you as a floater? I don't like not knowing where you are." He swatted her behind just as they rounded the corner into the cafeteria.

Grabbing two trays, she handed one back to Nick. They followed the metal bars through islands of food lines. She acted distracted over the varied rows of lunch choices to avoid his eyes. "You can reach me in the hospital.

Same as always. Text me, page me, ask the hospital operator to page me. Hasn't been a problem yet, has it?"

"Nope. Make sure it doesn't become one."

Rita giggled. "You're silly. Text is best. I know you don't like hospitals. Most don't—but it won't swallow me whole. A touch of the phone, I'll respond, like magic."

"I'm grounded about two weeks, unless someone calls in ill."

She hid her delight. Two weeks, time to help out Dr. Towers and the detectives. "It'll be great to have some evenings at home alone with you. We'll work on wedding plans."

"And I'll keep that body of yours occupied." His pupils soaked in every inch of her before he spoke again. "Mom and Chris are joining us tonight for New Year's Eve dinner. You'll need to be a vision of perfection."

Rita placed silverware and napkins on her tray and stood in the cashier's lane in front of him. "Can't wait."

She watched Nick pay, and then followed him to a booth.

He waited for her to empty her tray on the table and sit. "You're distracted."

"As I should be when you announce a meal with your family—I'm not just meeting them—I'm eating with them."

"You have a problem eating?"

"Don't order me anything with spinach or poppy seeds."

Nick tossed his head back and laughed. "What else?" He unloaded his tray, grabbed both their trays and set them on the table across from them.

"What'll I wear? What'll they think about me and the quick engagement—they don't know yet, remember?"

"Typical woman. Your beauty will outshine anything you wear. Although I prefer you in just the ring." Nick kissed her cheek before sliding into his side of their booth. "Dress classic."

Rita cringed at his dressing, conversation, and behavior directions. She struggled to enjoy her meal—the fact Nick fit the Double Cross Killer profile couldn't be plucked from her brain. She reminded herself she could account for every minute they spent in Sarasota. She relaxed and scooped another forkful.

\* \* \* \*

Eyes darted across the conference table until Rita made her hasty exit and Rabbit's deep voice asked the looming question.

"How well do you really know Nurse Rita Rose and her fiancé, Nick Archer?"

Dr. Towers cleared his throat. His head slightly cocked at Rabbit, one eyebrow lifted, both eyes slightly bulged. "Best skilled nurse I have ever worked with. It has been just this past month. Detectives have, in one way or another, known her for several years." He aimed his head purposefully toward Jaq.

"We met—I've lost track—about five—years ago in yoga. I feel like she's always been in my life, like family." Jaq studied Dr. Towers.

Dr. Towers picked up the cue. "Trusting Rita is simple. I assigned her exclusively to work on these murders because she is that good."

Jaq continued. "She was accused of vehicular homicide a few years ago. We investigated. Her former fiancé—real piece of work—set her up for an accident he caused. She was cleared, he's in prison. She has lingering trust issues."

"Not so lingering she avoided finding another fiancé," Rabbit said.

Jaq pulled her lips to the left. "Rita's working her way from jaded to positive."

David interjected. "Nursing Board suspended her license for two years because alcohol was involved. She suffered a concussion and didn't remember what happened. Jaq was really the only one who seriously investigated it. Jaq's instincts were on target."

Jaq twisted a chunk of hair around her fingers. "We've worked out regularly since we met, and spent other time together. Lots of things describe Rita. Murderer is not one of them."

David exhaled and nodded. "Damn fiancé drove blind drunk, hit a jogger, then placed unconscious Rita behind the wheel. Police got involved after his coward-ass found his way safely to his bed. He claimed they'd had a fight, and she drove home alone. We trust Rita."

Rabbit bounced the tips of his fingertips against each other. "Unfortunately, human nature often lends itself to trusting the wrong person. And, history repeats itself."

Jaq twirled her hair around her finger. "Rita has worked hard to avoid that. I've watched for signs; zilch."

Rabbit stopped bouncing his fingertips and left the circle formation. "It's curious. Nurse Rose travels with her Delta pilot fiancé, flying direct Detroit-Sarasota. Her fiancé also has layovers in Sarasota." He paused. "We should begin with them."

"Them?" Dr. Towers asked. "I do not know the fiancé, and do not give a damn about him. Is Rita now a suspect?"

Rabbit shook his head. "Abel and I are not emotionally involved. We can't ignore the fact that your Nurse Rita may be an unknowing participant, an innocent bystander, who can or already is a killer's alibi." Rabbit hesitated. "It's possible she has a silent nagging. Subconsciously, she suspects it's him, but after what you just told us, I'd guess, she can't believe she picked the wrong man again. Her subconscious simply brings it to you."

Jaq scrunched up her face in contemplation. "Excuse me?"

Rabbit began. "Nothing good can come of this. Rita will keep questioning her surroundings, the murders in two states as she travels more frequently with her fiancé. She's smart. She can't help but ask questions, good ones. Eventually, she'll ask the right one, find something, or worse yet see something."

Abel nodded. "She could confront him—think she is helping. Or, do the typical girl pushing buttons 'we need to talk about our relationship thing'—Jesus, I hate that. Anyway, if he's the perp, she'll be—could be, right now, in grave danger."

"If he's not the perp, we hope he has a sense of humor and we owe them an enormous wedding gift." Jaq rubbed her forehead.

"Rita may be in danger, regardless of the scenario." Dr. Towers sighed. "There is something else. I should have told you—"

Jaq stared at him. "Spill."

"I have not liked the way Rita has been looking—really dragged out."

Jaq nodded. "I just mentioned that to her as well, she brushed it off."

Dr. Towers held up a finger to make a point. "I have the idea, especially now, that there is already something foul."

Jaq frowned. All eyes focused on Dr. Towers. "Like what?"

"Does poison fit the profile? Would he drug her into submission or oblivion?" Dr. Towers began. "My gut tells me there is an issue—unless she is suffering from a grave illness."

David gaped at Doc. "Doesn't fit this killer's profile."

"She appeared fine today. Si?" Abel asked.

Jaq bit her lip. David and Dr. Towers nodded. "Could be makeup tricks, she's a master." Jaq cleared her throat. "She looked worn, but so do we. We'll watch her closely." She leaned into Dr. Towers. "That's us. We're the closest and see her the most."

"So noted." Dr. Towers grinned and nodded. "That is the most serious assignment I have ever been given."

Jaq tapped a finger. "She's smart and loyal. A dangerous combination."

"Recipe for blind peril and absolute vulnerability." Rabbit tapped his fingers together again. "Alarming."

"Investigate her fiancé immediately. Please." Dr. Towers maneuvered his glower toward the ceiling, then back down. He rubbed his hands together and shook his head. "If anything happens to that sweet girl, I will never forgive myself."

"We'll detail units to watch her." David paused and jotted a note. "Home, work, any place she frequents. She won't be aware she's being watched."

"Added bonus—we'll know where the fiancé is," Rabbit said.

"Right." David scribbled another note and closed his notepad. "Chief may regret authorizing extra man-hours."

"It'll keep everyone off our collective butts." Jaq snickered. "We need to keep Rita in Michigan. No Sarasota travel—can you do that, Doc?"

"Surely, except for weekends, quick in and out flight," Dr. Towers said. "To take care of that I will increase her hours—tell her you are so close I need her available seven days a week."

Jaq bit the corner of her lip, then shook her head. "Mandate on-call, with her cell and pager on her at all times. We'll swap your pagers. Give her one of ours with a GPS tracker."

David nodded. "Tell her the idea resulted from this meeting. She'll believe that—Doc?"

"Sounds right. She is very anxious to help. Really invested in the outcome."

Abel turned toward Doc. "Why these murders?"

Jaq interrupted. "These are the first murders she's ever been involved with."

Dr. Towers raised his eyebrows. "I am hoping she will decide to permanently make a career shift."

"Rabbit, in less than twenty-four hours, I trust you. You will pull this rabbit out of a hat," Jaq said. "If your gut tells us to follow the fiancé in Detroit, David and I are on it like rabbits on a carrot."

Rabbit chuckled. "Feels like home already. Seriously, surveillance, now, is mandatory and past due." He paused. "I could be wrong."

Jaq met his eyes. "We'll all sleep better if you're right."

Abel's cell rang and he clicked and read a text. "Bennie texted. Jonathan Walters traveled to Michigan with his daughter and grandchild on three separate occasions to close the estate of his late wife. Itinerary arriving now, via fax."

Jaq bounded toward the door. "I'll run down and grab it. Back in a flash."

Abel nodded and read another text. "Bennie's at Delta obtaining travel records from all Sarasota-Detroit travelers we identified as likely victims of the Communicator-Double Cross Killer murders."

David sat taller. "How long will that take?"

"Just texted that question, Bennie responded that Delta headquarters promised everything in twenty-four hours. Suggested your Michigan judges sign the same warrants and get those faxed over so the search will be complete."

"I'm on it," Jaq said. "Here are the three Walters itineraries—he sent a copy of their warrants, I'll get the same language on ours and be back in a flash. Don't do anything like solve the case without me."

David wiggled his fingers goodbye. "We promise to be statues until you return."

Abel scanned the faxed documents, passed them to David, then looked up. "Jonathan Walters flew the same direct route as Katherine Quinn. Sarasota-Detroit, Delta Airlines. Quinn-Riley family flew coach. Walters family upgraded to first class."

Rabbit grabbed the passenger list Veronica Riley had reviewed. There it was at the top. He handed the paper to Abel, who handed it to David. "I'm handing you the passenger list we had the daughter of one of our victims look at. Delta flight. Pilot—"

"Clear as the blue sky," David said. "Captain Nick Archer."

"Gotcha." Rabbit said.

David shook his head. "Either we get ahead of him or the Feds are on us faster than flies on shit and they'll take it away from us that fast. Another stiff, more warrants, with any sign this is a serial murderer crossing over state lines, there'll be so much jurisdictional red tape it'll look like a Christmas-redo at the Fourth of July fireworks."

Abel frowned. "And smell like the red tide."

Nods of agreement caused Rabbit to lean into Dr. Towers. "Sir, you must pin Nurse Rose down—her schedule, dating plans, whatever she'll talk about."

"I will try." Dr. Towers wiped his brow with a handkerchief. "She is like my own child. We need to warn her."

David folded his arms. "No. That could get her killed."

"I agree." Jaq reentered the room and sat. "Warrants are being typed. They'll be signed and delivered shortly."

David paused and motioned to Jaq. "Ask Rita about Nick's habits, quirks. Each of you can obtain different kinds of information about him, work different angles." He rubbed his hands together, his face flushed. They were finally going to close in, have their way with the Double Cross Killer. "I'll call reinforcements to tail him, watch the trail the pilot leaves on land."

"Bueno," Abel said, smiling. "My gut tells me this is his end—eh, Rabbit? My gut follows where the Rabbit goes."

"I'll ask our team to research his Siesta Key activities." Rabbit walked toward the map.

Abel set his hands on the table, palms down. "I hate vulture-lawyers eating our hunches. Working both states will bring hard evidence and conviction."

Jaq flipped her pen and let it drop with a thud. "Amen, add a halleluiah."

Rabbit snickered. He popped the circle of his fingers into a loud clap. "They won't just graze—we'll have enough hard evidence to choke the defense lawyers."

# Chapter Twenty-nine

"NEW YEAR'S EVE DINNER, FAMILY and fun, quick and painless, as promised." Nick helped Rita on with her coat, then tucked the corners of his wool scarf inside his jacket.

"No complaints, but you have to agree that a few hours was short notice. You mention it at lunch, then poof, I meet the family." Rita tightened the belt on her coat and fingered in her leather gloves.

"When I want something to happen, I work fast. I keep my promises."

"You have big connections to get last minute dinner reservations on New Year's Eve."

"My mother has connections. Award-winning chef in her time. It's always fine dining when she makes the reservations," Nick said. "I listened to what you wanted. New Year's Eve, simple, with a special twist."

Rita chuckled. "Very memorable."

"It was good of Chris to take Mom home a bit early so we could have alone time for our nightcap."

"I see why you brothers are close." Rita felt relieved.

They stepped out of the restaurant and into the fresh air. "I love your family." She placed her arm through Nick's and they strode toward the parking lot with her head on his shoulder.

"You'd better." Nick kissed the top of her head and drew her body in closer to him. "It's a package deal."

"One I cherish."

Nick opened the car door for her. "He that loveth his wife loveth himself. The wife must see that she reverence her husband."

Rita met his eyes before climbing into the passenger seat. "I understand." She thought she did—family was important to both of them, and he had just proven it by involving her with his mother and brother, the closest people to him. She fingered the pager in her coat pocket before buckling her seatbelt.

Nick flashed his white teeth at her. "Put that pager away. I'm tired of seeing it. We're going to have a celebratory nightcap at a special little place I know because you make me so happy."

"Okay—but I'm on call." Rita held her breath and pushed out a smile.

"No way—you promised to coordinate your schedule with mine." He adjusted the mirror and paused for a long minute while he stared into it. "New Year's Eve is like Christmas Eve; the whole world is practically closed. You owe me alone time."

Rita was thankful for the umbrella of night and Nick's sharp eye on the road. "I assured you I'd meld my work schedule with yours for travel. We're understaffed over the holidays. It's the height of accident and illness season. I'm on call the next thirty days. Sorry."

"Straight?" He released a loud sigh.

"Yes—doesn't mean I have to work—just stick around, in case."

"Broken promise." His voice was low and tight.

"No, I'm keeping it and my job." Rita tried to stay calm. She clenched her teeth, looked down, and was certain even in the darkness that under the gloved hands, clenched so tightly, her knuckles and nail beds were white.

"If you love someone, you will be loyal to him no matter what the cost. You will always believe in him, always expect the best of him, and always stand your ground in defending him."

Rita pressed an outward smile. Another argument she wouldn't win. She was tired of Corinthians. "You're right, of course. I'm sorry."

"I've changed my mind. We're going straight home." Nick exhaled. His voice was stiff and cold. "Get whatever this streak of defiance is out of your system *before* we're married. Before plans go any further, I need to believe we share the same faith."

"Nick, I love you. I have faith in you—and in us." Rita leaned into him, and kissed his temple. "Truth." Her fingers crawled into her pocket and felt with reassurance her pager and next to it her cell phone. "The New Year is ours, and it's about to arrive."

Nick removed his right hand from the steering wheel and gave her a playful squeeze on her thigh. "You'll make it up to me, nonetheless, prove just how much you love me."

Rita's teeth were grinding in the back. She clenched them and smiled, her face beaming into his. She edged herself as close to him as her seat belt would allow and rested her head on his shoulder. "Whatever it takes."

"You can be sure of that, all night long."

Rita bit the inside of her cheek in the dark, hearing his foot press harder on the gas pedal. The taste of blood oozed from the inside of her mouth. She heard the inner nagging and vowed single, engaged, or married, to stay strong, alert, and true to herself.

\* \* \* \*

Rita stirred. The murders were haunting her sleep; either the murderer was beside her or Nick was working with the murderer. She fluffed her pillows and straightened the covers. Nick was quirky, but a killer? He was mostly normal, wasn't he? Could the killer be a regular passenger, another pilot, flight attendant—someone, anyone, from another airline?

Ethically bound by confidentiality, loyalty too, she couldn't confront Nick—besides, it would end their relationship. Without reasoned explanation, Rita pounded her fists in the dark. Any truth was scary because trusting her gut told her she was tied to the killer more than by working on the victims, being intrigued by the cases, and shifting pieces of evidence together. If she was wrong she lost Nick, if she was right she lost—maybe her life, maybe someone else's life—or lives.

Sleep was as futile as debating herself with the hope of rational answers. Annoyed at her quandary, Rita carefully slid from the bed, slipped on her robe, and tiptoed to the kitchen to avoid the risk of another disagreement.

Armed with a small pan, milk, and chocolate syrup, she turned toward the stove, clicked the burner on low and began pouring ingredients. She stirred and stared into the whirlpooling milk. Complicating matters was the realization that Dr. Towers and the detectives were privy to information she couldn't know. Why Doc's sudden interest in Nick earlier today, their relationship, wedding plans, travel—what they enjoyed together?

As tiny milk bubbles formed, she reached for chocolate and a mug. What had she missed? An icicle might as well have dropped into her nightgown—Doc suspected Nick. Did the detectives—Jaq?

Rita's eyes followed long streams of chocolate; she squirted one after another into the steaming milk until a dark, rich color gurgled back at her.

Rita's inner nagging haunted her. Had she been set up? Maybe he was being set up—not out of the realm of possibilities. Either one of them could know something without knowing they knew it. He was very social, talked with coworkers, jogged and worked out with them. He was too visible, too predictable, too caring about other people to be the perpetrator...

She poured the hot chocolate into a tall mug.

"Did you make enough for me?" Nick's voice boomed into the kitchen behind her.

Rita jumped, almost dropping the pan and mug. "How long have you been there? You scared me."

"Long enough to wonder what planet that inquisitive brain of yours had traveled to."

Rita retrieved another mug from the cabinet and poured. "My brain's overtired. Hoped warm milk would put me to sleep, but I heard the call of chocolate."

"Loud call, lots in there. Tastes great." After another long, loud sip Nick sat on the bar stool next to her. "Bad dream? Talking helps."

Rita took a sip and let the milk's warmth travel through her before speaking. "I don't know what it is—like the calm before the storm."

Nick's eyes narrowed, his mouth frowned. "I'm not good at word games. I'm not following."

"I'm not sure how to answer your question or explain." She paused before beginning again. "I feel like something is about to happen. I can't figure it out. I don't know what—something good or bad, should I worry or not? Does that make more sense to you?"

Nick nodded. "Perfect."

"Really?"

"Take time off from work. You're nervous about floating and this on-call business, planning our wedding in between. I'll cover your bills. We'll travel, relax."

"That makes some sense." Rita's pointer finger went around and around the rim of her mug. She formed her next words slowly. "I have been worried about the wedding. My brain's lost in the clouds; tell me if you find it as you fly by."

"I've flown the same flight patterns for years. I'm a trained, highly skilled pilot with thousands of flight hours. But, when I'm called to fill in for someone who's ill or on vacation, to fly a different route, maybe with a copilot I don't usually fly with, I can't sleep."

"Really?" She drank half the mug, eyes fixed on Nick.

"I use the flight simulator. I wake up the night before with nagging angst. I get out of bed and review maps. I memorize everything, plot backup landing plans. Only then do I relax enough to sleep through what might be left of the night."

"I've seen you. I didn't realize." She ran her fingers through her hair. "You never mentioned—how long have you been flying the Detroit-Sarasota route?"

"That's an odd question." His eyes focused on Rita.

Her mouth formed the outline of a smile. "Just wondering how long I'll be able to hop flights to Sarasota with you."

"Don't worry, I've enough time in. Even if my flight routes change, I'm not selling my condo. We have our whole lives to spend on the Sarasota white beaches we both love. We can fly flight-available anytime."

Rita set down her mug. "Fact is, as much as I love Sarasota and Detroit, I'm worried about both cities having serial murder headlines. I'm scared we could become victims. I couldn't live without you, now that I found you."

He kissed her on the top of her head. "You worry too much. Anywhere we travel to or live in will have murders. No place in the world is violence-exempt. Police and media blow things out of proportion."

"It nags at me."

"Lunatics are everywhere. We will live our lives as directed. Don't tell me the outgoing extrovert I met and fell in love with is a homebound introvert? That will not help this relationship." His tone, full of disdain, lowered with each word.

Rita bit her lip, then spoke slowly, clearly annunciating each word. "I have this crazy feeling the serial killer in Detroit and Sarasota is the same person. I can't seem to shake it."

Nick stared at her in such a way, she wondered if she should duck. He was prone to bad moods, at times for no apparent reason. She froze, certain her heart skipped a beat.

He burst into gales of laughter. It grew stronger, louder. His shoulders began to shake.

Confusion flushed over her, and relief triggered a smile. "Before you fall off the stool and hurt yourself, I give. What's so damn funny? This laughter of yours will wake the building."

Tears streamed from the corners of his eyes. "You playing detective. So damn cute. You need to stick to nursing and pleasing me in bed. You'll sleep better. We both will." He wiped the tears from his face and kissed the nape of her neck. "I know one way to make you sleepy."

Rita shivered feeling his hand slide under her nightgown. Eyeing him, she laughed. "Last one to the bed makes breakfast."

Biting her lip teasingly, Nick announced. "Haven't you learned? I never lose."

They hopped off their stools and leapt toward the bedroom. "Cheater," was the only word Rita could murmur before he plucked off her nightgown. She'd worry about everything tomorrow.

* * * *

Hitting the alarm clock as the initial shock of morning bombarded her senses, Rita struggled to open her eyes to the first day of January. She prayed for a serial-killer-free new year. She wasn't sure if she wanted to relish or forget last night; her plans for the future were clear one minute, and then filled with billows of fog the next.

Cocooned by pulling soft sheets over her head as an evasion tactic, she slid her leg in search of Nick. Rita found cold empty space, confirmation that significant time had passed since he'd absconded. No breakfast aroma emanating from the kitchen—it was hers to make this morning. Where was he?

She tossed the covers aside. Letting her pupils adjust to the light, she stretched and ran one hand through snarled hair while the other placed pressure into her scalp. Her temples suddenly pounded as if poked by searing spears. Her head felt heavy atop her limp body.

Getting up in the middle of the night didn't agree with her. Perhaps she was getting ill. Or, hot chocolate hadn't settled well—was that even possible? Weird dreams, oversleeping, headaches, and nausea. As a nurse, she should be able to diagnose these symptoms, right? She grabbed her robe, quickly padding to the bathroom medicine cabinet. Washing down two migraine tablets, then two for cold and flu, just in case, she gulped a few cups of water to ease her parched throat. She bent down with her head between her knees to keep from fainting. When her blood pressure rose, she ran back and hid under the covers.

Leaning back against the pillow, she placed another pillow over her pounding head, hugging the covers. Where was Nick?

As she slipped into slumber, the nightstand telephone ring jolted her.

"Hello?" The word stuck. She realized her throat was not only parched but felt swollen.

"Rita?"

"Dr. Towers?"

"Happy New Year. I am sorry. You were trying to sleep in this brisk morning."

"Same to you. I'm fine." She lied. "I woke up with a major headache, sore throat. I took something."

"Can I call something in for you?"

"No. I'll be fine." Rita was careful to keep her voice steady. She didn't need him to think she had a New Year's hangover. "Did you need me to work?"

"Not if you are ill. If you are up to it, yes, come in for a few hours. Another victim is being transported."

"Double Cross Killer?" Rita almost forgot the pounding in her temples. Her eyes crossed the bed. No Nick and a Double Cross Killer victim.

"Discovered early this morning. I will begin full autopsy after lunch."

Rita pushed at the covers. "Bad?"

"Clean, like the others. If you are not up to it, just let me know."

"Work is a good distraction for what ails me." She heard Dr. Towers click off.

"New boyfriend?" Nick asked.

Rita blinked. Her mind raced through the conversation with Dr. Towers. What could he have overheard?

"Excuse me?" She slowly cradled the telephone.

"Who are you making plans with? We are spending the whole long weekend together. Right?"

"Remember, I'm on call," she said. "I'm due in at one."

"You are having memory lapses now. This floating thing, your crazy schedule, you being upset, unable to sleep—you promised to take leave, travel with me, plan our wedding? We agreed."

Rita sat at the edge of the bed placing her back to him. She felt compelled to move around the room. She wanted to shout, her brain went into overdrive: *Are you kidding me?* But, she couldn't utter an angry word—rocking the good mood of last night was not her style.

"I need to go to work and figure out the details. I want to retain my job and overtime pay today."

"Time? More time? Money? What does that say about us?" Nick visibly hardened, his voice darkened. "That I'm much more invested in our relationship than you." He pointed a stiff finger at her.

Rita met his staring eyes. They were icy, solemn. His body message was cold, his eyes sending dangerous daggers at her. She understood the issue was closed. He pursed his lips, folded his arms while the veins in his neck bulged like an over-wound clock.

Nick's body language signaled his game. Rita didn't want to play. She blinked away quickly several times, then refocused her gaze on him. She wrapped her body around him and placed her hands on his head, working the muscles, the warm spots, the sensual spots. She moved him as he began to relax, toward the bed. Her college psychology professor was right: if you want to change the dance, change the music. She rolled on top of him, kissed him, used light touches on the head, and chest, kissing him teasingly, with each touch of the points, he became increasingly aroused. She withheld, until she changed the game—at least on her terms, for now.

* * * *

The rawness and ache was worth it. Rita began to feel relief from the medication and Nick was relaxed in her arms, but her nausea had not dissipated.

"I'm only working a few hours," she whispered. "Anyway, last night, you said you had odd errands to run this afternoon. I'm truly sorry."

His eyes closed, he clasped her wrist tightly. When he finally spoke, his voice was insipid. "Just go. You owe me a five-star dinner, your body for dessert, and an outstanding breakfast. Don't make a habit of this. I don't often have this many days off without putting in for actual vacation." He released her wrist.

She rubbed the ache in her wrist. "I want to spend my time with you. I'll leave work early—" She paused, kissed him before quickly adding the escape clause. "If I can."

He rolled over, slid out from under the sheets with his back to her. "I'll be in the shower."

Rita observed Nick limp toward the bathroom. "Are you hurt?" She leaned forward and edged toward the end of the bed. "My God, you're cut. You didn't say anything. Can I look at those wounds?"

Swiftly, his head popped out from the bathroom, into the bedroom. "Nothing serious. It was dark when I took my morning jog. I fell over some lost yapping puppy. I didn't see or hear it soon enough."

"I wondered where you were when I woke up," she said. "My head ached so much I forgot about your daily morning jog."

"I've asked you to jog with me. Real exercise, not that fru-fru yoga—might help with your headaches and foul morning moods."

"Yoga's about strength in body, mind, spirit—"

"Not working."

"I jog. I can't keep your jogging schedule." She pulled in her anger, but wanted to hit him with his shoes. He submerged fully inside the bathroom. Rita retorted knowing it was futile, to feel better. "Hey, maybe you should tell your hands I'm in such bad shape."

Shower water running—incessant pictures slammed through her. How clumsy was he? He'd been injured multiple times while jogging. Was he overdoing jogging, experiencing textbook endorphin hypnosis so he didn't recognize pain or maintain awareness of his surroundings? Or, was something else going on? Her fear heightened.

She headed into the bathroom and stood next to the shower door. "I just have to ask, if you look like that, how's the dog?"

"Damn collie—sturdy enough to growl, bite me, then scamper off. Should've jogged at sunrise. Damn street lamps were still off. Scrapes and bruises—nothing needing the emergency room or your nursing bag." He paused. "Save the dramatics."

"Wear reflective clothing." Rita folded her arms. "I could clean out the scrapes with antiseptic—look at the bite. Dog bites require a rabies shot—"

Nick cut off the shower and pulled his towel robe from the hook. "Hear me: Not your patient. Don't touch my clothes. Don't buy me anything. I own jogging suits. Reflective clothing's just not cool."

"Did you see the direction the puppy went? Should we call animal control?" She met Nick's stare in the bathroom mirror.

With an unblinking glare, he covered his face with shaving cream, lifted his eyebrows, streamed water into the sink and began to shave. She was dismissed.

Rita pivoted out, retreated into the bedroom and noted the clock. One hour to report to work. She noticed the pile of jogging clothes on the floor next to his side of the bed, turned her head toward the bathroom. Not seeing Nick, she quickly lifted them and gasped at the bloodied lining. She dropped them and inspected them to insure they landed exactly as she'd found them. She took a giant step away. There was more to this story.

Small breaths steadied her as she sat on the edge of the bed. What she hadn't seen, she'd felt when they went to bed. The bloodied clothes were a yield sign that their relationship lacked trust, plus he belittled her career. She removed her engagement ring. Maybe a stop sign. She wiggled it back on, but it didn't slide easily in that direction.

Uncontrollable trickles of warm tears slid. Rita cast them away and donned her hospital scrubs. A bottle of Excedrin tossed in her purse to ensure the final retreat of her headache and she was ready to refocus her energy. The Double Cross Killer had struck again. Her problems were small in comparison.

\* \* \* \*

Dr. Towers studied Rita as she entered the lab. "Good afternoon. How are you feeling?"

She blinked. "Better."

"How often do you have headaches?"

Rita thought back for a moment before answering. "When I don't sleep well, I wake up with a headache. These Double Cross Killer cases are getting to me. I'm dreaming about them. Sorry."

Dr. Towers furrowed his brows. "Stress, maybe, but you need to get checked out by a neurologist."

"No thanks. Not ready to get my head examined." She laughed. "It's Double Cross Killer mixed with wedding stress. Pretty normal."

Dr. Towers unfolded his bifocals. "Have you always endured stress migraines?"

"No." Rita hesitated. "Except for these headaches, I hardly ever take medication."

"How do you account for the change?"

"I can't."

"I want them checked out because they are increasing. Humor an old man who cares about you like a father." Dr. Towers' face was serious, and his eyes locked with hers. "Could be something other than stress."

Rita kissed him on the cheek. "For you, I'll go—Dad."

Dr. Towers beamed a prideful red. "Rita, the sooner the better. I will refer you today."

Rita nodded. She rubbed her temples.

"Okay to work?" Dr. Towers leaned into her face and flashed a penlight into one eye, and then the other. He clicked it off.

Rita blinked. "Two more Excedrin. And I'm perfect."

"I will grab you a bottle of water," Dr. Towers said. "Then, we need to get gowned."

Rita nodded. She watched Dr. Towers leave the office. She closed her eyes, relieved for a few minutes alone. She hadn't realized until Dr. Towers asked, that her headaches significantly increased after sex with Nick. She made the corner into the hall, ran through the bathroom doors and vomited.

\* \* \* \*

"This cold sterile room's beginning to feel like our new office." A blue mask covered Rita's mouth, her eyes behind safety goggles. "I missed the morning news on this latest victim."

"If there was a blurb, it was small. Very little detail could have been given. Media is holding off, pending notice to the family. The papers were already put to bed when the victim was found," Dr. Towers said. "Our assisting team is waiting to be called in for photos of the organ removal."

"Does snapping pictures interfere with your thought process?"

"No. It is like wallpaper. Protocol requires documentation of each step. Avoids scrutiny, and makes clean court testimony."

"Why?" Rita asked. Talking distracted her brain from thinking about Nick.

"First, it avoids exhumation after burial. Families do not always agree, and court orders have to be obtained. We are respectful of the dead and their families. When someone is taken early, families take longer to heal. Second, a good defense attorney will tear apart our work if the tiniest detail is left out or appears contradictory. Over the years, mistakes were made, cases lost, procedure improved. That simple."

"Makes sense."

"Ready? Detectives want this quickly, as usual. With so many bodies backed up and this maniac on the loose, I decided to call in a team earlier to get us out of here earlier. New experience for you. The team will enter when I signal. They will take photos and label the dissections and slides as I make them. The microphone remains overhead, but I still have one attached to me for clear dictation." He paused and flagged the ready signal to Rita. He didn't begin speaking until she stopped organizing and counting surgical equipment. "Once everyone is in and I turn it on, the conversation needs to be limited only to this cadaver."

"Understood." Rita frowned. "Team's doing most of what I did. What will you expect of me as your assistant?"

"Follow my lead, like my third and fourth arms. They now perform the busy-work. You are ready for hands-in."

Rita's eyes widened. "Triple gloved."

Dr. Towers laughed. His fingers pointed, his hands flowed over everything. He walked around the room. "I run through everything in my head, including process each time. It deletes errors. My curiosity peaks with each new case, so my mental checklist prior to autopsy keeps me absolutely focused."

Rita snapped on her final layer of gloves and mask.

"Into work we go." Dr. Towers buzzed the outside and watched the door as the team filed in gloved, masked, and garbed in blue.

* * * *

Rita admired the stack of slides and rows of vials, then realized it was almost four o'clock. The autopsy was quick, clean, and similar to other surgeries. The outcome to the equation was merely different: autopsy resulted in answers of how death occurred, surgery hopefully resulted in extending life. After a few minutes into the autopsy, she forgot that twenty hours earlier the cadaver had been a living human being with a future and a family. As Dr. Towers told her, the cadaver had a story to tell, one she wanted to listen to. Her newly found career path was both insurmountable and exciting. What if she made it permanent? She would reserve explaining her decision to Nick for the future.

Rita wasn't drained. To her surprise she was energized, anxious to begin testing with Dr. Towers. Impressed by his precision, his almost artistic flair, Rita's empathy for the victim quickly transitioned into puzzle solving. "You were amazing in there. I understand why you enjoy it. It's fascinating work—clues only the body can answer, why you say the dead talk." Rita placed a file of notes on the corner of Dr. Towers' desk and sat across from him. "How long has he been dead?"

"Since very early morning. The red areas we documented were from blood settling based on the positioning of the body, not bruising. That is all part of the final profile we will put together."

"Early morning—maybe around the time the newspapers are delivered—hour or so before sunrise?"

"Exactly the parameters I was thinking. Double Cross Killer gets in and out under cover of darkness and soundness of sleeping. The family finds the victim when they expect him to be awake and is not."

"Is that what happened? He was found by a family member?"

"Yes, from the background the detectives gave us. The wife found him when she returned from working third shift."

"Home alone?"

"His stepchildren were sleeping. A neighbor took them in while the Crime Scene Investigative Units were there."

"Double Cross Killer strikes again and leaves very little to go on," Rita said. "It's eerie."

"Looks that way," Dr. Towers agreed. "Detectives are working with profilers and will be here later."

The sound of boots clomping came from the outer hallway. Dr. Towers and Rita shifted their attention to the office door.

Jaq walked through the open office door. "Double Cross Killer confirmation?" The other detectives trailed in behind her.

"Detectives travel in packs these days." Dr. Towers pushed up his bifocals, not answering the question. "Very tight quarters, but take a seat."

"Thanks." Jaq sat in the chair next to Rita. "We missed the special challenge New Year Yoga this morning, how about tomorrow?"

Rita tipped her head and shrugged.

David lifted files from the corner of Dr. Towers' desk, then dropped them center. He plopped his blue-jeaned butt in the empty angle. "I'm fine right here." He grinned.

Rita winced at the file thud and realigned her attention to Jaq. "Headache. Sorry. Woke up too late to even text—figured I'd see you and we'd figure out our schedules, and here you are."

"Have you brought me a present?" Dr. Towers asked.

All eyes focused on the black garbage bag in Rabbit's arms.

Rabbit and Abel were still standing. "A little victim."

Rita gasped, putting her hand to her mouth. Seeing the size of the bag, she blurted, "Not a baby."

"Sort of," Jaq said. "Found in the bushes—a puppy."

"Then you need a vet," Dr. Towers said.

"Not exactly," Rabbit said. "We're hoping you would necropsy the dog. Hunch is the dog got in the killer's way."

"Not surprised," Jaq said. "Number one Christmas gift this year in Wayne County—any guesses?"

Rita squinted as if she was trying to recall reading the list. She remembered an article that Christmas was second only to Valentine's Day for engagements. "Should we know this?"

"Yep." Jaq nodded. "Since the rise in crime and these serial killings, dogs were the number one Christmas gift. Big article about a record number of adoptions of dogs at the Humane Society this year—Wayne County even pulled dogs in from other counties—big spread in the Local and State section the Sunday after Christmas—Read a paper."

David focused his attention toward Dr. Towers. "Recon found the dog and went nuts."

"Dog's dead," Rita stated. She could barely utter the words or move her eyes from the bag. She pictured Nick as she stared at it.

David frowned. "Hence the black bag."

Jaq grimaced at David, then patted Rita's hand.

"I just—" Rita began, then stopped.

"David," Jaq said. "We don't want to scare her off. Doc can use all the help he can get."

Dr. Towers stared at Rita. "Rita, could you log and tag the carcass and put him in the freezer? We will get to the necropsy as soon as we can, but not on New Year's Day. My wife expects me home sometime today. But before that I want to review the autopsy slides."

Rita gripped the bag from Rabbit and trudged out of the office. Rabbit followed behind her. She placed the bag on a stainless-steel counter before grabbing the logbook. "What do you think happened?"

"Puppies like to play. Initially, he wanted to play, and then instinctively, likely very quickly, he realized danger lurked, and bit the perp. That got him thrown against the wall."

"Makes sense."

"Dog hairs and trace blood were found on a hallway wall. Poor mutt undoubtedly died on impact. But, that's for Doc to confirm."

Jaq headed toward Rabbit and Rita in time to overhear the end of the conversation. "Beautiful collie. Six, nine months, maybe a year—I'm no dog expert, but I know it's a puppy."

"Poor thing." Rita squeezed her eyes together tightly. She wished she could remove the image, but this morning's memory clicked in full force.

Rabbit stared at Rita. "You're pale."

Jaq steadied Rita's shoulder. "Yeah. Sit down, head between your knees."

"No. I'm fine." Rita pulled her sweater tightly around her. "Puppy didn't have a chance." Her heart pounded loudly, she felt her breathing become shallow. Coincidence—one too many? Wild imagination—Nick's roar still rang inside her.

Rita flashed back. They spent, all—correction—most, of their time together. She never missed him—except when she slept hard, awoke suddenly. He jogged. So did millions. She and Jaq jogged.

A thought slinked through her. Barbiturates. Damn him. She reran her change in sleeping habits, her headaches, her parched throat and mouth, her eerie dreams. Love didn't make her sleep. Damn him, damn him, damn him. Was she his alibi—was her mind running crazy? How long did barbiturates stay in your system? Her forehead wrinkled recalling her minimal nursing school pharmaceutical training. She needed to ask Dr. Towers for a drug test without sending up flares.

"Will the carcass be in refrigeration?" Rabbit asked. "Or will Doc tackle it now?"

"Refrigeration, but you will have results soon." She faced the clock and panicked. No explanation would satisfy Nick if she worked much later.

"It's New Year's Day. You and Nick must have plans—You clearly didn't intend to spend the whole day here. You still have to catch me up on your New Year's Eve." Jaq appeared and looped her arm through Rita's.

Rita laughed and her cheeks pinked. "I do have stories to tell. Truth is, we're having a special meal at home tonight." She looked away.

"Jaq, you did say evidence of the dog was found inside the home? But found by Recon outside?" She knew the answer, but she needed to hear it again.

"Yes, from the blood and hair samples. They're in another bag to be delivered by the CSI team." Jaq's arm hugged Rita's waist. "Killed in one spot, discarded in another."

Rita couldn't shake her discomfort. The collie Nick ran into jogging was outside. Coincidence-not likely. "There must be thousands of collies in Detroit," she muttered.

Rabbit narrowed his eyes at Rita in clear scrutiny, then met Jaq's stare.

"Probably," Rabbit stated simply.

\* \* \* \*

Abel stood at the office door frame to ensure immediate notice of Rita's return from handling the dog. "Doc, did you speak with Nurse Rita about her fiancé?"

"Briefly, last night. Today, she and the cadaver arrived within minutes of each other and we began autopsy almost immediately. When I called her in this morning, she had a migraine, took something for pain, then arrived."

"Was the fiancé there?" David asked.

"I assumed—it sounded like they were together, the way she whispered, but that could also have been the migraine. You could be barking up the wrong tree. Rita spends so much time with him, it would be difficult for him to have time to orchestrate all of this."

David threw up his hands. "Fiancé's the best tree we got."

Abel smacked his lips and shook his head. "If it's another pilot or a crew member they know, either one or both could be in harm's way, especially if they realize Rita has this much contact with us."

"On that, I am ahead of you." Dr. Towers couldn't stop wringing his hands together. "I spoke with hospital administration. Rita will remain listed as a floater."

"Did you swap pagers?" David asked.

"Yes, unknowingly she has your GPS pager. The rest is up to her common sense and good ethics," Dr. Towers said.

"Si, for the moment, maybe she is safe." Abel slapped his hands together. "My mama always say, people in love do and say strange things. We need to push this guy into making a mistake."

Dr. Towers shuddered. "If it is him, we need to know now."

Rabbit walked into the office and slammed his large body into his seat. "Hey, talking with Rita gave me an idea."

"It did?" Rita asked. She trooped in behind him and grabbed a form from the corner cabinet. "I'll return in a few minutes to catch up."

"Yup." Rabbit rotated toward the group, then continued. "Rita's questions to me about the dog made me think about the perp's hurried exit. Hallway was dark, probably didn't see the blood and hair on the wall when he tossed him outside."

Jaq nodded. "If he had, likely would've cleaned it up, given his attention to detail and his propensity to leave clean crime scenes."

Rabbit pointed at Jaq. "Got nervous—there wasn't time to look the area over and clean it up."

"Could've heard the wife coming home or one of the children stirring," David said.

"We can begin to operate with the assumption he doesn't know if the dog is dead or alive or if there is any trace evidence." Rabbit paused, then began to pace back and forth. "His desperate game to clarify his message is crossing wires with his confidence and making him sloppy. If that theory's true, the unknown leaves room for us to play. We can plant facts that are not in the media. If we're clever enough, he'll think we're right behind him— win-win."

"You might send him to a third state or back to Sarasota," Jaq interjected as Rita reappeared and returned to her chair.

Rita tapped her nails on the table.

"Good point." David nodded.

Dr. Towers peered out from behind his bifocals and looked around between them.

"First and foremost." Jaq stopped, reached out and grabbed Rita's tapping fingers and placed a hand over them to quiet her. "We can't discuss what we're doing."

Rita understood immediately. She lifted the hand under Jaq's, put it on her chest near her heart, then spoke without hesitation. "I already promised."

Jaq balled her hands into fists, banged them together in front of her, then spoke. "It could mean the difference between your safety and your peril."

"Excuse me?" Rita couldn't decide if she should be surprised, agitated, or both.

"The Double Cross Killer going to another state isn't the biggest problem, it's—" Jaq gulped in air and held it a moment. "Be aware you likely know him. Multiple leads direct us to Nick's airlines and regular flight. You and Nick socialize with the other pilots and crew members, at a minimum."

Rita saw spots, tears burned but she held them back. Fingers almost engulfed her mouth. Behind them her voice was barely audible. "True." She tried to hide her own growing concern.

"We were in conference with the profilers earlier. Perp's confidence means bodies will quickly multiply—" Rabbit said.

Jaq interrupted. "God-like confidence: he believes he will not, cannot, be caught." Jaq paused.

Rita not only met her eyes, but also wrinkled her forehead and nose at her. "What? What are you trying to say to me?"

"I thought back to things you've said about Nick." Jaq paused, pressed two fingers over her lips. "I don't want to break any confidences."

Rita tilted her head at Jaq. She ignored the others. "No problem. Say it. I can take it."

"You've said more than once the one thing that drives you crazy is Nick's constant bible quoting."

"Yes—I also said, I loved the fact he knows the bible and was raised in the church. That he's honest and caring," Rita said. "No crime there."

"Agreed," Jaq said. "I just want you to know—"

"That I've made another mistake."

"No." David interrupted. "We're concerned for your safety. The profile could fit a lot of people, but everything seems to fit what we know about Nick."

Rita focused on her shoes. Numbness kept her eyes there. She wanted to scream and vomit at the same time. She clasped her hands around her waist and listened.

"Rita, we have to investigate him. We want you—no, we need you to be careful." Jaq rubbed Rita's shoulder. "Can you walk out if you have to—call me if you need to?"

Rita returned a half-moon smile. "Of course." Neither woman blinked. Neither spoke. Neither looked away, they grabbed each other's hands and neither let go.

"What else did the profilers say?" Dr. Towers asked. It was obvious he was giving Rita time.

"All of the victims had children living in their home or had recent visits with family who had children. He sees himself as a protector of children."

"How so?" Dr. Towers inquired.

"Both Sarasota and Detroit reported either police response calls or involvement by Protective Services or the Department of Human Services, either formally or informally. A few have Family Court custody or parenting-time battles," Rabbit explained. "Regardless, there were problems between the adults, relating specifically to children in the home."

Dr. Towers frowned. "That is interesting, because it means, for the most part, there are some, although minimal, open court records anyone can review."

"The Protective Services or DHS records are, for the most part, confidential. Judges in both states signed orders. Profilers and police detectives have compared the confidential records. There's little doubt," Abel added. "This perp has a notion of being their protector."

"So, the Double Cross Killer commits one homicide at a time? Why not kill all the adults in the household?" Dr. Towers asked.

Rabbit nodded. "Perp targets the one viewed as harming the child."

"How does he obtain this kind of information from two states? That is a lot of work and visibility unless he has those kinds of contacts or special access." Dr. Towers frowned. "Seems he is a bit of a magician."

"Right. That presumes he's getting his information from court records. There must be other sources. Simpler methods, even being a good listener," David said.

Rabbit looked through the circle he'd made with his fingers. "Passengers speak loudly on planes without realizing it, and pilots often greet passengers as they board or deplane."

Jaq cocked her head to the side. "If a pilot saw or heard something undesirable, it wouldn't take much to figure out who the passenger was and from there, where they lived. Pilots have access to records, or at least to the people who maintain the records."

"Getting personal information would take bribes and breaking federal law—someone inside the airlines would know something and—" Rabbit clicked into the Internet on his cell. "We don't have time to interview and subpoena everyone in there—but a pilot could manipulate things to grab a carry-on luggage tag, especially of someone visiting the cockpit."

"Dead end from the start regardless because anyone who talks will likely lose their job." Jaq huffed. "Even if we offer immunity."

Dr. Towers' sigh landed on Rita as he spoke. "Not all, but many victims had other adults in the household. How does the Double Cross Killer decide which adult to kill to protect the child?"

Rabbit pulsed his fingers off one another. "That is a curiosity."

David shook his head. "Not that odd. We have two families where the children wrote letters to Santa asking for help. Then poof, the so-called bad parent's dead."

"God, Santa, plagues, the military, pilots—sounds more like a list for a scavenger hunt." Rabbit wrinkled his forehead, tapped his fingers together, paused and peeked through them. "The post office—isn't that where Santa letters go to die?"

Rita remained silent, entangled between detectives and her reel of conversations with Nick. Nick's words reverberated so loud she unconsciously blurted them. "It's like Bernard Shaw said: the question of who are the best people to take charge of children is a very difficult one, but it's quite certain that the parents are the very worst."

All eyes upon Rita, the conversation stopped.

"That's exactly right." Rabbit's voice was soft, but firm. His fingers held their circle while he shifted toward Rita. "Perfect summation of an angle the profilers have of the Double Cross Killer. What made you think of Shaw?"

Rita bit her lip, shocked she'd said it out loud. "Just struck me. I—we— Nick and I, had a conversation after reading the paper one morning about crime and murders—leaving children without parents. Nick's quote—it impressed me. Fit our conversation perfectly."

Dr. Towers explored the faces in his crowded, silent office, and then stood. "It has been a very long day, now almost evening. I promised my wife a lovely New Year's Day dinner. I am leaving. As to you, ladies and gentlemen, we are concluded for the first day of the year. Happy New Year to all of you."

"Can I just say two things before you leave?" Rita again wrapped her arms around her stomach against the rising queasiness.

Dr. Towers stood still. Ten expectant eyes aimed toward Rita.

"I love and trust Nick." Rita fluttered her lashes. "But, you should know, his brother Chris, works for the post office."

# Chapter Thirty

JAQ TOSSED HER CRUMPLED AMERICAN Coney Dog wrapper in the corner basket of the conference room. She was panicked. Already January 2, and reflecting on New Year's Day spent with Dr. Towers and Rita, she was underwhelmed with their progress, their time had been underproductive, they were still under scrutiny while time ticked away and bodies kept appearing. Locked in the conference room with the other detectives for the evening felt wrong with a killer on the loose, ready to strike. Jaq was frustrated they weren't cruising neighborhoods, personally following Rita and Nick. The weekend would be long and unsafe for her friend. Jaq's training was useless if she couldn't protect and defend Rita. She was terrified the demand for increased surveillance wouldn't be in place in time.

The course was set—an undercover detective CSI tech was assigned to work with Dr. Towers and Rita for additional undercover protection, and, thanks to her, they were also investigating not only Nick, but his brother Chris.

Nick Archer's honorable discharge from the military prompted David and Abel to join forces in negotiating with local FBI and Department of Defense Homeland Security personnel to persuade Delta to allow a military undercover pilot to be Nick's new copilot.

"No surprise the rosaries could have been connected to the military during a time Nick Archer was active and deployed with a Michigan unit," Jaq said. "We should've tagged that sooner."

"Easy to second-guess it. Wasn't obvious." Rabbit pushed his wrappers to the center of the table and pulled files toward him. "We have to forage through each detail to untangle this and stop him with a conviction that sticks."

"Military is taking too long preparing the names of units who had the rosaries," Jaq said. "It's frustrating—all we want to know is Archer's unit."

Rabbit nodded. "It gets more frustrating. The military didn't keep an accurate list—it was a family support project and a disposable item. I found a chaplain to assist—brigade chaplains were unit distribution points."

"So, if a large batch went missing—" Jaq began.

"It might be remembered." Rabbit clasped his hands together. "Long shot, worth the effort."

"Search warrant for Nick's home, car, locker needs to be prepared." Jaq clicked her pen end several times, then stuck it in her ponytail. "Sarasota condo, too."

"Bennie ran a check. No military connections between the victims," Rabbit said. "The rosaries fit with what Rita told us and the profilers' analysis. The plague theory fits in a weird twisted old-world meets modern world interpretive sort of way. On God's mission. Children's savior. Wants the world to change, one family at a time."

"And, the imprint of the cross on the throat—his way of blessing them?" Jaq squinted her eyes.

Rabbit shook his head. "No. He's telling everyone that these life-takings are by His direct action—remember in the bible the plagues are divided between Moses and God."

Jaq wrinkled her face. "So, he wants us to know these were done by His hand—meaning he equates himself with God."

"Best I got—the last murder, leaving dead fish, was almost like a scene from The Godfather." Rabbit stopped, plucked out his cell phone and punched in a few buttons. "The Catholic Encyclopedia talks about the first plague turning water into blood so the Egyptians couldn't drink it."

"Yeah?" Jaq stood and grabbed a marker, then wove her way to the boards.

Rabbit grinned. "Says, even the fishes died."

Jaq made that notation on the combined wall map and stepped back. "It's complete. Every homicide in Michigan by location and date tagged by orange flag. Same for Sarasota tagged by yellow flag. Archer's flight schedule tagged by hot pink flag—perfectly in sync. Not every victim's family travelled between Detroit and Sarasota—but over half that we've identified so far did."

David gathered his dinner remnants and tossed them in the wastebasket. He ran his fingers along the bottom of the wall map. "Great visual of how the homicides and evidence merge."

"Bueno." Abel wiped his mouth and fingers on a napkin, then tossed it aside, leapt to his feet, and twirled Jaq around. "Defense attorney's nightmare. Solid evidence—circumstantial anyway." He twirled back to the table and grabbed another Coney dog, followed by another, washing them down with gurgling sounds of root beer.

Rabbit cleared his throat, then focused on Jaq. "One more set of markers we need to add, and, it's your job to get the information."

"Sounds daunting."

"Meet with Rita. Get her personal and work schedule since she met this Archer character. Find out where she was the night of every murder, by time frame." Rabbit paused. He walked up, then back, studying the evidence wall. "I mean by the hour, half hour—every fifteen minutes if you can do it."

"She's not an accomplice—" Jaq's mouth gaped open. It was apparent she was searching for the next words.

"Suspect, no. Alibi." Rabbit stood and looked through his lens hands, moving it slowly on the boards. "Nick knows Rita perfectly, predictably. You described her, for months as notorious because of her former fiancé. She was in the newspaper—became a bit of an unwanted celebrity because her fiancé framed her for driving drunk, causing death." He paused on the map. "He learns her routine before they meet. Dating her now, he slips in and out of her home when she's unaware—she's an easy alibi."

"Sleeping." Jaq gasped. "Because we know and trust her—we believed in her before, we would again."

Rabbit pulled his hands apart and clapped. "Exactly."

David threw his arms up. "Touchdown theory."

Rabbit paced. "Save the praise till this devil-in-a-pilot's disguise is in custody."

"His brother could be an accomplice," David said.

"Maybe an accidental accomplice. Rita never mentioned much about the family except he has a mother and brother and both seem very private." Jaq bit her lip and considered the wall clock. "I'm nervous about Rita. We've been truthful, but not exactly clear with her. We need to get her away from Nick until we apprehend or clear him."

"Don't let your friendship compromise our investigation and arrest of Archer." David locked eyes with Jaq while Rabbit nodded in agreement. "At this point we can't do much more for her until we have hard evidence."

Jaq crossed her arms with a sour face. "I can and will pull her out of there—we can put her in protective custody."

Rabbit nodded, holding his hand up. "I can't shake a conversation I had with her."

"When?" Jaq asked.

"When we brought the dog in, I had a real sense she knew something, maybe suspected something."

Abel frowned. "Si? Another hunch?"

"No. She asked a lot of questions about the dog, hesitated at odd places, maybe withholding information, trying to figure something out."

David flipped through a stack of evidence photos. "Could be she's a dog lover."

Jaq nodded. "She's sensitive that way."

"That's not it," Rabbit said. "And the clincher was that biblical quote she recited from her fiancé. Fits the profiling perfectly. I still have goose bumps from the words, the essence of their meaning."

"We all felt it." David pulled out a close-up of the dog. They joined in nods.

Jaq sighed at David and Abel, then met Rabbit's gaze. "I know we haven't known each other long, but I trust you when you say something's not right. Even with the GPS pager and the extra detail assigned to Rita, we need to take our own shifts following her and the fiancé."

David nodded. "We'll pair up. If they separate, so will we."

"Sounds like a plan," Rabbit said.

Everyone agreed but Jaq still couldn't shake the panic. This was her friend. It was personal. "Thanks," was all she could utter before she read the text messages on her cell.

"What is it?" David asked.

"Two texts. Chief and Doc." Jaq felt queasy. "We're needed ASAP with Recon, not to talk to anyone, not the media and not Rita Rose."

"Say why?" David asked.

"Nope," Jaq said. "I've got a sick feeling—"

"We'll be happy we've already eaten." Abel grinned, stretched, rubbed his stomach and belched. He wiped the mustard from his face, collected the last of the trash, tossed it, then donned his jacket with the rest of them.

\* \* \* \*

Recon heeled awaiting David's command. They crossed the yellow crime-scene tape which with emergency and CSI vehicles had blocked in the area parade-style.

Abel observed the full view before marching forward. "This is different from the Double Cross Killer-Communicator crime scenes. No house, just a vehicle in a ditch."

Chief Hanusack walked toward them in the darkness with an outstretched hand. "Happy New Year. Nice to meet you again."

Abel and Rabbit nodded, the men shook hands. Rabbit was both distracted and direct. "Are we assisting on a different case?"

"Unlikely. CSI photographers and footprint experts are finishing. Dr. Towers was paged in by a photographer who recognized similarities to the Double Cross Killer homicides." Chief stepped forward. "Doc's supervision of the removal of this victim could be critical."

"And you were called in as well." Jaq wrinkled her forehead.

"Not for the obvious reasons." Chief took a few more steps.

"Copycat?" Rabbit squinted one eye at the Chief.

"Could be—I doubt it." Chief Hanusack extended his arm and motioned them forward. "See for yourself."

Harness in hand, David nodded toward his side. "Ready for Recon?"

"After you see the victim." Chief Hanusack pointed a sharp finger at Jaq. "You'll be most interested."

Jaq skirted ahead to the vehicle, pressing past the investigators. She felt their eyes as she bent into the vehicle and studied the victim.

"Fazul?" Jaq stepped back, motioned David in, and then the others. "Rita. We have to get to her."

"I was afraid you were going to say that." Dr. Towers rubbed his forehead. "I haven't heard from her since she left work. She was so pale, I offered to drive her home. She declined."

"Doc, cause of death?" David asked.

"Homicide."

"Double Cross Killer-cide is the real question?" David asked.

"Yes—from my preliminary review. Same markings. I need to complete the autopsy."

"But how does Zeke Fazul fit into this?" Jaq watched the team begin to remove Fazul. David scribbled notes and Recon padded about the area.

"Remind us, exactly who is Zeke Fazul?" Rabbit interrupted.

"Former Doctor Zeke Fazul, former fiancé of Rita Rose, who set her up to take the fall on vehicular homicide charges." Jaq turned to the Chief. "And still in prison?"

"Good behavior, early release. Paroled." Chief Hanusack shrugged.

"I'm surprised Rita didn't mention it. Parole Board's required to send notice." Jaq snapped the gloves off and stepped back. "She mentioned nothing to me. If she knew, I'm certain she would've." She swallowed hard, then turned to Dr. Towers. "Any idea of time of death?"

Dr. Towers put up a stop-sign hand. "Rita did not do this. I will vouch for her. No worry there. Time of death approximately four to six hours ago. I cannot present a narrower time range until autopsy, but we were all together during that time."

"I—we're not suspecting Rita." Jaq twisted around at the others who stayed silent on the issue. "She couldn't—"

Rabbit was looking at the scene through his finger lens. "As I said, his alibi makes sense, killer too much of a stretch—"

Jaq interrupted. "You don't know her like I—"

Dr. Towers interrupted. "We—"

Jaq nodded. "Right, like we know her. Rita couldn't harm anyone."

"Agreed." Rabbit tilted his head awkwardly. "Archer has access to her mail. Rita never saw the Department of Corrections letter because he intercepted it by plan."

Jaq met Dr. Towers' eyes with matched fear. "Doc, can you get to the preliminaries right away? Confirm copycat or Double Cross Killer?" Jaq bent toward the others and motioned David and Recon over. "We need to step up surveillance."

"Recon found footprints. Similar to the smaller size we have sets of." David commanded Recon to sit next to him. "Footprint guys already cast and will match."

"One more thing," Dr. Towers said. "Obvious alcohol bottles."

"Roger that. And?" David asked.

"Victim has a rosary stuffed inside his mouth."

"Fazul was in the military." Jaq paused and reflected. "I recall a dishonorable discharge based on what he did to Rita, and of course having a felony record. But before that, he was putting in his time because the military paid for part of his education—served in Afghanistan."

"I'm betting Archer and Fazul served together," Rabbit said. "Rita Rose is our connector."

Jaq shook her head. "She has no connection whatsoever to the victims—"

"Until now." Rabbit's fingers were rapidly bouncing off each other. "That makes her critical to the investigation and changes the playing field."

David nodded. "Doc, can you call her in early in the morning and keep her occupied without giving her Double Cross Killer matters to work on?"

Doc rubbed his temples, his fear clear. "Yes. Rita has been on call for thirty days including the whole Christmas and New Year's holiday and this upcoming weekend. She returns, like most of the world, Monday, January 5."

Recon's growling silenced everyone on scene. David pulled at the harness, then patted her head and rubbed her neck and back. "What's up, girl? Are you suddenly spooked?" David followed the dog's stare. Her body became rigid and her barking increasingly fierce.

"Police Officer. Stand back," David shouted in the darkness. The world was silent. "Stand clear." David's orders followed. He held Recon and spoke to her in a low calming voice. "Good Girl." He rubbed her head. Recon calmed immediately.

Everyone on scene safely backed away. David and Recon pushed cautiously forward. David cocked his weapon and aimed it ahead of them. Hearing what sounded like air coming out of the tires, he finally exposed the sound. "Jaq, radio Animal Control. Looks like we have a nest of snakes."

"Snakes? That is not random winter find," Jaq said. She gulped. "Our killer is watching us. This has to be a message."

"We've worked hundreds of cases," David said. "Any angry perp could have left the snakes."

"No case like this." Jaq extended her forearm. She had goose bumps and her arm hair was elevated. "I feel it to my core."

"She's got that sixth sense, like Recon," Rabbit said. "I agree with them."

"Well, if she starts barking, we might have to search for caffeinated kibble," David said. His tone was light but his expression darkened as they watched Jaq call Animal Control.

# Chapter Thirty-one

EVEN AFTER A LOVELY CHRISTMAS and New Year's, Rita awoke Friday torn. She was on shaky ground about Nick. She'd been fooled by one fiancé and vowed to never again feel like the punchline to a joke—by being publicly or privately humiliated.

She trembled, but stood stalwart. Nick was promised to his mother for brunch, and with Rita not feeling well, she was thankfully able to decline. She stepped into her bathroom, slipped off her nightgown and tied on her terry robe. Her agenda was a search for answers—assurance she wasn't crazy—or living with a murdering maniac—then a shower.

There was no middle ground and no turning back. Time for her own investigation, it was her home after all. A chill rippled across her scalp.

She desperately needed to believe the collie was coincidence, even as her nagging gut knew it couldn't be. There was no one to tell, at least not right now. She feared Nick's response as much as Dr. Towers' and the detectives', even Jaq, who always supported her. Investigating on her own was her only solution, and her feet carried her plan forward. Her life, in so many ways, was on the line.

She stared at the pair of his and hers hampers. A guilty twinge cut through her. With defiance, she opened the forbidden his lid and found it empty. In hope of an error, she dumped her hamper out and sifted through the clothes. Without surprise, she returned the clothes. They all belonged to her.

She sat in the middle of the bathroom floor pondering. What exactly was she looking for? His outfit was dark, but the white lining had been blood-covered. Logic dictated one of two things: soaking them to get the blood out or discarding them. Nick would discard them. He liked new, fresh clothing. He discarded anything old, tattered, or stained. He was meticulous about the way he looked, what he wore. He kept identical sets of new jogging suits so he could replace the whole set or any one piece at any time.

Rita stood up and retied her robe. What would Nick have done with the clothes? The garbage. Checking every bin, she was not surprised to find each one empty. Nick emptied the trash every morning before he left, tossing the garbage down the chute next to the elevator. She always appreciated this gesture—until now, she decided, entering the bedroom closet.

It was time to go through his clothing. Unwavering in her determination, she reached into each jacket and pants pocket. Clean. Not so much as a fleck of lint, stick of gum, or a coin. She eyed his shoes, perfectly lined up, spit-shined and polished. His running shoes, brand new and unlaced. He changed pairs like washing socks. She pictured Nick tossing the box in the recycle bin in Florida. The last two pairs were purchased on their last trip to Sarasota. Was the other in his workout bag?

Rita scrutinized the perfectly lined clothes on his side of the walk-in closet, careful to note exactly how far away from each other his clothes hung, then pushed an entry way through the clothes. Nick hated wrinkles, barely allowing his clothes to touch as they hung—unlike her jammed closet side. She didn't realize he'd brought so many personal items into her space so quickly. When did all this happen in what—a five-week relationship? She began to breathe heavily.

Invigoration and adrenaline stepped up the scared side of her and pushed her forward. She ducked under and in between the clothes. She crept her hands along the wall, under the shelf above the clothes bar. There was nothing hidden or out of the ordinary. *What am I looking for, anyway?* Rita muttered over and over. She adjusted the ill-fitting access door that led to the shower plumbing in the adjoining bathroom. What a stupid place to put an access door. She frowned and made a mental note to again demand the maintenance man make an adjustment. She'd be upset if a sleeve or a dress hem got caught in that sloppiness. She'd ask for a knob to pull it forward into place for a tighter fit, she decided, tired of it falling off the wall. Realigning Nick's clothes, she marveled at his crisp uniforms and absolute organizational skills.

Stirring toward the two dresser drawers she'd given him, she opened them one at a time. Careful to leave everything perfectly intact and in position, she held her breath. Fingers, shaking, they crept throughout without trace of their prowl. Nothing. Her breathing returned to normal. Relief.

Rita returned to the bathroom, untied her robe, and tossed it on the hook. She paused at the shower door before stepping in, recalling vividly

Nick's bloodied jogging suit piled there. Closing her eyes, she focused on exactly what she had seen. There were no holes, rips, tearing of any kind on his clothing, only blood, but she hadn't seen the clothing up close, and it was black. Would she have seen any fabric shredding? She didn't recall shoes. She opened her eyes and stepped into the warm shower.

She closed her eyes into the mist. Bandages, antiseptic, and cotton balls. He would've used those things. Blood could've gotten on any washcloths or towels, even his robe, but the apartment was blood free. No missing towels or bandages. Going through garbage was the last thing she wanted to do. She wished she could borrow Recon.

Hot water pounded against her while questions wove their way alongside facts she knew. Had he been drugging her, then leaving to kill? Was she his alibi? She would have to testify that as far as she knew he was in her bed—except for jogging. Was that enough time to kill? Was he marrying her so she couldn't testify against her husband—was that a rule, or did that only exist on television?

What had she actually seen? Bloodied clothing—likely meaningless in the grand scheme of things. He had an explanation: attacked by a scared puppy. He regularly changed running shoes. So do good athletes.

Nothing out of the ordinary or unexplained.

Nick simply couldn't be the murderer. He loved her. She was letting her mind wander too far. "Wake up," she yelled at herself. She twirled around under the thrust of the hot, then twisted the knob and shocked her system with cold water. *How's that for a reality check?* Rita laughed, shut off the water, toweled-up her hair and stood in the silence with closed eyes.

At times controlling, Nick was always kind. If something were wrong she would feel it, wouldn't she? In that instant, she knew—why doubt what she knew. Fact: he drugged her. She was sure of it. He left while she slept. She was the alibi. She was the alibi for a murderer. Time to listen. She twisted the nozzle as hot as she could stand it and let it pour over her back and shoulders, then her heart, until she felt light-headed from the sheer heat.

Finally, out of the shower she slipped into her terry-robe. No more worries. Nick would be stopped. If he wasn't the Double Cross Killer, the system would work, like it had for her.

"Hey, Angel-teeny." Nick blasted into the bedroom like fireworks below an avalanche. "You are feeling better. I called a few times—you didn't pick up. Got worried you took a turn for the worse—so I left early—here you are all warm and cozy for me."

"Couldn't hear the ring over the shower water." Rita let her robe hang open on her moist flesh. "I'm glad you are home, in my arms."

Nick sauntered toward her. He pushed off the towel on her head and the robe with one hard jerk, then loosened his shirt. "We're happy to hear that."

\* \* \* \*

Startled by eerie darkness and the acute dryness in her throat when she awoke, Rita swallowed hard. She peered through the inky room. Just as she opened her mouth to call out to Nick, a dark figure at the foot of the bed moved.

Rita gasped. It felt like a cheese grater was in her throat.

The figure was silent.

The pounding in Rita's ears was so loud she doubted she could hear if he did speak. Her eyes focused. She realized the shadow was Nick. Why was he just standing there? Could he know she suspected him? She wanted to scream, dial 9-1-1. She needed to bluff. *Be strong, Rita. You're smart.*

The whites of his eyes shone toward her in the dim light.

She breathed faster, too loudly. She struggled to maintain control, but a cold sweat covered her.

Nick still didn't speak.

Rita exhaled. She had to follow his every move. She made her voice sensual. "You scared me, Nick. What on earth are you doing staring at me in the dark?" Her voice was a rumbling melody. She was a siren. "Come back to bed. It's cold in here without you."

"I'm watching my lovely girl. You were tossing in your sleep, mumbling. Woke me up."

Rita cocked her head. Could she do come-hither in a pitch-black room? To a pair of eye whites? "I'm sorry, my love. I remember nothing. What did I mumble?"

"Not one sensible word." Nick's voice was monotone.

"Sorry I woke you—in one way." Rita rested herself on her elbows and rolled slightly toward him. "We're both awake—" She patted his side of the bed.

He didn't move.

*He needs to be in control. He won't come because I want him.* She rolled back and covered herself. "I'm actually feeling dizzy, and my throat's so dry—it's sore. I need sleep." She closed her eyes.

"Can't have you ill. You don't look right. Let me get you some water with whatever cold magic you say—you're the nurse."

Rita nodded. "Excedrin. Headache throbbing." And she did feel ill—mostly terrified. She heard him step toward the bathroom; she read the clock—three thirty-seven. They'd had a few hours of sleep. No wonder she felt ill. It was too early to be awake. She'd only consumed what she'd prepared when he arrived home. Was she influenced by the suggestion she was ill or was she actually ill?

She didn't remember falling asleep—she hadn't intended to sleep, but after a few rounds of sex, a moonlight cheese-and-mushroom omelet she'd made, they must have both fallen asleep. Could he have dosed her? Damn it, her throat was parched, why didn't she know the difference between illness and being poisoned via drugs? *I'm a nurse, damn it; think back to training, pharmacology…*

"Take these. Then, I'll join you to ensure you're warm." In the darkness Nick handed her a bottle of cold water and two pills.

Rita nodded, palming the pills. "What'd you find?"

"Excedrin, as ordered."

"I have a scratchy throat, headache, no fever. I hope I'm just tired, not ill."

"Wishful thinking. I didn't find a thermometer or I'd take your temperature." Nick placed a hand on her forehead. "Anytime you need different meds, I can go to the pharmacy."

"Sleep."

"In the morning, call one of those fancy doctors you work with and get a prescription."

Rita put her hand to her mouth, chugged down half the water bottle, then handed the bottle to Nick. "Thanks." She curled on her side to sleep.

Nick kissed her forehead, then arched back over to place the water bottle on his nightstand. Rita dropped her hand and slipped the pills between the mattresses. She wasn't sure what they were, but they were not shaped like her Excedrin. She'd taken that bottle into work and hadn't replaced it. She'd take these pills to work and ask Doc what they are.

"That's my girl." Nick slid his bare body next to Rita's, spooning their bodies into one.

"Mmm." Rita felt Nick's warmth against her. She clasped her hands around his. She prayed morning and the safety of the light would come quickly.

"I'll hold you while you fall asleep," he whispered in the darkness, softly stroking her hair.

* * * *

Her own coughing awoke Rita to an empty bed. Reaching to her nightstand for the water bottle, she remembered giving it to Nick. She sat up to reach over him and discovered him missing. She grabbed the bottle, chugged it, then deposited it into the basket alongside her bed. Her throat was swollen. She was ill. Stress-induced. She pressed her fingers to her neck and found enlarged glands.

Across the room the halo from the bathroom nightlight allowed her to see the open bathroom door. She rolled toward the alarm clock face, almost five o'clock. Nick's disappearing act was more than a bad habit. It had always been there, she wasn't wrong. Too dark to jog. He'd promised, after the puppy incident, he'd wait till sunrise. Jaq needed to know—what would she say—*hey Jaq, I can't choose a decent man, but I solved the case...* It was Saturday, they were meeting for eight o'clock yoga. She grabbed her cell, sent a text to Jaq, placed the cell in the nightstand drawer and tossed a pillow over her throbbing head.

* * * *

Jaq paced the unmarked car slowly. It wasn't hard to keep Nick in sight. Rabbit in night vision goggles looked like a perched Halloween mannequin. They studied each jogged step.

Rabbit spoke through gritted teeth. "Backup's outside Rita's building. I texted David and Abel our location and that we're cruising."

"He's one cool number. Jogging like he doesn't have a care in the world," Jaq said.

"He doesn't. Thinks he's immune to getting caught." Rabbit pointed a finger. "Taking a shortcut through the alley."

"I'll go around the corner, catch up with him on the other side. If we follow behind him, he'll see us," Jaq said. "Not easy to track someone on foot in Detroit. Alleyways, unlit streets, broken street lights, make it difficult."

Jaq manipulated the corner and approached the opposite end of the alley. Rabbit changed positions for a wider view. "Damn. Lost him, even these night vision goggles don't show anything moving in the shadows."

"What'd he do, catch a flight on Wonder Woman's invisible plane?" Jaq griped, nodded, and picked up the car radio. "I can't handle another corpse announcing our defeat. Gotta find him."

"Sometimes a jog is just a jog." Rabbit's voice was calm. He didn't move the goggles from his eyes as Jaq drove. "On the other hand, when it comes to naughty children and criminals, nothing means something." The last three words ended in song.

"Is that a southern saying?" Jaq teased Rabbit, thankful he made her feel better.

"He's military-trained. He plans, never acts on impulse. He jogs, surveys, even takes inventory, figures a precise striking time. Likely carries a stopwatch, times everything perfectly: gets in and out, no witnesses. Rita's his faithful naive alibi."

Jaq huffed. "Like right now while she's sleeping."

"She's credible. When questioned, she'll respond to law enforcement, any judge, under oath, he was home with her all night. We can't prove otherwise."

"Until now." Jaq picked up her buzzing cell. *I pray this isn't Hanusack.* She released a deep sigh. "Text from Rita. She's ill, can't make yoga. I'm texting back announcing my arrival at her door with medicine."

"And if he's there?"

"I'll deal with that then. The three of you have a wide net ready to drop. We'll be fine. I want to get her out of there."

"I don't like it." Rabbit shook his head. "David'll fire me when he hears you changed the operation."

"I'm not Miss Muffet. I don't sit and wait when I know my friend is in trouble. You three will cover me."

Rabbit grumbled, still scanning the area. "Follow the crumbs back and we may find him. Order extra undercover officers to monitor this area. Where he jogs is the next victim."

"I'll call in the request after I pull over. If you're right, he'll jog past here." Jaq knew patience prevailed despite its frustration and while following police procedure and logic was important, waiting was challenging.

"A new stiff is due any day and—" Rabbit pulled down the goggles and faced Jaq. "My odds say it's Rita. This jog is too close to home."

"Not happening." Jaq pounded a fist into the dashboard.

Rabbit covered his eyes with the goggles. He became distracted between looking out into the darkness and at his watch. "Over there. He's headed back." He pointed. "We can move behind without detection. He's headed home."

"Will do," Jaq said. Her knuckles ached but the pain surged a power switch inside her.

"Based on the time and distance he's been jogging, his prey is within two miles—still betting it's Rita and this route is simply camouflage."

"Look how smoothly he glides into the building. Stays in the shadows, creeps inside doorways, away from direct light sources." Jaq pulled the vehicle over and snapped off the lights. "The whole jog he was hardly visible, unless you know to look."

"Cat eyes." Rabbit lifted the night vision goggles and stared across the parking lot at the tall, dark figure entering the apartment building.

\* \* \* \*

Rita woke again, her sinus cavity now filled to match her swollen neck glands. A chill gripped her, but not from the onset of the illness settling inside her; the chill that pulled through her was from Nick. His flesh was as chilled as the shivers from the fever charging through her. Goose bumps, questions and realization taunted her into calm fear. *What would happen first, a page calling her into work or reading another headline?*

She trembled, rolled to the edge of the bed, and then held her breath hoping she hadn't disturbed him. Sleep would bring healing and clarity; morning was almost here.

\* \* \* \*

"Wake up, sleepy-head," Nick said. "Feeling better?"

Rita opened one eye, then the other. "Mmm. Not great. I had a terrible night. You're right, I have a fever, or else we have some incredibly warm blankets."

"Perhaps the two of us together are combustible?" Nick reached under her sheer nightgown and playfully tweaked her nipple.

"Always." Rita tried to smile. "I'm tired. I kept waking up."

Nick's brow furrowed. He rolled onto her and placed his nose almost touching hers. "What do you mean you kept waking up? You should have slept through." He paused. "After the Excedrin, your body should've felt better, relaxed into sleep."

"Chills. Night sweats. In and out of weird dreams."

"That's the fever."

"I wanted you to keep me warm, but I couldn't find you."

"You were dreaming. I was right here next to you all night." Nick kissed her. "It's cute, you worrying about me leaving you. You know I'll never leave you, Angel-teeny, don't you?"

Rita gave him a half-smile and nodded at him. "You're right, as always. Thank you for taking such good care of me."

"First, I like taking care of you. Promise. Second, I'm going to make you hot tea with honey and a good breakfast. Stay in bed, sleep off that fever." Nick rolled off her.

"Are you going for a jog?"

"Why do you ask?"

"I can shower and get ready while you jog. I'll nap while you shower."

"You plan too much." Nick flashed a grin, then widened it to show full perfect teeth. He slipped on his robe. "Relax. Stay in bed. We're spending the whole day together without distraction—no work, no jogging. Take the time to be sick."

"Thank you. What would I do without you?" Rita sat back and watched Nick turn into the bathroom. Carefully, her fingers fished out the pills she'd tucked between the mattresses. They looked like aspirin, she thought, turning them over. But they had different markings and were larger than any brand she knew. Reaching for the purse she'd tossed on the other side of the nightstand, she slipped them into the small hole in the lining that needed repair. Surely, Dr. Towers or a pharmacist would know. She bit her lower lip. This could explain a lot.

Half an hour later, smelling bacon, eggs, and toast—but mostly because of the aroma of coffee—Rita put on warmer pajamas, cleaned up, and headed to the kitchen. "Can I help?"

Nick frowned. "Back to bed."

"I can't sleep."

"I'm surprised you smell anything with that congestion. You were supposed to stay in bed and wait for delivery. Are you feeling better?"

Rita's nerves were getting the best of her. A queasy stomach and a head-cold, the flu? "A little."

"Good. Take something else and some vitamins."

"Excedrin, maybe?" She scrutinized Nick closely as he poured two mugs of coffee. Rita motioned Nick to sit next to her. "What did you give me last night?"

Nick clapped his hands together, then folded them. "Check your cabinet. I don't recall the brand. Mom always gave us plain aspirin. Nothing fancy needed, just something for aches, pains, and fever." Nick placed a stack of toast, a jar of jam, and a dish of butter in front of her. She reached for a slice.

"Thanks, I'll check."

"Why the interest, Angel-teeny?" Nick passed her a platter of eggs and bacon, then sat on the stool next to her.

"I can't ever buy that brand again."

He placed his elbows on the table and matter-of-factly clasped his hands. "You're the nurse: Excedrin, aspirin, Tylenol, for what you have, brand is irrelevant. Eat."

Rita buttered her toast. "Sometimes I don't sleep well when I take cold tablets, like last night." She ripped off an edge of toast, dunked it in her coffee and let it melt in her mouth. "Just curious." She picked up the remaining toast, with a bite of egg. She waited. Bait.

Nick stared across expressionless.

A chill of venom spiked through her.

"I'm just an old-fashioned guy who gave you an old-fashioned remedy. Anything wrong with that?"

*I need to stay alive to figure you out.* "Not one thing." Rita leaned closer into him and kissed him.

"Don't fall off the stool and break something." Nick steadied her shoulder. "We don't need to spend our day in the emergency room. You have too many headaches, now you're sick. Ask a doctor to write you stronger meds or stick to real exercise, like I've said."

Rita nodded. "Did you get the newspaper?"

Nick reached over and grabbed the still-rolled paper. He removed the plastic and the rubber band, kept the first section, handed her the Local section, and tossed the remainder. "Good thing we're getting married."

"Why do you say that?"

"Reading the paper instead of talking over breakfast. It's very married." Nick snapped his section open.

Rita laughed. "I'm going to make hot chocolate." She stood, and minutes later returned with a marshmallow-topped mug. "Anything interesting in your section?" She opened the Local section and began to read, waiting for the cocoa to cool.

"Drink your cocoa." Nick retained full attention on the headlines.

Rita squinted her eyes at the back of the paper as if she had x-ray vision. "What's so interesting?"

He breathed out a loud huff. "Detectives have a lead on the serial murders you're so interested in."

Despite hearing his annoyance, she ventured. "Who?"

"Doesn't say. Another victim, his dog, and bloody clues—DNA—this time."

"Really? Please toss it to me when you're finished." Old news to her; his reaction, fascinating news. Intimate then clinical, psychopath pattern. Time to shed him.

"Doesn't say much else. Just forget it. You know how you get. Nothing to be afraid of. Promise. I'll protect you, Angel-teeny." Nick pointed to the seat beside him. "Sit down. You're very pale."

She nodded. "Okay."

"I'll always protect you, as God expects." Their eyes met as she sat. "Husbands, in the same way be considerate as you live with your wives, and treat them with respect as the weaker partner and as heirs with you of the gracious gift if life, so that nothing will hinder your prayers."

Rita shrugged. "I bet the killer's victims had someone who was their protector, too. But everyone has to live their life—no matter how close they are." *I need protection from you.*

"Your point?"

"We work. You can't be with me every minute."

"Some people aren't worth protecting. They are bad people." Nick pointed at her. The last few words were drawn and deep. "Truly bad people never change."

Rita's heart pounded inside her head, she feared hyperventilation was near. "You really believe that?" She gulped, then plunged forward. "An innocent animal was also murdered." There, now she'd done it, dared herself to challenge him into giving her information, maybe insight. She drew in a breath.

Nick ignored her and returned to the paper. His voice was bland, she was dismissed. "Animals aren't people. Sometimes they simply get in the way."

Rita pressed. "What kind of dog was it?"

He didn't look up at her. "What?"

"The dog. Does it say what kind of dog—just curious."

Nick crunched the paper down. "Are you suddenly a dog lover? Your empathy is admirable, a dog's a dog." He lifted the paper, turned the page and added softly, "Collie. Dogs, they're all the same. I'll protect you, as I'm directed to do. Promise."

Promise was amplified and surged through her.

Rita contemplated Nick's reaction to collie. She noticed he didn't look back at the article to read the type of dog, in fact, he'd already turned the page. She hid the tremble in her body by gathering dishes, laying them in the sink and prepping them for the dishwasher.

"Back to bed." Nick ordered. "You're shaking." He put his hand on her forehead. "Fever. I'll get aspirin. It's eight thirty. I'll wake you for lunch."

# Chapter Thirty-two

"**I**S JAQ ON HER WAY?" Dr. Towers faced the three male detectives, then ushered them into his conference room, took his seat at the head of the table, and extended his hand toward the center. "Fresh coffee, rolls—courtesy of my wife. Help yourself. Least I could do after texting you to be here at nine on a Saturday morning."

"Been on duty for hours—a welcome change, Doc. Rabbit dropped Jaq off at Rita's. Hoping to pick them both up when we're finished." David grabbed a roll. "Extra surveillance teams are watching Nick and the neighborhood."

Rabbit scratched his head, then rubbed his neck. "Good news, Bennie locked in the Archer-Fazul connection." Anxiety spread as pens clicked, knuckles cracked, and mugs sat.

Doc peered over his bifocals at Rabbit and leaned in. Rabbit cleared his throat and clasped his palms together. "The two fiancés knew each other in the military. Then Captain—Dr. Fazul, signed off on part of Lt. Colonel Nick Archer's medical evaluation."

"This relationship is noted in Archer's military records?" David almost gulped his eyeballs. The intersection cut through him with icy alarm.

Rabbit continued. "Soldiers' medical records are regularly reviewed—pilots, more often. Dr. Fazul recommended Archer for a psychological evaluation, and then medical discharge."

"Archer figured he had an axe to grind with Fazul." David cracked his knuckles.

Abel winced. He rubbed his forehead. "Rita ends up with both of them? By chance?"

Rabbit shook his head. "Hand selected her. Archer's records revealed special psychological warfare training with clearances to access of all sorts of special training, toys, confidential military records and information."

"Like doctor records—like the fact that Captain—Dr. Fazul, decided and documented that Archer was crazy enough for discharge," David said.

Rabbit tapped at a paper in front of him with his pointer finger, then pushed it at David who handed it to Dr. Towers. "Archer, a decorated unsung hero, was released honorably, with a bar to reenlistment."

"And the psychological?" Dr. Towers asked.

Rabbit began bouncing his fingers off each other. "Buried. No record found." Rabbit said. "Archer agreed to leave, Brigade Commander said all issues against Fazul were military, barred and closed."

"Archer patiently finds Fazul, sets him up, sits back and waits until a jury finds him guilty. Researches Rita and latches onto her to complete the revenge?" David wanted to rush out, pull Jaq and Rita from the killer's lair, but waited to hear the rest. He shouldered into his chair.

With crinkled eyes, Doc tipped his head to David. "Why would Archer wait for Fazul to go through the long judicial process to do all of this?"

David abruptly jerked forward. "Doc, the profiling suggests that's exactly what he would do—he loves the game."

"Archer kills Fazul anyway. Why not just kill him initially and be done?" Dr. Towers' stare held David. He stood frozen as David contemplated his question.

"Archer must have really fallen for Rita and wanted Fazul completely out of the picture. In his sick mind, he sees himself as her savior too." David rubbed his temples.

"Danger level—elevated—red." Rabbit held up ten fingers.

David cracked his knuckles. "Jaq and Rita are with him." He cracked his knuckles again. "We have to act fast."

"And the victims?" Dr. Towers removed his bifocals and wiped sweat from his brow. "How do they fit into this overall scenario?"

"Working on that—this is the right path." Rabbit flipped his notes. "Bennie's property search shows Archer owns his Siesta Key condo across from the public beach. It's been under surveillance. No new Sarasota serial murders since he's been here."

"Where does his Condo fit into the Sarasota grid?" David asked.

"Ten-mile radius, collectively, of the homicide victims," Rabbit said. "Jogging ten miles is a stroll for him."

David nodded. "Similar to Detroit."

"Yep," Rabbit said. "We'll be able to lock and load this with absolute certainty with the victim airline travel dates and his vacation dates."

Dr. Towers pointed to a stack of files. "I will contribute as well. Thanks to Recon, luminal and DNA. And a rush on the DNA pairing."

"I wager, based on all this, a judge will sign search warrants for anything Captain Nick Archer ever touched." David arched a questioning brow at Dr. Towers. "Doc?"

"I was on the horn with Dr. Milano very early this morning. We exchanged files by PDF, others by fax. We matched some of what you need," Dr. Towers said. "Likely, you know from the print guys, footprints in both cities are different sizes and different brand shoes."

"That makes six different shoe sizes and several different brands of running shoes—cheap to very expensive," David said.

"Si." Abel nodded.

"Even with the inconsistency in the footprints, every expert estimates the same weight, regardless of size." David twisted his watch. "Same intruder."

Rabbit looked through his finger-scope. "Wears his own size, except when he commits a homicide run, then it's any size, but his own."

Dr. Towers pointed to two stacks of reports. "DNA, blood, and toxicology samples are noted in these reports. Dr. Milano and I compared them separately and together. Concluded the same thing. Two of the crime scenes match: the old woman in Sarasota, who tried to fight him off, and the Detroit victim with the collie puppy. Dr. Milano also worked some off-the-record magic and obtained Archer's DNA from the military. Confirmed match." Dr. Towers paused. "Any indication he's a smoker?"

David stiffened. "No. Why?"

"Remember the dog you brought in? No question death occurred on impact. Take a look," Dr. Towers said. He opened a file in front of him and began laying pictures across the table. "Photographs of the skin and skull of the collie. Note the forehead." He paused. "Note these marks." He pointed. Detectives followed his finger. "Burns, consistent with marks from a burning cigarette."

"Burned into the dog after he died?" Rabbit asked.

"Yes. Seven burn marks in the shape of a cross. Five down, one on each side."

"A cross." Rabbit stood and began to pace. "Fits Jaq's religious nut and plague theory as well as the profiler's and our theory of escalation."

"He is getting anxious, desperate to be credited for his work and message—" Dr. Towers sighed, his voice more stern. "Might be his time to surprise or taunt you. Make sure our Rita is protected whatever happens."

Rabbit broke in: "Escalating's an invite for us to make our move. With the dog, he couldn't leave neck-cross bruising, didn't bring an extra silk cross, so he burned it in."

"Si. Serial killers, the more special they think they are, the more the same they are. Not getting caught earned him confidence and makes him sloppy."

The table nodded. "We need to undermine his overconfident ass and pull Rita and Jaq—out now," David said.

Doc clasped his hands. "Do that now, verify all this later—"

Rabbit interrupted, "Jaq has her weapon. She's not afraid to use it. She's protecting Nurse Rose."

"Bennie is faxing over Archer's blood type, height, weight, and shoe size from the military medical records," Dr. Towers said. "I paged Rita to come to work early."

David sat upright and turned toward Doc. "Maybe Rita and Jaq are on their way." He checked his cell. Nothing.

Doc frowned. "Rita called before you arrived and said she wasn't well—flu, fever, had a headache, wanted to stay in bed with the drapes drawn. She declined my offer of a prescription or making an immediate doctor's appointment. She wanted sleep." He paused. "No mention of Jaq."

Rabbit shrugged. "Likely hadn't read the text."

"She looked pale but fine on Thursday." Abel winced. "It's possible she's really ill—are you doubting it?"

Dr. Towers stopped in thought. "I'm concerned her fiancé is dosing her."

"Let's not be too disruptive, cause Archer to suspect. I'll text when I get back there," Rabbit said.

David grabbed his cell phone and followed the mapping, then looked up. "GPS monitoring shows Rita at home—"

"Accessible to a killer—let's cruise," Rabbit finished David's sentence, then stood.

David nodded, then continued, "Doc, please secure all information in a separate file away from Rita. Can't have a potential witness work on it."

"Agreed. And better for Rita to figure out she is living with a sadistic murderer after he is arrested." Dr. Towers closed and stacked the files. "If indeed she has that luxury."

Rabbit's fingertips were nervously pounding each other. "Let's find her an escape hatch—unless Jaq already has."

Icy doses of alarm shrieked inside David. "I want them out, now." He pushed his chair away from the table and stood next to Rabbit.

Abel grabbed a roll for the road. "Gracias."

* * * *

Jaq rang Rita's doorbell. She waited, and then rang again.

Eyebrows raised, Nick opened the door. "Yes?"

Jaq's eyes crinkled as the corners of her mouth stretched up. She extended her free hand. "You must be Nick. I'm Jaq—Rita's yoga buddy. I understand she's quite ill. I'm here with supplies."

Nick grinned, then shook the extended hand. "Ah, the famous Jaq. We finally meet. Can I help you with those bags?"

"Sure." Nick grabbed the bags. Jaq followed him into the condo. She shed her coat, hung it on the coat tree behind the door, then removed her boots. She felt awkward as he stared at her. She arranged her boots, tucking the laces inside them to give her a moment to survey the room. Nothing appeared out of place.

Jaq stood up and grabbed one of the bags from Nick. "How's Rita?"

"Sleeping. I gave her aspirin and sent her to bed. She can't be disturbed."

Jaq leaned in closer to him. "You take great care of her. I can see why she loves you so much. I can stay with her if you need to get out." She neither waited for response or permission. She headed toward the kitchen like she had condo ownership. He tagged behind.

Jaq couldn't see the glower in his face or the crinkles of hatred in the corners of his eyes at her words as he followed her. She instinctively knew they were there because she'd taken control.

With one giant step, he leapt ahead and clicked on the kitchen light.

"Actually, I do have a few things I need to take care of. I'll be back for lunch, please join us." Nick flashed his slow, easy, pool-boy smile.

Jaq tilted her head. "No promises." She unpacked the bags they'd set on the kitchen table. Nick watched her. She placed bottles of Vernors in the refrigerator, a pastry box in the center of the table, and lined up cold relief items.

"Lot of flu going around. Take care." Nick's voice was cool as he exited the kitchen. A few minutes later, he called out. "See you later." And Jaq heard the front door slam.

Geez—the outside looked like a normal boyfriend, Jaq thought. She stood in the doorway of the kitchen to make sure he was gone.

Jaq latched the front door, doubled checked the locks, then the condo to insure he was gone. Finally, she found Rita tucked safely in her bed.

Sitting down at the edge of Rita's bed, Jaq felt her forehead. Fever—low. "Rita?" Jaq whispered. She didn't want to alarm her, but she needed her to wake up. She called her name again louder. She needed assurance she was truly ill and not harmed. "Rita?"

Rita opened one eye and rolled it toward the sound. She closed her eye, then opened both eyes. "Jaq—"

"Your text. I got worried, brought supplies. It took you being sick for me to meet

Nick—"

"Nick—where?"

"He's running errands. He'll be back to have lunch with us."

Rita seemed to relax hearing that. "I'm so sorry I'm sick. Work—"

"Everyone gets sick. Rita, can you answer a few questions—they're important—"

Rita nodded. She tried to sit up. "I'm really queasy." Her head flopped onto her pillow.

"Glass of water, Alka-Seltzer and Vernors headed your way. Grandma's recipe." Jaq hopped off the bed and glanced back at Rita. Her eyes were closed. She thought she heard a snore.

Jaq fixed a tray for Rita and set it on the counter before heading out of the kitchen. She reached into the back of her jeans, pulled out her cell and hit David's direct dial number.

David's frantic "you're out of my sight-line" voice answered. "About time. Batman about to embark."

"I'll let you know when you need to send in the Batmobile with characters, but for the moment we're fine."

"Who's we, exactly?"

"Rita has a mild fever—she's really ill. I'm making her grandma's get-out-of-bed tray. I met the fiancé—he took a hike almost immediately once I arrived. I'm hoping our tail's on him."

"Tail, yes. We just left Doc. Abel and I are almost to my truck. Rabbit's outbound, headed your way. Great updates—what the fuck—"

Jaq understood the sounds of explosives. Her brain fractured.

"David. David?" She shouted into her cell, it hadn't disconnected, time was still counting but there was only silence. What was going on? Cold sweat broke out, her heart pounded loudly in her ears.

She clicked off her cell and redialed David.

No answer. She panicked.

Jaq dialed Abel, then Rabbit, finally Chief Hanusack. No answer—just messages. She sent a group text, slipped the cell into the rear pocket of her jeans, picked up the filled tray and checked on Rita.

Jaq set the tray on Rita's nightstand and sat next to her. Rita didn't stir. Jaq's cell vibrated, she grabbed it and read a text from David. Truck exploded. Bomb squad called in. All okay. Proceed with plan. Get Rita out NOW. Rabbit on way to you.

Jaq grabbed Rita's neatly folded blue jeans and sweater from the corner chair, fished through Rita's drawers for undergarments, then returned to Rita and began shaking her. "Rita, honey, you need to be seen by a doctor. Let's get you dressed."

Rita's eyes opened, her lashes fluttered and her pupils rolled back. She squeezed her eyes closed.

"Rita. Try again. Open your eyes. I have your clothes."

Rita felt Jaq's arm, grabbed onto it, then opened her eyes and with Jaq's help turned herself out of the covers. Her feet spilled onto the floor, Jaq steadied Rita's feet into her slippers, then peeled off her nightgown. They dressed her, then slid to the bathroom to work on grooming Rita.

"I'm feeling a little better." Rita paled.

"You look like crap and your fever's officially scaring me." Jaq opened the Motrin and watched Rita take two. "Wild hair." Jaq flipped Rita a hairbrush.

Dressed in warm winter gear, Rita and Jaq opened the door to the condo.

"Exactly where are you two going?" Nick asked.

Jaq manufactured a look of understanding concern. "Rita's fever is exploding and she needs a doctor. She has an appointment with mine—he has limited Saturday appointments, it's at eleven. We've less than an hour to get there—you're welcome to come along." She paused. "In fact, you should come, she might pass out. I'm very worried."

Nick pushed them back inside. "If Rita needs to go, I'll take her. What she needs is rest. Cancel it. She's not going outside in the frigid cold of January. Not your place or your decision."

Jaq narrowed her eyes and clenched her teeth. They were walking out, one way or the other. She locked her arm around her friend. "Rita, let's go."

Rita barely reacted. She could hardly stand, and her eyes kept fluttering. "You two work it out. I just need to sit." She had Gumby knees.

Nick flashed an I-win grin at Jaq.

Jaq hated him. Killer or not, he wasn't the man for Rita. Jaq would make sure of that.

"Fine. I'm not leaving until I'm confident she's on the mend."

"Suit yourself." Nick lifted Rita, tossed off her winter coat and boots, then steered her toward the bedroom.

* * * *

David hated to be driving a black-and-white, and the thought of dealing with the insurance company hurt him almost as much as losing his truck. He refocused and gripped Recon's harness. His wallet with badge and search warrant were in his pocket. His free hand was ready to pull his Glock if needed. Watching his Explorer detonate like the Fourth of July finale, meant leaving nothing to chance. Police officers were in rear position and around the house. David gave the nod. Abel reached over and rang the doorbell.

The door opened. David's eyes focused on a sixty-something woman. "Ma'am, does Nick Archer reside here?"

"He's my son. He lives between here and his fiancée's home. He's not here. Can I help you with something?" Evelyn asked.

"I'm Detective David Maxwell. This is Detective Abel Mendoza."

Abel stepped forward from the other side of the door. He raised an eyebrow, then stepped back into position.

"Has there been an accident?" Evelyn's hand slapped over her heart. "Nick wasn't scheduled to fly. What's happened?"

"Ma'am, we have a search warrant for these premises." David handed her the document. "Please step aside."

"I—I am about to sit and eat my lunch. I don't understand—you do what you need to do. You can find Nick at his fiancée's—"

"Our next stop, ma'am." David took a giant step inside. "We have a warrant for Chris Archer. Does he live here as well?"

"Yes, my other son." Evelyn made the sign of the cross. "He's upstairs."

"Ma'am, here's the warrant to search his premises." David showed her the second search warrant.

"Excuse me, please." Evelyn purposefully turned her back to them.

"Ma'am, you can go about your business. I'll assign an officer to accompany you. Safety reasons. I'm sure you understand." David walked into the foyer and directed a pair of officers to follow Evelyn and the remaining four uniforms to follow him. "We'll begin upstairs, Nick's bedroom, then Chris."

She craned her neck back. "That dog better not make a mess in my house or my yard."

David waved her off.

She wriggled her nose at the array of officers. "Oh dear. Neither of my boys likes anyone touching their things. Can't this wait until Nick comes home? Chris is upstairs."

David paused and turned slightly. "When might that be, ma'am, that Nick's coming home?"

Evelyn bit her lip. "I'll reach him on his cell."

"Ma'am, you can call him. We'd like to speak with him, but we're proceeding." David marched up the stairs.

Evelyn headed toward the stairwell and climbed slowly up the stairs. The two uniformed officers trailed Evelyn within a pace. Evelyn pointed to Chris' room. "There." She stepped forward and knocked rapidly. "Chris, please open the door. I need you. Please, now."

"What's up?" he called through the closed door.

"I need you out here. There are officers, lots of them. Police officers, they want to search Nick's room and talk with you. They have search warrants."

The door swung open. "What?" Chris stepped into the hallway, and then into Nick's room. "May I help you?"

"We have search warrants for you and your brother. Please step aside. We'll access your room soon," David said. "You can read all about it in the warrants we left with your mother downstairs."

"We have rights—" Chris glowered.

"Si. Read." Abel pointed.

Chris grabbed the search warrant from David. Evelyn had one hand over her heart, the other over her mouth. Chris gritted his teeth together. "Look where you will. There's nothing to find. Let's get this over with. I've got work to do."

Chris put an arm over Evelyn's shoulder and the pair stood silently, watching through the doorway.

Officers began with Nick's bedroom. They put rubber gloves on before methodically taking photographs, spraying, and powdering chemicals over the whole room.

A tall, dark-haired officer neatly placed samples in small bags before he sealed and labeled them. Another officer put the smaller bags into a larger bag.

A stocky officer with large, gloved hands opened the closet door and entered it. He searched pockets, bags, and boxes, and pulled out an array of articles. Moving inward, he disappeared behind the clothes, then reappeared holding a box. He opened it and cautiously pulled out papers, spreading them in rows across the bed.

"What's that?" David snapped gloves in place and stepped toward the bed.

"Found these in the closet behind a moveable panel. Whole box," the stocky officer said. "The box I placed at the head of the bed is filled with letters in envelopes. The letters I spread underneath that box were in a separate, large, white envelope I've set to the side on the right with the letters on the left. Each letter has a news article clipped to it."

Abel reached a gloved hand into the box and pulled the first three letters out. "Kids' letters. To Santa." Abel flipped through the box. "Some addressed to Saint Nick, others to Baby Jesus."

"Letters to Santa?" David asked.

Chris walked in, and one of the uniformed officers held a hand up to stop him. "Hey, those are mine. If that's what this is about, I'm guilty, not Nick."

"Hush." Evelyn put her fingers to her lips.

"What exactly are you guilty of?" David asked. "Maybe I should read you your Miranda rights?"

Abel and the two uniformed officers stopped and stared at Chris.

"No rights—I took those from the dead-letter office at the Post Office. I work there. I'm guilty. I didn't think that was a crime. They were set for destruction," Chris said. "I understood stealing what is essentially garbage isn't a crime."

David contemplated, nodded, and curled his lips to one side. "Why would you do such a thing?"

"I write computer games. I look for trends in toys. You know, what kids are interested in. It's like having my own private focus group."

"These are in your brother's room," David said. "Did you give them to him?"

"He destroys the ones I don't want. Uh, that's what I thought he did." Chris rubbed his right ear lobe. "I'm confused. I watched him shred them. Probably didn't get to all of them. He's very busy. No big deal."

"Clearly didn't destroy all of them. Had no intention to, from the looks of things." David pointed. "Your brother has a private collection. Saved his favorites."

Chris nodded. "No crime there either. Like I said, they're garbage, destination shredder."

David stared at him, then refocused and shuffled through the letters. Chris watched.

"See, some are to Santa, but others are to Saint Nick, Baby Jesus—my brother's very religious. My guess is he prays for the kids at Mass. You've got things all twisted, whatever you're thinking. He's a solid citizen."

David raised his brows and directed the officers, "Take pictures. Then list the box, letters, and news clippings on the inventory. Take more pictures than what you think we need."

"We take letters and clippings with us when they're finished. Si?"

David nodded. "Let's see what twin brother's room has to reveal."

They followed the same procedure in Chris' room. When they were finished, David confronted Chris. "You are under arrest for suspicion of murder—"

"No!" Evelyn turned deathly white. Abel put a hand on her shoulder.

"—conspiracy to murder, and aiding and abetting. We'll see what else we can come up with, and the judge will let you know at arraignment." David handcuffed Chris, read him his rights, and released him to a uniform. "Take him downtown to lock-up. I'll contact the prosecutor when we're finished so the paperwork will be ready for the Judge to arraign him in the morning."

"Murder?" Chris shook his head. "You guys are nuts. I want a lawyer. We'll sue."

Abel directed to another uniform, "Find a new home for the mother for a few days."

"Until we've gone over every crevice, this house is a crime scene." David motioned the officer and Abel downstairs.

"Man, this is unbelievable." Chris just kept shaking his head.

"Let's cruise." David curved his head to the remaining uniformed officers and ordered, "Call me when everything's completed. Until you're finished, I want an update every hour."

Evelyn rocked herself. "Arrest me if you want. My boys have nothing to do with the crimes of this house. You can't do this."

"Bueno. We can and we did."

"I'm calling my lawyer." She didn't have enough breath to yell, only a whisper came out.

David stiffly stated back to her. "A lawyer is a great idea. Your boys will need a good one. In fact, when you speak to your boys, ask them how they feel about wearing jumpsuits for the rest of their lives."

"Detective, you are very wrong, my sons were just boys." She took on a pleading tone. "Don't prosecute them for the sins of their mother. I was the fool who married him and didn't divorce him."

David shook his head. "Every family has problems."

She looked confused.

David pressed on. "From all those shoe boxes in Nick's closet, he wears a size twelve shoe? Is that correct?"

Evelyn stepped back. "So do millions of men."

"I'm only concerned about your boys. Twins? Maybe they both wear size twelve?"

"You've got it all wrong—what's going on here? I have very good boys, best sons in the world. A boy protects his mother, nothing wrong with that. That's the way it should be." Evelyn's voice was low and harsh. Tears streamed down her face, but she stood tall and unblinking. She scooped her purse over her shoulder, stepped into the boots by the door and grabbed her shoes. A tall uniformed officer handed her a coat and escorted her outside of her home.

David checked his watch as the search of the house continued. It was one thirty, time to get mom downtown to talk about "sins of this house."

\* \* \* \*

Evelyn sat in the tiny interrogation room as David and Abel placed the recorder in front of her, watched her sign her rights after they'd read them to her. She didn't want a lawyer. She had a story and it was time to tell it. There was no crime, only self-defense. Okay, the story through a victim's eyes. David and Abel wanted to hear it.

David pushed the recorder closer to Evelyn. "Ma'am, no disrespect—"

"You've disrespected my home, my family, my sons." She clasped her hands and released a long sigh. "But I should have come forward a long time ago. It is a sin of the mother of the house. Punish me. I am old. I knew better. I should have told when they were boys, protected them."

"Ma'am?" David tried again to interrupt her ramblings and watched tears fall.

"I was being beaten. I didn't know—didn't think the children, my Nick, anyway, knew. One night, it was bad. He protected me. Hit his father until I could get free of him."

"Did he know how much he'd injured his father?" David asked.

She shook her head. "He simply ran—his head hung low, ashamed to have struck his father, a man he adored, loved." She stopped, pulled tissue from the box, and blew her nose. Wiping her face as tears fell, she continued. "I didn't see Nick until the next day. Chris slept through everything."

Abel leaned back in his chair. "Do you know where he spent the night?"

She shook her head. "We never discussed what happened that night. Ever. Nick grew up protecting people, respecting the helpless. He is a good man. Served our country honorably. You have all of this wrong, so wrong."

Able scratched notes into a pad. "And your husband?"

"I was beaten, bleeding myself. But, he was dead. I had been gardening. I used the shovel Nick had grabbed and dug a deep hole. Buried him right there under my prize-winning roses."

"You never reported any abuse." David didn't see any reaction to that as he stared at her. He pressed on. "You never reported your husband missing."

"The children and I waited for him to come back. I couldn't tell Nick he killed his father protecting me."

"Self-defense, defense of another is not a crime." David spoke softly.

"A man and his father. That is not simple. Legal or otherwise." Evelyn stared between the men. "So punish me. I am guilty for hiding it. Not my sons. I confess."

"One more thing." David opened a file and lined up a series of pictures. "Have you ever seen a cross with this patterning in your household?"

\* \* \* \*

"Exactly what were you thinking going through my things?" Nick demanded.

Rita's anger rose, but this time the fear brought clarity. While her adrenaline surged, her face dulled in its affect as his voice cut into her. It was quarter to twelve. Sleep and the Motrin had helped the fevered disorientation but the illness kept her unsteady. Her unwavering eyes held his. She tried to focus, think quickly. She felt her wrist bare of the bracelet she'd left at the lab.

"I thought I lost my favorite silver bracelet. Last time I wore it was dinner with your mom and Chris. When we left the restaurant and walked to the car, you let me put my hands in your jacket pocket to keep warm. I thought it might've come off then, and it would still be in your pocket."

"We've been together nearly every minute since dinner with my family. Why didn't you just ask me?" Nick pressed. "I know where all my things are. What I don't mark, I code. I never leave things to chance. Military tactics and surveillance are my specialty. I know every time you so much as brushed by my things. You actually had the guts to open my hamper, my drawers, go through my pockets?"

"Fever. I didn't think."

"No, you didn't." His voice was stern, harsher than Rita had ever heard it.

"I was so happy to remember where I last wore my bracelet, I just began searching. It's the illness, honestly."

"I can't abide lying or liars," Nick said. "A false witness will not go unpunished, and he who tells lies will not escape."

"I really am truly sorry. It will never happen again." She pushed her head against the pillow, unsure how to calm his intense fury. She changed the subject. "Is Jaq still here?"

He glared.

She rambled to fill the void. "When did she leave—did she say anything? I want to thank her for stopping by. I'm happy you two finally met." Rita sensed she had to buy time till she knew what was going through his mind.

"How long have you known?" Nick's voice was deep and raspy. He sat on the bed, his shoulder touching hers, he reached onto the bedspread, found her kneecap sticking up and put his hand on it. He clamped his fingers like a wrench tightening a lugnut.

Rita felt crowded. He smelled of a recent shower, fresh cologne and wore a fresh jogging suit. His voice was calm, warm; his eyes were cool, distant. Her leg felt impaled.

Nick's demeanor instantly zapped her energy and replaced it with sheer fear.

"What's bothering you?" Rita placed a hand on Nick's head and began stroking it. She shifted to begin cranial manipulation. "I love you. There isn't anything we can't work out together." Rita kept her voice as gentle as her touch, despite severe cramping in her knee. Nick abruptly released her.

"A false witness will—A false—" Nick raised his arms and ignored her. "A false witness will not go unpunished, and he who breathes out lies will not escape."

An inner chill froze her flesh. "Please. Don't shut me out. I thought we were doing great." She realized it was a small plea for her life.

Nick placed his hands on her shoulders, his fingers pressed hard. "Wrath, when used of man, is the exhibition of an enraged sinful nature and is therefore always inexcusable."

"Nick, I don't understand." Rita didn't blink back. Nick's stare was foreign to her.

"You understand too well." Nick's voice was calm, steady, octaves lower than usual. "You've never been truthful."

"I've always—"

Nick pressed his fingers on her lips. "But ye are forgers of lies, ye are all physicians of no value. You never told me about Dr. Zeke Fazul, your past."

Rita's body arched back, her shoulders perched higher, her eyes widened. "How—? I've not uttered his name since he—"

"Set you up. I know everything. I do read newspapers." Nick snickered deeply. "And Zeke the sneak, a name he earned in the military, filled in all the blanks I needed about you."

"Me?" Rita bit her lip, felt her body waver between chills and perspiration. Rushing adrenaline kept her focused.

"We didn't meet by chance. I knew all about you. Zeke bragged about what an angel he had, that no one could find better."

"He, he did?" Rita said. "When—how—did you meet him?" Rita felt like she was in a dream. It wasn't possible—they knew each other? She'd been duped by both of them? Anger lined her fear.

"Afghanistan. Captain Fazul performed all pilot physicals before certain flight operations. We became friends, until he became my enemy, recommended a psychological evaluation, and they grounded me."

"I don't understand." She had to buy time. Where was Jaq?

"That little sneak followed me. I had a mission to help the local women and children—rid them of their tyrant men. I protected them."

"You've always been a kind and gentle man." Rita kept her voice calm, her mind engaged in finding an opportunity to run to freedom. "I'm sure he knew that."

Nick laughed. "Poor trusting, innocent Rita. There was the military mission, and then there was my own mission, my real duty. No woman or child should suffer at the hands of men. They had to be extinguished."

He killed innocent people, not soldiers. She searched his face. She could no longer see the man she thought she liked—loved. His handsome features had morphed into true evil.

"No one misses malevolence. Doctor-Captain Fazul didn't understand that. I should've extinguished him the night he followed me, but then I never would've had you—women always idolize the dead they loved and lost."

"He didn't really care anything about me. If you read the articles, you know." A tear slid down her face, but she held her own.

"Don't you know by now? Nothing gets past me. I was there that night. I followed you home from the party. I saw the accident."

Rita blinked hard, refocused, and stared. "Why didn't you come forward? I almost went to prison."

Nick laughed a jolly-St.-Nick laugh, as if she'd just told the best joke ever.

Rita felt like molded plastic. She wasn't sure if she was actually breathing.

"Poor Rita." Nick stroked her hair and tucked long waves behind her ears. "It was a very bad turn. Bit of oil on the road made the curve difficult to maneuver. I was the first to see the accident. Stupid jogging idiot wasn't wearing any reflectors. Zeke couldn't drive in a straight line. Zeke couldn't see him, a true accident." An evil laugh emanated.

"What?"

"You were both passed out. A little shot guaranteed some extra sleep time." Nick grinned a slow hungry smile.

"You planned every detail?" Rita found it difficult to breath.

"Bad timing of that jogger, I found. Too bad no one saw me place him there—already dead by my car. I dragged Zeke into my car, placed the tangled jogger under your wheels, and then popped you into the driver's seat. Neither one of you ever quite remembered what happened that evening."

"You? He told me the truth?" Rita shook her head rapidly back and forth. "Why Nick? I don't understand."

"Zeke needed to lose something he loved, like I lost the military. Like I almost lost my pilot's license. I waited a very long time for everything to perfectly fall into place." More evil laughter erupted from him.

"But you left the military with an honorable discharge. You showed me the papers and you didn't lose your pilot's license." Rita's eyes didn't waver from his, her tone was firm but gentle. She felt both inner and outer strength finally gel and she wasn't frightened. "You fly for Delta."

"I cut a deal. I'd leave military service without backlash, no complications either way, and the military would simply release me, honorable discharge, with my twenty years' full retirement but a bar against reenlistment."

"Zeke didn't set me up. You did." Rita sighed. Hearing the words out loud, her face crinkled, she stood, her hands formed fists, and she struck at Nick. "No. No. No." Adrenaline pulsed through every nerve.

Nick grabbed her wrists firmly. "The law of truth was in his mouth, and iniquity was not found in his lips. You're just like your fiancé, you think you know truth, but you're surrounded by venom and lies."

"Nick, he was gone. I've never uttered his name since his trial."

"So you became a master of deception with your detective friends." Nick bitterly pulled at her.

"Jaq? My best friend—"

"Your friends have been following me, interrupting my mission. Just like Fazul." Nick pulled her forward toward the desk. She pulled a wrist free and grabbed her robe from the edge of the bed.

"I'm cold." Nick watched as Rita stubbornly tied the robe around her, then stepped into her slippers. He pushed her to the chair at her desk.

"Hurry up." Nick's voice was dark. "Sit."

"Nick? Your mission to kill innocent people? You aren't making any sense." Rita looked for an opening around him to run out the bedroom door, but he blocked her view.

"You all think you know better. You don't. I protect those who can't protect themselves." Nick clenched his hands around her arms, then raised one arm and placed it around her voice box and began to squeeze.

"Nick. You're hurting me. Please release me." Rita began to lose air, and then he released her. Rita's whole body was trembling.

"Let the lying lips be put to silence."

"Nick, I don't understand," Rita said. "Please. Where's Jaq?"

"Exactly where you put her. We've things to do." Nick's eyes were glazed. Rita no longer recognized his voice. Putting her hands together in one of his, he reached over her and grabbed a scarf from the back of the desk chair and looped it around her neck. Her hands were freed, but her neck was caught in his makeshift noose.

Immediately, Rita grabbed at the scarf. "What's this for—Nick?"

He pulled tighter.

"Ah, silence. A perfect sound. I told you, I cannot, will not, tolerate liars, impurity. I'm always able to protect the innocent, take every measure to defend them. You are no longer innocent, nor is your lying friend. You're deceitful."

Rita opened her mouth, sound leaked out but no words.

He tightened the scarf.

She was scared to remove her fingers because they were allowing morsels of oxygen to be drawn in.

"Lying can be done with words and by silence. You've done both. I can only prevent further evil, because you are not able to rectify your mistakes."

Rita kept her eyes on him.

"Focus. Take out a piece of your stationery, and write as I dictate. Or, I'll simply watch you turn blue, and do it myself," Nick said. "Cross me, and I'll not be as merciful as I was to the others, including your fiancé. Understood?"

Rita blinked at him as she sat in the chair. She knew exactly where the stationary was, but took her time opening drawers looking for it. Could she find a weapon?

"That's right, grab the good stuff."

Shaking, Rita smoothed her hands over the paper, with tears streaming and hands trembling, she formed the dictated words.

*I cannot live in this world without Nick, the love of my life.*
*I'm sorry I had to take Jaq, but she tried to stop me.*
*Please tell Jaq's family, my family and friends, I am very sorry. Rita*

Nick picked up the note and read it. "You couldn't handle our breakup. Suicide was your only way out. Sad you felt you had to take your best friend with you."

"Where's Jaq?" Rita's voice was strained but she was able to speak, the scarf loosened just a bit as he read the note.

"Right where you left her, sitting near the front door, attached to her Glock."

Rita tried to understand, but couldn't. "What?"

"Too bad you didn't have the stomach to pull the trigger yourself. Next person who opens the door will unwittingly cause her weapon to fire." Nick sniggered with overtones of hoarseness. "It might take me weeks to get over that little shock. Accidentally killing a cop and finding that you killed yourself."

"That's not suicide, that's murder—double homicide."

"No, that's perfection. As to you, Angel-teeny, after a few months playing the distraught fiancé, you'll hardly be remembered. Your fingerprints will be found on Jaq's Glock."

"You've thought it all through." Chills peppered her. Since they'd met, every relationship morsel premeditated—everything a lie. Zeke had never betrayed her. Her mind raced. Anger, clarity, prayer rushed in. The detectives were right to suspect him. Nick, a serial killer, with others, so many, victims, murders.

Rita's eyes roamed the room for a way out. Praying to God for Jaq, to direct detectives, send Dr. Towers who said he'd check on her. If she didn't answer the telephone, surely Doc would come. Surely, detectives would appear if Jaq didn't emerge. A tear fell on the paper.

Nick grabbed the pen from her.

And if Nick was telling the truth, when they opened the door, they would kill Jaq. She had to find a way out and save them both.

Nick led Rita into the closet. "Step up on this stool." He put it under the clothes rod. "Sturdy high closet rods. Tall enough, for your tiny frame to swing from. An inch or two is all we need."

Rita stiffened, making it more difficult for him to tie her hands behind her back. She struggled and tried to position her wrists so there might be room to slip out.

"Good thing you like these silky scarves. They won't leave much of a mark." Nick tied and laughed. "Very sturdy."

She tried to make sounds, but what little came out was not loud enough to be heard. Seeing the rage in Nick's dark eyes, she stopped all movement. Resolute in her determination to survive and save Jaq, she looked around the closet to ensure she was familiar with exactly what was nearest to her. She stayed still, reserved her energy.

"That's my Angel-teeny. It'll be over before you know it. I'll be back from my jog too late to save you and become aghast at Jaq, shot—since you rigged the door." His voice was low and slow with a determined fire in it. "And as it's appointed unto men once to die, but after this the judgment."

His words seared through her and prompted a stream of silent tears. "You won't get away with it. You can't leave." She had to delay him.

"Poor naïve Rita. Angel-teeny, I always work backward." He laughed. "Fire-escape."

With the ease of expert hands, Nick tied the ends of the scarf to the rod and tested it. He pulled the cross from his shirt, pressed it into her forehead, then untied her hands, and pulled the stool out from under her. The silk tightened and her feet hung above the floor.

He didn't look up. He didn't look around the room. He didn't look back. Nick simply closed the closet door as if he'd just hung a suit.

Rita's desire to save Jaq and live, coupled with her nurse's training, engaged into overdrive. Adrenaline surged through her. She kicked a leg backward, and her foot landed on the ledge of the plumbing access door. She pushed back on the ledge and secured her foot, then lifted her body upward just enough to gain some air.

The access door fell to the carpeted floor with a dull thud prompting her to lift her other leg onto the trim. Awkwardly, with both feet braced, she pushed her body upward. Feeling the cool rod against her cheek, she rested her head to let her body calm. How long could she stay at this weird angle, she wondered, surprised it had worked at all. She grabbed the bar and used one hand to work its way to the knots. Damn, they were tight. She had to find a way to untie them.

Rita closed her eyes and focused. Thankfully, years of meditation and yoga had made her strong in mind and body. She pictured pages from medical books and heard emergency-room voices explaining why hangings are painful and slow.

Most hanging victims die from suffocation, not a broken neck, as one would believe. The words of her forensic professor's lecture years before gave her a glimmer of hope. She felt her teeth gnash against her cheek, and she tasted blood. Her hands steadied.

She maintained her balance, and her fingers crept around the ridges of the scarf between it and her neck. The scarf was snug, but it was not cutting into her yet. Her eyes adjusted to the darkness. She looked for something, anything to help free herself.

Hyperventilation. Her medically trained brain continued to catalogue cause and effect. If she didn't stay calm and it took over, it would be her demise. Her fingers and toes would curl from lack of oxygen, and her body might begin to tremor. Could she shift her neck enough to find a position to allow enough oxygen in? Any tremor whatsoever could cause her to lose her balance and her footing.

What would Nick do if they were still alive when he returned?

\* \* \* \*

"Let the uniforms finish inside." David clasped Recon's harness and headed for the front door with Abel following behind. "Let's take Recon for a walk around the perimeter of the house, then follow Rabbit to Rita's."

Abel nodded. "Si." Abel closed the door of Nick's home behind them.

David stopped. He frowned as he read his text. "Surveillance team's outside Rita's unit. Another's following Nick, he's jogging again. No sign of Rita or Jaq." He clicked onto the GPS map. "Rita's still at home." David turned left. A few giant paces and they followed Recon as she scampered into the back yard.

"Heard from Rabbit?" Abel reached inside his jacket for his cell and scrolled through it.

"Negative. We need to get inside Rita's place." David's attention remained focused on Recon. "I can use Recon's sensory training to run interference."

"That bomb spooked me." Abel put away his cell. "No message. Cell silence irritates my nerves, bad vibe."

David called Recon back. "Recon will finish the yard later, doesn't look like she's ready to go."

Abel nodded. "Maybe she smells reindeer tracks."

"We'll bring her back to sleigh that scent trail later." They laughed. David grabbed Recon's harness and they hurried to the marked vehicle. "Buckle up and hang on, Abel. We're going to cruise." David charged the ignition, hit the lights and sound, then pressed the gas pedal.

Abel read the vibrating cell phone on the console between them. "Doc just sent a text. No answer at Rita's. He's headed to her condo. He pulled the extra key ring she had hidden in her desk; he thinks it has both her car and condo key."

"Smart man," David said.

"Do you think the mother or brother tipped Archer off that we were at his home?" Abel asked.

"It's possible, brother's computer savvy. Could've easily sent a message during the search. Once he learns we searched his mother's home and arrested his brother, there's no telling what he'll do. Something's more wrong than normal."

"Do you think it explains the bomb in your truck?" Abel asked.

"No time to have planned the explosion so close in time without sophisticated equipment. I'm betting the bomb squad will find it was on some kind of timer or remote." David half faced Abel.

"Did he want to kill us or scare us?"

David winced. "Delay tactic." He stomped on the accelerator.

\* \* \* \*

Dr. Towers' wool coat hung open and his head was bare of the usual wool cap as he clutched his medical bag and ran toward David, Recon, and Abel. "I have never known you to drive a marked vehicle."

Before anyone could answer, Rabbit approached them from the back of the building. "We've got problems."

David interrupted. "Have you spoken to Jaq or Rita 'cause I couldn't—"

Rabbit interjected. "No, I haven't been inside. When I arrived, I saw Archer, at least I think it was him, jogging from the back. I radioed and surveillance confirmed, he's out jogging again."

David frowned. "So, why not move in and get them out?"

Rabbit held his microscopic lens fingers up and peered through it as he stared up at the building in the direction of Rita's condo. "Getting nearly blown-up's a game-changer. I'm suspecting booby traps herein out."

"Yeah, so, we have to get Jaq and Rita out." David strode toward the front door.

Rabbit grabbed David's shoulder. "No, like I said, I got a very bad feeling after your truck blew."

Dr. Towers frowned. "Blew? Blew-up?"

They ignored Dr. Towers. "So what? We all got that bad feeling. Lucky we weren't scorched," David snapped. "Jaq and Rita need out now."

Abel grabbed David's other shoulder. "Hey man, gotta listen. Rabbit, he's great at this. What's up man—say it straight so we can get in there."

"Everything, everyone says that the Double Cross killer—Nick—stays in the shadows, is a creature of habit. Not today. He's jogging a second time, exiting from the back of the building. I ask why."

David frowned. "We're wasting time. I've got Recon—you're not understanding—"

"Slow down. I walked back there, found a fire escape near the balcony. I think he used that exit."

David froze. "Booby traps."

Rabbit shook his head. "His profile coupled with his military jacket, then watching that bomb detonate made me think of recent mass shooters. Snare in the lair fits."

David grabbed Recon's harness. "Recon worked bomb squad for two years. She's highly trained." They sprinted into the building. David dialed Hanusack and left him a message to join them with a parade of extra detail. "Doc, you stay rear, ready treat or call in medics."

Dr. Towers cleared his throat. "Right. I called ahead and asked the Condo Association office permission to pick up a copy of Rita's key under medical emergency if one of these keys are not to her condo." He dangled the keys from her desk on his forefinger.

Taking the stairs two at a time, they finally reached the third floor and rushed down the hall to Rita's unit.

David directed Abel and Rabbit to stand back. He leaned down, disconnected the leash and whispered to Recon. "Recon search."

All eyes on Recon, she sniffed the hall, then a few feet to the right, and then the left of the doorframe. She pulled David back from the door. Each time David made a lunge forward, she blocked him and growled.

David cocked his head. "Stand back. Abel, you and Doc get the uniforms to start clearing the building one floor at a time. Then, follow us. Unclear what we're dealing with, but Recon found something and I'm thinking of my former vehicle." David pointed toward the back-exit sign. "Rabbit, let's take her to that back balcony and fire escape and see what her reaction is."

Rabbit, David, and Recon sprinted to the back of the building to locate the fire escape nearest Rita's unit.

\* \* \* \*

Once around the building, David counted windows and floors, then pulled down a fire escape ladder leading to the third floor and climbed up with Recon to Rita's balcony. David wasn't fond of heights, rickety ladders, or anything covered in ice that wasn't a chilled glass. Fear of losing his partner and best friend kept pushing him forward. In minutes, they were on site. He directed Recon to jump onto the balcony and sniff. When Recon calmly sat by the patio door and looked up at David, he jumped over.

"Good girl. Now let's find our girl." David couldn't see in with the curtain drawn. He gripped the handle and slowly slid the heavy glass door open an inch.

He waited. No response from Recon.

He edged the door just wide enough to slide in sideways. Recon followed him in. He held Recon's leash wrapped in one hand clutching his cell phone in flashlight mode, his Glock cocked in the other.

Lights off, daylight streamed into the living room. He focused, then stepped into the room with the caution and center of a snake about to capture its mouse. Recon aimed toward the front door and froze. In sync,

David did the same. They heard the familiar low hum of Jaq's voice. David began to edge toward her, but Recon bumped him back, then growled. David aimed his flashlight slowly around Jaq, then up and down her. Her mouth was duct-taped shut. Her limbs affixed to the chair she sat upon. He followed the frantic movement of her eyes. Recon growled again, louder.

"Holy shit. Recon, you just saved our lives—well, Jaq's for sure." He spun back and called down to Rabbit. "Call EMS, then sprint up here."

David flicked on a light switch, and waited for Rabbit. Recon stood guard, without flinching.

In minutes, Rabbit was through the sliding glass door. He recognized the situation. "Rigged it so the opening of the door will trigger a bullet in her, but any slight movement will set it off as well."

David's eyes darted around the room. "Set up as volatile as nitro."

"Move along the walls to the kitchen. Bring back something to protect Jaq's head. I'm going to figure the angles."

David instructed Recon to stand guard, then he disappeared to retrieve armor.

"Hang on, Jaq." Rabbit slightly tilted his body and rotated his head. Further movement was Russian roulette, and not an option.

David returned with a large baking pan filled with boards and lids. "Work it and pray."

Rabbit pointed. "On the couch. Any floor clunk could trigger it." Rabbit pulled out his penknife and crawled to Jaq. "Jaq, I'm going to free you, but don't move until David and I have everything in place. When I say 'drop.' Don't think, just drop, 'cause if you flinch, we see your brains." He sliced Jaq's hands and legs free. "It's gonna hurt, but you can pretend you're at the salon for a wax."

Jaq fixed her eyes on David.

Rabbit plucked the tape from her mouth immediately placing his hand over her lips to stop the burn and the scream. Tears streamed, but her composure held.

Jaq blinked away tears that stopped as quickly as they'd started. She remained focused on David.

David held her stare until she was settled. "Recon, stand down." David and Rabbit took their positions on each side of Jaq.

"Drop."

Jaq fell to the floor.

David traded his weight for Jaq, put up the makeshift kitchen shield and Rabbit grabbed the Glock to change its trajectory.

In the same instant, the weapon fired.

Jaq gaped at Rabbit. "Damn fine math skills."

David slapped Rabbit on the back. "Glad you're on our team." He reached down and gave Jaq his hand. "Jaq—"

She latched onto his hand and stood on wobbly feet. David wrapped his arms around her and said, "You scared me."

Jaq breathed him in, then stepped back. "Thanks for the rescue." She rubbed face, then her wrist. "Rita. Last I knew she was in the bedroom."

\* \* \* \*

With Recon in the lead checking for booby traps, David, Rabbit, and Jaq followed into the master bedroom. The unmade bed was empty. Jaq inspected the nightstand. She picked up a piece of stationary by its corner. "Here."

"Suicide—or so he wants us to think." Rabbit read the letter over her shoulder.

"Part of the setup." Jaq put the note down and turned around the room. She headed toward the closed closet.

David put a stop-sign hand up as she passed him. "Recon gives clearance. Paw and sniff test. She hasn't been wrong yet."

Rabbit grabbed his revolver, cocked it and followed David and Recon.

Jaq marched ahead. "I'm cutting in for this dance." Arm held high as she moved in, she struck a Statute of Liberty pose at David. "Remember the last time we had a closet with a body—Rita's practically my sister. My call." She did an about face. "Rabbit call Doc."

Jaq patted Recon's head. She flicked the light on, then edged fully into the closet and gasped. Jaq shrieked Rita's name as she lifted her. "David—get in here. Rabbit—EMS—now."

David dashed in. His fingers immediately unknotted the scarf.

Rita's lifeless body was oddly bent. Her cheek had a deep mark melded into it from the clothes rod, and her feet and legs were positioned awkwardly.

"David—" Jaq couldn't finish.

David laid Rita on the carpet. He placed his ear against her chest and grabbed her wrist. He tried to feel a pulse. After a minute, he spoke, "Barely warm. She's still in there."

Dr. Towers and Abel entered the room. "Stand back." Dr. Towers dropped his medical bag, snapped his stethoscope into place, then lowered it onto her chest. "I need oxygen and a gurney STAT." His fingers were crawling along her head and neck. He began CPR.

"EMS down the hall." Rabbit turned. "I'll direct them in." He was gone.

Within seconds of the CPR, Rita's eyes fluttered. Dr. Towers put his fingers to her mouth. "Your body has been through enough. Your neck is swollen. Do not speak."

Tears formed. Her frantic blue eyes made a line from Dr. Towers to Jaq.

Jaq rushed to her. "Doc, she's trying to tell us something."

Dr. Towers nodded. "Rita, remain calm. You are safe. Try not to speak. Jaq can ask you a few questions. Blink once for yes, two for no. Can you do that?"

Rita's long lashes blinked once. Her face crinkled in distress.

Jaq held her hand. "We've a great story. They saved us." She presented a reassuring face to her friend. "In a minute, you'll be on a stretcher to the hospital. Doc says you'll be perfect." Jaq paused. The women stared at each other. "Rita, do you know who the Double Cross Killer is?"

She blinked once.

"Is it Nick?"

She blinked once.

"Do you know for certain?"

She blinked once.

"We wanted to tell you, but we weren't definite, until now. I'm so sorry." Jaq brushed her hand over Rita's hair.

Rita closed her eyes. Tears spilled, and she shook her head. Her fingers pointed to Jaq.

Jaq put her hands to her face and hair. "Rita. I'm fine. Truly."

A corner of Rita's mouth went up.

"We'll get him," Jaq said. "And you'll have police protection until he's locked up for good."

Dr. Towers reached for Rita's hand and squeezed it tightly. "You have suffered some trauma to the neck. You will be achy for a while. You will be fine."

Rita opened her eyes, smiled, then winced in pain. She motioned Jaq closer in need of whispering something to her but in that second Jaq and Dr. Towers' attention shifted, as they simultaneously spun toward the bedroom door at the incoming EMS crew rolling in a gurney and oxygen tank. Uniformed police officers followed with Chief Hanusack, who marched in with Abel.

Everyone stepped aside while they stabilized Rita and prepared her for transport.

Chief Hanusack bellowed toward David. "Abel tells me you've all solved my brother-in-law's murder, but our serial killer is still out there?"

"We're about to tie up that loose end, Chief," David said. "I just checked in with the surveillance team. They lost the perp on his jog. Does tricky shadow jogging."

Rabbit pounded his fingertips as he spoke. "Headed back here to finish what he started."

Jaq cocked her head. "That's right, sir. Left me to get blown to bits with the movement of the front door and Rita to die strung up in the closet as an apparent suicide."

Chief Hanusack frowned at Jaq. "You look like you need a ride in that ambulance."

"No, thank you, sir."

Chief Hanusack nodded, his eyes finally gazed downward. "Is this Rita who was strung up in the closet—how is she?"

"From the looks of things, about ready to be transported to the hospital." Jaq shook her head. "Short version. Rita is his fiancée—incredibly, she hoisted herself up just enough to breathe. She regularly practices yoga and core strength training. Unbelievably, it saved her. Would've died otherwise."

"Chief, we've got him. He's going down on several counts of murder and two counts attempted murder," David said.

"Trials and prison occur after capture." Hanusack's voice was loud and unhappy. "This feels like my wife's premature labor. Call me when apprehension's real." He made an about-face and stomped out.

EMS turning the stretcher's wheels toward the door, Rita now stabilized, again motioned Jaq and Rabbit to her. They bent closely toward her face, Rabbit lifted the oxygen mask slightly. They leaned their ears close to Rita's lips. "Nick's returning." Her voice was low, rough and broken. Rabbit replaced the oxygen mask, then questioned Rita.

"Now?"

Rita blinked once.

"To make sure you and Jaq are dead?" Rabbit asked.

Rita blinked once.

She pulled him in again, then whispered. "To finish setting the stage."

"Is that what he said?" Rabbit asked.

Rita blinked once.

Rabbit patted Rita lightly on the shoulder. "The hospital will take great care of you. Don't worry about anything. Okay?"

Rita blinked once.

Dr. Towers stood next to Rita. "I will follow the ambulance to the hospital."

Rita blinked once.

"Doc, could you stay just a minute or two?" Rabbit pointed at Doc's bag. "I need use of your medical supplies."

"Certainly." Dr. Towers observed EMS wheel Rita away, then focused on Rabbit.

Rabbit picked up the silken scarves from the floor, held them up and edged toward Jaq, David, Recon, and Abel. "Let's make a big rattrap."

The room stared back.

David excused the officers and directed them to pull all emergency vehicles out of sight leaving only unmarked vehicles and plain-clothed officers in place.

# Chapter Thirty-three

D AVID STOOD AGAINST THE WALL outside Rita's door and played a game on his iPhone. Recon sat by his side.

"Can I help you?" Nick asked. It was clear he was about to enter.

David looked up as if only half interested. "Oh, yeah. You must be the fiancé." He typed as if shutting down his game and slipped the iPhone into his pocket. He stretched out a hand to Nick. "David Maxwell. Jaq's partner. Recon and I were supposed to pick her up at two, it's two thirty. Just like a woman to be late. Are Rita and Jaq behind you?" David looked behind Nick as they shook hands.

Nick frowned. He released David's hand, then unzipped his thermal running jacket.

"I knocked. I called. No one answered. Figured you all went out together. Were you jogging?"

"I jog alone. Rita's very ill, probably sleeping. Last I knew, Jaq was leaving to get her some cold medicine. I went for a jog to keep those cold germs away from me."

David nodded and waved an agreeing hand. "I hear ya. Girl talk and germs. Best to get out while you can." David kept his eyes on Nick's hands. "Mind if I come in? You can check on Rita. I'll wait for Jaq?"

"No offense buddy but I'm allergic to dogs, and I'm going to hit the shower. Maybe you want to come back when Jaq gets here or go to Jaq's. I doubt she's with Rita. When I left, Rita had a high fever." Nick eased one hand on the knob and turned to open it. "That's odd. It wasn't locked when I left."

David watched his hands.

Nick knocked on the door. No response. He called out. "Hey, Rita, let me in."

"What, no key?" David chuckled. "You piss her off or something?"

"I don't carry a key when I jog and she's home." Nick slid him a sideways glance, rattled the knob again, then toggled his fingers along the edge of the doorframe. "That's odd." He squinted.

"Yeah?" David studied him.

"We have a hidden key in the doorframe. Carved it in myself." Nick closed his left eye and peered in the crevice with the right. He stuck a groomed nail inside. "It's either fallen inside or it's been removed."

"Sounds like your girl might be sending you a message. Maybe she's sick of you." David gave Nick a half smirk. "Might want to check the balcony to see if your toothbrush took a flight."

Nick frowned at David. "Take a hike. I'll find Maintenance and get in. We'll let you know if Jaq shows up." Nick paced down the hall.

David shifted his posture as if he was satisfied and prepared to leave. "Let's get home, Recon." He and Recon followed Nick. David kept a firm grip on Recon's harness with one hand, fingers firmly planted on his Glock under his jacket with the other.

David and Recon stayed paces behind Nick as he stomped down the stairs. They stopped on the landing above Nick, who abruptly stopped a short, stocky, dark-haired man in a grey Maintenance jacket.

"You there." Nick grabbed the man's arm.

The man in the grey jacket steadied himself on the railing and jerked his head toward Nick. "What's the rush?"

"I need in my condo now. My fiancée is ill, and there may be a problem." Nick's hand remained firmly planted.

The man's eyes looked at the hand on his arm, then at Nick's eyes. "Got ID? I don't recognize you."

Nick looked up at David and Recon.

David looked down at Nick. "Don't look at me. We just met. I don't know you—remember you weren't going to let strangers in. Back at you, Bud." David and Recon strutted past Nick. David whispered, "I'll have Jaq call you when we hear from our Rita."

\* \* \* \*

"Stand down, Recon," David ordered. They stood on the balcony and waited.

David heard the bullet rip out of the barrel, and the door opened. David gripped onto the harness and held his breath as he peered in.

Nick shouted, "What the hell—" He rushed in behind the Maintenance man, nearly knocking him over.

The key ring swung loose in the doorknob. The Maintenance man ignored it, reached in his pocket, and shouted orders into his phone.

Nick ignored Jaq's flailing body taped to the chair with blood spurting from her head and splatted around her. He ran to the bedroom.

A robust bareheaded officer tossed off the Maintenance jacket and cap, grabbed a long jersey sweater from the coat rack by the door and wrapped Jaq's head. Glock in hand he paused until David signaled him forward.

Jaq peered out. She remained positioned until David and Recon were in line outside Rita's bedroom door. "My Rita. Rita, honey, where are you?" Nick entered the bedroom, then shut the door. He spun around the room. He stepped toward the bed, picked up the note, and tossed it next to the telephone. He closed his eyes, dialed 9-1-1, and with a tearful voice of panic shouted into the receiver. "Hello? Hello. I have a situation here. I need help." Nick's back was to the door. He sat on the bed.

David opened the door and peered in.

"Emergency Center. Where's the problem?" the voice encouraged.

"I just came home. I went out for a jog. I came back. It's my fault."

"Sir, what is the address?"

"Yes, my fiancée. Rita Rose. Her name is Rita Rose. My fiancée," Nick repeated. His voice trailed as if disoriented. "Her friend, too. I think they're both dead… murder-suicide. I don't understand myself. There's so much blood, a note."

"Okay, sir. A unit is on its way with EMS. You need to stay calm and give me an address. I need you to help me here."

"I don't know. I think it's too late. Oh God. I just went out for a run. My fiancée and I had an argument. She, well, she left a note. Suicide. She hung herself in the closet."

"Sir, put the phone down. Can you check to see if she's still breathing?"

"I—I'm going to go be with her now," Nick cried into the phone. He set the receiver down, but didn't cradle it. Despite the distraught voice, he walked with up-curved lips. "Get here. Hurry. Please." He shouted from the center of the room.

Nick grabbed the stool in front of the closet door and reached for the handle. He opened it.

He squinted.

He frowned.

He reached in.

He began removing fallen clothes from overtop the body.

"Rita." Nick cried. His voice loud, shrill as he tossed clothing. Abruptly, he stumbled backward and motionless, his face contorted.

"You'd agree, Nurse Rose is much prettier than I? Si?" Abel appeared from the closet, moving toward a dumfounded Nick.

Rabbit appeared behind Nick. "Nick Archer, you are under arrest for the attempted murder of Jaq McSween and Rita Rose and the murder of several others in Detroit. After trial, you will be extradited to face murder charges in Sarasota, Florida for several other murders in that jurisdiction." He slapped and tightened a handcuff on Nick's right wrist, grabbed his shoulders and circled him around. Nick twisted and jabbed Rabbit with his free elbow. Despite getting jabbed, Rabbit clung onto Nick's wrist, continued speaking and reached for Nick's left arm but missed the moving target. "You have the right to remain silent. Anything you say or write can be used against you. You have the right to an attorney—"

Nick, agitated, rotated his body, struck Rabbit's ribcage with a left hook. Rabbit bent forward, his voice choked. Nick turned to run but met David's weapon center spine. Rabbit caught his breath, stepped forward and placed a solid knee to Nick's backside next to David's Glock. Rabbit placed an arm on Nick's right shoulder, wrapped his fingers around his left wrist and twisted Nick's left arm behind his back and pushed. Momentum plugged the three of them to the floor. Rabbit handcuffed his wrists together behind his back. "As we were saying. You are under arrest," Rabbit said. David kept his Glock pointed at Nick. "My friend here missed target practice this morning. Anything you move, gives him a reason to practice."

"Nick Archer, as our Florida partner just said, you are under arrest." David continued to imprint the barrel of the Glock into his spine. "Let me begin to tell you a story about how you flinched and I had the necessary pleasure of making a memorable hole in you. Please—feel free to flinch any part of your despicable murderous body. Like my partner said, any reasonable excuse and I pull the trigger." David's teeth were clenched but his voice was loud and clear. "And because of your love of dogs, I'll order Recon to bite." He chattered his teeth together directly in Nick's ear for full biting sound effect. "When Recon bites, there's no release until I give that command. Oh—you'll live, painfully." David sneered with his upper lip and held it.

Jaq traipsed in, stood in front of Nick, hands on hips. Nick scowled. "I want my lawyer."

Abel marched over to the telephone and addressed the 9-1-1 dispatch operator, while Rabbit reread the Miranda rights and conducted a pat down body search. "This is Detective Abel Mendoza. Everything's secure here.

We have all the assistance we need. You can help by making a note and formally request that the Wayne County Prosecutor and Chief of Police want a copy of your conversation with Captain Nick Archer preserved to use as evidence."

"That was sweet," Jaq said. "I'll play Halloween and be sprayed with blood anytime."

Rabbit winked. "We're barely into the New Year. Let's not think about Halloween."

"Yeah." Jaq laughed.

Nick looked toward the sky, closed his eyes, then uttered clear words in a deep throaty voice. "You know not what you do. I shall hide my face from your sins and blot out your iniquities." His expression bland, controlled.

"Tell it to a guy in a robe. You've got two good choices. A priest and a judge." Abel grinned, then looked outside through the bedroom window. "Bueno. Crime scene unit's here." He rubbed his hands together very fast. "I was promised Coney dogs on our way to visit Rita."

"I have a hunch." Rabbit disappeared inside the closet and pulled away more of the clothing.

Nick continued his blather, "Behold, tomorrow I will cause it to rain a very grievous pain, such as hath not been since the foundation thereof even until now those this departure from good will cleanse a necessary evil from us as we begin again." His eyes opened, he stared blankly, trancelike.

"Move out," Abel ordered Nick to step out with the plain-clothed officer and the additional uniformed officers, who had emerged into the room and surrounded his exit.

Jaq interrupted the sudden silence in the room. "No more costumes, including duct tape, silk, and blood." She lifted up strands of her hair. "I need a shower."

"That's disappointing—the silk, I mean." David moved a wet curl and tucked it behind her ear and bent down. "The shower sounds like fun." His voice dropped to a whisper. He felt her heat with the rise in cheek pink. "Think. Victoria's Secret box. Valentine's Day—pink silk—I was hoping my gift would be a fashion show." He squeezed her hand.

Jaq squinted her eyes toward the closet. Curious at what Rabbit was looking for, she peeked inside.

Several minutes later, after demanding a flashlight, Rabbit emerged still on his hands and knees. His was face flushed, his forehead filled with perspiration. "I got the idea from following Nick's pupils while he was being cuffed. That and the report on the search of his bedroom closet in his mother's house." Rabbit untangled himself from the closet. "Typical serial killer—he keeps his tools and his trinkets in close proximity, same hiding place."

All eyes studied Rabbit as he stood. He held out a garbage bag.

Jaq frowned. "Halloween continues after all. Trick or treat. The trick was his hiding it. The treat is finding it and using every piece to convict him of murder, over and over again."

Rabbit widened the bag and everyone bent forward. "Clothes and shoes the Captain didn't have time to destroy."

A Halloween pumpkin's grin was no match for the one planted on Abel. "Rabbit out of a hat, I tell you. I tell everyone."

"Abel, no hot dogs, no food, no drink." Rabbit cocked his head. "Wait until you take Jaq to get cleaned up. David, Recon, and I have a little work to do. We'll meet you in Rita's hospital room. We need a few hours. *Comprendes*?"

\* \* \* \*

"No hospital food." Abel entered the hospital room. "Put down that fork." He pulled away Rita's hospital tray and set down a large white paper bag. Jaq released her tottering tray of drinks, then glued herself to Rita.

Rita giggled. "So happy you're here." Her voice was a hoarse whisper. "Dr. Towers said there's enough evidence to insure no release from prison, ever. Congratulations."

Jaq covered the bed table with Coney dogs, fries, and drinks. "You have to share 'cause we're starved." Abel grinned and helped distribute the food from the bag.

Rita grabbed a fry. "Did you leave anything for any other Detroiters at American Coney Island?"

"Look little lady, I plan on eating my share till we're on the plane." Abel stuffed a Coney dog in his mouth, then licked his fingers and grinned.

"I owe my life to all of you," Rita said. Her blue eyes were swimming in tears of gratitude. "When will everyone else be here?"

"Soon. There was some cleanup work to do." Jaq walked over to Rita and gave her another hug. She whispered in Rita's ear. "Angel-teeny? Really?" Their eyes met and they shared a laugh. "We need to chat."

Rita didn't blink. She simply brought Jaq back over to her with a wag of her forefinger and returned a whisper. "Girlfriend code—no explanations for dumb dating decisions we've both made."

They laughed.

"Spill."

Rabbit considered the women, then David, and spoke with a half grin. "Guess that's why you're single. Read between the lines. Easier to get a confession out of hardened criminals than information out of these two."

Jaq raised an eyebrow, nodded, then elbowed Rita. "You owe your life to quick thinking and your strong body. You're amazing."

"Yoga. I kept focused on relaxation breathing techniques—living proof it works. Strength in body, mind, and spirit," Rita said.

Jaq hugged Rita. "You're soooo very right."

"I couldn't die, let him get away with it, especially after he told me he targeted me before I even knew him."

Jaq's eyes focused on Rita. "What?"

"I'm so stupid. Nick told me he knew Zeke."

"Rita, he's a very sick man," Jaq said. She held her arm around Rita's shoulders. "We didn't know the particulars, but we learned in their military files they crossed paths."

"I've been so upset with Zeke." Rita shook her head. "I have to talk with him."

"Honey." Jaq placed a hand on Rita. She leaned into Rita and met her eyes almost nose to nose. "Zeke is gone. He was released from prison early—good behavior."

"Then find him—"

"He's dead. There's evidence to believe Nick—"

"Like the others—Nick?" Rita's face scrunched.

Jaq nodded. "We think so. Yes."

All eyes on Rita, the room went silent. "Oh my God." Rita blinked away tears.

"There's more, if you're up to it," David said. He leaned over Rita and waited.

Jaq and Rita locked their hands together. Rita nodded at David to continue. Abel grabbed three dogs.

"Recon was extremely bothered by the front door. So, Rabbit took his pen knife and continued to cut along the opening Nick made where he claimed he placed an extra key in the door frame."

Rabbit interrupted. "Just before he walked out in cuffs, Nick spewed some crazy biblical-ish quote about same time tomorrow he'd be causing it to rain grievous pain—a serious issue, given the history here."

David rubbed his hands together and aimed his chin toward Jaq. "Explosives were concealed, shaped in a cross, tied together with a silk rosary."

"Nick's final plague," Jaq said. "Destruction, death, and darkness of your whole condo building—to erase everything about you. Juror, judge, and executioner, with God-like control."

Rabbit sat at the foot of Rita's bed. "Remember the ten plagues were a divine demonstration of power and displeasure designed to persuade Pharaoh to let my people go. Since the time Nick killed his father, he tried to deal with it by righting wrongs."

Rita wrinkled her forehead.

"We searched his mother's home," David began. "Nick's problems began in his childhood."

"Growing up without a father?" Rita bit her lip.

David cracked his knuckles. "The brothers are completely different. Clueless Chris spends his time writing nonviolent computer games for kids. He gets ideas from letters to Santa."

"From the post office?" Rita asked.

David nodded and continued, "Their father was very religious and extremely strict. A violent drunk, who frequently beat his wife. As the boys got older, Nick decided being mute made him his father's silent partner. One night he got in the middle of the beatings."

"Oh my God." Rita covered her mouth with a hand. "How horrid. Never said a word." She squeezed Jaq's hand until both their knuckles were white.

"Domestic violence never has a good outcome," Jaq said. "Children, hit or not, have a lifetime of scars. Chris withdrew into his computers, so he wasn't affected."

"Maybe that was his way coping." Rita blinked. "Deep down he knew, too."

"But one night, when mom was being choked into unconsciousness, Nick grabbed a shovel his mother had been digging with in the rose garden. He hit his father on the back of the head until he lay dead and bleeding on top of her," David said. "Then he fled."

"Mother drags dad into the garden and buries him, cleans up the mess. Tells the boys dad left to cool off, and they would wait in the house until he returned," Jaq said.

"How did you even think to look for dad in the rose garden?" Rita asked.

"Recon began sniffing around during the search," David said. "We went back after the uniforms were done. We couldn't keep Recon out of the garden. Even in the snow, it quickly became apparent why."

"We're awaiting final results from Doc, but mom broke down after she and Chris were arrested," Rabbit said. "Chris was clearly baffled. He just kept pacing, scratching his head, and saying things like: no, why, and oh my God."

"Decided to arrest all three to get the true picture. Nick's the only one charges will stick to, but the arrests caused them to talk," David said.

Rita put a hand on her cheek. "Mom's really in jail?"

"For now, out on bond—in reality, she was the victim. And, at least for this first killing, Nick killed in self-defense, or arguably defense of another." David cracked his knuckles. "There'll be an inquiry, it's a formality."

Jaq chimed in. "They needed family counseling back then. Maybe Nick would've grown up without feeling the need to protect children from harm."

"He talked a lot about that." Rita sighed. "Protecting people who can't speak for themselves. I thought it was admirable."

Jaq nodded. "Usually is—until he became judge and jury."

"We showed Nick's mother the cross he was wearing at the time of arrest," Rabbit said.

"I only ever saw a gold chain." Rita put her hand over her heart. "Another quirk, he never took it off, no matter what."

Rabbit gave Rita a moment. "Mother identified it as his father's. Said she'd buried dad with it. When mom saw it, she had to sit down."

"So how did Nick get the cross?" Rita's eyes were wide, her shoulders set back in her pillows.

"Mom recalls Nick planting new rose bushes as a Mother's Day gift to her and thinks he found the body," Rabbit said. "With his profile, if we consider his activity in Afghanistan and the escalation here with the Santa letters, triggers, timing, it all fits."

"Mother's Day finding, awakened the realization that he'd killed his father," David said.

"Nick was really just one big screwed-up kid." Rita focused her words on Jaq. "I was too screwed-up to recognize even one symptom."

"Rita, you've nothing to be sorry for." Jaq squeezed Rita's hand.

"That's why you need to know this." David kept his voice tranquil, eyes between Jaq and Rita. "You were targeted and couldn't have prevented anything. We owe you a thank you for your insight."

"You posed the Florida-Michigan connection." Abel reached for another Coney dog and grinned. "You likely saved lives and allowed me to taste these delicious Coney dogs."

Rabbit interrupted. "Nick hid critical evidence in your condo."

Rita stared back at Rabbit. "Really?"

"Your closet is a mess, but I worked my fingers over every inch of your sloppy plumbing access area that was reachable. I found a black velvet pouch," Rabbit said.

Jaq jumped in. "He pulled out the crucifix."

"Crudely made, but looks like the one he was wearing. He welded the cross in the center of two four-inch metal rulers with levels at each end—"

"What?" Rita asked. She frowned. "He wore a crucifix? Attached to a gold chain around his neck?"

"Yes," Jaq said.

"He never let me touch or see what was attached to the chain around his neck. He always had an excuse. Said the chain was fragile. I never knew where he placed it when he slept or showered—" Rita paused. "It like magically disappeared and reappeared. I forgot about it after a while."

"Nick was good at creating illusion," Jaq said. "And instruments of destruction."

"Like the level you mentioned," Rita interrupted with a shiver. "Actually, you said levels, you meant like the kind with a bubble in the center, used for building things?"

Rabbit nodded. "Crudely designed to give him exact imprint control and depth perception of the marking he wanted to achieve."

"That's how the crosses were so faint in the beginning and became so increasingly clear with each victim," Jaq explained.

Rita raised her hand. "Let me get this straight. He wore his father's crucifix, he made a cross with a crude crucifix in the center to imprint his mark on their throat, ensuring each victim bore his cross mark, and he left a silk hand-knotted rosary on each victim?" Rita asked. She held up three fingers and stared at Jaq.

"Yes, that sums up what we found," Jaq agreed.

"So, Nick's more of a *Triple* Cross Killer?" Rita's mouth remained in a half-opened smile.

"Hey, no renaming our collars." Jaq bumped their shoulders together. "Doc said the cuts increased because the crude level crucifix was so roughly made compared to the smooth original."

"But it's a match according to a jeweler who preliminarily tested it with a cast," David said.

"It's too much." Rita pursed her lips. Jaq rubbed her arm lightly.

Dr. Towers poked his head in and interrupted, "I heard you down the hall."

"Plenty of Coney dogs left," Abel said.

"You are not stressing out my girl, are you?" Dr. Towers held a package and promptly handed it to Rita.

"It's better to know. I feel like a big weight's been lifted." Rita spied the white box. "For me?"

Dr. Towers smacked his lips. "Open it. There is good news and better news."

Rita lifted the top of the box and handed it to Jaq. She pulled out a crisp white lab coat with her name embroidered under Wayne County Medical Examiner's Office. "Thank you?"

"Not the thrilled reaction I hoped for, but here is the rest of the story. You are fired from Henry Ford Hospital—"

"Fired, I—"

Dr. Towers put up his hand, and Rita stopped talking. "Okay, permanently laid off. You are hired as my full-time assistant." He reached into his pocket and handed her an envelope. "A grant to continue your education. Physician's assistant—medical school—consider concentration in forensic pathology."

Rita nodded and put the envelope over her heart. "Thank you." Her eyes filled with tears. "I accept." She held her arms out. Dr. Towers entered for a momentary hug.

Dr. Towers stepped back. "Wonderful. I paid extra for the embroidery."

"Our case shaping up forensically, Doc?" David asked.

"I will continue running labs, but you know Nick's evaluation in the *Center for Forensic Psychiatry* will take several months. Plenty of time to deliver trial evidence to the prosecutor."

Rita shuffled under her covers and repositioned herself against her pillows. "What'll happen in Sarasota?"

Rabbit and Abel shot affirmation to each other, then to Rita. "We've work to do, but Florida will extradite him when Michigan's finished." Rabbit raised his brows, then looked around the room. "We've a bet on how many life sentences he'll serve."

"Enough talk of bad things. I spoke with your doctor, reviewed your chart before I came in. I understand my new permanent assistant will be released soon." Dr. Towers grinned at Rita. "Feeling well enough?"

Rita nodded. "Yes, a week at most, then another to recuperate, a third to list my condo and move out."

Dr. Towers held up his pointer finger. "My wife expected that. We hope you will consider staying in our guest room for as long as you need—garage and basement storage. She most certainly closed the stores this evening buying new sheets, towels—do not deprive her of the shopping adventure she loves."

Rita crossed her arms over her heart. "You've all been so wonderful."

"I also know detectives who work cheap and will help you move." Jaq squeezed Rita's hand.

Everyone turned to the heavy shoes at the door.

"Chief." David stood and shook his hand at the door.

Chief Hanusack stepped into the room. "Hello everyone." He held up a glass globe filled with plants and flowers. A lone balloon floated above it on a pink ribbon. He placed it bedside next to Rita, and then hugged her. Out-of-character tears shone in the corners of his closed eyes. "A small token. You risked your life—the Department, my family, we're all grateful. You deserve more." He drew in a breath.

"I'm honored you're here. Very sorry for your loss." Rita pinked and shook his hand. "Thank you."

Abel almost swallowed his Coney dog whole, wiped fingers on his jeans, then stood up and grabbed the plant from her. He set it on the windowsill next to several other plants, flowers and balloons, then returned to his seat next to Rabbit.

"I didn't mean to intrude. Get well, Rita." Chief Hanusack nodded to his officers and swung around to the door. "Jaq, David, walk me out?"

Jaq arched a brow to David, kissed Rita's cheek, then followed behind the men. "Get some rest, Rita."

Chief Hanusack strolled into the hallway with Jaq and David. After several paces down the corridor, he stopped and faced them, his lips pursed tightly before he spoke. "Thank you. I, my family, is very grateful to you." He cleared his throat, shook their hands, then pulled them into his chest for a hug and a back slap. He lunged back from them, drew in a breath and spoke in almost a whisper. "Be forewarned. There's talk of a public award ceremony."

Jaq squinted. "We don't like public—"

The Chief nodded, then raised his hand to cut Jaq off. His face was stern, but the worry lines were no longer there. "Just tell me, I don't put any stock in locker room talk—your intimate relationship didn't delay, interfere with, or compromise this investigation."

David grabbed his wallet from his pocket and flipped out his badge. "Investigation, always our first priority." He lifted the Chief's right hand and pressed his badge into it. "Chief, send us a postcard. You just made our decision easy." David grabbed Jaq's badge from her hand along with two letters she pulled from her pocket. He kept one letter. Passed the other with the badge to Hanusack.

Jaq reached for David's hand and squeezed it as she spoke. "Truth is we've been debating this since it was personally delivered by the Governor's top aide."

"What are you two mumbling?" Chief Hanusack pocketed the badges and focused on unfolding the paper and reading it.

"We have been invited to be one of the first of ten detective teams appointed to serve in the State Detective Special Forces unit in a statewide united effort to fight against crime." David made the announcement eye-to-eye with the Chief who dropped the letterhead to his side. David turned to Jaq. "Rabbit and Abel have been made an offer as well. We are accepting."

Jaq nodded. "Today, but after we take a nice long vacation."

"Thank you for everything, Chief." David slapped him on the shoulder as Jaq leaned in and kissed Hanusack's cheek.

David's hand still in hers, he pulled her into him, kissed her long and hard, then they locked arms and strode down the long hallway toward a dinging elevator without turning back.

CPSIA information can be obtained
at www.ICGtesting.com
Printed in the USA
LVOW12s1325260118
564131LV00001B/27/P